5/24/12

To Brad —
Enjoy the Adventure!

Michael D. Travis

Melozi

by Michael D. Travis

PO Box 221974 Anchorage, Alaska 99522-1974
books@publicationconsultants.com—www.publicationconsultants.com

ISBN 978-1-59433-150-3
eBook 978-1-59433-151-0
Library of Congress Catalog Card Number: 2010908763

Cover adapted from a photograph taken by Ned Rozell, July 2009.

Manufactured in the United States of America.

Dedication

To Leonard and Patricia Veerhusen—may their
pioneering spirits live in the hearts of all Alaskans.

Michael Travis is also the author of
El Gancho
A saga of an immigrant family's journey out of Mexico

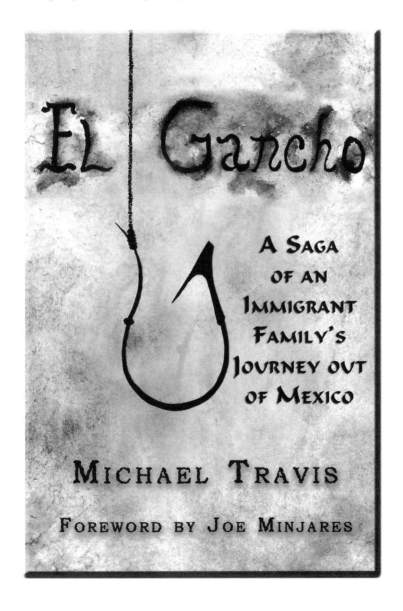

- Point Barrow

- Kotzebue

- Nome

- Melozi Hot Springs
- Fairbanks

- Anchorage

- Juneau

- Ketchikan

Contents

Dedication 5

Introduction 11

Chapter 1 .... The Ad 13

Chapter 2 .... Welcome to the Bush 23

Chapter 3 .... The Proving Grounds 41

Chapter 4 .... The Turning Point 65

Chapter 5 .... The Land 85

Chapter 6 .... The Taming of Happy 119

Chapter 7 .... The Responsible Man 135

Chapter 8 .... Unconventional Guests 163

Chapter 9 .... Swans 195

Chapter 10 .... Hobo 215

Chapter 11 .... Another Lifestyle 245

Epilogue 265

Acknowledgments 271

Bibliography 277

Photos .... Reflections of Melozi 279

Introduction

After thirty-seven years, my mother lamented, "What on earth were we thinking? A complete stranger offers to fly you into the Alaska boonies to work with people we never met for the entire summer. Now, does that sound like responsible parenting to you? You had just turned sixteen!" She was right, of course, but the adventure that resulted from my parents' lapse in judgment changed my life forever. In their defense, times were different in 1973 within the little town of Fairbanks, Alaska. A handshake still bonded a man's word and people judged you by your actions, not by your clothes or possessions.

This is a true story reconstructed from memory, letters, newspaper and magazine articles, books, and interviews. It offers a glimpse into a time when Alaskans were not shackled by regulations and government oversight. When people could strike out on their own with only their dreams and carve a life out of the Alaska bush. I hope this book encourages our youth to work hard and pursue their passions with a fearless heart.

Chapter 1

The Ad

My pen smacked the period onto the small piece of paper and I pushed away from the kitchen table to admire my work. On a three-by-two-inch form, I scrawled the following, "HIGH SCHOOL JUNIOR interested in outdoor work such as carpentry, gardening, etc. Mike Travis. 452-4642."

I was responding to an advertisement in the June 9, 1973 edition of the *Fairbanks Daily News Miner*. The newspaper stated it would run a free "Work Wanted" ad for high school and college students seeking summer employment. The offer limited each advertisement to twenty words—a restriction I struggled through several drafts to meet.

The ad intrigued me. It featured a girl my age who was obviously excited about landing the summer job of her dreams. As a boy who turned sixteen on this day and who had struck out for the past two weeks trying to find summer employment in the little town of Fairbanks, Alaska, I was green with envy. *She's got a job*, I thought to myself. *How come I can't find one?*

My family had arrived in Fairbanks only seven months before from Montana. My father worked for the Federal Aviation Administration as a Flight Service Specialist. Although my parents suffered from wanderlust, my Dad was certain this would be a lasting move. Since this was the third time we had moved during my high school years, I was skeptical at best. The net result of our relocation had placed me and my three brothers in a town where we knew no one outside of our newly acquired school friends. Coupled with the fact that the Fairbanks economy was in the doldrums between the rapid pipeline construction shutdown of 1969 and the promise of restarting someday soon, jobs for sixteen-year-olds were scarce and saved for lifelong residents. Thus, this ad meant everything to me.

Today was Saturday and I had to wait two agonizing days until I could submit my literary work for publication. At 8 a.m. on Monday, I rode my orange Schwinn ten-speed bike down Cowles Street to First Avenue where I hopped onto the bike path that paralleled the Chena River. With my precious scrap of paper carefully nested in my sweatshirt, I crossed the river on the Cushman Street bridge and rolled down to the office of the *Fairbanks Daily News Miner*. The office was located close to the Alaska Railroad terminal and across the street from the ruins of Saint Joe's Hospital and the Immaculate Conception Catholic church.

I strode up to the counter where a man in a neatly pressed plaid shirt sat behind a nearby desk and looked over his reading glasses at me. "And what can I do for you?" he asked.

I reached inside my sweatshirt and produced the slip of paper that contained my future and proudly replied, "I am responding to your free work-wanted ad. Here." I pushed my cutout form toward him.

The man did not seem to understand. He cocked his head, rose, and walked to the counter. He picked up the paper and pushed his glasses up the bridge of his nose. He read my ad with casual interest and, much to my relief, it seemed to jog his memory. He took his glasses off, held onto the paper, and said, "You look a little young to be a carpenter."

I straightened my six-foot skinny frame and answered defensively, "I took VO-TECH classes in school."

The man almost snorted. He lifted my ad in the air and said, "okay. We'll run it."

Relief flooded my body. "Thank you. Will you place it in tomorrow's paper?"

The man gave me a condescending smile and replied, "In a few days." With that, he turned back to his desk carrying my ad. I reluctantly left the office knowing my fate was in somebody else's hands.

———◆◆※◆◆———

The *Fairbanks Daily News Miner* was an evening paper and the paperboy usually stuffed it in our screen door around 5 p.m. I met him on our porch on Tuesday and Wednesday and practically yanked it out of his hands. I immediately sat down on the steps and ripped the paper apart until I found the work-wanted ads and then meticulously read each entry. I was devastated that my ad was not printed. By Thursday, the paperboy had wised up and threw the rolled paper at me as he peddled by on his bike. My ad was still missing. Then, Friday, I caught a looping pass from the paperboy and braced myself for another disappointment. With my finger tracing each line, I stumbled across my ad. "There it is!" I shouted and ran into the house to show my parents. I announced to my brothers that the phone would be ringing off the hook with offers, but much to their glee, it remained silent through the evening.

The *News Miner* printed the ad again on Saturday. This time an elderly lady called and asked if I would be interested in some yard-cleaning work. I said yes and she told me that she had to clear it with her husband first and she would call back. I never heard from her again.

The ad posted a final time on Sunday. Dejected, I sat in the living room watching television when the telephone rang. My mother answered and called out to me, "Michael! It's for you."

As I rose from my chair, I heard a brother mutter, "I bet it's that yard lady."

I solemnly took the phone from my mother and said, "Hello?" My mother stood in front of me and watched my face.

A man answered with a question, "Are you the high school junior looking for outdoor work?"

I cleared my throat and replied, "Yes I am. My name is Mike Travis and I am looking for a summer job."

The man answered in a pleasant tone, "Well, I think you could help me. You see, I have a business relationship with an older couple to build a wilderness lodge at Melozi Hot Springs, but I can't get free this summer to help them out because I am building some homes along Badger Road. So, I need to send someone in my place. Are you interested?"

Interested? I thought. *Heck, yes! I am way more than interested. When can I start?* Then reality struck and I knew I had to remain cool if I was going to convince my parents to let me go on this one. With my mother still watching every line on my face, I smoothly replied, "Yes sir, I am, but if you are serious about this, I need you to come over and meet my parents. Then we can decide how to proceed."

"Not a problem. Just give me your address and I will come at three o'clock tomorrow."

When I hung up the phone, my mother kept her eyes glued to my face. "What did he say?" she asked.

"Well, Mom, he wants me to help a couple build a camp outside of Fairbanks. Sounds like a great job!"

Over the course of raising four boys, my mother had witnessed every sort of subterfuge known to man. Thus, she had developed the knack of getting to the heart of the matter. "How far out of town is the camp?"

I could tell that this conversation was deteriorating, so I elected to be evasive. "I don't really know, Mom," I answered, "but the man is coming tomorrow at three to meet you and Dad and discuss the details. Let's see what he has got to say, okay?"

My mother appeared mollified. "All right," she said. "But your father has to work tomorrow afternoon, so he will have to deal with me." I gulped and wondered if this was good or bad news.

————◆•※•◆————

Promptly at three in the afternoon, a light green panel van pulled in front of the duplex my family rented off Airport Way. A beautiful dog of husky/setter mix sat in the passenger seat and panted out the open window. My dog Mickey snarled a greeting to it from the porch. A young man with close-cut black hair and a complexion darkened from outdoor work got out and walked around the front. As I came down the stairs to meet him, my mother and brothers lined up on the porch to watch. I stuck out my hand and said, "Hi. I am Mike Travis. Thank you for coming."

The man grasped my hand with a solid grip formed by years of pounding nails. He smiled and said, "Hello, my name is Doug DeFelice and I am pleased to meet you."

I motioned for him to come up the stairs to meet my family. "Mom, this is Doug DeFelice, the man who called last night. Doug, this is my mother, Carmen Travis." Much to my relief, my mother greeted him warmly and invited him in. Then, I introduced my brothers, "Doug, these are my brothers Steve, Greg, and Jeff." Doug shook their hands, too.

My mother directed Doug to sit in the living room chair that faced the couch where my mother and I sat. My brothers and Mickey positioned themselves on the floor surrounding the couch. The arrangement pitted Doug against the six of us. If he felt uncomfortable, he did not show it.

My mother politely asked about his occupation. Doug replied he was an independent contractor building houses in the area. She and Doug exchanged pleasantries about the weather and the happenings around town. Soon, she delicately steered the conversation to my potential employment. "Now where exactly is Melozi Hot Springs?" she asked.

Doug smiled and replied, "Melozi is about seventy miles northeast of Galena." When Doug saw the quizzical look on my mom's face, he added, "About thirty miles north of Ruby off the Yukon River."

"Oh," my mother feigned understanding. "And how would Michael get there?"

Doug answered with directness, "He would fly to Galena on a commercial flight and then take a bush plane to Melozi." My mother seemed bothered by this revelation, but it only boiled my anticipation higher.

"Look, Mom," I said, "the planes won't be any smaller than the ones Dad flies." My father had his commercial and instrument ratings and flew us around when he could afford to rent a plane.

Sensing that my mother had major reservations, Doug moved quickly to assuage her misgivings. "The Veerhusens will take good care of him. They are responsible and caring people. I am offering to pay Mike $350 per month plus pay for his airfare."

"Mom, please!" I begged. "It's the most perfect job in the whole world!"

The room went silent. My mother looked into my pleading eyes. Then she looked around her and saw every face waiting for her answer. Even the dog laid back her ears and stretched her muzzle toward her in sympathy and support. Finally, Mom decided on the same course of action taken by millions of women before her. She looked at me and said, "Go ask your father." Her response was not an outright denial and offered some ray of hope.

With the matter put on hold, I walked Doug back to his van and tried to reassure him that all was not lost. "I will talk this over with my dad and get back to you this evening."

Doug smiled and said, "That would be fine. I hope things work out. You have a nice family." His dog was standing on the driver's seat as he opened the door. "Slide over, Tasha." The dog hopped over and Doug got in. He rolled down the window and said, "Make sure you call me tonight. I need to know one way or the other." Then he drove off and left me standing in the street with the sinking feeling that I had my work cut out for me to convince my dad to let me go.

The van had no sooner turned the corner when I leaped on my ten-speed bike and headed toward the east ramp of the Fairbanks International Airport where my father worked. I followed the sidewalk along Airport Way to University Avenue and turned left past the Safeway store that had rejected my box-boy application. Here, the pavement deteriorated into a narrow gravel road. My speed slowed as I negotiated loose rocks and potholes. After a mile, I pulled in front of the flat-roofed FAA Flight Service Station at the airport. I propped my bike up along the wall and ran inside.

I skated down two tiled hallways and slid into the briefing room where I saw my father leaning over the counter reviewing weather forecasts with a pilot. Usually, I would have waited until my father was done, but my excitement killed my patience. I blurted, "Dad! I got a great job offer!" My loud voice startled them out of their concentration. I quickly gave my father a thumbnail sketch of the details and then let the dice of fate play out.

My father had a slight smile as he stared at me for a second while he sought the words to gently let me down. His blue eyes were sympathetic and seemed to understand my excitement. He remembered what it was like to be young and full of wild hopes. As he opened his mouth to speak, the pilot interceded. "Lloyd, I just flew in from Melozi. It's a great place. Len and Pat Veerhusen are good people, too. They're honest and hardworking. I know they would take good care of him." This information surprised my father. He looked uncertain and the pilot sensed it. So, he stated an overlooked benefit of working in Melozi. "Heck, Lloyd, you will at least know where he is at. It's not like he could wander off somewhere."

As the father of four boys, my dad thought that was a definite plus. He turned to me, nodded, and said, "Okay. You can go."

I leaped for joy. "Thanks, Dad! I gotta race home and tell the guy I'll take the job." I started to run down the hallway and then remembered to thank the pilot. I turned to him and waved.

He winked and grinned back. "Have fun, son," he said. "It'll be a grand adventure." I nodded and bolted for the door.

My mother knew something was up when I came screaming into the house. I knocked over a kitchen chair as I lunged for the telephone. I jammed my shaking hand into my pants pocket and fished out the scrap of paper that contained Doug's scrawled phone number. With a rapid-fire motion, I twirled out the number on the rotary dial and held my breath for a few long seconds until I heard a distant ringing. Doug answered on the third ring. "Hello?"

"Hi, Doug," I replied breathlessly. "This is Mike Travis. My father said yes. So, when do you want me to go?" *Soon*, I hoped.

"Wow! That was quick! I just got in the door." Doug's voice seemed to contain a mixture of disbelief and humor. "You can leave as soon as you want."

"How about tomorrow?"

Doug laughed and replied, "Tomorrow is a little soon. I will stop by tomorrow after work with a plane ticket and instructions on how to charter a flight to Melozi. Okay?"

I felt a little crestfallen. "Yeah, okay. I will see you tomorrow then." My voice dripped with disappointment. Doug said goodbye and I hung up. I turned and found my mother staring at me. Her eyes radiated shock tinged with fear.

"Your father approved?" she asked.

"Yeah, Mom, he did. Honest." My mother learned long ago to trust but confirm pledges of honesty. She went straight to the telephone and called my father. I did not stay around for the ensuing conversation or the one that surely occurred when my dad came home.

Early the next morning, my father told me that Mom would take me to J C Penney and buy me some work clothes. I thanked him and after he left for work, Mom and I piled into the car and went shopping. Within one hour, I had a new Levi jacket, a couple pairs of work gloves, and a new pair of jeans. Then we stopped by Foodland where I bought some jerky, a bag of candy orange slices, and Cutter's insect repellent.

We came home and I immediately went downstairs to my bedroom and started packing. Mickey followed me, sat to the side, and watched me empty my dresser onto my bed. Then she looked upset when I hauled out my duffel bag and canvas backpack and started stuffing my belongings inside. Mickey slept on my bed with me at night and she sensed that this arrangement was coming to an end.

Around noon, my mother brought me freshly washed underwear. I smashed these into my duffel bag and proclaimed that I was done. All I could do now was wait for Doug to arrive.

Around six in the evening, Doug's van drove up with Tasha wagging her tail and sticking her head out the passenger window. Mickey made sure she stayed in the van. I jumped off the porch and ran to Doug. "Hey, Doug. Please come inside. My father is here and I'm sure he wants to talk to you." Doug smiled and followed me into the house.

I introduced Doug to my dad and then my entire family including the dog settled in the living room with Doug, once again, positioned in a chair facing us. After some cordial discussion, Doug handed me two envelopes and then explained what they contained. "One envelope contains your ticket to Galena. I have you booked on the 10 a.m. flight on Tanana Air Taxi. The return flight is an open ticket, which you will use when it's time for you to come home. So, don't lose it, okay?" I answered by nodding. Doug continued, "The next envelope is for Norman Yaeger. He runs Galena Air Service. After you arrive in Galena, carry your bags down to his business, tell him you need to go to Melozi, and hand him this letter. He's a fantastic pilot, but his personality can grate on your nerves. Just let his comments slide off you like water off a duck's back and he'll take care of you. Any questions?"

I had about a million questions, but I chose to appear strong and confident to ward off any misgivings my parents might be having and said, "Nope. I think I can handle it. Thank you."

Doug smiled as he stood up to leave and said, "That's good. I am hoping you can give me two good months of work. That would really help me out."

I rose with him and stuck out my hand to strike the deal. "You can count on me. Thank you for the job." Doug maintained his smile as he clasped my hand. For the first time, I could see a tinge of doubt in his eyes and it unnerved me. *Have I bitten off more than I can chew?* I wondered as I released my grip. Doug turned and shook my dad's hand and said goodbye to my mom and brothers.

I walked Doug to his van and thanked him again for coming . He opened his door and then turned to me and said, "Just do the best you can and stay with it. Things will work out." Then he jumped into the van and drove off.

I stood there thinking as I watched him leave, *Why did he say that?*

Chapter 2

Welcome to the Bush

On the early morning of Wednesday June 20th, I awkwardly shook each brother's hand goodbye. Never before had we said farewell to each other, so our emerging male bravado tried to dampen our feelings of separation and love. We smacked each other on the shoulders and made rough jokes about running off with bears and never returning. To hug each other was unthinkable. Out of the corner of my eye, I saw my father grinning at the sibling exchange.

Next, I knelt down and stroked Mickey across her head. Then I put my arms around her and gave her a hug and kiss. Mickey responded by smooching me and wagging the tip of her tail. My brothers deemed this display of affection appropriate and made no comment.

Saving the most emotional parting for last, I stood tall and stiff and opened my arms for my mother. I was her first child to leave the fold for any appreciable amount of time and she felt the significance of the moment. Her eyes teared as she wrapped her arms around me and buried her face into the rough fabric of my new Levi jacket. I heard her quiet, muffled voice say, "You be careful, Michael D."

"I will, Mom," I answered in a choking voice. I gently put my arms around her and bent my head down to hide my misting eyes. "I'll write as soon as I can." I felt my mother nod, but she maintained her hug.

"It's time to go," my father said. He was going to drop me off at the airport on his way to work. My mother and I held each other for a second longer and breathed each other's essence in an attempt to forever rivet the memory into our thoughts. Then we released our embrace and I turned to pick up my duffel bag and backpack while my mother wiped away her tears. Dad held the door open as I carried my luggage to our 1966 white Ford Galaxy 500. I threw them on the back seat and turned to wave to my family. My brothers, mother, and dog stood on the porch and said their final goodbyes. My brothers had a few derogatory comments. My mother had some sweet loving words. Mickey had some woeful looks. As we got in the car and drove off, I felt like I had left a piece of me on the steps of our house.

My dad and I drove in silence to the airport. When we pulled in front of the off-white terminal, I got out, unloaded my belongings, and turned to my father. My grandfather Travis had been a strict authoritarian and never told my father that he loved him. Although my dad did not possess his father's reserve, he still found it difficult to put his emotions into words. So, we stood stoically facing each other, struggling how to appropriately say goodbye. "Got your ticket?" Dad asked.

"Yep," I replied as I patted my coat pocket. An awkward silence prevailed. I had to say something, so I added, "Thanks, Dad, for letting me go." My father seemed to have second thoughts and, for the first time, I almost wished he would retract his permission and tell me to bag it.

Then the cloud of doubt passed from my father's face and he said, "Make sure you write your mother as soon as you can. She will worry if you don't."

"I know, Dad." There was nothing further to say.

My father shook my hand and said, "I have to go. Enjoy yourself."

"I will, Dad." He nodded, got back into the car, and drove off. A sudden feeling of loneliness attacked me as I watched him leave. I shook it off, grabbed my gear, and marched inside. I walked up to the Tanana

Air Taxi counter and deposited my stuff on the floor. A lady of Athabaskan descent took my ticket.

"Very good, Mike," she said with an easy smile. "Slide your bags over this scale, so I can get a weight and tag them. Is your final destination Galena?"

"I am supposed to go to Melozi Hot Springs by Galena Air Service," I replied as I lifted my duffel bag onto the scale. This information did not appear to surprise her.

As she studied the scale for a moment and jotted down the weight, she said, "Okay. You will find Norm a few buildings down from the Galena passenger shelter."

"You mean terminal," I corrected her.

She smiled again and asked, "How much do you weigh?"

I filled my chest with as much air as it would hold and lied, "160 pounds." This was about ten pounds heavier than I weighed wet. She wrote it down and told me to take a seat in the lobby next to the counter. I found a chair and looked around me. There were two men dressed similar to me and a woman with two children. Everyone looked as normal as anyone would flying to Seattle.

Within half an hour, the pilot walked into the lobby holding a logbook and a clipboard of passenger names and weights. He announced the flight, "Everyone headed to Tanana, Ruby, and Galena, follow me." I rose and followed the pilot out the door and onto the tarmac. There sat a beautiful Piper Navajo waiting to carry me to my adventure. All my misgivings evaporated as I bounded for the door. The pilot caught my arm and stopped me. "Wait a minute, kid. I want the mother and her two kids in the back first. Then, I want you to sit over the wing. The weight will balance better."

I took a step back and let the woman and her two children get in the back. Then I got in and folded my lanky frame into the seat. A man strapped in next to me and the pilot and the last man crawled into the cockpit. After a quick preflight, the pilot checked our seat belts and told us not to smoke. Then he started both engines, taxied to the runway, and took off to the north.

The Navajo vaulted into the sky like a smooth flying arrow as we sailed over Fairbanks and gently turned to the northwest. Within minutes, we flew over the last vestiges of civilization and then there was nothing but wilderness as far as I could see. About 15 minutes later, the pilot throttled back the engines to cruise and trimmed the airplane. I looked out the window and gawked at the vastness of Alaska. Lakes, rivers, forests, and tundra stretched from horizon to horizon. The Tanana River looked like a thick blue rope along the left side of the plane. I felt strangely alien to this world. Nothing looked familiar and everything appeared foreboding like a strange planet waiting to swallow me up.

Forty-five minutes later, we descended toward the wide junction of the Tanana River with the much larger Yukon River. We roared over Manley Hot Springs and then we flew diagonally across the shallow and rapid Squaw Crossing at the mouth of the Tanana River. The plane veered to the north as we crossed the Yukon and lined up for the runway at the village of Tanana.

The Tanana Airport was a maintained gravel strip with a couple of buildings along the apron and a flight service station. The village stretched along the river-side of the airport. The woman and her children departed from the airplane, but we gained another woman passenger. She said she was a nurse stationed at the Indian Health Service Hospital in Tanana and needed to visit some patients in Galena. Within a few minutes, the pilot was shutting the doors and restarting the engines.

We flew a few thousand feet above the Yukon River as we followed it downstream to Ruby. Rolling hills and mountains confined the big muddy river to a channel that ranged from a quarter to half a mile wide. I spotted fish wheels turning slowly in the current along the banks trying to scoop up migrating salmon. Twice I saw riverboats skimming the surface and creating large v-shaped wakes behind them.

Soon, the pilot gently brought the plane down for a straight-in approach to the Ruby airstrip. Like Tanana, Ruby had a graded gravel runway that paralleled the Yukon River. Most of the village was built above the strip on a north-facing bluff overlooking the river. Many of the homes were built from large logs taken from river islands and along the shore. About a dozen villagers greeted the airplane. Most rode bicycles or walked. Only one man drove a pickup truck.

The pilot got out and waved to the man in the pickup. Then he unloaded a mail bag and tossed it into the truck bed. I could tell they knew each other. I watched them through the window exchange a few jibes before the pilot crawled back into the cockpit and closed the door.

We took off without any fanfare and headed for Galena. After a half an hour, the pilot reduced the throttle and we began our descent into the massive floodplain below us. In the distance, I could barely make out the faint outlines of buildings. As we drew nearer, the details of Galena became clearer. A giant dike surrounded most of the airfield and separated it from the small town. Galena was an assemblage of haphazardly placed homes and buildings built along the riverbank. Some homes were plywood/tar-paper shacks while others looked as modern as any found in established cities of the Lower 48.

The pilot flew us over the dike and smoothly flared over the paved runway. It seemed immense after landing on the two previous gravel strips. As we taxied toward the apron, I realized Galena was also an air force base with enormous hangars, dormitories, and large support buildings. The air force manned a control tower that was framed by two colossal totem poles with a sign that said, "Galena AFS. The Biggest Little Base in the World. Elevation 152. On the Edge of Nowhere."

The pilot pulled in front of a cabin made from weathered logs. Along the roof eaves were the words, "Northern Consolidated, Wien Alaska." A sign hung from the roof peak that said, "Galena." Over the top of the front door, another sign read, "Alaska Airlines." The pilot stopped the plane and shut the engines down.

A man walked out of the log building and opened the door. "Welcome to Galena," he said. I unbuckled my seat belt, snaked my long legs between the seats, and exited the plane with as much grace as a stork crawling through a culvert. I blinked in the hot morning sun and looked around me. The airport was vast with a few huts to the east and the Air Force complex sprawled along the west.

The pilot and the man began unloading the plane and placing the luggage on a push cart. When I saw my pack and duffel bag unloaded, I walked to retrieve them. Suddenly, a deafening siren screamed and several uniformed men by the hangers began running. Seconds later, two enormous hangar doors lifted and two F4 Phantom jet fighters emerged with engines roaring and canopies closing. The jets quickly taxied to the end of the runway and took off like fireballs into the sky. Their afterburners produced thunderous roars that seemed to shake the whole earth as they flew away. The pilot and baggage handler scarcely looked up during the whole spectacle.

Stunned, I stood momentarily dazed at what I had just witnessed. Then the pilot brought me back to reality. "What bags are yours?" he asked.

I shook my head to clear it, pointed to my luggage, and answered, "Those two."

"Okay," replied the pilot. He grabbed them and then pointed to a shack two huts away. "I understand Norm is going to fly you to Melozi. You will find him in the second building. He should be there. His 185 is parked in front."

I thanked the man, put on my backpack, threw my duffel bag over my shoulder, and strode toward the next leg of my journey. I walked up to the blue and white ramshackle building and took a serious look at it. The structure consisted of two shacks that were hammered together with plywood. A rickety, lopsided porch led to the front door. A large sign nailed to the top of the flat roof read, "Galena Air Service—Chartered Flights." A Chevron gas sign was attached to the lower right side of the billboard.

I walked up to the building and propped my pack and bag against the wall next to the porch. As I stepped onto the deck, I noticed a small sign on the weathered door that read, "Come on in. If I am not here, wait outside." Two folding chairs were positioned under a dirty window that overlooked the porch. I glanced through the window and could not see anyone, so I knocked on the door.

A low gruff voice replied, "Come in. I can see ya." I opened the door and stepped inside. Sitting with his hands behind his head and his feet propped on a desk was a short, stout man glaring at me. I guessed him to be in his mid-thirties. His receding crew-cut hair and crisply shaven face gave him an air of authority. His piercing eyes looked me up and down and then hardened. I had a hunch that he resented my height. This meeting was deteriorating fast.

I cleared my throat and said, "My name is Mike Travis and I am looking for Norman Yaeger."

Some disdain rose in his eyes as he answered, "I'm Norm."

"Great," I said as I stuck out my hand, "good to meet you."

Norm maintained his laid-back posture and ignored my hand as he held me in his gaze. "What do you want?" he asked.

I awkwardly dropped my hand and produced Doug's letter from my coat pocket. "I need you to fly me to Melozi Hot Springs. Here's a letter that I am supposed to give you that explains the situation."

Norman put down his feet, sat up, and took the letter. As he unfolded the paper out of the envelope, I suddenly realized that I had never read it. The letter was not meant for me, but surely concerned my future. Nonetheless, I believed that reading it would have been an egregious violation of privacy. Thus, its contents were a mystery to me.

As I watched Norman read the letter, I saw his face turn red and his hands almost crunch the paper. He swore and threw the letter down. Using my best inverted reading skills, I glanced at the letter and interpreted the sentence fragment, ". . . I will pay you later when I can." I went silent as a wave of anger rippled through his head. Then as quickly as it came, the rage passed. Norman stood up and ran his hand over his short hair before putting on his baseball cap. "Come on," he said as he walked out the door, "we might as well get some lunch before flying."

Astonished, I hesitated for a moment before quickly following behind. Norman led me to a nearby mobile home and walked straight inside. We entered the kitchen where a little girl sat at the table eating a hot dog and potato chips. A younger boy sat in a high chair and was completely immersed in his finger food. A young Native woman looked up from the stove and smiled. Norman took off his cap and hung it on a hook and said, "Mike, this is my wife, Rose. Rose, I'm going to fly Mike up to the Veerhusens' after lunch. Should be back by this evening."

I said hello to Rose and suddenly felt like I was intruding. Rose seemed to sense my apprehension and waved me to a chair at the table. Norman was already seated and was spooning pork and beans onto his plate. Rose gave me a warm smile and said as she pointed to her children, "Please make yourself at home. This is Vicky and our son's name is JJ"

I greeted the kids and helped myself to the hot dogs, beans, and chips. Then I ate in silence as Norman and Rose conversed about activities around Galena. I grasped that some sort of party called a "potlatch" was planned, but I failed to understand what it had to do with a funeral.

Suddenly, Norman halted the tranquil discussion as if he had enough and pushed away from the table. "Gotta go," he announced as he stood and put on his cap. I took this as my signal to quickly put my dish in the sink and thank Rose for the lunch. She smiled goodbye as Norman whisked out the door with me in close pursuit.

Norman went straight to the shack attached to his office. He quickly came out with a few boxes and a canvas mail bag—all addressed to "Veerhusen" or "Melozi." Norman carried these to his Cessna 185, a beautiful white and red tail-dragger airplane built for landing on rough strips, and loaded them into the back of the fuselage. Then he turned to me and said, "Go get your pack and bag." I quickly retrieved them and brought my luggage to him. He snagged the bags out of my hands and roughly threw them in the back of the plane.

Without wasting a second, Norman slammed the baggage door shut and started untying the plane from its moorings. As he put his hands on a strut and began pushing the plane toward a couple of drums, Norman barked over his shoulder, "Don't just stand there! Give me a hand."

I jumped at his command, grabbed the free strut, and threw my weight and strength into it. The plane shot forward causing Norman to stumble. He barely caught the strut before falling. His cap flew off as he swung his legs forward and firmly planted his feet to brake the plane. The plane spun and the tail almost smacked the drums. Norman exploded in a ball of red flame. "Damn it, kid! Watch what the hell you are doing!" I stepped back horrified at what I had done.

Norman stomped to his baseball cap, swooped it up, smacked it against his leg to knock the dust off, and firmly shoved it back on his head. Then he strode to the side of his building and grabbed a folding ladder that was propped against the wall. A funnel with a chamois cloth wired across the top and a hand pump were stacked on top of the drums. Without saying a word, Norman used a wrench to remove a drum bung and inserted the hand pump. Then he positioned the ladder under the wing and climbed up with the funnel in his hand. He quickly took the fuel cap off the wing and inserted the funnel.

"You think you could hand me the hose without wrecking the plane?" His voice dripped with sarcasm. I leaped at the chance to redeem myself. I grabbed the hose nozzle that was connected to the pump assembly, but something held it in place. My eyes frantically searched for a latch while feeling Norman's glare bore into my skull. Then I saw the thin baling wire looped over the pump. I quickly slipped it off and removed the nozzle. When I handed it to Norman, he impatiently snatched it away and placed it in the funnel.

Norman looked down at me and said, "Now, work the handle." Again eager to please, I grabbed the handle and began to pump back and forth with gusto. Within a few seconds, the fuel shot out of the nozzle under considerable pressure. Fuel ricocheted off the funnel rim and showered Norman. "Damn it, kid! Stop! Stop!" he screamed. I instantly froze. Norman's expression told me that if he had not been teetering on a ladder with a fuel hose in one hand and a funnel in the other, he would have jumped down and taken a swing at me. His face turned such a deep red that I thought he would ignite his gasoline-soaked clothes.

An uncomfortable minute ticked by before Norman could speak, and when he did, it was through his clenched teeth. "Pump with slow, full strokes." Trembling, I nodded and slowly moved the handle back and forth. This time the fuel flowed smoothly into the funnel at a rate that allowed the chamois to remove any water or particles before entering the tank. By the time Norman told me to stop, my arm felt like it was going to fall off. I took the hose and funnel from him as he stepped down. Then much to my dismay, he set the ladder under the other wing and climbed up. I handed him the funnel and hose and reassumed my position at the pump with my other arm working the handle. By the end of the refueling, I was spent.

After climbing down and handing me the hose and funnel, Norman walked back to his trailer without saying a word. I rehung the nozzle and set the funnel on a drum. Then I carried his ladder back to the wall. A few minutes later, Norman emerged with a new shirt. He opened the passenger door and told me to climb inside. "Okay, kid," he said as he pointed to the rudder pedals. "I don't want you to touch these, got it? That goes for the yoke, too. Make sure you got the seat pushed back far enough." I double-checked that my seat was scooted back and lowered to miss all the controls. Then I fastened the five-point harness and cinched the straps tight.

Norman climbed into the pilot seat. He had to move the seat forward so his short legs could reach the pedals. He seemed a little small to handle such a large and powerful airplane, but his manner was all business and he rapidly went through his preflight check. Satisfied, he put on his headphones, looked around, and yelled, "Clear!" Then he immediately turned the starter and the engine roared to life. After a quick glance at the instrument panel, Norman taxied the Cessna toward the eastern end of the runway.

Norman appeared relaxed and confident as he talked to the tower while taxiing. As we reached the threshold, Norman smoothly applied power and accelerated the plane into a sweeping arc onto the runway. When the plane aligned with the runway centerline, Norman shoved the throttle into the instrument panel. The plane lurched forward and seconds later leaped into the air. The ground fell away as the Cessna rocketed into the sky.

After a few minutes, Norman eased the throttle back, leveled the plane, and set the propeller pitch to cruise. The engine noise dropped to a tolerable level.

I turned to Norman to see if I could engage him in some conversation, but one glance told me he was not interested. So I looked out my window and gazed in amazement at the vastness before me. As far as I could see was rolling hills, lakes, and rivers without a trace of civilization. I noticed that we were angling away from the Yukon River and headed to a small mountain range in the distance. After thirty minutes, the mountains loomed before us. Norman turned the plane north to follow a large river upstream. I could see where the river squeezed into a narrow canyon causing the water to boil and froth against the rocks. A short ways upstream of the canyon, we encountered a large tributary flowing out of the mountains. Norman parted from the river and followed the creek.

Norman reduced the power and we began to lose altitude. I looked around for a camp, but all I saw was wilderness. We descended until we were only 500 feet above the trees. Suddenly, three log cabins in a clearing appeared straight ahead. Norman quickly dropped another 400 feet and we buzzed the camp. I snapped my head back and saw two people run out of an old log cabin and wave. Norman screwed the propellers forward and shoved in the throttle. The plane shot into the sky and pulled away from the terrain. Norman banked the plane to one side of the valley and then entered into a gentle 180-degree turn. He reduced power, lowered the flaps, and aligned the plane with what looked like a rough river bar. As we flew by the camp again, I saw a man driving a small bulldozer and pulling a trailer behind. A small woman walked briskly in front with a wild-looking dog bouncing beside her.

Norman skillfully floated the plane to a flat spot within the rough strip and flared. The plane glided and gently touched down on all three wheels. It was a perfect three-point landing. Then the plane rolled into a rough stretch with cobbles and water-filled potholes. The Cessna shook and bounced until we came to a stop. Undaunted, Norman applied power and lifted the tail off the ground as he spun the aircraft around and taxied back to our landing spot.

My excitement exploded and I could not wait to get out and meet my new employers and explore this new country. I unclasped my harness and put my hand on the door handle. Norman reached out and stopped me before I could unlatch it. "Wait, kid, until I get out. I will open the door for you." This was the first time he had spoken to me since we left Galena.

I watched Norman jump out and walk around the front of the plane. He seemed to be waving at something in the air as he approached the door. In addition, the grimace on his face told me that he was experiencing something uncomfortable. Puzzled, I waited for Norman to open my door and I climbed out. A cloud of buzzing, stinging mosquitoes pounced on me. I could not tell if they were attracted to me or the plane so I ran to edge of the runway and buttoned up my jacket. My short jaunt gave me a two-second reprieve until they found me again.

I started swatting bugs when I heard a woman's voice say, "Hi ya, Norm! How's Rose and the kids doing?" I looked up and saw a petite woman who looked like she was in her early fifties. She wore a sweatshirt that said "Ruby, Alaska" and blue jeans that were much too large for her. She had a pink hair band that pulled her shoulder-length graying hair back and framed her face. Her eyes struck me as intelligent, kind, and confident.

"Oh, they're doing just fine, Pat," replied Norman. Norman smiled for the first time since I met him. "The kids are growing like weeds."

Pat walked up to him and gave him a hug. Norman seemed to like the hug and, for an instant, showed some cracks in his angry shell. Pat pulled away from Norman and noticed me for the first time. "And who's this?" she asked.

Norman replaced his smile with a sneer and said, "Doug hired this kid to help you guys out this summer. It didn't work last year and probably won't this year."

I tried to stand up straight, but the mosquitoes were relentless. I managed to stick my hand out and say, "Hi, my name is Mike Travis." Pat carefully took my hand and squeezed it. Her grip surprised me. Before she could reply, an enormous dog stepped between us. It looked like a cross between a large husky and a Norwegian elkhound, but it had a back almost an axe handle wide and an enormous head. It snarled at me with menacing wild eyes.

"Happy!" shouted Pat, "Behave yourself!" Then she looked at me and said, "Hello, I am Pat Veerhusen and this is Happy. He's just making sure you're okay." Her relaxed smile made me feel welcome.

Something caught Happy's attention and snapped his head back toward camp. The dozer and trailer emerged from the woods and rolled onto the strip. Happy ran back to the man driving the equipment. Pat watched him go and turned back to me with an expression that read, *Oh dear!*

I was about to ask Pat about her sudden misgivings when Norman started throwing my pack and duffel bag on the wet ground. I ran and picked them up before my luggage became waterlogged. As I turned around, a man drove a small dozer next to the plane. He smiled and yelled, "Hi ya, Norm!" and jumped off the tractor. His six-foot frame, broad shoulders, and deep chest filled the grey coveralls he wore. He covered his grey thinning hair with a faded green cap. Thick coarse white stubble enhanced the ruggedness of his face. I judged him to be about sixty years old.

Norman smiled back and shook Len's outstretched hand. "Howdy, Len. I got some mail for ya." Unlike my bags, Norman carefully removed the mail bag and boxes from the cargo compartment and placed them in the wagon. "Your equipment parts finally arrived. Jackovich said he sent you a message on Trapline Chatter a week ago." I walked to the trailer and threw my bags on board. My movement caught Len's attention.

"Yeah, we heard the message," replied Len. He wagged his head toward me and asked Norman, "Who's this?"

Norman seemed to relish the moment before he spoke. "Why, he's your new help, Len. Doug hired him. Just the *man* you were looking for, huh?" I felt my embarrassment rise with the way he sarcastically said "man".

Len looked at me disbelievingly for a second and then turned to Pat and said, "For the love of God, Pat, he's a boy!"

"Now, Len," began Pat in a soothing voice.

Len turned back to me and continued his tirade. "What the hell am I going to do with a boy?" Norman appeared to enjoy the scene and my obvious discomfort.

"Len!" scolded Pat. Len threw his hands in the air and walked straight into the woods. Happy followed Len and stopped at the edge of the forest. He turned and growled at me before continuing after his master.

Norman let out a bellyful of laughter, slapped me on the shoulder, and said, "Welcome to the bush, kid." Then he turned to Pat and said, "I will be in the area within a week or two. I can bring his tail back then if you want."

Pat lifted her chin and firmly replied, "We will do just fine, thank you." Norman shrugged, but maintained his sneer as he waved good-bye and pushed his plane clear of the dozer. He jumped in the cockpit and fired up the engine. Within minutes, Norman Yaeger bounded down the airstrip and roared into the sky. Pat and I stood watching him fly down the valley and out of sight. Then she sighed and said, "You can leave your gear in the wagon. Len will eventually take it back to camp. Come on. I will show you around."

With the sound of Norman's airplane still echoing across the mountains, I followed Pat to the end of the strip. She stepped onto a rough equipment trail that veered into thick black spruce. We walked along the trail in silence until we came to a fast-running stream that was about 10 feet wide. Pat pointed to a row of large, flat rocks that crossed the creek just upstream of the trail ford. "Be careful here," she warned. Pat deftly leaped from rock to rock until she reached the other side. Having longer legs, I was able to step across the rocks without much trouble. Pat waited until I was safely across and began walking up a small hill.

As we reached the top, the camp rolled into view. I saw a large rough-hewn building that looked like a shop and farther to the right

I saw an antiquated sawmill with piles of sawdust, wood debris, logs, and neatly stacked rows of lumber. On my left, a new three-sided log cabin perched on a steep hill overlooking the larger creek. On my right was a nearly completed lodge that was also made from cut logs. The lodge still had plastic sheeting for windows and planks to the front and back doors. Beyond these buildings was an old log cabin. Its logs were weathered grey and black and the roof sagged from countless snows. The structure suffered from dissimilar settlement over the ages causing its arctic entry to bend upwards. In the distance, I could see a greenhouse and steam rising from a bluff. I also detected a whiff of sulfur.

Pat headed for the older cabin. She pushed in the spring-loaded door on the arctic entry and held it for me. When I grabbed it, she walked inside and pushed the next door open. The entry walls were adorned with rain gear and coats. I continued to walk down the slight incline until I entered the cabin.

After my eyes took a few seconds to adjust to the feeble light, I began to look around the cabin. The ceiling was lined with cardboard. The log walls were adorned with Alaska art including paintings and Native crafts. I noticed that a large tarp hung from the ceiling and separated the cabin into two rooms. The Veerhusens used the back as a bedroom. The front room was larger and functioned as a living room, kitchen, and dining room. A distinctive pungent smell wafted by me. Then I spotted a Pic insect repellent coil burning on the plywood dining table.

The kitchen stretched along the west wall. A screened window vented the wood cooking stove and provided light. The cupboards were cut from plywood with bone knobs for handles. Not all of the cupboards had doors. Some had curtains that covered the shelves.

Pat waved me to a chair and said, "I bet you're hungry. We finished dinner about an hour ago, but I can warm you up some leftovers. While I am doing that, why don't you tell me a little about yourself." She was right. I was hungry, but I was still spun up from the unusual activities of the day. Talking helped me relax and Pat proved to be a good listener. She politely asked questions about my family, smiled and shook her head when I said I had three brothers, and sat silently as she watched me wolf down a plateful of meat and gravy over potatoes. The meat tasted good but different—like something wild that I never had.

Pat started asking me about my job experience when we heard the tractor drive up. A minute later, Len pushed open the door and strode solemnly inside. Happy followed with his thick curly tail wagging until he caught sight of me. Then he flattened his ears and snarled. "Happy! Go lay down. Now!" commanded Pat. Happy shot me another threatening look and trudged off to his pillow in the corner of the room.

Len wasted no time getting down to business. "Breakfast is at seven a.m. sharp. You miss it, too bad. Work starts at 7:30 a.m. sharp. Understand? And I mean work!" I gulped and nodded. "Come on, I will show you your bed." I got up, thanked Pat for dinner, and followed him outside.

Len walked past the trailer without grabbing one of my bags. I scooped them up and continued following Len to the new cabin. He pulled the screen door open, slid the moose antler bolt to the right, and pushed the thick wood door. It gave on heavy hinges and swung open. I carried the bags inside. The cabin had two rooms. The first room had two beds made from rough-cut lumber with complete bedding. Curtains hung from handmade wooden valances above each window and the walls were adorned with small wooden shelves and a moose antler coat rack by the door. I saw a small closet by the door to the back room.

The back room had a sunken, pink bathtub with a hand-carved wooden plug sticking into a black plastic pipe protruding where the faucet should be. A honey bucket sat in the corner next to a stool made from a large spruce burl that had been split in half. The back door opened to a small deck overlooking the creek below.

I placed my bags along the wall. Len took a look around as if he was memorizing the initial condition of the cabin. Satisfied, he turned to me and said, "Seven o'clock." He left without saying another word.

I watched him through the window march back to the old cabin. Within seconds, I could hear his voice carry through the screen. "He's just a kid! What the hell was Doug thinking?"

"Now, Len," reasoned Pat, "Doug associates with all sorts of young people. He probably didn't give Mike's youth a second thought."

"Yeah, right," countered Len. "I bet he never met him before. Doug probably saw an ad in the newspaper or something. Look what happened last time. That kid last year was useless. When is Doug going to wise up?"

As the argument raged on, I sat down on my bed and pulled the bag of candy orange slices out of my backpack. I opened it, removed an orange slice, and popped it in my mouth. As I savored the sweet taste, I resealed the bag and replaced it in the pack. For the first time, I had a chance to review the day's events and analyze my feelings. I had seen a lot of new country and I was starting to comprehend my remoteness. I relived my screwups with Norman Yaeger and believed I deserved his disdain, but his contempt went deeper than it should. Now, Len, my new boss, was greatly upset at my arrival. *There must be something else going on here*, I thought. *I never had a chance to prove myself.*

There was another unfamiliar feeling twirling in my gut. I thought a few moments about it and realized I desperately missed my family. For the first time in my life, I was truly on my own. There was no telephone to call home, no brother to discuss problems, no parent to assist me with solutions, and no dog to hug—just me. As I started to chew the candy, I felt my eyes mist up and a hard lump form in my throat. "What did I get myself into?" I asked out loud.

As if on cue, I heard Len bellow, "Well, I'm going to work his butt off!" I sighed, took off my boots, and lay down on the bed. I had no problem drifting off to sleep in the bright daylight of the Alaska summer solstice evening. Tomorrow was another day and I would have a chance to make this right.

Chapter 3

The Proving Grounds

I awoke startled for the fourth time and quickly glanced at my watch. Without an alarm clock, I was on my own to awake at the proper time. My wind-up Timex strapped to my wrist by a thick black leather band said 5 a.m. My tired head fell back on the pillow and I gingerly closed my eyes for a little more sleep. The sun shone brightly through my windows as if it was midday and the birds sang loudly.

My plan was to rise at 6:30 a.m., wash up, comb my hair, and be waiting at their cabin door at five to seven. There was no way that I was going to be late. After a few more abrupt awakenings, I gave up and rolled out of bed at five thirty. I found an empty water jug in the bathroom, carried it to the small stream I had crossed last night, and filled it next to the rock ford. The streambank appeared flattened and worn bare of vegetation from similar water collections. I lugged the heavy jug back to the cabin and poured some ice-cold water into the basin on the bathroom shelf. My mother had packed me a towel and washcloth. I wetted the cloth and used a piece of old soap that I found on the shelf. The coldness refreshed me and snapped me awake.

I combed my hair, smoothed out my clothes, and tried to look as presentable as possible. Satisfied, I grabbed a pair of work gloves and slipped a squeeze bottle of Cutter's into the breast pocket of my Levi coat. A quick glance at my watch confirmed it was still early—only five forty-five. So I decided to take a walk around the camp to prepare myself for the upcoming day.

My first stop was the shop. Len had built the spacious building into the side of a hill. The north wall was completely buried. The west and south walls gradually protruded from the hill. The west wall had a large double door and two windows to provide light. The walls were made from horizontal three-sided logs to a height of four feet. The remaining five to six feet were constructed from vertical six-inch logs. The roof was flat and protruded a few feet above the south wall.

I pushed the door open and peered inside. A large generator sat a few feet from the door. A thick work bench complete with a heavy machinist vise was attached to the south wall. Every beam and support post had machine belts, tools, and extension cords hanging from nails. A portable arc welder sat amidst stacks of welding rods, cans of flux, and assorted debris. I had a feeling that I would get to know this shop well. I closed the door and continued with my tour.

I followed a worn cat trail to the south and found the sawmill that I had spotted last evening. The mosquitoes also found me, so I put on a few drops of Cutter's and took a look around. The mill consisted of a large metal frame constructed from angle iron. A long, thick belt connected a gasoline engine with a circular saw in the middle of the frame. I noticed the rollers on top of the frame and surmised that the logs slid along the top and were cut into lumber. A mountain of sawdust sat next to the mill. I also saw neatly stacked piles of fresh logs next to a stout rack made from thick logs. Piles of stripped bark lay near the rack.

A small foot trail led from the mill to the back door of the lodge. I followed it to the door, walked up a plank ramp, and went inside. The back entry opened next to the kitchen and a new wood cooking stove. The cabinets were made from plywood that was singed with a hot roller, sanded smooth, and varnished. The treatment gave the wood a rustic look and accented the bone handles. The kitchen had a double sink with ample counter space.

I stepped into the main room and looked around. It was still under construction, but I could see that the workmanship was superb. The high ceiling had large natural logs for rafters that stretched across the room. A liquor bar was roughed in along the south wall. Sawhorses and tools littered the floor.

Turning back toward the kitchen, I found a bathroom and two other rooms. They appeared to be nearly completed bedrooms. One room had a bed with a bare mattress. The bathroom had a sink and a lone dry toilet.

I decided to cross the large room and exit by the front door. A large homemade wooden bolt secured the massive door. To exit and enter, a person had to lift the thick block of wood by a lever. When the door closed, the block slid over the catch and locked in place. I lifted the block and pushed the door open. Then I stepped onto a plank that served as the entrance ramp and closed the door behind me. I heard the block thump into place before continuing down the ramp toward the eastern part of the camp.

The greenhouse was straight ahead. A clothesline was erected on the south side and a garden on the north. As I approached the building, I noticed water was streaming from under the door. The greenhouse was a wood frame covered with two layers of Visqueen. I popped the door open and went inside. The musty humid air hung like a blanket with the pungent smell of rich organic soil. Several benches lined the walls and held pots and troughs of dirt with tomato plants, peas, carrots, and lettuce. I noticed something had punched through the plastic sheeting along the wall and someone had repaired it with grey duct tape.

Heat ventilators were placed along the dirt floor and connected by black plastic tubing. The ground sloped slightly toward the door. Hot water flowed through the pipes and discharged outside. I exited the greenhouse and walked around the back.

About 50 feet behind the greenhouse, I found the source of the hot water and sulfur smell. A hot springs bubbled up from a crater about eight feet in diameter. The springs fascinated me. I swatted a few more mosquitoes as I looked it over. The water flowed from the springs and cascaded over a bluff that overlooked the creek. I knelt down and slowly moved my hand through the vapor rising above the water. It was warm, but not searing hot steam. Cautiously, I brushed the surface and found the water hot, but not unbearable. Then I immersed my whole hand. I discovered that I could hold it in the water for several seconds before my hand became uncomfortable.

I got up and hiked down to the bottom of the bluff. Looking along its face, I could see multicolored fungus and algae growing on the rocks. Obviously, the primitive plants owed their existence to the warm mineralized water falling down the cliff. I spent several minutes gazing at the 20-foot-high bluff when something stirred in the creek below. I strained to look closer into the small pool at the base of the cliff and saw several large arctic grayling rolling near the surface. Their large, long dorsal fins swayed along their backs as they fed on the plentiful insect life swarming around the pool.

I continued to watch them for a few minutes longer and then checked my wrist watch. It read six forty-five—still a little early, but time to start back. I walked up the hill and took another look around. I noticed the hot springs was located above the entire camp. It was five feet above the greenhouse, which allowed the Veerhusens to siphon the water to the building. It was also about 10 feet higher than the cabins and the lodge. Thus, I assumed Len used gravity to pipe the hot water to them.

As I started to return to the cabins, I passed the garden. The Veerhusens had planted cabbage, lettuce, potatoes, two squash plants, and a pumpkin. Some of the plants looked like a buzz saw had attacked them. The ragged edges indicated a moose-sized mouth had chomped the leaves to the stems. I also noticed two black hoses that moved hot water under the full length of the garden to warm the soil.

I walked down the trail back to the old cabin. Since I was about ten minutes early, I sat outside the arctic entry on a large round chopping block with an axe embedded in the surface and shooed away more bugs.

Within a few minutes, I heard some activity in the cabin. I knocked on the door and heard Pat tell me to come inside.

I pushed on the spring-loaded door, walked through the arctic entry, and entered the cabin. Pat was busy making a fire in the woodstove. She already had a coffeepot brewing on the Coleman burner. Len was silently putting his shirt on in the back room. Pat looked up to me, smiled, and asked, "Howdy, Mike. How did you sleep?"

"Not bad," I answered. I stood awkwardly next to the kitchen table not knowing what to do.

"Have a seat, Mike," Pat directed. "I will fry us up some bacon and pancakes, shortly. Do you want some coffee while you wait?"

"No thank you," I replied. "I haven't developed a taste for coffee, yet." Happy emitted a low growl and watched me from his pillow with eyes that glowed like embers.

Pat smiled as she grabbed a pitcher on the counter, handed it to me, and said, "Here. Why don't you fill it up with some ice-cold water from the creek we crossed last night? We don't drink from Hot Springs Creek because of the sulfur taste. I'll mix you up some Tang when you get back."

Relieved to have something useful to do while I waited for breakfast, I said, "Sure. I will be right back." I hotfooted it out the door and away from Len and Happy. By the time I came back, Len was drinking his coffee at the table and I could smell and hear bacon sizzling on the stove. The smell made my stomach rumble with hunger.

Len pointed to an empty five-gallon gas can with the top removed that sat next to the stove and said, "From now on, it's your job to make sure that can is filled with kindling, understand?" I nodded and the conversation died.

Pat heated her griddle on the woodstove until the Crisco skittered across the surface. Then she poured her batter into perfectly round pools. Her griddle was large enough to make two pancakes at a time. When she served up the first batch with bacon, I passed the plate to Len and sat looking at the walls while she cooked more. Finally, Pat handed me the next plate. I slopped some butter on the cakes, poured

Aunt Jemima syrup over them, and proceeded to devour my food. Within seconds, it was gone.

"How did you like the sourdough pancakes?" asked Pat. I suddenly realized that I had scarcely tasted them. I subconsciously ran my tongue across my mouth to recapture any residual taste.

"They were really good!"

Pat laughed and asked, "Would you like some more?"

"Sure!" I almost shouted. Len never looked up from his coffee. Pat made two more and flipped them on my plate. "Thank you," I said as I repeated my preparations to eat them. This time I ate them more slowly and savored the mild sour taste. I washed my breakfast down with a glass full of cold Tang and wiped my face off on the napkin. I could have downed another two pancakes, but I had a hunch asking for more would be pushing my luck. So, I turned to Len with a look that proclaimed that I was ready. Len continued to drink his coffee and finish his food.

I took this moment to prove to Len that I could be useful. I stood up and took my dish, utensils, and cup to the sink. Then I grabbed the gas can and carried it outside. I wrenched the axe out of the block and proceeded to split the cut logs that were piled nearby into kindling. Within a few minutes, I had filled the can and I proudly marched back into the cabin with the load. As I set the can next to the stove, I heard Len say, "Next time, put a few more chunks in there. That spindly wood burns too quick."

Crestfallen, I nodded and emitted a flat-toned, "okay."

Len got up and said, "Well, we best be getting to it." He placed his plate in the sink and grabbed his hat from the peg on the wall. Then he opened the door and proceeded through the arctic entry. I caught the door before it swung shut and followed close behind.

I heard Pat call out, "Have a good day!"

Len made a beeline straight for the shop. He opened both doors and walked to a center post where two hoops leaned against it. A stack of beveled slats lay next to the hoops. Len put his hand on the hoops and appraised his work for a moment before he spoke to me. "I want to raise the elevation of the hot springs by another four feet. So, I decided to build a tank and set it over the well. See these hoops? I want to set these precut slats inside the hoops and have the water rise inside." I nodded that I understood his approach.

Len looked at me for a moment and then asked, "I have sixty slats. What angle should I have cut each side of the slat?"

I looked at him and answered, "Three degrees."

Len blinked and, for the first time, gave me a quick smile. "That's right," he replied. "Let's get these materials up to the hot springs. Then we will string an extension cord from the generator to the work site to power the drill." Len rolled a wheelbarrow inside the shop. I loaded as many slats as I could and wheeled the materials up to the springs. Then I made two more trips until I moved all the materials. Meanwhile, Len strung extension cords from the shop.

Finally, Len and I walked back to the shop and Len demonstrated how to start the generator. "This is a cold-hearted beast," said Len as he set the choke. "It takes a few cranks of the cord." Len slipped the knotted end of the rope into a slot on a drum connected to the crank and wrapped the rope around it. Then he braced his foot on the timber holding the generator and yanked the rope with a grunt. The generator lay lifeless. Len repeated the process two more times before the generator coughed. He adjusted the choke and cranked it again. This time the generator fired and roared into life. It ran loud but strong.

Len looked like he was out of breath as he took his hat off and wiped his brow. He studied the generator for a minute longer before nodding his head to leave. We walked back to the springs and Len plugged the electric drill into the cord. "Okay," he said as he threw a hoop over the springs, " we have to clear the rocks away from the hoop so we can push the slats into the springs. I want to make a watertight seal along the bottom the best we can."

Using picks, shovels, and pry bars, we laboriously carved a circular trench around the springs. It was hot, sweaty work that seemed to attract hordes of mosquitoes. As I frequently shook my head to clear my face from the milling insects, I noticed Len snorting mosquitoes out of his nostrils. Holding on to tools made it difficult to swat at them.

After removing the rocks, Len had me hold the slats against the bottom hoop while he screwed them in place with the drill. The mosquitoes made the tedious task almost unbearable. Two hours later, we finished the first hoop. The slats fit perfectly together within the hoop. Len and I admired the work. The spring water had already risen six inches before flowing through the slats.

"Let's take a short break," suggested Len. I tried to feign reluctance, but I think Len could tell it was bravado. We walked back to the cabin and away from the mosquitoes. Inside, Len had coffee and I had another glass of Tang and a Pilot Bread cracker with jam. As we sat quietly, Len took out a tobacco can and cigarette paper and began rolling a cigarette. He did it without much thought, but when he was done, the cigarette was perfect. "Here you go, Pat," he said.

Pat came away from the laundry she was soaking in the sink and took the homemade cigarette. She lit it with a paper match and drew heavily until the end had bright red ember. She closed her eyes and seemed to relish its taste. When she opened them, she found me staring at her. Pat slowly pulled the cigarette from her mouth and said, "We love a good smoke. People say it's bad for you, but I don't believe them. We've never been healthier."

Len patiently rolled another cigarette and held it up to Pat when he was done. She lit it with her own cigarette and handed it back to him. Len took a deep drag and slowly exhaled the smoke above his head. He also had the look of sheer bliss. Soon the cabin was a mix of breakfast, burning Pic, and cigarette smells. The three of us sat in silence for a few minutes until Len looked at me and said, "You need a hat, don't ya?"

I self-consciously ran my hand over my mosquito-bitten scalp and replied, "Yes. I could use one."

Len took one last long drag of his cigarette and snuffed it out in an old butter can. He exhaled and said, "I got just the ticket. Let's go." We got up and went back outside. I followed Len back to the shop. He rummaged around the work bench and uncovered an orange hard hat.

He handed it to me and said, "See if that fits." I put it on and it swam on my head until I found the adjustment strap. After a few tugs, the hat felt heavy, but fit well. "Got it?" he asked. "Good. Now let me see it." I handed it back to him and Len poured 10/40 motor oil over the hard hat until he coated the entire surface. "There you go," said Len as he handed it back to me. "This will keep the mosquitoes off your face. You will have to clean them off the hat from time to time and apply more oil, but it works."

I shrugged my shoulders and put it back on my head saying, "It's worth a try."

Len started out the door. "Let's get that upper hoop on before lunch." The second hoop proved to be much more difficult than the lower one. Len wanted the hoop to be perfectly level as he attached it to the slats. He placed a carpenter's level across the top and directed me to hold the hoop so the bubble of the level stayed in the center of the sight glass. Three factors conspired against me to accomplish this task—the hoop was heavy and awkward, the mosquitoes were still relentless, and the immersed slats and bottom hoop were becoming buoyant. Thus, keeping the top hoop level was next to impossible.

Within half an hour, Len had reached the end of his patience. "Damn it! I told you to keep that end up." I wisely chose not to say anything. As the minutes dragged by, Len's vocabulary deteriorated. At a little past noon, I saw Pat come up to get us for lunch, but she abruptly halted when she heard Len's swearing and decided to leave us alone. Finally, after three agonizing hours, the hoop was secured to the slats. The wood fit snugly together and the water rose another foot within the newly formed tank until it streamed through the slats and under the bottom.

We were exhausted as we stood back and examined our work. Len wiped his brow and said, "The water will rise higher once the wood swells and becomes watertight. We will need to shore up the bottom, too, but that can wait until after lunch."

I took off my hard hat and wiped my forehead with the back of my sleeve. Then I examined the hat and was shocked at what I saw. The entire helmet was covered with mosquitoes glued to the oil. The coverage was so complete that it was no longer orange, but gray-black from the insects. I carried it away from my body and deposited it on the chopping block in front of the cabin.

Then I excused myself and went to my cabin to wash. I poured the cool water into the wash basin and washed the sweat, insect repellent, and smashed bugs off my face, neck and hands. As I dried my face, I studied my reflection in the mirror and took stock of my condition. I had large welts from mosquito bites rising on my ears, neck, and especially along my left wrist. My wide watchband had provided the bloodthirsty villains with a portal to climb inside my coat. I took my watch off and threw it on my bed. I had just experienced five hours of hard work without complaining and, therefore, I concluded that I was still in good shape. I hung the towel on the rack and went to join the Veerhusens for lunch.

Pat had homemade soup and sandwiches ready. Len was already eating when I sat down. Pat ladled soup into a bowl and set it in front of me. It tasted good with the meat sandwich and I devoured it and the soup within seconds. Pat was just sitting down with her own bowl of soup when she saw me drain my bowl. "Would you like more?" she asked.

"Sure," I said. "I can get my own." I poured the rest of the pot into the bowl and grabbed a Pilot Bread cracker.

As I sat down, I noticed Len and Pat staring at me. Len muttered as he stirred his soup, "I'm going to have to kill another moose just to feed him." Pat gave me a sympathetic smile.

Lunch ended with Len and Pat enjoying another hand-rolled cigarette. I noticed the gas can was empty of wood, so I got up and reached down to get it. I froze when Happy growled at me from the corner. I was aware of Happy in the background wherever I went. He watched me warily from a distance and made sure that I did not pull any shenanigans. Apparently, Happy thought stealing the gas can was an offense worthy of a bite. This time, Len set him straight, "Happy! Leave him alone." Happy put his head between his paws and glared at me.

I picked the can up and carried it outside. I returned a few minutes later with it filled with kindling and larger chunks. When I sat down, Len was stubbing out his cigarette. "Okay. Now, I want you to haul sand and rocks up from the creek and fill around the bottom of the tank. Try to stop the water from bubbling up from underneath, understand? You might have to pile some rocks on top to weigh the tank down." I nodded.

As we left the cabin, I grabbed my hard hat and took it to the shop. I found an old rag to clean it. The layer of insects made the oiled surface hard and crunchy. Then I applied another coat of oil and put on the helmet.

I retrieved the wheelbarrow and went down the steep trail to the banks of Hot Springs Creek. Here, I shoveled sand and gravel into the wheelbarrow. Then I grabbed the handles and pushed with all my strength to move my load. I had to gain some momentum before I hit the trail incline or I would not make it up the hill. I was worn out by the time I completed my first round trip. I knew this was going to be a long afternoon.

As the hours passed slowly, I gradually shored up the bottom of the tank. As Len predicted, as the water rose in the tank, the tank's buoyancy increased. To counter this force, I hauled loads of rocks and piled them on planks that straddled the rim. By the end of the day, the water had risen three feet above its original elevation and I was so tired that I could barely raise my arms.

Len came up to me to appraise my work. Using his foot, he tamped down the sand around the tank and then stood back and watched the water bubble in the springs. "Well, this is about as good as we are going to get it," he said. He pointed to a black-capped nipple protruding from one slat. "That's where we'll hook the pipe to supply the lodge with hot water. I'm hoping for a sustained two feet of head to push the water through this opening. Once we connect all the hosing, I will install a hydraulic ram below the springs to increase the water pressure."

I looked at Len quizzically and asked, "What is a hydraulic ram?"

"I will show you in a couple of days. Let's tie things up before dinner." We gathered the tools and extension cords and loaded them into the wheelbarrow. Then, I shuttled the materials to the shop and parked the wheelbarrow inside. As I closed the door, I felt tired and filthy, but strangely good with the knowledge that I had held my own throughout the day.

Len and I walked in silence to our respective cabins to clean up. I took my muddy boots off at the porch and shuffled inside. I peeled my sweat-soaked shirt off my back and removed my dirt-caked pants. Then I washed the grime and insect repellent off my body. My hands stung from blisters that formed under my work gloves. I put on clean clothes and hung my dirty ones over the front porch railing. Finally, I slipped on a pair of tennis shoes and walked to the old cabin for dinner.

Len was just sitting down when I came in. Pat was finishing her dinner preparations over the woodstove. Without looking up, she said, "Mike, you should fill up a pitcher with creek water if you want cold milk for dinner."

"Okay," I said as I grabbed the Rubbermaid pitcher from the counter. "I will be right back." Halfway to the creek, the mosquitoes found me, but I was determined not to use Cutters. I had washed off the stink and I was not going to use it until tomorrow. I quickened my pace, which evolved into a run. I scooped out a pitcherful of water and ran back to the cabin with a black cloud of mosquitoes behind me.

I stopped in the arctic entry to catch my breath and calm myself before entering the cabin. As I came inside, Pat was putting the pots on the table. The smells made me ravenous. Pat smiled a thank you as she took the pitcher and mixed powered milk in a tall glass. As I sat down, I found a feast spread before me. Pat had cooked canned meat in a gravy sauce to be served over rice. She had also picked and cleaned lettuce and carrots from the garden and greenhouse. Plus, she had made a loaf of bread which was still warm from baking.

I could scarcely contain myself as Pat sat down and began to serve the meal. I wolfed down two platefuls until I felt Len's and Pat's eyes on me. "Dear God," muttered Len. I felt my face flush red, so I put my hands on my lap and looked away. Len shook his head and returned his attention to his meal.

An uncomfortable minute ticked by until Pat motioned with her head to the food and said, "There is plenty, Mike. Go ahead and serve yourself." I was torn between two emotions. One was pride. I wanted to push away from the table, declare myself finished, and preserve a few shreds of my dignity. The other emotion was absolute hunger. My stomach felt like I had a tapeworm devouring everything I put in it and screamed for more. I settled for a compromise. I spooned up a small helping of rice, drizzled some meat sauce over it, and ate it slowly. When I finished, I carefully rose from the table, placed my plate in the sink, and sat back down.

Len and Pat finished their dinner in silence. As Pat was getting up, she asked me, "How did you like the moose meat, Mike?"

I looked at her in surprise and said, "It was really good! I've never had moose meat before."

Pat smiled and said, "Well, that's good because we canned a whole moose last fall and we still have a lot of it."

Len rolled his eyes and said, "For the love of God, Pat, the way this kid eats we will be lucky that it lasts till the end of the month."

Pat squared off to her husband and said, "Mike's a growing young man and the way you are working him he is going to eat a lot." Her statement made Len angry, but before he could fire back, something outside caught Happy's attention. He let out a loud bark in the cabin and ran to the entry. He quickly hooked his paw on the door, threw it open and bolted through the arctic entry. Within seconds, he was outside barking up a storm. Pat looked out the front window and immediately saw why Happy was upset.

"She's back!" hissed Pat through clenched teeth. "She's back with her brat calf. I swear I'm going to butcher the two them where they stand!" Pat grabbed a broom and zipped out the door. I looked back to Len and saw his expression change from anger to amusement.

"A cow moose and her calf are munching Pat's garden again," he said. I ran outside to see the spectacle. Pat was running fearlessly toward a tall gangly moose that was prancing in the garden with Happy. Its neck hackles were straight up and its ears flattened. The calf was standing next to the greenhouse looking unsure which way to run.

"Get out of here, you mooching varmint!" yelled Pat as she waved her broom. The cow paid no attention to Pat. Instead, she tried stomping Happy, but he was too quick for her. He darted and veered away from her killer hooves. Finally, the moose and calf trotted off and headed back to the woods. Pat lowered her broom and took a deep breath. Happy came marching triumphantly back.

"That's showing her who's boss, Pat," laughed Len. Pat made a face at Len and then walked back to the cabin with Happy.

Pat's aggression surprised me and when I asked her about it she responded, "That cow thinks she owns the place. I work damn hard to grow vegetables and she thinks it is all for her. Last week, she saw fit to stick her head right through the plastic sheeting in the greenhouse and helped herself to my tomato plants. Took me a full day just to patch up the wall with duct tape." Pat took some deep breaths to relax her and then continued, "When she and her calf browse in the north field, I usually greet her and speak softly to her about her baby. But sometimes she gets too bold and wants a luscious snack. Then I have to set her right."

Pat was spun up and was having trouble settling down. So she grabbed a water jug and filled a pot. Then she fired up the Coleman stove and set the pot on it to warm. "I'll be glad when you guys hook the hot water back up. It sure makes washing dishes easier."

Pat's comment caused me to look at the kitchen sink more closely. Sure enough, there was a black hose with a wooden stopper protruding from it. It looked like the one in the bathtub of the cabin where I was staying. "You mean you guys pipe water from the springs into the cabins?"

"Yep," answered Pat, "the water comes out of the springs at 135 degrees and it's the perfect temperature for washing dishes and clothes. It is even great for bathing. Once you guys hook the water back up from your new tank, you can take a bath in your cabin. Luxurious, uh?"

I fought an urge to ask Len if we could hook it up now. Len was settling down in a chair next to a window screen with a paperback book. He obviously was going nowhere. I subconsciously let out a sigh and looked out the window at the mountains in the distance. Len interpreted my sigh as boredom and said, "Not much happens around here in the evenings. Mostly read. Then listen to some radio. You're going to have to get used to it."

I looked at the wall clock and it read seven thirty—too early to go to bed. So I asked, "May I turn on the radio?" Len shrugged and returned his attention to his novel. I walked to a bench built into the log wall. A tall AM radio sat next to a side-band transmitter that was equipped with a microphone. Both radios were hooked to a 12-volt car battery stored underneath the bench. I gave Pat an inquisitive look.

"We use the side-band when we need help or call for a plane," explained Pat. "Two years ago, I came down with an infection that paralyzed me. Len called the air force base in Galena for a helicopter to take me to Fairbanks. That radio was a lifesaver. Before that, I had to call for help to look for Len. Turned out he broke his leg several miles from here when he tried to remove some parts from a bulldozer we left on the trail from Kokrines. Without the radio, he would have been a goner."

Pat's explanation evoked many questions in my mind and the possibility of exciting stories, but she returned to her chores as if she had nonchalantly described the weather. Len never looked up from his book. Disappointed, I refocused my attention on the AM radio. I noticed the antenna was removed and a wire led outside to two old black spruce poles that separated our cabins. A long antenna wire was stretched across the poles to improve reception. I flipped the power switch on. A few seconds later, KIAK, the country western station broadcasting on 970 AM from Fairbanks transmitted clearly through the radio speaker. Though I was a rock and roll fan, the country music and commercials were a link to the life that I had just left behind. I took a chair and listened for a while.

Pat looked at the windup clock on the counter and said, "We'll listen for messages on Pipeline of the North. It comes on at eight forty-five. Then we switch to KNJP on 1170 AM to hear Trapline Chatter. Trapline Chatter broadcasts at nine twenty."

That's a neat concept, I thought. *Messages over the radio.* "So, how does it work?" I asked Pat.

Pat wiped her hands on a towel as she thought about her answer. "Well, if someone wants to send you a message, they call up the radio station and give it to them. Then when the time comes, the deejay reads it on the air. For instance, if someone was sending us some supplies, they would tell us when to expect the plane. Or someone could get a message to us if there was a family emergency. Remember, we don't have phones in the bush."

"Do the stations carry the same messages?"

Pat smiled and said, "Not really. Pipeline of the North sometimes sounds like Peyton Place and the messages can get a little racy. KJNP is a Christian station. So, they watch their content. Every once in awhile, we will get the same message on both stations. People will post messages on each program just to make sure we get them. KJNP boosts their power in the evening, so their program comes in the clearest."

I sat down and suffered through the country wailing. Promptly at eight forty-five, the music ended and the deejay announced that it was time for the Pipeline of the North. Len put down his book and Pat sat down to listen. The first message was for someone in Huslia to fly back to Fairbanks for a medical checkup. Others talked about meeting a plane or boat at a designated point. Then, out of the blue, came the message, "From Lucy in North Pole to John in Allakaket. I'm pregnant. What are you going to do about it?" Len and Pat found this highly amusing with Len slapping his knee in delight.

"Wow," I said. "They'll say anything, won't they?"

"That's nothing," replied Pat as she wiped the tears from her eyes. "Wait until they repeat it." Sure enough, a few minutes later, the deejay announced that was the end of the messages and would repeat them after a few words from their sponsors. After the commercials, the deejay slowly and clearly repeated the messages without missing a beat. Lucy's message was hilarious the second time.

At nine o'clock, Pat tuned in KJNP, which was broadcasting. The station clearly boomed on the speaker. Pat turned down the volume and resettled on the chair. KJNP played soothing Christian music which I listened to without complaint. At nine twenty, the music stopped and a deejay announced that KJNP was the "gospel station at the top of the nation" and that it was time for Trapline Chatter. The format for Trapline Chatter was similar to Pipeline of the North. Some of the messages were the same, but Lucy's was missing.

By nine forty-five, my eyes grew tired. I wished everyone good night and without waiting for a response from Len, I went to bed. Before I undressed, I sat on my bed, popped another candy orange slice in my mouth, and thought about the day. I had the satisfying feeling of holding my own. Len did not seem so harsh by the end of the day and Pat clearly stuck up for me. I made a resolution to try hard again tomorrow. I still had the dull ache of homesickness, but I could manage it. I got up, brushed my teeth, washed, and went to bed. Exhaustion took the last of my worries away.

My head snapped up as my mind flooded with thoughts that I had overslept. A quick glance at my watch said the time was six thirty. I rolled out of bed and took stock of my body. My hands were raw with blisters and my arms ached, but further examination showed that I was no worse for wear. I got up, washed, and slipped into my dirty jeans and work shirt. The mud had dried, so I stood outside and brushed the dirt off the best I could.

I strolled to the cabin at five minutes to seven and rapped on the door. I heard Pat telling me to come in. I pushed the arctic entry open and walked inside. Pat was busy stirring a pot of oatmeal on the Coleman stove. "How did ya sleep, Mike?" she asked.

"Like a log," I answered. I grabbed a water pitcher and said, "I'll be right back." I jogged down to the creek, filled up the pitcher with ice-cold water, and walked briskly back.

"Thank you," said Pat as she spooned up the oatmeal into bowls. I noticed she had bread toasting on a wire stand over the stove. "Why don't you sit down. Len will be here in a minute." I noticed Len putting his shirt on by the opening in the curtain to the bedroom. Pat slid a big steaming bowl of oatmeal in front of me. "We've got canned milk that you can pour over the top and sugar." As I prepared my cereal, Pat put a plate of buttered toast in front of me and a big glass of Tang. Len came to the table looking a little stiff. We ate in silence.

At the end of breakfast, I fetched the gas can and filled it with kindling and split wood. When I returned, Len had my day's assignment ready. "Can you drive a tractor?" he asked.

"Yep!" I answered. I quickly took out my wallet, removed my Montana Work Permit, and handed Len the laminated card. I had taken a week-long course in Belgrade, Montana and learned to safely operate farm equipment. The card certified that I demonstrated proficiency in driving tractors and other mobile equipment.

Len scarcely looked at the card before sliding it back across the table. "Okay," he said with a trace of disbelief. "Let's go and find out." Len rose, gave Pat a kiss, grabbed his hat from the wall peg, and walked out the door with Happy close behind. I put my dishes in the sink and ran after him.

We walked straight to the sawmill. The John Deere C60 tractor sat exactly where I had last seen it two days ago. Len waved his hand toward the tractor and said, "Start it up." I walked up to the C60 and took a look. The driver's seat was a molded metal stand with two brake levers for steering. I also saw levers by the dashboard that controlled the throttle and the hydraulics to the blade. The tractor had been modified with tracks that replaced the wheels. I had driven similar equipment in Montana.

Before climbing into the seat, I walked around the tractor and performed a quick inspection. I pulled the dip stick and checked the oil. I took off the gas cap and saw the tank was three-quarters full. I unhitched the engine cover and checked the fan belt. Finally, I jumped on the tracks and took the tin can rain guard off the exhaust pipe. Turning around, I saw Len watching me. I half expected him to look impressed, but his expression was bland.

I sat down in the metal seat, shifted the transmission to neutral, set the choke, and added a little throttle. I was ready. I pushed the silver starter button and the tractor chugged a few times, but did not start. I pushed the choke halfway in and tried a restart. This time the tractor caught and rumbled to life.

Len waited a few minutes for the C60 to warm up before shouting to me, "I want you to back the cat up to that trailer over there and hitch it up."

"Okay," I answered. I put the tractor into gear, added more throttle, and slowly let out the clutch. The C60 smoothly moved forward and began plowing a ditch in front of me because I forgot to lift the blade. I threw in the clutch and pulled the hydraulics lever to raise the blade. I could feel Len's scrutinizing eyes upon me, but I never looked back. I resumed my trek forward and drove to the trailer. I turned in front of the wagon and backed the tractor so that the trailer hitch lined up with the ball on the cat. I jumped down, lifted the hitch, and connected it to the tractor. Then I stood up and proudly beamed back to Len.

Len nodded and said, "All right. Now drive over to the woodpile and back into it." This was a harder maneuver because you have to feel the tractor push the trailer into position. I steered the tractor past the woodpile, stopped, shifted in reverse, and gingerly tried to back the trailer into a narrow slot by the pile. I missed on my first try. I drove forward and tried again. This time I slid the wagon into place.

"All right," said Len when he observed my driving skills, "I want you to load up the waste wood and stack it neatly by the log rails down the trail. I can use the big pieces for paneling inside cabins and cut the other pieces for firewood. See you at lunch." Len turned around and left. I killed the engine and set the brake.

At first look, loading the debris did not seem to be such a big deal, but the freshly cut wood dripped fresh sap and the bark seemed to embed itself into my clothes. By the time I had loaded the wagon, I was covered in pitch, dirt, and splinters. Only the weather cooperated to ease my labors by clouding and becoming noticeably cooler. The lower temperatures seemed to decrease the cloud of mosquitoes bugging me.

The day wore on in the tranquil silence of the Alaska wilderness. I frequently found myself gawking at the rugged untamed mountains around me. This country was more than beautiful—it was mesmerizing. The dark and bruised cumulus clouds seemed to bounce between the rocky peaks that were still splashed with snow. A light wind blowing through the tall spruce trees signaled a change in the weather.

My morning-long hard work scarcely dented the waste pile, but I kept whittling away at it. As I was backing the trailer up to the debris pile for the umpteenth time, I suddenly heard Pat yell out, "Time for lunch!" My head snapped up and I saw her standing by the lodge. I waved to her and shut down the equipment. My stomach growled in anticipation.

We walked back to the cabin with Happy by her side. Happy watched me with a scrutinizing eye and made sure I behaved myself. "I'll be right over, Pat," I said, "I've got to wash up." I took my helmet and coat off and placed them on the porch to my cabin. Then I tried to scrub the pitch off my arms and hands. I finally gave up and walked to the large cabin for lunch.

Len was consuming his stew when I walked inside. As I sat down, he asked, "Tractor running okay?"

"Yep." I answered as Pat scooted a bowl of moose stew in front of me. With a spoon in one hand and a Sailor Boy Pilot Bread biscuit in the other, I attacked it. Within seconds, it was gone.

"For the love of God . . ." muttered Len.

"Would you like some more, Mike?" asked Pat.

Since I had not taken a break during the morning, I reasoned that I had earned another bowl. "Please," I answered without embarrassment. Pat smiled as she took my bowl and filled it up. This time I ate more slowly and savored the rich meaty taste. I buttered another Pilot Bread biscuit and used it to help shovel the stew into my mouth. When I was done, I washed the remnants down with a tall glass of Tang.

"Thank you," I said to Pat as I stood up and put my dishes in the sink. Then I carried the gas can outside and filled it with wood. When I came back inside, Len was rolling Pat a cigarette. Not wanting to loiter in smoke, I announced that I was going back to work and left Len and Pat in their tobacco ecstasy.

By the time I got back to the tractor, the wind had started to blow. Within minutes, I felt the first sprinkles of rain splatter on my face. I buttoned my coat tighter and pressed on. The rain increased and soon it began to come down hard. Not wanting to quit, I jumped on the C60 and started driving to the off-loading point. Then the rain came down in sheets. "I'm done!" I yelled above the storm as I stopped the engine, threw the can over the exhaust pipe, and jumped off the machine. Water streamed off my hard hat as I ran for the back door of the lodge. I flew up the ramp, raced inside, and almost smacked into Len. He had been watching me from the back window.

Len looked me straight in the eyes and said, "Even an animal knows when to get out of the rain." I would remember his caustic remark for the rest of my life.

The hard rain killed the rest of the workday and another chance to prove myself. Still smarting from Len's barb, I sought refuge in an old wood Chevron AV-Gas box that contained a heap of paperback books. Most were secondhand copies with torn covers and bent pages—signs of many owners. I flipped through the Louie L'Amour westerns and various romance novels until I found a cover that captured my imagination. The book was *The Alaskan* by Robert Lund. Under the title were the words, "Women and gold, and a raw, new country— the brawling, lusty, turbulent story of a man who challenged an untamed frontier." The cover displayed the back of a rugged young man, broad at the shoulders and trim at the waist, carrying a partially clothed native woman. Her expression wavered between unconsciousness and ecstasy and her left arm, adorned in Indian bracelets, wrapped around his torso with her nails raking his back.

Oh, yeah, I thought as I sat down and opened the cover. The inside page contained a note written in a woman's hand that read, "Damn good book! Verna." The next page read, "A BIG Book, A MAN'S Book, A Book as Vital and Earthy as the Wilderness Itself. Nineteen-year-old Wade Carlson came to Seward, Alaska, with nothing but his hard muscles and the clothes he stood up in. He fought for his place among the brawling, hard-drinking sourdoughs, the old-timers. He ripped gold out of the earth with his bare hands. He was a man to whom women came easy. This is his story and the story of an untamed new land." *Okay*, I thought, *I'm hooked.*

Within the first pages, I began to identify myself with Wade Carlson, the fictionalized character of Robert Lund's brother who arrived in Seward in the 1920s in search of work. I was only three years younger, on my first Alaska adventure, and in a similar situation having to prove myself to an Alaska sourdough—not to mention my teenage mind fantasied that I could strike a similar pose in my Levi jacket as Wade on the cover. After establishing that Wade and I were kindred spirits, I quickly became engrossed in the story.

"Did you find a good book, Mike?" asked Pat. Her soft voice pulled me out of my make-believe world and I suddenly flushed red with embarrassment. I nodded and showed her the cover. She smiled and said, "Oh, yes. I read that one. Len picked it up in Galena. It's a good story." I felt relieved. I half expected Pat to yank it out of my hands and reprimand me for reading inappropriate material.

"It looked like an okay story," I lied. "Gives me something to do." Pat nodded and returned to her sewing. I read a few pages more and checked the time—eight o'clock. Still forty-five minutes until Pipeline of the North. I put down my book and asked Pat, "Do you mind if I turn on the radio?"

"No. Go ahead," replied Pat. Len scarcely lifted his head and nodded. I flipped on the radio and KJNP crisply broadcasted through the speaker. The music was a combination of gospel and old melodies. After listening for half an hour, a soothing baritone sang *"The Last Waltz."* Pat put down her sewing, closed her eyes, and swayed slowly to the words. "Engelbert Humperdinck," she cooed, "We love Engelbert Humperdinck. We tried to see him once at a concert in

California. It didn't work out. Hope to see him someday. Do you like Engelbert, Mike?"

"Ah, honestly, I have barely heard of him."

Pat continued as she moved to the music, "Well, he is a bit before your time." Len put down his book and listened to the song with his wife and, for a brief moment, I witnessed something special between this couple who I had known for only two days. When the song ended, they opened their eyes and smiled at each other—the acknowledgment of sharing a touching memory and love. I sat quietly, not wanting to disturb the moment, but I felt that my mere presence desecrated it. Then slowly they resumed their activities.

Pipeline of the North and Trapline Chatter proved to be uneventful. I gathered my novel and excused myself for the evening. Much to my surprise, Len bid me good night to which I immediately replied, "Thank you!"

As I sat on my bed and ate another candied orange slice, I reviewed the day's successes and failures. I thought, *Do wild animals really have more common sense than I?* The revelation shook me, but the sourdoughs in my book were accusing Wade of the same fault. They even called him a strange name—*Cheechako. I just got to work through this like Wade.* Then I thought about what Doug told me the night he gave me my plane ticket. "*Just do the best you can and stay with it. Things will work out.*"

I started thinking about my family and how much I missed them. Another lump formed in my throat. Then I got up, washed, and got ready for bed. As I slid under the covers and got comfortable, I felt myself becoming tranquil like the wilderness around me, and before I fell into the realm of sleep, I whispered, "Something will break for me. I've got to keep at it."

Chapter 4

The Turning Point

Finishing breakfast, Len announced that he would be using the C60 to drag logs he had cut during the winter to the sawmill. While he was gone, Len wanted me to dig a trench to bury the new pipeline from the hot springs to the cabins and the lodge. This meant a day of swinging a pick into the rocky ground, but the weather was still cool and breezy so I knew that I would survive.

I started digging next to the wooden tank. The pick pinged on the rocks and sent tingling vibrations up my arms. Progress was slow and miserable. Within an hour, new blisters began to form inside my gloves. I gritted my teeth and continued. The light wind gave me some reprieve and kept the mosquitoes at bay.

Len was working along the northern edge of camp, not far from my work site. The terrain dropped quickly with unstable tussocks that pitched and rolled the tractor as Len drove. Every now and then, I stopped to catch my breath and watched Len wrap a steel cable around two or three logs and slowly drag them back.

Around ten o'clock, I faintly heard the tractor bog down, idle, and finally quit. Suddenly, Len's cuss words carried across the distance and seared my young ears. I looked up and could see the C60 resting on the side of a hill in an awkward tilt. Len was kicking the right track in disgust. I threw down my pick and jogged over to the tractor.

"What's the matter, Len?" I asked.

Len held his hat in his left hand as he pushed both fists into his hips and scowled at the track. "I broke the lower track support! The cat slid sideways on the hill and couldn't handle it. Damn it all to hell! I gotta fly a welder in from Galena to fix this and it's gonna cost me big time! Damn it!"

I took a quick look at the damage and saw an eight-inch-wide by four-inch-thick metal bar snapped in two. The break looked clean, but the pieces were pulled far apart. I stood up, cleared my throat, and said, "I can fix it."

Len turned his head and looked at me in disbelief. "Say what?"

"I said I can fix it." To bolster my claim, I quickly added, "I saw you had a portable arc welder and some rods back at the shop. If we collect all the extension cords, we might just have enough to connect the generator to the welder. I also saw you had some scrap metal under your work bench. I can fashion a brace from it."

Len scratched the stubble on his chin as he studied my face for a moment and then looked back at the tractor. He sighed and said, "What the hell! I've got nothing to lose. Okay. Let's do it."

"Great," I said as I turned and started walking back to the camp. I looked up to heaven and asked God for a miracle. Truth be told, I never was a good welder in school. I barely managed a passing grade because I had a hard time producing a good bead on a vertical surface—the exact surface where I needed to weld the brace. But here was my chance to shine and I went for it.

When we arrived at the shop, I started collecting and coiling every extension cord I could find. No matter what the length, we were going to use it. Soon I had a wheelbarrow full. As I started shuttling and stringing the cords to the tractor, Len said he knew where he had stashed a few more in the lodge and ran off to get them. When we connected the last one to the gangly and unmatched line of cords, we had only 10 feet to spare. *Well, we cleared the first hurdle*, I thought to myself. I secretly worried that the long procession of haphazardly connected cords would create an electrical short or loss in power, but there was nothing I could do about it.

Next, we loaded four hydraulic jacks into the wheelbarrow. We needed the jacks to align the tracks and the break. We also collected several broken planks to serve as foundations for the jacks to prevent them from sinking into the tundra. These items created a heavy load and completely overwhelmed my teenage strength. Len walked alongside the wheelbarrow and helped pull it across the rugged terrain. I was spent from the effort and we had one more trip to make. Suddenly, Len let out a deep sigh and announced it was time for lunch.

Thank God, I thought as I grabbed the empty wheelbarrow and pushed it back to camp. My forearms and back throbbed from the strain. I set the wheelbarrow next to the cabin door, threw off my hard hat and Levi jacket, and ran to my cabin to wash. My reflection in the bathroom mirror showed dirt and sweat streaking down my face. The cold water in the basin felt good as I washed away the first layer of dirt.

Lunch was a silent affair. As we sipped our soup, Len had a faraway look as if he was contemplating our next move. I diverted my attention to my soup to hide my uncertainty. I was committed to my claim as a welder and there was no backing out. Pat sensed our apprehension and determined it best to let us brood quietly.

After a half-hour reprieve, we resumed our rescue of the tractor. We went back to the shop and lifted the arc welder into the wheelbarrow. Then I pulled a piece of scrap metal from under the bench. It was a thick piece of steel about two-feet-long and six-inches-wide. I placed the metal in a machinist vise that was bolted to the bench. Len watched me remove the uneven ends with a hacksaw. Finally, I smoothed the edges with a file and removed the metal from the vise. I rotated the metal once in my hands and inspected it. I found no flaws and deemed it acceptable as a brace. I placed it in the wheelbarrow along with the file.

Then I collected the necessary equipment required to make the weld. I found the welder's mask, gloves, and hammer and put them in the wheelbarrow. The final item I needed was a welding rod. Len had several different types stored upright in an old 55-gallon drum. I chose a standard diameter rod with coated flux. I loaded five 2-foot welding rods into the wheelbarrow and nodded to Len that I was ready.

"Okay," he said, "Let's do it." Much to my surprise, Len grabbed the wheelbarrow and pushed it out the door. I almost ran to keep up with him. I helped him negotiate the rough terrain up to the tractor and set it down about four feet away from the C60.

Len took his cap off and wiped his brow with his sleeve. Without looking at me he said, "I guess we need to slide the wood and jacks under the dozer." This meant he wanted me to crawl over the cold wet tundra and position the jacks. The space was tight and thus I was the logical choice.

I took a deep breath and took off my hard hat and jacket. I pushed a few planks under the tractor and wiggled after them. I immediately felt ice-cold water squish out of the spongy soil and seep into my clothes. This was going to be a miserable job. I laid the planks as level as possible under the broken bar and the carriage. Then Len passed me the jacks. I placed the four-ton jacks under the tractor and the smaller one-ton jacks under the track and broken bar. Finally, I helped Len by guiding the crank with a long extension to each jack and holding it in place while Len expanded the jacks so they fit tightly. The whole process took about 20 minutes and I was soaked and chilled by then. I slid out from underneath the tractor and put on my coat.

For the next two hours, we jacked up the C60 and built cribbing from logs to slowly move the track into place and align the broken bar. When we finally brought the broken bar together, it was time for me to demonstrate my welding skills. Using a few old rags, I carefully cleaned the bar and the brace. Meanwhile, Len set up the arc welder. I selected a welding rod and connected it to the electrode holder. I put on welder's gloves and mask and clipped the negative wire to the broken bar. I grabbed the welding electrode with my right hand and held my mask up with my left. "Okay, Len. I'm ready to go. I'm going to run a bead down the crack before I put on the brace. Please switch the transformer on when I'm in position."

I saw Len nod as I knelt and positioned myself. Len switched the welder on. Then I dropped the mask over my face and slowly brushed the rod against the metal. Nothing happened. I continued to stroke the metal and still no arc of electricity leaped from the rod. *The long extension cords must be dropping the voltage*, I thought. Suddenly, a bolt of searing hot electricity and molten metal shot from the rod. The rod splattered on the bar. I quickly recovered and brought the arc along the crack of the broken bar.

Laying a good welded bead required finesse, a steady hand, and the correct speed. I had none of these, but I struggled to make it work. I knew I had to go slow enough for the molten rod to penetrate into the crack and weld the pieces together. I consciously slowed my breathing and mustered all the concentration I could. Gradually, I walked the bead down the crack. The last two inches of the bead would have made my shop teacher proud.

"Done!" I yelled. Len switched off the transformer. I flicked up my mask, pounded the slag off the weld with a welder's hammer, and inspected my work. The first inches were a disaster with molten metal splattered everywhere, but my weld improved with distance. If Len was upset he did not show it. I filed the weld down and told Len I wanted to redo the bead on the top. I got into position again, Len flipped on the transformer, and I redeemed myself with a good weld.

After filing the weld again, I arranged the brace on the bar with C-clamps. I inserted another rod into the holder, put on my mask and gloves, and announced, "First, I'm going to tack the brace in place. Then I will run a bead around it." Again, Len nodded. I situated myself so I could move around the brace and yelled, "Ready!" Len turned the machine on and I began stroking the rod against the metal. Knowing what to expect this time, I kept striking the rod until the white hot electric arc leaped to the brace. I kept my composure and quickly placed six tack welds around the brace. "Done!" Len turned the transformer off. I removed the C-clamps and cleaned the welds.

"This time I am going to make four long welds around the brace. I will have to stop halfway through and insert another rod. So here we go!" I flipped my mask down and prepared to make a bead along the top horizontal edge of the brace— the easiest weld. The rod burned smoothly and, within a few minutes, I had made a perfect weld. The two vertical welds were much harder. The upside-down weld along the underside of the brace was nearly impossible and I made a mess of it.

When I was done, Len inspected the welds. He rubbed his chin as he studied the brace. Then without saying a word, he stood up, walked behind the dozer, and grabbed a sledge hammer. He took a step back and let the hammer fly against the brace. Much to my relief, it held. Len smiled and said to me, "Good job, Mike! I think it will work." Len's words were music to my ears. I suddenly did not feel cold, tired, or hungry—just happy, content, and a bit vindicated.

We quickly removed the cribbing and jacks. Len fired up the tractor and drove it out of the muskeg. The brace worked beautifully. Len came back a few minutes later towing the trailer. We loaded the equipment and drove back to camp in style. Len stopped the C60 in front of the cabin and ran inside yelling, "Pat, Mike fixed the tractor! Isn't that great!" I felt a little embarrassed as Pat came outside smiling at me as she was drying her hands on a dish towel. Len pointed to the brace and showed her how we fixed the break.

Pat looked up to her husband and said, "See? I told you Mike would work out."

Len put his arm around Pat, looked at me, and said, "Why don't you drive the tractor back to the shop and put away the gear? Then we'll call it a day."

The significance of his words was not lost on me. Len trusted me to carry out his directions without supervision. My eyes misted as I nodded and climbed onto the driver's seat. As I drove away, I heard Len and Pat laugh and walk back into the cabin.

As I sat on my bed munching on a rationed orange slice candy, I shook my head in amazement over today's events. I had started the day like a prisoner at a labor camp and ended the day feeling like I was part of a tight family. Dinner was enjoyable listening to Len talk about some of the characters living in Galena. Pat reminisced about her time as a secretary to the commanding officer of Galena Air Force Base. Then we topped the evening off with a lively episode of Pipeline of the North. Even the fictional character, Wade Carlson, of my novel had won acceptance in his new Alaska home. His friends Mitch, Boots, and Jack were helping him learn the hard lessons of the Alaska bush.

For the first time since I arrived, my stomach did not hurt from homesickness. I missed my family terribly, but I also had an excited feeling about what tomorrow would bring. I reached across my bed and grabbed the marvelous gift from Pat —an alarm clock. I could now sleep soundly without fear of waking up late. I wound the spring, set the alarm for 6:30, and placed it on the window sill.

I got ready for bed and lay awake for a few minutes listening to Hot Springs Creek babble in the quiet daylight evening. "Thank you, God," I whispered, "for making the weld hold." Then I fell into a gentle sleep.

After breakfast, Len announced that we were going to install the hydraulic ram. "Oh, good!" exclaimed Pat. "I've got a ton of clothes to wash and I don't want to use the old scrubbing board. Mike, I bet you got some filthy pants and shirts by now, too."

"Yeah," I replied sheepishly, "they kind of stand up by themselves."

"Well after you guys get the hot water flowing again, give them to me. I will wash them with our stuff."

Len and I walked down to the shop. Len opened the door and went straight to a large box supported by a wood frame. He grabbed a pry bar and popped the lid off. Inside was a large cylindrical pump with two metal V-shaped springs that spread from the sides. The pump was painted a bright red. What struck me as odd was that I saw no electrical cord protruding from the base. I looked up to Len and asked, "How does it work? It doesn't appear to use electricity."

Len smiled and replied, "The ram will use the momentum of the falling water from the tank to power it. In fact, it has only two moving parts."

"Wow, that's neat," I said in amazement, "but I still can't envision how it works."

"Come on. Let's load it in the wagon and connect it up and I'll show ya." The hydraulic ram was surprisingly heavy, but we managed to slide it into the wagon. Len fired up the tractor and we drove it to the hill below the hot springs.

Len had chosen a spot just uphill from the old cabin to install the ram. We off-loaded the pump and placed it next to the trench I had dug the day before. I estimated the hot springs was located about eight feet above us. Len uncoiled the black plastic pipe and we strung it from the tank to the pump. "We'll hook this end up last," said Len. We then connected the output end of the pump with the pipe to the cabin. After Len inspected each connection, we returned to the tank. Len said, "Okay. Let's see how well this works. I want you to unscrew the cap on the nipple and I will jam the hose over it. Ready? Go." I used a pair of channel locks to twist the cap off. Hot water sprayed out and drenched us. With clenched teeth, Len forced the hose over the nipple and cinched it tight with a hose clamp.

Len wiped his face with the back of his sleeve and turned to walk back to the pump. "Let's take a look." At first, nothing happened. Water sputtered from the pump as the falling head of water pushed the air from the pipe. Then suddenly, a miraculous transformation took place. The water pressure slowly moved the piston inside the pump, spreading the spring bars. I heard a distinct "click" and the springs snapped back, spraying copious amounts of water in each direction. Then the process repeated itself every few seconds.

We watched it for a few minutes before Len explained what was happening. "The pump has an internal valve that allows the water to fall through the pipe and build up speed. Then the valve slams shut. The water rams into the closed valve and develops pressure. Hence the name, hydraulic ram. The pressure forces open a second valve and shoots the water to the cabins. As the pressure falls, the first valve reopens and the second valve closes and the cycle repeats itself. The pressure in the cabins increases almost tenfold, but it comes at a cost. As you can see, over half the water is wasted in the process." Len was right, I could see a small stream developing as the wasted water cascaded down the hill and into Hot Springs Creek.

"Why do you need such increased pressure at the cabins?" I asked. "Pat said she could operate everything just fine with the pressure naturally generated from the hill."

"That's right," replied Len, "she can, but I've got other plans that need water pressure. We are going to plumb the lodge and install a flush toilet this summer. The toilet needs at least twenty PSI to operate. Then, eventually, I'm going to build a swimming pool. The falling head from the tank won't operate showers there."

I was stunned. "A swimming pool?—Wow! Where do you plan to build it?"

Len took off his cap, wiped his brow, and pointed in direction of the shop. "Across from the shop in the woods between the trail and the creek. I've got sheets of fiberglass already stacked there. Took me forever to drag it from Kokrines."

I looked at Len with new admiration. *Is there anything he can't do?*

Len looked at me for a second and laughed. "Come on," he said as he playfully smacked my back. "Let's see how the water flows into the cabins." We walked back to the old cabin and entered. Pat was heating a bucketful of water for dishes. Len walked up to the sink and pulled the plug from the black plastic pipe. Air rushed from the pipe before water spurted out. Within seconds, hot water gushed from the pipe. "Well Pat," said Len, "You won't have to heat water anymore."

Pat smiled at Len and said, "Music to my ears, honey. So, can you and Mike drag the washing machine out and I will run a few loads of clothes?"

Len replied, "I think Mike and I can handle that request. Come on, Mike. Give me a hand here." We walked outside to a tarp covering a hidden pile alongside the arctic entry. Len grabbed the tarp, flung it off the heap, and revealed a white tub washer machine with a wringer on top to squish water from clothes. Len said, "Let's drag it to the front of the entry." We wrestled it out of the storage area and scooted it to the front. Pat met us at the door with a hose.

"That's fine right there," she said. Pat put the hose inside the tub and went back into the cabin to fit the hose onto the black pipe. She yelled from the cabin, "Mike, please bring me your clothes after you start the generator."

Len wagged his head toward the shop and said, "Come on and I'll watch you start it." We walked down to the shop and Len let me fumble with the starter cord and the choke. After five wrenching pulls, the generator reluctantly coughed and rumbled to life. Len pointed to a black extension cord hidden behind the generator. "That cord is buried between the shop and the cabin," he yelled above the noise. "Pat will plug the washer machine into it. You need to connect it to this outlet." Len pointed to a small panel on the generator. I nodded and plugged the cord into it. "That should do it," said Len. "Now go get your dirty clothes and take them to Pat."

I jogged over to my cabin and collected my clothes. After three days of outdoor work, they were mired in mud, wood pitch, and sweat. I was embarrassed to hand them to Pat. She took them from me without repulsion. By now the washing machine was nearly filled with hot springs water. Pat separated the clothes and threw in blue jeans and work shirts. She added some detergent and flipped on the machine. The tub immediately began agitating the clothes.

Pat turned to me and said, "This sure beats my scrub board. I rapped my knuckles more times than I want to remember on that thing. It should be outlawed! It's a housewife's nightmare." Her comment made me realize that even the simplest convenience was a big thing in the bush. Nothing should be taken for granted. I excused myself and went to find Len.

Len and I spent the rest of the day plumbing the lodge for the hot water. We hung the plastic pipe underneath the lodge from the floor joists. Len planned to use the water for heat, kitchen cleaning, and to flush a toilet. The latter proved to be amusing.

When we finished, Len connected the piping to the main line off the hydraulic ram. Within a few minutes, the surging water purged the air from the lines and the toilet began to fill. Len and I waited until the tank was full and then we ceremoniously flushed it. Steam gushed from the bowl as the hot water swirled inside. "How about that?" laughed Len. "You sit down and get a steam bath, too!" I felt the heat emanating from the tank and wondered if hapless users would get branded when they sat down on the seat. I decided to continue visiting the outhouse until the inaugural event proved otherwise.

Len looked pleased with the day's progress. He announced, "Let's wrap it up and take the tools back to the shed. We'll knock off a little early today. It being Saturday and all."

Cool, I thought. I could use a little free time to explore around the camp. We walked to the shop and put the equipment away and then made our way back to the old cabin. As Happy stood guard, Pat ran freshly washed underwear through the rollers to remove excess water. In the distance, I could see clean laundry hanging to dry on a clothesline next to the greenhouse.

Len put his arm around Pat's waist and said, "We're done for the day. We thought that you might want to be the first one to use the new toilet. What do you say?"

"Uh, Len," I cautioned, "you might want to take it kind of slow on that. The seat felt awfully hot."

Pat seemed amused as she gathered her laundry in a basket and prepared to carry it to the clothesline. She looked up to Len with a teasing smile and said, "You know, Len, if I get burned down there, you are going to be unhappy for a long time."

Len's smile vanished. He removed his arm from her waist and scratched the stubble on his chin as he contemplated his offer. "You know what?" he said after a long moment. "Perhaps we ought to wait a day just to see how the toilet holds up."

Pat shook her head and sighed as she picked up the basket. "I thought so. On another subject, why don't you have Mike catch us some grayling for dinner? We haven't had fish in a while."

"You bet!" I shouted a little too loudly. Fishing was one of my favorite hobbies. My grandfather had taught me how to fly-fish along the Montana rivers and I loved it. I had noticed two fly rods propped against the cabin wall when I arrived three days ago. I could hardly wait to try my luck with them.

"Sounds like a plan," said Len. "Come on, Mike. I'll get you fixed up." Len went inside the cabin for a moment and returned with a small bag of flies. Then he chose a fiberglass pole with a manual reel. "Here. I prefer the black gnat, but you take your pick."

Len had a limited selection of tied flies. I remembered the grayling below the hot springs were feeding on the surface, so I selected a White Ruff dry fly that would float. The black gnat was a wet fly that would sink. Len seemed amused at my choice. "Well, let's go see what ya got."

On a lark, I grabbed my little Kodak Insta-Matic camera and stuffed it in my coat pocket before meeting Len at the top of the cliff where the hot springs water fell to the creek. I shielded my eyes with my hands to reduce the glare coming off the water. Within a few minutes, I could detect the faint outlines of fish swirling in a back eddy close to the bank. I pointed to the school and said to Len, "Over there is a group. I'm going to sneak upstream and let my fly drift over them."

"Okay. I'm going to stay here and watch." I had a hunch that Len thought I was going to fail, so I detoured far away from the creek before I crawled back to the bank. I popped out of the brush about 20 feet upstream where I had last seen the fish. Casting from the kneeling position, I dropped my fly directly in front of me and let it drift over the fish. Wham! A grayling pounced and took off with it. I set the hook and held on. The fish jumped a few times and started running downstream. I let it go for a short distance until it halted from the drag. Then I carefully pulled in the line. Within a few minutes, I was holding the largest arctic grayling that I had ever seen. I spread its multicolored dorsal fin and held the fish up to show it to Len. He nodded with approval. Then I opened my knife to measure it. From the base of the handle to the tip of the blade, the knife was eight inches long. The fish measured two knife lengths. This was a giant compared to the little grayling I used to catch in the high Montana lakes.

I cut a willow branch and slipped it through the gills to hold the fish before continuing to try my luck again. I had to dry the fly by rubbing it on my shirt so it would float. Then I swung it into the creek and let it drift down again. Another fish whacked it and caused my reel to scream. Within fifteen minutes, I had caught a total of four grayling, all between 12 and 16 inches long. My fly was shredded from the strikes.

"That should be enough," said Len. "You need to leave some for next time."

"Okay," I replied with a big smile. "I'll clean them here and bring them up."

"I tell you what," said Len as he walked downhill to where I was standing. "I'll take your picture with your catch." Len took my camera and backed away as he framed me in the viewing sight. I stood tall and held out my catch that was hanging from the willow branch. My last fish was still flipping. I was wearing my new Levi jacket and the orange hard hat which contrasted sharply against the blue sky and beautiful distant mountains. So outfitted and posed, I held my catch as Len snapped one of the most memorable pictures of my life.

Pat fried the grayling in seasoned flour, bacon grease, and Crisco. I never knew fish could taste so good! When I pushed back from the table with my ravenous appetite temporarily sated, I rubbed my stomach and said, "Thank you, Pat. That was delicious. I could eat fried grayling every night."

"Whoa there!" replied Len as he wiped his mouth with a napkin. "You have no idea what you just said. Two years ago, we ran low on food while waiting for a plane. For two weeks we ate nothing but oatmeal, rice, and fish. It took me a long time to even look at a grayling again and I am not fond of oatmeal either."

Sensing that the mood was right for conversation, I asked Len a question that had been burning in my mind since I arrived. "Len, how did this place get here and how did you find out about it?"

Len took this opportunity to kick back and leisurely roll a couple of cigarettes. After a few minutes of silence, I thought he had not heard me or did not want to answer, but it turned out that he was consolidating his thoughts. As he licked the second one closed, Len began his story. "Melozi is a shortened version of Melozitna, which means 'river whose headwaters flow backward' in Athabaskan. The name refers to the Little Melozi River that flows north away from the Yukon to form the Melozitna. Natives, fur trappers, and prospectors have been coming to Melozi Hot Springs for centuries to soak in the mineral springs. People usually followed the 16-mile-long winter trail from Kokrines—a small village just upstream from Ruby on the north bank of the Yukon."

"In the early 1900s, the U.S. Army established a telegraph station at Kokrines. Military men would take dogsleds from the village to spend a few days around the springs. They built two small log bathhouses next to the hot springs. Supposedly, the bathhouses had wooden tubs and sweat chambers that could hold up to twenty people. Then, in December of 1911, the military built this cabin to accommodate visitors." Len paused as he lit his cigarette and passed it to Pat. He then lit his and took a deep drag before letting out the smoke. He watched the blue haze swirl to the cardboard ceiling and spread into thought-provoking wisps before continuing.

"Around 1920, Melozi became a winter headquarters for a reindeer-herding business. You can still see the fence posts for the old corrals around the camp. Old-timers say they had several thousand reindeer during their heyday. Herders would slaughter their animals and ship the meat to markets in the Lower 48. They apparently made good money until the Depression hit in the 1930s. The demand for their products slumped, but what put them out of business was the cattle-men. The cattle industry got jealous of the reindeer competition and lobbied Congress to pass the 1937 Reindeer Act. Overnight, white businessmen found their herds under the management of the Bureau of Indian Affairs, or as we call them, the BIA. The BIA then trans-ferred the ownership of all reindeer to Alaska Natives.

"Bankrupted, the white men opened their corrals and released their reindeer. The deer mingled and bred with the surrounding caribou. The resulting hybrid was a smaller caribou. This is why no trophy caribou are ever taken out of this area."

Len stopped to inhale another pull from his cigarette. Judging from the look on his face, he found it deeply satisfying. Then he smiled like he was remembering a fond memory and continued with his story.

"In November of 1965, I was playing poker at Hobo's Bar in Galena. A conversation started up about different government land programs a person could apply for and get tracts of land. There were homestead-ing programs, Native allotments, mining claims, and what not. In the middle of the discussion, some guy says that the BLM (Bureau of Land Management) is going to offer leases to develop hot springs around Alaska and Melozi was one of them."

"Now, I've heard of Melozi, but I had never been there. So, I got talking to Hobo about it."

The name intrigued me. "Who's Hobo?"

Len took a short pull on his cigarette before laughing. "Hobo is the nickname of Frank Benson. Great guy. Give you the shirt off his back, but he has a knack for getting in trouble."

Pat blew smoke into the air as she took her cigarette out of her mouth and added, "That poor man has been shot, stabbed, beat to an inch of his life, and damn near drowned in his own bar during the big flood two years ago and he still lives to see another day. He's a living miracle."

Cool, I thought. *I need to find out more about him.*

Len continued, "So, Hobo and I hired Harold Esmailka from Ruby to fly us out here in the dead of winter. We could see the steam from the hot springs rising ten miles out. Harold landed us on skis just downstream of here. We took a look around and thought we could develop it, so we came back to Galena and filed for a twenty-year agricultural lease from the BLM. Hobo had second thoughts, so I decided to do it myself."

"When did you guys move out here?" I asked.

Len took another drag on his cigarette and said, "It wasn't all at once. We kind of did it in stages. You see, at the time, I had a contract with the Air Force to keep the Galena runway clear of snow and ice. It paid well and kept me busy—sometimes day and night."

"And I had a job as the secretary to the commanding officer," added Pat.

"Right," continued Len. "So, we couldn't just up and move to Melozi. BLM finally issued the lease in late May of 1966. On top of all this, my son Dan and I had just finished building a hotel in Galena. We called it the Galena Yukon Lodge and it was doing real well . . ."

"Until it blew up!" exclaimed Pat with great delight. Her eyes danced with humor.

"What?" I asked with surprise. These two people were filled with incredible stories.

"Uh, thank you, honey, for bringing that to our attention," Len replied with a glint of mischievousness on his face. "We'll save that story for another time. Well, like I was saying, we had commitments that we could not walk away from. I also needed to build an airstrip to fly supplies in, so we decided the first order of business was to drive a cat in here during the winter."

I asked, "Is that the C60 you have here now?"

Len shook his head, "No, that was my second try. The first time, Bob Moore and I moved a rebuilt TDA-18 International from Ruby to Kokrines by Yutana Barge. Then we tried to walk it along the trail to here during the winter of 1966. We made 10 miles before we got stuck in a gawd-awful melt hole. We ended up leaving the cat and walking the remaining six miles to the hot springs. We damn near froze to death. The hot springs saved our lives."

"We tried again in the early spring of '67 and this time we were able to walk that C60 in here. The first thing that I did was build the airstrip, so we could get supplies flown in. We have been living here full-time ever since."

"Did you ever go back and get the TDA-18?" I asked.

Len snubbed out his cigarette in an old butter can. "Nope. Never did. It's still sitting out there. I tried to get some parts off it during the summer of 1970. That venture ended in disaster! I planned to walk there and back in one long day. So, I traveled light—no gun, a few sandwiches, and a coat. I took Hap with me, which turned out to be the smartest thing that I ever did.

"Well, I got there in good time. So, I went to work removing the engine part that I needed. I was standing on the track when I decided to jump off and get a tool from my pack. My leg slipped between the track and the frame. I fell backwards and snapped my leg bone. I could hear it as plain as day. God, did it hurt!"

"So there I was—laying on my back about ready to pass out from the pain without a way of contacting anyone. My pack laid about fifty feet away and Happy was dancing around me."

Len's story enthralled me. I could feel a piercing pain creep up my leg and the hopelessness of the situation. I needed Len to rescue me from his dire tale. I asked breathlessly, "So, what did you do?"

A mountain threw a shadow over the cabin as the evening sun dipped below its peak. Len looked at me with hard eyes through the dimming light and said flatly, "I fought panic. I knew that whatever I was going to do within the next hour would determine if I lived or died. The first thing I had to do was immobilize my leg. I noticed my pant leg was soaked in blood. So I rolled up my pants and there was this gawd-awful jagged bone sticking out of my skin. I damn near passed out just from the sight of it. When I couldn't get the bleeding to stop, I realized that I had no other choice. I had to set the break."

I released a deep shudder and reluctantly asked, "Did you do it?"

"Yep. I figured the only way to set the break was to pull my leg apart and align the bone. So I crawled over to the cat and slipped my leg between the track and the wheel. I was sitting up and thought that if I just fall backwards the leg would stretch out and line up. What I did not count on was passing out from the pain when I fell. When I came to, the leg had snapped back into place and the bleeding had stopped. I guess I was lucky. The doctor said that I did such a good job that he did not have to reset it.

"I managed to bandage up my leg and crawl to my pack to get my coat. Then I had to wait for help. The cold nights were the worst. I kept trying to get Happy to lie with me, but he was too nervous to come close. He would lie just out of my reach.

"On the second night, a bull moose came snorting and stomping around. Happy chased him away."

I looked over to Pat and asked, "So, when did you call for help?"

Pat had picked up her knitting and was intently listening to the story. Without looking up, she said, "I wasn't going to at first. I thought he had run off and wasn't coming back." Then she looked up, gave me a teasing smile, and continued, "When Len didn't return the first night, I thought something was wrong. So, I gave him until the next morning to come home. When that passed, I radioed Harold and asked for help."

"Harold took his Super Cub and flew the Kokrines Trail. He found Len lying next to the cat and radioed the location to the Air Force rescue helicopter. I was worried sick about him."

I marveled at Len's story. It had everything a teenage boy wanted to hear in an adventure— tragedy, perseverance, a faithful dog, a monster moose, and a flying rescue. "Wow," I exclaimed, "that's a great story, Len."

Len nodded and then looked at me with serious eyes. "You're welcome. Don't think that I will ever want to repeat it, but one thing is for certain. That little episode taught me that even the best plans can go bad very quickly. You can't let down your guard in the bush." As I read Len's stubbled face, I realized that he had just given me an important and hard-earned lesson about living in the Alaska wilderness.

⬥➤⬥

I was amazed how good a bath felt. I lay back in my private tub, sucked on a candy orange slice, and soaked in the hot mineral water. Its soothing goodness melted into my bones. My mind drifted through Len's incredible story of survival. Then I thought about Wade Carlson's troubles in Seward. He had just learned that his beautiful Native wife, Alice, was an alcoholic and it was shattering their marriage. I shook my head free of his grief and vowed not to read the novel tonight. I was engrossed in the story and took the characters way too seriously.

I could hear the melodious sounds of Hot Springs Creek babbling in the background. Occasionally, I heard the clunk of a rock tumbling over in the stream. For the first time since I arrived, I felt relaxed and accepted. It was a good feeling and, coupled with the fact that Len said I had tomorrow off on account it was Sunday, life just couldn't get any better.

Chapter 5

The Land

I awoke fully refreshed into the glaring daylight of the early Alaska morning. I lay quietly for a few minutes listening to the splashing sounds of Hot Springs Creek and the buzzing of mosquitoes on the window screen. My alarm clock read six forty-five and Pat said breakfast would be ready around nine. I rolled over and tried to bury my head into my pillow, but my stomach began to growl. Day off or not, I had to get up and munch on something.

I swung my feet over the bed, sat up, and thought about food. Suddenly, an idea flashed through my head. *Jerky*, I remembered. *I've got some jerky in my pack for emergencies*. Well, this was an emergency. I rummaged through my pack and found my unopened package of jerky. I took out my pocket knife, slit the plastic open, and popped a slice of dried smoked meat into my mouth. *Ah*, I thought to myself as I chewed the tough meat, *the perfect snack for the perfect time.*

Temporarily sated, I decided to get up and face the day. The air through the window screen felt warmer than yesterday. So, I wore my thin denim shirt under my broken-in Levi jacket. The mosquitoes seemed to bang against the screen with renewed urgency and reminded me to liberally apply insect repellent before leaving the refuge of my cabin.

I stepped outside and sucked the beautiful day into my lungs. The world seemed tranquil and inviting. Suddenly, I heard a deep growl to my left. I snapped my head toward the sound and saw Happy next to the cabin lying in ambush. His piercing eyes seemed to beg me to try something bad—just anything bad to give him an excuse to set me straight. I extended my hand to him and said as soothingly as I could, "Come, Happy. Let me pet you." Happy would have none of it. He remained unstably tense like a stretched rubber band against a knife. "Okay, Happy. Have it your way." I backed off and started walking toward the springs.

I reached the bluff and looked up the valley and marveled at the sweeping vista. The quiet, peaceful view stretched as far as I could see and seemed to beckon me to explore. The scene invoked a couple of verses from a Robert Service poem *The Call of the Wild* from the recesses of my mind . . . "But can't you hear the Wild?—it's calling you . . . And the Wild is calling, calling . . . let us go." I could feel the pull—it was almost irresistible.

As I stood completely mesmerized by the land, Happy came to the bluff and seemed to share my awe. We stood still and silent, each in our own thoughts, when a dog barked twice from the woods. The sound surprised me and I shook my head in disbelief, but Happy had heard it. His ears stood straight up as he stared transfixed at a location about half a mile upstream and slightly up the mountainside. For several minutes, neither of us moved a whisker. We never heard it again or saw any movement, but the experience left me with an eerie feeling.

Happy forcefully exhaled like he suddenly lost interest in the subject and trotted back to the cabin. I still had an hour to kill, so I sat down on the rocks and watched the grayling below feed on surface insects. Their long dorsal fins swirled in the current. A few minutes later, a river otter humped his way through the tall grass along the bank and dove into the creek. It resurfaced halfway across and swam to a small slough on the other side. I was beginning to realize that this country teemed with wildlife. You just had to look for it.

Fresh smoke rose from the stack above the old cabin, indicating Pat was fixing breakfast. I got up, walked to the arctic entry, and rapped on the outer door. Pat's cheery voice told me to come in. I pushed the door open, walked through, and heard each door snap shut behind me. Pat was dressed and making coffee. Len was putting on his flannel shirt.

Pat smiled at me and asked, "Couldn't sleep in much, huh?"

I shook my head and answered, "Tough to do when the sun is burning high in the sky."

"Ain't that the truth?"she said as she began to make a pot of oatmeal.

Len came to the table and sat down heavy. I let him drink a mug full of coffee before I asked him about the dog bark. I told him what happened and he listened without comment until the end. Then he smiled and said, "I believe you just heard your first wolf."

Len's revelation shocked me. "Wolf? I thought wolves howled, not barked."

Len refilled his cup and said, "Nope. Wolves are complicated creatures and in some ways they behave much like dogs. They communicate, play, and fight with each other. You just heard one talking to another. Happens all the time. Only once in a great while will we hear them howl and when they do, they echo off the hills like something fierce."

Pat put a bowl of steaming oatmeal in front of me. "Wow," I said as I spooned some sugar over my cereal. "There are wolves living around us. I hope I get to see one."

"You just might," Pat said as she sat down to join us. "You gotta keep your eyes open, though."

I thought about what Pat said as I gulped down my oatmeal. Then I spoke what was on my mind. "I was thinking about hiking up the creek today. Is that all right with you guys?"

Len smiled and replied, "I think that is a good idea. There is a spot about two miles upstream that is fantastic fishing, but first I need to check you out with that pistol hanging over there." Len wagged this head toward a pistol in a black holster with a belt that was looped over their bedpost.

"Okay," I said with a little excitement. I was familiar with firearms from Boy Scouts and I had passed my Hunter's Safety Course in Montana. "What kind of pistol is it?"

Len took another sip from his cup and answered, "It's a .357 magnum. Pat's son, Michael, got it for us a couple of years ago. It saved our lives last fall."

As usual, Len's matter-of-fact comment piqued my interest. "What happened?" I asked.

Len leaned back and ran his fingers through his grizzled hair as he took a very satisfying sip of coffee. Then he pointed out the window next to their bed as he recalled his story. "We were taking care of Wolf Hebel's dog, Minado. Minado and Happy got along famously. One seemed to support the other and raised their threshold of bravery.

"We had just gone to bed when we heard the dogs barking their heads off next to the river by the cabin. I got up with only a tee shirt on and peered out the window. There I saw a big black bear, and I mean big, slowly making his way up the hill. The dogs were darting back and forth, nipping at its heels, but the bear kept coming. It walked right up to the window, stood up, and looked straight at me without the least bit of fear."

Pat laughed and excitedly added, "So, all I could see was Len's bare bottom and this big black head looming above him. It was quite a view!"

Len flashed Pat a devilish grin and continued, "Suddenly, the bear drops to all fours and begins ambling around the front and pushing against the wall like he was testing it for an opening. I knew he was going to hit the arctic entry and find his way in here."

"So I ran half-naked to the front room just as I heard the first entry door push open. The door snapped shut and the bear was trapped inside! I threw my shoulder into the inside door and pushed with all my might. The bear suddenly slammed against it and knocked the door open several inches. I shoved it back. Then the bear rammed it open again. This went on for a few seconds until Pat joined the battle to keep it closed.

"I yelled for Pat to get my rifle. She got it off the hook, worked the action to slide a shell into the chamber, cocked it, and handed it to me. When the bear pushed the door open again, I shoved the rifle inside and pulled the trigger. Nothing happened! It had jammed!"

Pat took a sip of coffee and shook her head as she recalled the event. "You should have heard the slew of cuss words that flew from my husband's mouth. My ears are still burning."

I sat spellbound. My heart was thumping faster and I started to sweat. I asked breathlessly, "What did you do?"

Len nodded toward a peg in the wall about halfway between the front door and the bedroom. "I told Pat to grab the pistol from the wall. Until then, I had never used it, but I had loaded it. Pat pulled the pistol out of the holster and handed it to me just as the bear started making an all-out effort to come inside. He poked his snout through the door and was trying to wiggle inside the cabin when I pushed the pistol above his head and fired a blind shot."

"We heard the most gawd-forsaken groan you've ever heard. It was almost human. Then it went quiet. We waited for a minute before cautiously opening the door. There was the bear lying on the door sill barely alive. I had to shoot it in the head to put it out of its misery."

"Len," I said with wide eyes, "that was the most incredible story I have ever heard!"

Pat replied, "I'm glad you think so, Mike. I wrote it up and submitted it to the Alaska Magazine for publication." She got up, rummaged thorough her desk that held a manual typewriter. Pat found a folder and said, "Here it is." She gave it to me to read. I opened the folder and found a manuscript titled, *We, The Intruders*. "The magazine said they would publish it next summer. We'll see."

"Weren't you scared?" I asked Pat.

Pat shook her head as she finished her coffee. "Not at the time. It happened too fast to be scared, but later on, after I had time to think about it, I started shaking. If those dogs had not given us a warning or if that pistol had not been ready to fire, we would have been goners. Len retrieved the smashed bullet from inside the skull and I sent it to my son as a thank you."

Len added, "The bear dressed out over three hundred pounds and measured more than six feet long. All hell would have broken loose had it gotten inside. Now I make sure that all the rifles are well oiled and loaded, ready to go. And you can see, the pistol is holstered over our bedpost."

I thought to myself as I took a gulp of Tang, *I'm definitely not in Montana anymore.*

— ◆ ✕ ◆ —

After breakfast, Len took me behind the lodge to the dump for some target practice with the pistol. I had fired .22 caliber pistols, but this gun was three times as heavy and looked like it would buck hard in my hand. Len set three tin cans on a log at a distance of twenty paces and told me to shoot them off. I held the pistol with two stiff arms and pulled the hammer back with my right thumb until the cylinder rotated and the hammer cocked.

"Pull the hammer back faster to cock it," said Len. "This is a single-action pistol. You can't just pull the trigger. Remember that."

"Okay," I answered in a low voice as I concentrated and aimed at the first can. I slowly squeezed the trigger as I struggled to keep the gun sights centered. Suddenly, the gun boomed and the recoil threw the barrel up. The sound was deafening and a little unnerving. The bullet struck two inches below the can and blew out a huge chuck of wood from the log. The cans shook from the reverberation.

"Again!" shouted Len.

I took aim again and this time I pulled the hammer back with more authority. As the hammer moved backward, the cylinder rotated to the next live chamber. The barrel pulled to the right as my finger compressed the trigger. The gun fired and the middle can flew off the log. My ears were ringing now.

Len nodded and yelled, "Keep going."

I took a deep breath and shook my head to clear my ears. Then I re-aimed at the first can. This time I smoothly pulled the hammer back and kept the barrel lined up. I gently pulled the trigger. The gun fired and the can disintegrated before my eyes. Now completely deaf, I swung the barrel toward the third can, took aim, and confidently cocked the gun and squeezed the trigger. I winged the can and sent it flying. I looked at Len and saw him smiling and saying something to me. I could not hear him, but he seemed pleased.

Back at the cabin, I put some tied flies, insect repellent, some matches, my pocket knife, and my camera into a small backpack that I had borrowed from Len. My hearing had gradually returned, but my ears still rang. Pat gave me a sheet of folded tinfoil that held a wad of butter mixed with salt and pepper. She told me to spread the mixture over a freshly cleaned fish and wrap it in the foil. Then I could cook the fish over hot coals.

Len handed me the pistol and holster. I wrapped the belt around my hips, slipped the leather strap through the buckle, and pulled it tight. The holster barely fit my rail-thin waist and it felt heavy on my side. I consciously leaned to the left to compensate for the weight and when I walked I could feel the gun brush my right thigh. Although it was cumbersome, the pistol made me feel like a gunslinger.

Len seemed to know what I was thinking. He pointed to the pistol and said, "The hammer is resting on an empty chamber. I call it the 'Alaskan Safety.' The gun's safety is off, but it won't fire if you stumble. If you need it in a hurry, all you have to do is aim and fire. Take it from me, sometimes a fraction of a second counts. Understand?"

I nodded and said, "Yes. Thank you and thanks for the fishing equipment."

"No problem," answered Len. "You best be going." Len and Pat walked me outside. I picked up a fishing pole from alongside the cabin. Len added, "Just follow the game trail along the bank for a couple of miles. You can't miss the fishing hole. You will see where the creek runs into a bluff and carved a deep pool."

I saw Happy standing next to Pat. "Hey, Hap. Do you want to come with me, boy?" Happy seemed insulted that I would even suggest that he should tag along. His eyes told me to forget it. I straightened my shoulders and waved goodbye to Len and Pat. With my backpack, fishing pole, and holstered pistol, I struck out on my first grand adventure.

Len was right. Just beyond the hot springs bluff, I found the game trail paralleling the creek. It was well worn and in places straight as an arrow as if a surveyor had laid it out. Len told me to be alert for animals moving on the trail, so I nervously looked around every bend to make sure I wasn't going to surprise something—especially something big and furry. But gradually, my anxiety gave way to the almost mystical allure of my surroundings. The land seemed to sap my worries and replace it with an awe that I had only experienced in the high Montana mountains. Each step took me further away from reality and deeper into a wild and untamed land of adventure. The land was mesmerizing.

The utter silence punctuated with bird calls was soothing to my soul. There were times that I shook my head to bring me back to reality and resume my vigilance only to lapse back into the land's spell. I was loving every minute of my walk.

After a half-hour hike, I noticed that the usual tranquil sounds of Hot Springs Creek had changed to distinct roaring and splashing noises ahead. As I drew closer, I saw the water turn around a bend and ram against a cliff face. Over eons of time, the water had carved a deep hole along the base of the bluff. Here, the water quieted and formed a long tranquil pool. *This must be it*, I thought as I parted from the trail and walked down to the creek.

As I approached the creek, the ground turned rocky and eventually gave way to boulders. I worked my way around the rocks and stood before the pool. The roaring water overwhelmed all other sounds. I looked up at the cliff of solid granite as a gull flew across the rock face and then I gazed down at the deep clear water. I thought, *This is truly a special place.*

Not wanting to waste any time, I threw off my pack and assembled my fly rod. I did not see any fish rising, so I chose a wet fly—a black gnat. Then I walked to the head of the pool and flicked my line into the water at the base of the cliff. The fly immediately sank in the turbulent water and drifted into the pool. Within seconds, a fish hit the fly and I set the hook. I played it for a while and gently brought the fish to the bank. It was a 12-inch grayling. I kept it in the water and popped the fly out of its mouth. The grayling finned briefly while it caught its breath and then darted back to the safety of the pool.

"Well, that was fun," I said to myself. I checked the fly and tried my luck again. Over the next thirty minutes, I caught so many fish that the novelty of it began to wear thin. The grayling I caught measured between 8 and 16 inches. Then, after catching countless fish, something smacked my line with such strength and ferocity that I knew I had hooked into something special. The fish dove to the bottom and was trying to shake itself loose in the rocks. I kept my rod high and strained against the 10-pound-test leader about as hard as I dared. Then the fish changed tactics and rocketed to the surface. It leaped into the air and twirled before hitting the water and diving back to the bottom.

The fish repeated its maneuvers several times over the course of ten minutes before I finally coaxed it to the bank. Then I scooped it up with my left hand and brought it to the rocks. As I held it, I stared in disbelief. This was the largest arctic grayling I had ever seen. I judged it to weigh more than two pounds. Its bluish-green body was slender—built for speed. Its long iridescent dorsal fin had a red border along the top.

No one is ever going to believe this, I thought. Suddenly, an idea flashed in my mind. I rummaged through my pack and found my knife and camera. I laid the fish on a flat rock and spread its dorsal fin out. Then I unfolded my pocket knife and set it next to the fish to give it scale. I took a picture of my displayed trophy. Afterwards, I measured the fish with my knife. It was slightly more than two and a half knife lengths long, which equated to more than 20 inches! Then I ceremoniously butchered it, wrapped it in the tinfoil that Pat had given me, and made a cooking fire within the rocks. The trophy fish tasted as good as it looked.

My hike back to camp was as amazing as the walk to the fishing hole. As I gazed down the sweeping valley, I saw the wild mountains bend Hot Springs Creek to the right toward the Melozitna River. The awesome view consumed my imagination. I noticed that the blueberry bushes lining the trail were heavy with blue-green berries. They would need another two weeks before they were ripe.

As I drew closer to the camp, I noticed smoke rising from the stovepipe. *Pat must be cooking dinner*, I thought. My stomach rumbled in anticipation. Judging by the angle of the high summer sun, I estimated the time to be five o'clock. Happy stood by the cabin and watched me come into camp. His face seemed disappointed that I returned. As I strode up to the cabin, Happy pushed open the door and went inside. I followed closely behind.

Pat looked up from her cooking when she heard the door slam a second time. "Mike! How did it go out there?" I saw Len sitting in his chair by the window reading a worn pocketbook. He was wearing a tee shirt and old blue jeans. He was freshly shaved and it took years off his face. Len laid his book down and looked at me like he was expecting a full report.

I smiled at them and exclaimed, "Great! I caught a ton of fish. One was a monster, over twenty inches!"

Len smiled and asked, "Oh yeah? What ya do with it?"

"I ate it," I replied with pride. "Pat, that tinfoil idea worked great. The fish was delicious."

Pat grinned and said, "I'm glad it worked out all right."

"Did you run into any bears?" asked Len.

"Only one or two," I teased. "Had to shoot one. Thought we'd skin him out after dinner."

Len nodded and reached for the pistol. As I took off the holster and handed it to him, I instantly felt ten pounds lighter and leaned to the right from a day of compensating for the weight. Len took the pistol out and examined it. Then he reholstered it and gave it back to me. "Looks good. Better hang it back on the bedpost," he said.

I did as I was told and when I returned Len had moved to the dining table with a deck of cards and a board with rows of tiny holes drilled in it. Len motioned me to the table and said, "We got some time before dinner, so I thought we'd play a game of cribbage while we wait."

"Okay," I said as I sat down, "but I don't know how to play cribbage."

Len nodded as he replied, "That's all right. If you are going to work in the bush, you best learn to play. Men play cribbage to decide who washes the dishes, who chops the wood, or any other chore they wish to avoid. And, of course, they play for money."

Len turned the board over and revealed a hidden compartment that was closed by a metal tab. He slid the tab open and knocked four metal pegs into his hand. Then Len uprighted the board and placed the pegs into four holes at the bottom left of the panel. At closer inspection, I noticed the linear, parallel holes resembled a race track that led the pegs to the top of the board and then back to the bottom. The first and last set of holes were set apart from the track and seemed to signify start and finish positions.

Len slid the deck of cards out of the cardboard box. He quickly thumbed through the deck and discarded the jokers. Then he carefully cut the deck and equally arranged the cards in his hands to shuffle them. It was then that I made a startling discovery. Len was missing most of his left index finger, which made it difficult to shuffle. I was amazed that I had failed to notice it sooner. Len spread the fingers of his left hand to compensate and performed an adequate shuffle.

Len placed the deck on the table and told me to cut it. I did and he dealt each of us six cards face down. "Okay," said Len as he turned both sets of cards over, "during a real game, each player hides his cards, but I'm going to walk you through a few hands. Now the object is to hold cards that will make points. Any group of cards that equal fifteen is worth two points. Pairs are worth two, three of a kind is worth six, and four of a kind makes twelve points. Straights are worth three or four points. Got it?"

No, I didn't, I thought. "Um, keep going."

"Now," continued Len, "since I dealt, I get the crib. That is, we both throw two cards face down on the table. I am going to put cards in it that I think will make points. You need to throw cards in that won't give me points. Are you with me so far?"

I gave Len a blank stare in response. Undaunted, Len leaned over and analyzed my hand. "See, you have a 4, 7, 8, 10, king, and an ace. This is a tough one. I recommend you throw your 7 and 8 into the crib. It will give me two points for the fifteen, but you still have two fifteen-point hands for a total of four points. Understand?"

"Not really," I answered, totally bewildered. "Let's play a hand." Len threw in a 5 and a 9 into the crib.

Len said, "Okay, you must cut the deck and I will draw another card before we play." I cut the deck and Len turned over a 10 of hearts. "Well that gives you a good hand."

Really? I thought as I stared at my hand. *I don't see it.*

"Let's start pegging. We need to lay down cards that will equal thirty-one. Since you cut the deck, you start. I recommend laying your 4 of clubs down." I did as I was told. "Now, I'm going to put down an ace. You need to play your 10 and that will give you two pegging points. Go ahead and move your first peg two holes up." I struggled through the thirty-one count and Len lost me when he counted my hand. "You got three fifteen-point hands and a pair for a total of eight points. Go ahead and move your second peg eight holes forward."

After Len counted his hand, he grabbed the crib cards and whistled. "Now see here? I caught a straight. I got one fifteen-count and a four-card straight for six points." He moved his peg forward on the board. "Now, it's your turn to deal."

I struggled to comprehend the game. Len won the game in a

landslide by pegging out forty points ahead. Len's ability to count the hands quickly and fluently navigate the complexities of the game amazed me. My head ached after the barrage of addition and strategy. Len put the game away and Pat set the table for dinner.

After a satisfying meal of canned moose meat and fresh vegetables picked from the garden, I helped Pat with the dishes and filled the gas can with wood. Len had settled down with his book, but I would not let him rest. I grabbed the cribbage board and set up the game. Len looked surprised and pleased that I was willing to jump back into the fray. He put away his book and sat down at the table as I shuffled the deck.

For the next two hours, Len trounced me. Every time I believed that I was getting a handle on the rules, Len would surprise me with nuances such as "Nobs" (laying down a jack of the same suit as the starter card), "Nibs" (the dealer turns over a jack for the starter card), "Muggins" (the capture of points your opponent fails to count—stealing as far as I was concerned), and additional pegging points for laying down matching cards after the opponent declares "Go."

After the final beating, Len put away the cards and turned on the AM radio. KIAK was getting ready for the evening's broadcast of Pipeline of the North. We listened to the ramble of messages to various people in the Bush, when out of the blue, the deejay announces, "To Len and Pat in Melozi Hot Springs, from Norm. I will be flying in your area tomorrow. Will drop off mail."

Pat looked up from her knitting and said, "Well, that was nice of Norm to let us know that he was coming. I've got some bills to pay and letters to write. Mike, you should write a letter to your folks."

"Okay," I said as I stood and yawned. I was starting to feel the effects of my outing. "I should probably go do that now. I'll see you guys in the morning. Thank you, Len, for teaching me how to play cribbage."

"Well, you haven't learned yet," replied Len, "but, you're off to a good start. Good night."

As I walked back to my cabin, I noticed the sky had cleared and the air felt much warmer. Maybe it was my imagination, but the mosquito activity seemed to have risen, too. I swatted at a few before entering the cabin. Inside, it was uncomfortably warm. I opened the windows to let the air circulate. The mosquitoes unceasingly pelted the screens. A few of them had sneaked in when I entered, so I hunted them down and smacked them before settling down to write my family a letter.

I pulled a small notebook and a pre-stamped envelope from my pack. I sat on the edge of my bed and composed my thoughts. A lot had happened during the past week and I struggled how to best describe the events. Finally, I put pen to paper and wrote, *"Dear family, I got here okay. The hot springs is really cool! Len and Pat have a dog named Happy. I hope everything is okay at home. Love, Michael."*

Being a young man of few words, I thought that this just about summed up my stay so far. I tore the paper from my notebook, folded it into the envelope, and sealed it. It would be two weeks before I discovered that my mother thought my letter was woefully inadequate.

I awoke to the blazing sun shining through my window and the patter of mosquitoes battering the window screens to come in and suck my blood. My alarm clock said five minutes after six and already I could feel the heat of the day building. I got up and recoiled in shock at the thick swarm milling outside the windows. Balls of mosquitoes were thick enough to obscure my view and I could feel my skin crawl.

Although I knew the day was going to be hot, I put on a long-sleeved work shirt and my Levi jacket to protect my body from the stinging insects. Then I liberally put on Cutter's insect repellent on my neck, ears, and hands. I grabbed my work gloves and hard hat and stepped out into the day. The mosquitoes immediately ambushed me. Their Kamikaze dive-bomb tactics blasted through my chemical defenses and smacked against my exposed skin. I shook my face to clear my eyes and ran for the old cabin. I lowered my shoulder and rammed the first door as I vaulted into the arctic entry. Then I crushed all the mosquitoes I could find that clung to my clothes before continuing inside.

Pat was just finishing the coffee preparations. A Pic insect repellent coil was burning on the kitchen table and it filled the cabin with a distinctive odor. She took one look at me and knew that I was being tormented. "Good morning, Mike. Looks like we got a bumper crop of newly hatched mosquitoes."

"Bumper crop?" I responded in dismay. "You mean a plague! Nothing seems to stop them."

Pat laughed and handed me the water pitcher, "You have a way with words. You think you can tolerate the bugs long enough to get us some cold water for milk? We're having oatmeal for breakfast."

I reluctantly took the pitcher from her and said, "I will be right back." I took a deep breath and ran outside. The mosquitoes attacked immediately, but I found if I ran fast enough, the swarm seemed to peel away and stay behind. I sprinted as fast as I could to the creek and shoved the pitcher into the ice-cold water. As I scooped up the water, the bugs found me. I shook my head furiously to knock them off and ran back to the cabin. Len and Pat were just lifting their coffee mugs when I burst into the kitchen, out of breath and miraculously with three-fourths of a pitcherful of water. Happy growled a greeting from his corner.

Len nonchalantly asked, "Bugs bad today, Mike?"

I set the pitcher on the counter and checked my ears for damage. "You can say that again! They almost picked me up and flew off with me!"

"Yep," said Len, "when the weather warms up they tend to come out in droves. Unfortunately, we have to peel logs today. That means standing in one place while you work, so the bugs have a chance to poke you."

"Great," I muttered as I sat down to my bowl of oatmeal. As we ate in silence, I swear that I heard the mosquitoes pummeling the window screens. The cabin was already warm from cooking and the day looked like it was going to be a scorcher.

Len seemed to read my thoughts and said, "Make sure you wear lots of repellent today. I mean spray your jacket and pants down good! Then get some string from the shop and tie your pant legs tight around your boots. Also make sure your shirt is tucked under your belt and you are wearing your gloves. The bugs are going to try to get the best of you. Just hang tough." I nodded and finished my oatmeal.

After breakfast, I started my preparations in the cabin. I buttoned my jacket up to my neck and made sure my shirt was tucked in. Then I sprayed my entire body with liberal amounts of Off insect repellent. I topped it off with Cutter's lotion rubbed on my ears and face. The smell radiating off my clothing was enough to make Happy backpedal away from me. I looked over to Len and announced, "I guess I'm ready."

"Okay," replied Len, "just a sec." He grabbed his cap, sprayed it down with Off, and put it on. "Let's go." We marched outside to face the day. The mosquitoes met us with full force. I instinctively bent forward as if I was walking into a gale. I grabbed my gloves and hard hat from the chopping block and followed Len to the shop.

The first thing I did was to apply a fresh coat of oil on my helmet. Then I tied string around my pant legs to seal them against my boots.

Len grabbed two hatchets and draw knives and motioned me to follow him to the sawmill. We walked up to a stack of logs alongside heavy wooden racks. Len grabbed one end of a log and lifted it onto the rack. Then he rolled the other end up. He selected a draw knife and said, "Peeling logs is really quite simple once you get the knack for it. You can use a hatchet or a knife depending on how many knots there are. I like to use a draw knife to cut the bark without scarring the log. Then, when the bark starts peeling, I switch to the hatchet and use it to pry the bark off. See?" Len expertly drew the knife toward him along the log to shave the bark off. Then he loosened the bark from the log with the hatchet. A large piece almost fell from the wood.

Len continued, "When you are done with each log, stack it on the far rack for curing. Now, let me see you do it." I took the draw knife from Len, grabbed the two handles, and carefully pulled it toward me. The edge bit into the bark and quickly sliced into the wood. I deeply nicked the log in several places until I got the knack of it. Len hung around long enough to satisfy himself that I was not going to hack myself to death. Then he told me that he would return shortly and left.

Within a few minutes, I realized this was going to be a long day. Pitch oozing from the bark began to cover my gloves, which made everything stick to my hands. The heat of the day slowly rose and I started to swelter under my protective clothing. Beads of sweat mixed with repellent formed on my brow and dripped into my eyes causing them to burn. But the worst hardship was the mosquitoes' relentless pestering. They constantly pelted my skin, flew inside my ears and nose, and occasionally into my mouth. I frequently shook my head to clear my face. While I worked in silence, I could hear their high-pitched whine.

Just when I thought the mosquito hordes could not get worse, they did. It felt like all the mosquitoes of Alaska had descended on me. The swarm was so thick that they blurred my vision. The sky went dark. I looked at my jacket and could no longer see the color of the fabric. A dull gray mass of mosquitoes coated my arms and seemed to move in unison. I lifted my arms and stared in horror as the bugs hung like bees off my elbows. My fear rose in my throat as I dropped my knife and started maniacally swatting the mosquitoes on my clothes. In response, they seemed to swarm with renewed intensity and attack with a vengeance. I windmilled my arms trying to find an escape. I was going insane.

Suddenly, I felt a hand grab my shoulder and heard Len's calm voice say, "It's all right, Mike. Don't let them get the best of you." I spun around and saw Len standing behind me holding a small net. He squinted against the mosquitoes pelting his face and handed me the net and said, "Here. Put this on. It will help."

I took a quick look at the net and realized it was a head garment. *Salvation*, I thought as I threw off my hard hat and grabbed the head net. As I fumbled with the opening, I noticed my hard hat was no longer orange, but grey black. It was completely covered with stuck mosquitoes. I slid the net over my head and arranged it so the elastic sealed around my neck. The netting had a hoop that held the fabric away from my face. Despite the fact that the head net dimmed my view, the mosquitoes no longer tormented me. "Thank you, Len," I said with great relief. "You saved me."

Len gave me a grimace for a smile and said, "Yep. A head net is kind of handy. I don't care much for them. I get too hot and claustrophobic wearing that net over my head all day. It's hard to smoke with it on, too."

At the moment, I believed anything was better than the relentless onslaught waged by the mosquitoes. The head net allowed me to regain my composure and go back to work. Len grabbed another log and started peeling beside me. I marveled at his toughness to tolerate the mosquitoes.

We worked in silence for an hour when Pat surprised me by arriving with a head net on ready to peel logs. Len placed a log on a rack for her and she attacked it with the draw knife. After a few minutes of steady progress, she began to talk to me. "Last winter, Len and I went to Fairbanks for a checkup. The doctor had me squeeze his hand as hard as I could. I darn near tore it off! He couldn't believe how strong I was. I told him it was from peeling logs and smoking hand-rolled cigarettes."

My wrists were already starting to ache from prying the bark off the logs. They were going to be numb by the afternoon. "Yeah, Pat. I can see how log peeling would toughen you up." Pat continued to talk about her children and grandchildren while she steadily ripped the bark off the logs. With my full concentration on the task, I could barely peel faster than Pat. Len was a machine—processing log after log without stopping. Finally, after three grueling hours, Len and Pat halted. Pat said she would start lunch and Len directed me to back the wagon into the work area and load it with bark. This proved to be a sticky and dirty job that took me more than an hour to complete. By the time I finished, I was filthy, hot, and famished.

I went to my cabin first to clean up before meeting Len and Pat for lunch. I furiously beat my clothing to drive the mosquitoes off before entering the cabin. I stripped off my head net and jacket just inside the door and made my way to the bathroom. I blanched at my reflection in the mirror. Sweat plastered my hair to my head and grime streaked down my face. Despite my precautions, mosquito bites had caused large welts along my neck, wrists, and forearms that rose in hard knots. I poured cool water into the wash basin and thoroughly cleansed my face and wounds. I combed my hair the best I could and went to the older cabin for lunch.

Pat had fixed a large tray of moose-meat sandwiches along with soup and fresh vegetables from her garden. My appetite flared at the sight. Within seconds, I was shoveling the food in my mouth with both hands. Len and Pat looked too tired to comment. After eating in silence for several minutes, I asked Len a question. "Len, do you ever get used to the bugs?"

My question caused him to smile. "I'm lucky I guess because I tolerate them better than most. I hardly swell up anymore. I actually moved to Alaska after World War II. I was a seabee with the navy. I traveled to various tropical places and managed to come down with a mild form of malaria. The frequent mosquito bites keep me from having a relapse. Many veterans come to Alaska for that reason."

Wow. I thought. *I never knew that.*

Len reached for the tobacco can and papers. He popped the lid and began making two cigarettes as he continued. "Some people just can't get used to the mosquitoes. You never know who might crack under the swarms. Sometimes it's the biggest guys that go down the hardest. In the late 1960s, a fella from New York came to Fairbanks to do a little fly fishing up the Chena River. He was a big guy—well more than six feet tall and weighed about three hundred pounds. He parked his car along Chena Hot Springs Road and walked in about a half a mile. Apparently, the bugs found him and drove him nuts. He panicked and started running. Then he got lost. The search party found his fishing pole the next day, but no sign of him. They kept searching and finally found him three days later lying under a spruce tree mindlessly swiping his hand across his face. They said he had lost his mind."

Pat added, "Nobody really gets used to them. You learn to tolerate them. We have good days and bad days."

"When do the mosquitoes die off?" I asked.

Pat answered, "By August, the mosquitoes taper off. Then come the gawd-forsaken gnats. Sometimes I think they are worse than the mosquitoes. They get into everything. When they really get bad, we have to build a smudge fire just to work outside."

"You got that right," said Len as he licked the last rolled cigarette. He handed one to Pat and lit it with a match. Then as he lit his own cigarette with the same match, he continued, "At least we don't have the white sox and noseeums that haunt other parts of Alaska. I used to homestead in Clam Gulch on the Kenai Peninsula. The white sox are flies with black and white stripes that bite like a mule, but the noseeums are worse. They are so small that they can fly through mosquito netting and window screens. Their bite feels like they just took a hunk of flesh off you. No sir! I will take the mosquitoes anytime."

To delay facing the mosquitoes, I challenged Len to a game of cribbage. Len accepted and skunked me within the blink of an eye. So within a very short period of time, I found myself repeating the morning's preparations of dressing tightly, spraying repellent, and going back to work.

By late afternoon, a light wind mercifully found its way down the valley. It brought lower temperatures and the mosquito hordes abated to the point that I could remove my head net and resume wearing my oil-coated hard hat. My wrists and hands felt like they were going to fall off. Len halted the peeling at five o'clock and told me to pick up the bark and haul it away. I finally finished my chores an hour later and called it a day.

My jacket, pants, and gloves were covered in pitch and it seemed to harden as the day cooled. I walked into my cabin and stripped. Then I pulled the wooden plug from the hot water pipe and filled the tub. I slid under the water and tried to soak the grime and pitch off my body, but I only partially succeeded. The rest required lots of scrubbing and soap.

When I showed up for dinner, I was wearing a clean shirt and pants and feeling much better. As we ate, Pat said, "I wonder what happened to Norman? I thought he would be here by now."

Len shrugged as he spooned up some more potatoes, "He's got about a hundred things going on right about now. He'll make it." About five minutes later, we heard an airplane buzz the cabin. We immediately got up and walked to the door. Happy led the way barking and dancing as he tried to hurry us along. I saw Norm's white and red airplane fly down the river with the flaps extended preparing to land. I ran into my cabin and grabbed my letter to my family and shoved it in my shirt pocket. As I came out, Len called to me and said, "Mike, bring the tractor and trailer down to the plane and throw an empty gas drum in. I'll see if Norm will sell us some gas."

"Okay," I said. I jogged to the sawmill where I had parked the C60 and trailer and fired it up. I drove it to the shop, picked up a 55-gallon drum, put it into the trailer, and continued down to the strip. As I crossed the last stream and entered the runway, I saw Norm talking with the Veerhusens and unloading the plane. Then he turned and saw me barreling toward him on the tractor. His expression changed to horror. Norman threw up his hands and frantically signaled me to stop. Len mistook Norm's hand waving to mean to turn the tractor around and back the trailer under the wing. So, Len twirled his hand in the air to clarify Norm's instructions.

I executed Len's command. As I turned the dozer around, I heard Norm gasp. Len gave him a puzzled look. I backed the trailer under the wing, turned off the engine, and jumped down. "Hey, Norm,"I said with great enthusiasm, "how are you doing?"

Norm glared at me before turning to Len and resuming his conversation. "Sure, Len. I can sell you about twenty-five gallons. I'll bring more next time. I got a little crank pump that can move the gas out of the wing tanks and into your drum. I'll get it."

Len replied, "Why don't you let Mike get it? He can climb up there and crank the pump easier than you or me."

"No!" screamed Norm. Then he collected himself and continued in a calmer voice, "No. I can do it. You know. Insurance reasons and all." Again,

Len gave him a confused look. I dead-panned my face and said nothing.

Norm opened the baggage compartment and retrieved a small pump and about 10 feet of rubber hose. Then he huffed and puffed as he scaled the airplane and inserted the pump into the wing tank. I climbed into the trailer, took the bung off the drum, and reached for the hose. Norm reflexively yanked it back. Len shook his head, took the hose from Norm, and placed it into the drum. Then Norm cranked the pump for a grueling fifteen minutes until the drum was half full. His face looked tired from the effort. He replaced the gas cap on the wing and jumped down.

Norm took off his cap with his free hand and wiped his brow with the back of his sleeve. Then he looked at me as he spoke to Len and Pat, "I guess things are working out okay? He hasn't burned down your camp or anything, has he?"

Pat lifted up her chin and said, "No, Norm. Things are all right. We got some mail for you, though." She handed him a stack of stamped and sealed envelopes neatly bound with a rubber band. I jumped down from the trailer and handed Norman my letter. Norm readily accepted Pat's stack, but loathed to take mine. He snatched it from my hand and stuck it underneath Pat's mail.

Len thankfully provided some respite from the uncomfortable scene by asking me to drive the tractor up to the shop. Len and I loaded the trailer with supplies. Then I quickly fired up the C60 and drove away. I had just crossed the last ford when I heard Norm's plane fire up. By the time I stopped in front of the cabin, I could hear the plane rumbling down the valley.

Len and Pat showed up a few minutes later while I was unloading the packages. Pat continued inside while Len stayed behind. "Anything you want to tell me?" asked Len.

I knew what he meant and I replied, "Norm and I got off on the wrong foot when we met. I thought he would have gotten over it by now."

Len scratched the stubble on his chin before continuing, "He thinks you are a screwup."

That comment stung. I gritted my teeth and said, "I think he resents my height."

Len broke a smile and replied, "Yeah, he does act like a little Napoleon from time to time. Just ignore his digs and be polite whenever you're around him. Deep down, he's really a good guy."

I nodded and continued unloading the trailer. As I grabbed the last package, I thought to myself, *Someday I'll prove to him that I'm not a screwup.*

━━◆━━

Even though I was dead tired, I stayed up and finished *The Alaskan*. I enjoyed reading about Wade's rough-and-tumble adventures, discovering gold, and hitting it rich, but I was not prepared for the story's ending. While celebrating in Juneau, Wade finds his estranged wife's body in a mortuary. Alice had succumbed to the ravishes of alcoholism, beatings, and exposure. Wade scarcely recognized her bloated face when the authorities asked him to identify the body. Alice was only in her late twenties.

Wade pays for her preparations and ships her body to her people so she can be buried in her tribal lands. Then, as Wade stands at a defining crossroads of his life, he decides to stay in Alaska and not follow his trusted friend Mitch back to the Lower 48. The book ends with Wade knowing in his heart that Alaska is his future and he would strive to make it a better place.

I closed the book and popped another rationed orange candy in my mouth as I reflected on the story. The wind had stopped and the sky cleared, allowing the sun to burn brightly in the late evening. I could hear the creek babbling in the background and the patter of mosquitoes on the screen. I identified with Wade and felt his peace with his decision. Then as I prepared to go to bed, I wondered if Alaska would be my future, too.

━━◆━━

The last days of June consisted of peeling logs and enduring the never ending onslaught of mosquitoes. My wrists slowly strengthened and my hide gradually toughened over the days. I became more proficient at peeling and now rivaled Len for top peeler. My skin also became more tolerant of bug bites and swelled less than at my first exposures. Despite these adaptations, I still wore the head net. I could not get used to the mosquitoes constantly pelting my face.

Evenings were spent learning the intricacies of cribbage. Len was a shrewd player and he delighted in pulling off a last-minute save or tricking (a smoother word for "cheating") me with some sleight of hand when he dealt or cut the cards. He claimed his tactics were necessary to teach me the dark side of cribbage. "When playing for money," said Len, "no moves are barred. You've got to be on your toes and watch closely for cheating. Some day, when you really get good, you should go where the serious cribbage players meet in Fairbanks—Pikes Landing. Only the best play there."

When we finished playing one evening and we still had an hour before the Pipeline of the North broadcast, I asked Len about the lodge he operated in Galena. My request generated smiles from Len and Pat. Pat suppressed a laugh and concentrated hard on her knitting. Len retrieved the tobacco can and papers and began rolling cigarettes. He used this time to gather his thoughts. Len finished the cigarettes, lit them, and handed one to Pat before speaking.

"During the winter of '64—'65, I had a contract clearing snow from the Air Force runway in Galena. Because I worked among the enlisted men, I was privy to inside information about future Air Force plans. One day, I overheard some men talking about a couple of large-scale projects that the government was going to award in the spring. People were saying a huge work force would descend on the town. Even though the barracks could accommodate some of the men, more temporary housing was needed. So, I decided to build a lodge to house them.

Len took a long drag on his cigarette and sent the smoke swirling along the ceiling. "I got my teenage son, Dan, and a few more laborers together and built a two-story hotel not far from Hobo's bar. I named it the Galena Yukon Lodge.

"We had gotten off to a late start building, so we finished in October—right when it started to get cold. Before we finished pounding nails, I had a couple of companies begging me for rooms to house their men. So we set up a bunch of bunk beds upstairs and stacked the men like cordwood.

Len chuckled as he continued, "The first couple of weeks, we didn't have the hot water hooked up yet. The men were getting their meals on the base. Sometimes they stumbled in at night and brushed the sawdust off their bedding before going to sleep.

"Hobo Benson was supposedly a certified plumber, at least that is what he told me. So, I had him hook up a large water heater in the basement. The plan was we would have a grand-opening dinner when the hot water was working. Hobo promised me he would complete the job by the upcoming Saturday. So, I had a bunch of turkeys shipped in and we cooked up a huge feast. We used picnic tables and plywood sheets on top of sawhorses as banquet tables. We had a full house so we had wall-to-wall men crowding around. Hobo had come up from the basement earlier that day and proclaimed the job done.

"We were just sitting down and spooning up the meal when all of a sudden it felt like we were having an earthquake! The whole building started vibrating as this gigantic tank began to emerge from the floor. It pushed over a table and food went flying! The tank looked like a rocket blasting off. Steam streaming from the bottom propelled the tank through the ceiling. Some guy had just gotten up from his bed on the second floor when the tank shot through it, rocketed through the roof, and landed in the alley behind the lodge breaking in half a 10-inch thick tree.

"We were all knocked against the walls when the tank shot through the dining room. I landed next to the circuit breaker, so I threw the main switch to turn the power off. The whole place went dark. When the tank blasted through the roof, it sucked the air out of the building. Every window imploded and even a wall fell off its foundation!

"Then suddenly, it was quiet. I mean you could hear a pin drop. Then I heard someone yell out, 'Hobo! You got five seconds before I beat the hell out of you!' I heard Hobo get up and run for the door. He barely made it outside when a man jumped up and chased after him."

I was stunned. In the week and a half since I had arrived, Len and Pat had told me some pretty good stories, but this one took the cake. "Oh my God, Len! You mean nobody got hurt?"

Len laughed and shook his head. "Naw. We got really lucky. Only Hobo suffered a black eye or two."

I still had a hard time believing Len's story. "So, you had to close the lodge after the explosion?"

Len took another drag on his cigarette and said, "Nope. We boarded up the windows and swept up the glass. It took us three weeks to fix it, though. Dan and I had a heck of a time getting the building back up on the foundation. All and all, I did pretty good with the lodge and sold it when Pat and I decided to make a go of it out here. But, for some odd reason, it burnt down in the fall of 1971. Rumor has it that the boiler acted up again, but this time it caught fire instead of blowing up."

I shook my head in amazement and said, "You guys sure live big out here."

Len smiled and replied, "Yep. Sometimes we do. We're just doing the best we can and sometimes things go a little haywire. That's life. You gotta roll with the punches." I nodded and Len continued, "You know, speaking of big, I mean to take you fishing tomorrow and show you how to catch really big grayling. How does that sound to you?"

"You bet!" I shouted. I had forgotten tomorrow was Sunday and the promise of a fishing adventure made the wait unbearable.

<hr />

I awoke to cool moist air seeping through the window screen above my bed. The air felt good and refreshing. I sat up, looked out the window, and saw low clouds hanging over the valley. The cooler weather seemed to quell the mosquito activity with only a few individuals slowly poking at the screen.

My stomach growled as I checked the time on my alarm clock. It read 7 a.m. Pat would not have breakfast until nine. Thus, I had some jerky to check my hunger and contemplated how to kill some time. Until now, I had not explored the land south of the runway and thought this would be the time to do it.

I threw on my clothes, slipped on my Levi jacket, and strode out of the cabin. The camp was quiet and the land appeared to be asleep shrouded in grey-blue clouds. I felt good as I set a brisk pace to the runway. I walked over the creeks and slowed my pace as I entered the strip and looked around. The country never ceased to amaze me. The wide open valley and the beautiful boreal forest with wisps of clouds gave the land almost mystical qualities.

Halfway down the runway, I made an important discovery. I found a cat trail that ran up the mountain and headed south toward the Yukon. *This must be the haul road from Kokrines*, I thought. Although it was cleared and easy to see, the trail was rough from dissimilar settlement of thawing permafrost and tussocks. Any bulldozer traveling the route would be severely tossed from rut to rut. Travel would be slow and tortuous.

I continued down the runway until I came upon four sets of hoof prints. Although my grandfather had taught me how to differentiate between deer and elk, these looked distinctly different. The prints appeared to be oval shaped with a split down the middle. The tracks were fresh—only a few hours old. The animals appeared to have waded Hot Springs Creek, crossed the runway, and continued up the mountain.

I thought if I hiked up the trail I might have a chance to see them. I went back to the trail entrance and started up the path. Within a few steps, I discovered walking was much harder than it looked. The compressed tussocks squished and squirmed under my feet. When I stepped between them, I sank into cold ankle-deep mud that held my foot as I pried it loose. After a few minutes of tortuous progress, I realized I needed to modify my walking technique. I decided to skip from tussock to tussock. With a little practice, I found that I could do this until I slipped and fell in the cold wet tundra. Then, I would stand up and try again.

The trail steepened as it led straight up the mountain and soon I entered the cloud base. The moist air caused me to shiver even though I was sweating from the exertion. My visibility dropped to a few hundred feet and soon I gave up trying to track the animals. I turned around and descended out of the clouds. I halted to catch my breath and took in the sweeping vista below.

The clouds extended up the valley and it was like looking through a tunnel. I could see the camp in the distance and it looked small in comparison to the vastness surrounding it. I noticed swathes of thick blueberry bushes along the slope. The berries were almost ripe with a light bluish-green hue. I tasted one and found it still had a tart bite. *Another week*, I thought as I continued downhill.

By the time I got to camp, smoke was rising from the cookstove. I rapped on the door and Pat responded with a cheery, "Come in!" I came inside and saw Pat cooking her famous sourdough pancakes. My stomach growled in anticipation.

Len was sitting comfortably at the table wearing blue jeans and a tee-shirt. He was sipping coffee and running his fingers through his thinning hair. "Good morning, Mike," he said in a relaxed tone. "I guess the mosquitoes zapped me harder than I thought. I got welts all over my head."

I laughed and said, "Len, I don't know how you can stand it without wearing a head net. I would go crazy."

He smiled back and replied, "Hard to smoke with a head net on. Today looks much cooler, so the bugs should be down."

"Yep. I went hiking up the mountain in back of the airstrip this morning. They didn't bother me much." I sat down and asked Len about the tracks I saw.

Len scratched his chin and said, "Sounds like you found a set of caribou tracks. We get small bands this time of year come up the valley and cross the creek by the runway. If you are going to be walking around early in the morning, I should give you a rifle in case you see one. We could use the fresh meat." I liked that idea and Len could see it in my eyes. He continued, "okay. After breakfast, we should do a few chores around here. After that, we need to search for those big grayling. Then I'll get you fixed up with a spare 30.06 rifle. That sound all right with you?"

"You bet it does!" I answered. Sourdough pancakes, fishing, and hunting—it just didn't get any better than that.

The early afternoon air was still damp and cool, but after several days of blazing sun, it felt refreshing. The sun still had not burned through the clouds, but the diffused light could not dampen my enthusiasm. I was following Len across shallow rapids about a quarter of a mile upstream of the camp. We were wearing hip boots and carrying fly rods. We waded up the far bank and struck an animal trail leading downstream. Len led the way, snaking through willows and alders until we came to a network of small backwater sloughs. The clear water was dark and deep with grass and brush hanging over the banks.

Len dropped to his knees and motioned for me to do the same. Then he reached inside his coat pocket and retrieved a small leather pouch. In a quiet voice that was slightly above a whisper, he said, "This is a secret fly that old- timers have known about for years. If you want to catch big grayling, you have to use this." He opened the pouch and showed me four large flies that resembled shrews. Each fly was made from deer hair. They were grey with a small tapered body and a two-inch tail.

I was incredulous. "You have got to be kidding me. You would use those for pike, not grayling."

Len smiled and said, "Watch this." He tied one on his line. Then from the kneeling position, he flicked the shrew fly onto the grass hanging over the opposite bank. Len waited a few seconds and then gently tugged the fly into the water. It plopped on the surface. Again, Len left the fly motionless for a few moments before retrieving it with slow jerking motions. Suddenly, the water erupted under the fly and something big yanked it under water. Len calmly let the fish have it before setting the hook. His pole bent double under the pressure as the fish fought him. The fish stripped the drag as it raced up the slough, turned, and came shooting back. It rocketed out of the water, flopped back, and slapped the surface.

Finally, Len was able to bring it to the bank and scoop it out. He handed it to me and I held it in disbelief. The grayling was at least 24 inches long and weighed more than three pounds. Unlike the slim torpedo-shaped trophy I had caught at the pool, this one possessed a thick girth. It was a monster!

Len chuckled and said, "Not bad, huh? We'll keep two of these granddaddies for dinner. I want you to clean it now and take a look at its stomach contents." I quickly killed the fish and gutted it. I noticed the stomach looked abnormally large and when I opened it I found remnants of a real shrew. I was amazed. Vindicated, Len nodded and said, "Now you try it."

I took one of Len's shrew flies, tied it to my leader, and flicked it onto some alder branches overhanging the bank. Mimicking Len, I waited a few seconds before tugging it on to the water. Just as I was retrieving the slack, a fish ripped the fly from the surface. I let the leader plunge before setting the hook. The water exploded in a twisted fury. The fish bucked the line, jumped, dove, and ran with a vengeance. I played it the best I could within the tight confines of the forest. Finally, it tired enough that I could pull it onto the bank.

I hefted it up and gawked at its size. The grayling was every bit as long as Len's, but a little fatter. It would easily go three and a half pounds. When I cleaned it, I found two shrews within its stomach. I would never had believed it unless I had seen it.

Len motioned that it was time to leave. "Let's leave these boys alone now. They probably produce most of the fish in this creek."

"Len," I asked as I twisted down the tight trail with the two big grayling in one hand and my fly pole in the other, "How do they get so big?"

Len answered, "I think they overwinter downstream of the hot springs. They don't spend the energy to migrate and food is plentiful year round. If they can nail a shrew or two a month, they got all they can hold. That makes for large fish."

We continued in silence—Len concentrating on his footing and me contemplating another fascinating fact of Alaskan life.

———◆◆◆◆◆———

True to Len's word, he loaned me an old Remington 30.06 rifle to carry on my early-morning walks. Its stock was weathered and the barrel had rust spots, but after a few hours of cleaning, I got the action to move smoothly and the gun looked years newer. I loaded the shells into the magazine and closed the bolt so that the chamber remained empty. Then I stored the rifle above my bed on pegs drilled into the log walls for that purpose. In an emergency, I figured I could jump out of my bed, pull the rifle from the wall, and chamber a shell in seconds. The thought gave me a strange feeling of confidence.

The next two mornings, I got up at 6 a.m., got dressed, slung my rifle over my shoulder and went hunting. My eyes strained with the anticipation of spotting a caribou along the mountains or the creek. After walking a four-mile loop each day, I came back empty-handed, but I always had a good time and could not wait until the next morning to try again.

After Tuesday's breakfast, Len announced that tomorrow was the Fourth of July and therefore a mandatory holiday. Len put down his coffee and asked me, "Do you want to do something special for the Fourth?"

"Sure," I answered. "What do you have in mind?"

Len rubbed his chin and said, "Well, Pat's daughter Sharon and her husband Hal are going to visit us in August and Hal and I are planning to float the Melozitna River to Ruby. I bought an inflatable raft to make the trip, but I have not used it. So, do you want to try it out? I thought we could pack it up to the fishing hole and float back to the camp."

"Wow! That's a great idea, Len," I exclaimed. I had never rafted a river and it sounded like a grand adventure. As I turned the idea over in my head, a stab of regret dimmed my excitement. The Fourth of July was my father's birthday. For the first time in my life, I was not going to celebrate this special day with him. Worse yet, I was in a remote location where I could not even call him. I felt that uncomfortable feeling of homesickness again creep into my stomach. I excused myself from the table and went to work alone to sort out my feelings.

———•◦✕◦•———

The next day, we completed our necessary chores in the morning and prepared for an afternoon of fun. Len and I packed our gear and tied the folded raft to the oars. This way we could carry the raft between us on our shoulders. We said goodbye to Pat and started our trek up Hot Springs Creek. We both had long legs with a similar stride, so we had no problem slinging the raft and making good time along the trail. The trip up to the fishing pool was uneventful and soon we were unfolding the raft next to the boulder field. Len had a foot pump to inflate the raft. We took turns compressing the air, but it still took more than an hour to fully inflate the boat.

Finally, we were able to load ourselves into the raft and push off from the bank. I sat in front and Len tried to steer us from the back. Each of us had an oar and we flayed the water in uncoordinated unison. The current grabbed us and led us on a journey careening over boulders with reckless abandon. Len finally learned to steer and I gave up and used my oar as a pole to fend off rocks.

As we started to relax and enjoy the trip, I looked up at the riverbanks and was surprised at how fast we were moving. I judged that we were floating faster than I could run. The vegetation was ripping by us. Within fifteen minutes, we spotted the cabins and the hot springs. As we floated by the camp, we yelled at the top of our lungs for Pat's attention. She must have been working inside and failed to hear us, but Happy did. He came bounding down to the creek bank and raced along side us to the airstrip. Here, we pulled out and dragged the raft to shore.

"That was fun, Len!" I exclaimed.

"Yes, it was," answered Len, "and I learned something about steering. Mainly, you don't have perfect control. That will make life interesting when Hal and I shoot down the canyon. Let's pack things up and take it back to camp." We deflated the raft much quicker than we inflated it. Then we packed everything back to the camp and stored our equipment in the shop.

When we got back to the cabin, Pat was putting the finishing touches to a feast of moose meat, potatoes, carrots, lettuce, and a cherry pie. She had the radio turned up and she was humming the tune of an old ballad. We had no doubt as to why Pat had not heard us yelling. "We tried to get your attention, honey, as we floated by" said Len as he plopped into a chair and stretched his legs.

Pat smiled and wagged her head toward the radio, "We got real good reception today. The station is just booming in."

Dinner was delicious and lively with Len and Pat recalling Fourth of July festivities in Galena. As the night wore down, so did I. I bade everyone good night and thanked them for a wonderful day. I walked back to my cabin with a heavy heart about missing my dad's birthday. I finished the last candy orange slice, crumpled the plastic wrapper, and went to bed.

As I fell asleep, a large boom startled me awake. I jumped up and looked out the window to see Len chambering a shell into his 12-gauge shotgun and fire another shot into the air. "Happy Fourth of July," he hollered to the countryside. Pat was standing next to him with her arms folded across her chest laughing. Their antics cheered me up and made me feel accepted in this wild land—until I spotted Happy. He was staring straight at me with menace in his eyes.

Chapter 6

The Taming of Happy

I watched Happy patrol the boundaries of the camp with military precision. The dog easily weighed a hundred and twenty pounds. His barrel chest and broad back were supported by strong legs. His body shape and gait gave him the appearance of a Sherman tank rolling across the terrain. Pat told me that Happy was half McKenzie Husky and half Norwegian Elkhound. This explained his enormous size, but he looked like he had something else flowing through his veins. His wild eyes and massive head indicated that he was also part wolf.

Happy ruled the camp with an iron paw. Nothing moved without his awareness or approval. Len said that before they got Happy, the camp was a regular parade ground for wildlife.

Len recounted that he found Happy as a puppy wandering lost around the streets of Galena in the summer of 1970. He gathered him up, fed him, and decided Pat and he needed a dog to guard the camp. So, Len brought Happy to Melozi Hot Springs in hopes that the canine addition would raise the overall safety of the lodge. Happy proved to be a mixed blessing. While he possessed a vicious bark, he lacked the backbone to drive a persistent animal away. Thus, bears eventually ignored him as if he were a pest disturbing their tranquil foraging.

Happy was loyal to the Veerhusens and, according to Pat, was slow to accept anyone else into his pack. I definitely was experiencing his mistrust. Over the past two weeks, I had made little progress in gaining Happy's acceptance. In Happy's eyes, I was no more than an annoyance that he could barely tolerate and would gladly bite at the drop of a hat.

Thus, I made a vow to convince Happy to like me, and I decided to use the universal tool for taming animals—food. My first training session started at the breakfast table. Len had trained Happy to lie on his pillow in the corner of the cabin while a meal was served. My plan was to secretly circumvent Len's command and offer Happy a tasty tidbit.

Pat had served up a stack of sourdough pancakes and bacon. While the three of us were eating, I nonchalantly offered Happy a piece of bacon with my left hand under the table. Out of the corner of my eye, I could see Happy focus on the treat. His eyes told me that he was torn between obeying his master, taking the treat, or biting me. I kept my hand still and gradually, over a few minutes, his resolve began to deteriorate. I watched him slowly and quietly get up and walk over to my hand. It took everything I had to participate in the breakfast conversation and not tip Len and Pat to the drama that was unfolding under the table. Happy quickly snatched the bacon and retreated to his pillow.

Relieved, I continued to finish my breakfast as if nothing had happened. As I was polishing off my Tang, I offered Happy a smaller piece of bacon. This time I presented it on my open hand. Happy needed less coaxing, but stopped short bewildered by the method of the offering. Then he leaned over and licked the bacon off my hand.

"Well, I think we peeled enough logs for a while," said Len as he drank his coffee. "It's time we start up the mill and make some lumber."

I wiped my hand off on my napkin and answered, "Okay. What do you need me to do?"

Len put down his mug, ran his fingers through his unruly hair, and said, "It's gonna take me a while to set the mill up. I haven't run it since last year, so the engine needs some attention. I also got to hook up the drive belt to the saw and lubricate the guides. So in the meantime, you could finish stacking the peeled logs so they dry, then give me a hand with the belt."

Pat held her cup with both hands and smiled at me over the brim as she said, "I'm glad we've got you. I don't have the strength to be much help on the mill. The boy we had last summer was a real disappointment and after he left, I had to pitch in and help Len. That wood is just too heavy for me to lift and move all day."

Len grimaced at the mention of the boy. "That kid was useless. He would sit on the riverbank all day playing his guitar while we worked. After a week of trying to get him off his butt, I threw him on an airplane and sent him home."

That explains my reception. "How old was he?" I asked.

Len shrugged as he took another swig of coffee and replied, "Probably a year or two older than you judging by the scraggly growth on his face." Len's comment made me subconsciously run my hand across my chin. A few wisps of hair had barely begun to sprout.

Pat noticed my gesture and laughed. She put down her coffee cup and said to me reassuringly, "Don't worry, Mike. You two are nothing alike."

I flushed with embarrassment at how transparent my thoughts were. I cleared my throat and said, "I guess I better get to those logs." I got up and began to collect my dishes until I saw Len glance down at Happy, who was sitting about two feet away from me. Len gave him a puzzled look but said nothing. I quickly put my dishes in the sink and strode out the door.

The freshly peeled logs shone white in the morning sun. Even though we had stacked most of them after we finished stripping the bark, the logs needed to be evenly spaced with slats placed under each row to allow air movement. This would ensure that the logs dried evenly. I decided to pull all of them down and start over. This process took the whole morning to complete. Meanwhile, Len revived the sawmill.

The mill consisted of an old tractor motor mounted on a frame. The motor turned a metal drum with a thick belt. The belt connected to a metal gear box on a large saw table. The gear box allowed the operator to engage the circular saw blade and mechanically feed the log. The operators would roll a log onto the table and secure it with clamps. Then the operator would activate the blade and guide the log forward and back by a control lever.

After I helped Len roll the belt onto the drums, he demonstrated how it worked. We secured a log on the table. Len used a metal guide to determine the thickness of the cut. He handed me a pair of goggles to wear and told me to stand back. He engaged the blade and it whirled into action. Then he applied pressure to the control lever and the table slid forward. When the log met the blade, the saw emitted a high-pitched screech. It quickly sawed the length of the log and lopped off a slat. Len slid the log backward until it cleared the blade. He stopped it and motioned for me to remove the clamp and roll the log 90 degrees. We repeated this process until we had a square log. Then Len carefully cranked the table to cut a two-inch thick board. This log yielded four planks about eight inches wide and eight feet long.

Len shut down the blade and began talking. It took me a few moments for my ears to stop ringing so I could hear him. "That's how we do it. It gets a little loud so we'll wear headsets. You've got to pay attention to what's happening. Know where your hands are and don't wear loose clothing for the equipment to catch. Understand?" I nodded.

"Okay," continued Len, "Let's get some lunch and see if we can't put in an afternoon of sawing." That sounded good to me. I went to my cabin and washed up. Pat had soup and sandwiches waiting. Happy was perched on his pillow and seemed to anticipate my arrival. I sat down and started eating. Then I slowly slipped a piece of sandwich under the table. This time Happy darted to my hand, snatched the morsel, and sat down next to me. His eyes and ears were alert to my every move.

I continued to eat without paying Happy any attention. After a while, I covertly dangled another piece of sandwich in front of Happy. He gobbled it up and then, much to my surprise, plopped his head on my lap. I pretended not to notice, but the more I ignored him, the harder he pressed into my leg.

Len was finishing his soup when he noticed Happy. "Happy!" scolded Len. "What has gotten into you? Go lie down! Now!" Happy reluctantly removed his python-like grip from my lap and wandered back to his pillow. Len looked at Pat and said, "What on earth has gotten into his head?"

Pat shrugged and said, "He's starting to like Mike."

Len shook his head and said, "That could be, but he knows better than that. Crazy dog."

I acted like nothing was wrong and I was as bewildered as Len. "Well, I guess I better start stacking the logs for the mill," I said as I rose to put my dishes in the sink. Some crumbs fell off my lap as I stood up.

Len saw them fall and a light came on in his head. He looked at me and asked, "Were you feeding Hap?"

Busted. I gave Len a sheepish smile and answered, "Yes."

Len looked at me sternly and said, "We don't feed Happy at the table. Understand? You start that and he won't leave any of us alone."

I nodded my head and answered weakly, "Okay." I left the cabin with mixed feelings of shame and triumphant elation. *Happy laid his head on my lap*!

<hr />

The next three days were filled with sawdust, sweat, bug repellent, and lots of mosquitoes. We started each day stacking fresh logs for cutting into lumber or two-sided building logs. Then while Len serviced the equipment, I shoveled sawdust into the wagon to haul it away. I marveled at how much of that moist, prickly material accumulated after a day's worth of cutting—easily three feet deep under the saw table.

The sawdust was only part of the story. I also had to constantly remove the accumulation of slats. As the days wore on, the stacks of slats grew into huge heaps around the mill. Len said we would later cut them up for firewood.

Each day, we sawed hard for four hours until lunch and then another four hours until we stopped to clean the site and prepare for the next day. Including the start-up preparations, we easily put in 10-hour days. Working with a hard hat, hearing protection, and goggles created a hot, humid, and muffled world. Moisture fogged my goggles and sweat permeated my clothing. The sawdust stuck to my perspiration and the mosquitoes were drawn to it. I felt miserable.

Thus, on the fourth day, I felt chewed up, filthy, and tired. Len and I trudged back to the mill after breakfast and started the preparations to fire up the engine. After Len checked the oil, gasoline, and coolant levels, he pushed the starter button. The starter could barely turn the engine. "Battery is low," announced Len as he took his cap off and wiped his brow. "I thought it felt a little weak yesterday. Mike, please go into the lodge and get the battery charger. We'll trickle-charge it while we clean up around here."

Great, I thought as I walked up to the lodge and entered through the back steps. *That means shoveling sawdust.* I walked into the main room. It was still unfinished, but it was slowly taking shape. Len had told Pat that we would probably activate the kitchen within the week, so we would eat in the lodge instead of the cabin. Pat seemed pleased with that option because the new kitchen was larger with more shelf and counter space and the woodstove was much easier to control than the old burner in the cabin.

I looked around the cavernous front room until I spotted the charger next to the wall by the front door. As I stooped down to grab it, I heard Happy barking ferociously outside. I couldn't see anything out the window, so with the charger in hand, I lifted the heavy latch and pushed open the door.

As I walked down the ramp, I saw Happy barking unceasingly at something in the middle of the clearing directly in front of the lodge. My first thought was, *when did Len erect a totem pole?* I gazed at the structure rising above the two-foot tall grass. The morning sunlight filtering through the trees bathed it in soft yellow hues. Suddenly, my mind snapped the scene into perspective. The totem pole was actually a grizzly standing on his haunches. The bear was completely motionless as it stared at Happy through transfixed eyes.

Within a heartbeat, the tranquil scene turned lethal. The bear sprang at Happy with incredible swiftness. Happy recoiled and darted around the field with the bear inches behind his tail. No matter what Happy did, the bear remained in close pursuit like a heat-seeking missile locked onto a jet afterburner. I stood slack-jawed at the base of the ramp with the battery charger in my right hand watching the death-defying scene unfold.

In the midst of his desperate twisting and turning, Happy suddenly looked at me across the field with eyes that radiated, "Michael, old buddy old pal, save me!" Then he bolted straight for me with the bear in close tow.

As I watched the two come screaming toward me with Happy's eyes bulging with fear, a wild thought flashed across my mind, *Hap is bringing the bear to me*. When that realization sunk into my mind, fear and adrenaline surged through my body, tunneling my vision and muting my hearing. Time seemed to slow down and my mind only comprehended snapshots of reality like a strobe light flashing on a screen. As I turned to run up the ramp, I clearly saw the charger tumbling in the air in slow motion as I threw it aside. I leaned forward on my toes and pushed off into a sprint. The ramp seemed impossibly long and my speed agonizingly slow like in a nightmare. As I hit the door and knocked the latch up, I felt an animal pounce on the ramp behind me. I shoved the door open and leaped across the threshold, but suddenly I was stuck in midair, unable to move any further. I glanced to my right and saw Happy had jumped at the same time wedging us in the doorway. Happy was squirming with wild eyes and all legs frantically flailing in the air to work himself free. I grabbed him by the rump and sent him somersaulting into the room. I fell on the floor and kicked my right leg to the door. My heel caught the edge of it and I hooked it back. The door swung shut as the bear charged up the ramp. The bolt closed and the bear smacked into the door pushing it against the hinges and the latch. The door seemed to hang in suspension for an eternity until the pressure relaxed and it fell into place. The door had held.

I exhaled forcibly and felt the adrenaline drain from my system. I got up and looked quickly around for Happy. He was gone and nowhere to be seen. Then I heard the bear popping his jaw and growling outside the door. I carefully peeked over the window sill and saw him stomping his feet and swinging his head in anger at the bottom of the ramp. I silently slipped away from the window and went to find Happy. I found him under the lone bed in the bedroom. One look at his fear-stricken face told me, *Stick your hand under here and I'll bite it!* I left him alone and went to tell Len what had happened.

Len looked up from the engine as I ran back to the mill. Judging from my scared look and no battery charger in my hand, Len knew something was wrong. "What's the matter?" he asked with trepidation in his voice.

I jerked my thumb back at the lodge and blurted, "A bear charged Happy and me."

Len reeled at the news. "Where is it?" he asked.

"He's in front of the lodge."

"Okay," said Len, "let's go see." After narrowly escaping death, I blanched at the idea, but Len was already jogging back to the lodge. So, I reluctantly ran after him. Len stopped at the front of the building and peered around the corner. Seeing nothing, he stepped around and walked to the ramp.

"He was right here, Len. Honest." I was perplexed and scared that the bear had vanished. I looked down at the soft earth and saw fresh bear prints. "Look, Len! See the prints! He's here somewhere." Len looked at the ground and scratched his chin in thought. A movement in the woods caught my attention. My eyes snapped to it and spotted the bear walking from behind the trees and heading for the east wall. "Len, there!" I whispered forcefully as I pointed. The grizzly looked at us menacingly before he disappeared behind the lodge.

Len watched it go and asked, "Where's Hap?"

"He's in the lodge."

Len nodded, turned toward the cabins, and said, "I want you to grab your rifle and meet Pat and me in front of the old cabin."

All I managed to say was, "Okay." As we walked briskly to the cabins, I began to feel the gravity of the situation. We had danger lurking in the camp. Len and I parted and entered our respective cabins. I snatched the Remington from the wall and checked the chamber and safety. The chamber was loaded and the safety was on. Then I walked back outside. Len and Pat were just coming out of the arctic entry. Len wore his pistol and Pat walked solemnly beside him with her arms folded tightly across her chest as if she was hugging herself for support.

Len looked at me and said, "Good. Let's go back." We walked side by side to the mill. The bear was nowhere to be seen. As we halted at the woodpile by the saw table, Len said, "Stay here. I'm going to get Happy." Pat stood close to me while we waited for Len's return. I suddenly realized that she was standing next to me for protection. The thought made me feel strangely concerned for her safety and determined to hold my own against anything lurking in the woods. This was a new feeling that I had never experienced in my life.

Len appeared a few minutes later with Happy wagging his tail as he followed close behind. Len looked around before saying, "All right. We'll work here together, so we can keep an eye out for the bear. Maybe the activity and the sound of the mill will persuade the bear to leave. Mike, what did you do with the battery charger?"

The charger! I thought. *I forgot it!* I steeled myself for what I must do and answered, "I threw it when the bear charged. I'll go get it."

"Be careful," Pat said. I nodded, clinched my rifle tighter, and walked quickly to the front of the lodge. I carefully peered around the corner. Seeing nothing big, brown, and furry, I quickly found the charger and jogged back to the mill. The relief on even Happy's face when I returned unscathed underlined the tension in the air.

During the next four hours, we worked looking over our shoulders. Happy sporadically barked and made false charges to the woods surrounding us. His antics kept us on pins and needles and told us the bear was still close and hidden.

When we broke for lunch, the four of us walked wearily back to the cabin heavily armed and cautious. Pat fixed a simple lunch of leftover soup and sandwiches. As we were eating, Happy began barking fero-ciously in the cabin. I looked out the creekside window and spotted the bear crossing the creek. Pat and Len came to the window and we watched the bear try to fish with his front paw splashing in the water. "Oh, the poor dear," exclaimed Pat. "It's starving. The salmon won't be in the creek for another month."

Len nodded and said, "A starving bear is a dangerous bear. He's gonna hang around for a while."

"The blueberries will be ripe in another week," I noted.

Len replied, "That'll help, but he's gonna need more than that. We need to be careful from now on."

After several minutes of fruitless fishing and Happy's nonstop bark-ing, the bear waded back to the bank and wandered off into the bushes below the camp. We watched it go with trepidation and silence. Len broke our thoughts with marching orders. "Pat, let's spend a few min-utes cleaning the kitchen and making sure all the scraps of food are picked up and dishes cleaned before we leave. We don't want the bear breaking in while we are working. Then we will carry the trash to the dump and burn it before we walk back to the mill together."

We agreed that was the best course of action and began thoroughly cleaning the kitchen. I helped Pat wash the dishes while Len swept the floor and bundled up the trash. When we were ready, Len and I carried the trash to the dump with Pat walking beside us and Happy leading the way. I had my rifle slung over my shoulder and Len was wearing his holstered pistol. We looked like armed traders trudging along the silk road with our load of goods while we searched the country for bandits.

When we arrived at the dump, the charred remains had been recent-ly stirred. Fresh bear tracks and Happy's growls told us that the bear had been recently rummaging through the dump. I collected some dry spruce branches and laid them over the ashes. Then we piled the gar-bage over them. Len retrieved a small can of weathered gasoline that he stored near the dump. He sprinkled the gas over the garbage and wood. Then he restored the can, stepped back from the garbage, and threw a match into the pile. The garbage and wood exploded into a flame with a soft "whoosh" sound.

We stood next to the dump watching the garbage burn for a few minutes before Len told us it was time to go to work. We trudged over to the mill and started cutting lumber. We worked hard for four hours while Happy patrolled the area. Several times we stopped as Happy came running back to the mill with terrified eyes and looking back over his shoulder at some hidden menace, but we did not see any sign of the bear.

We finally quit for the day and went back to the cabin for dinner. We ate a simple affair of cold leftovers and vegetables. Len thought Pat should not cook a warm meal to keep food odors to a minimum. After listening to Pipeline of the North and Trapline Chatter, I bid everyone good night. Len told me to make sure my door was bolted before I went to sleep. I could hear the concern in his voice. I cautiously stepped out the arctic entry and surveyed my surroundings. Seeing nothing ominous, I put my hand on my rifle sling and quickly made my way to my cabin.

Before I went to bed, I double-checked that I had securely stored the rifle on the wall pegs so that I could retrieve it at a second's notice. Then I ensured that I had set the door bolt. It was now ten o'clock and the evening looked as bright as ten in the morning. I felt tired, but edgy like something dangerous was about to happen. My cabin was hot and stuffy from the blazing sun, so I opened the window above my bed to allow some air to circulate. I got undressed and went to bed.

I slipped into unsettled dreams of charging bears and barking dogs. The barking was so real that I abruptly woke. In the daze of semi-consciousness, I could still hear the incessant barking out my window. Suddenly, I was aware that the barking was real. I jumped out of the bed and looked out the window. The grizzly was walking up from the creek along the old cabin and creeping its way to the kitchen window. Happy was outside the arctic entry barking a challenge to it. The bear ignored Happy's loud antics, stood up on his hind legs, and looked through the window. It pressed its nose against the window screen and appeared ready to crawl inside the cabin.

I shouted a warning at the top of my lungs to Len and Pat, "Wake up! The bear is coming inside!" I yanked the rifle off the wall and flicked the safety off. I kicked the door open and jumped onto the porch with my rifle leveled on the bear. Then I saw Len through the window screen with his pistol cocked and pointed at the bear's head. The bear seemed unfazed by the human in front of him and leaned into the window. Len shot it at point-blank range. A flame pierced through the bear's skull. The bear wheeled and sprinted past me with unbelievable speed. Happy took off in the opposite direction as fast as his legs could carry him.

Len bolted out of his cabin wearing only trousers and barefooted. We watched the bear vanish down the path. Then Len faced me and yelled, "Why didn't you shoot?"

The episode had shaken me and Len's question made me realize that I had not stepped up and acted like a man. I felt ashamed. I put my head down and said, "It happened so fast. I just didn't think to shoot."

Len shook his head and swore. Then he looked at me gravely and said, "Tomorrow, you may have to fire at a second's notice. Got it?" I nodded and comprehended the seriousness of his words and implications of my failure to shoot. We had a wounded bear in camp.

———◆◆✕◆◆———

Breakfast was a silent affair. We were groggy from lack of sleep and trepidation seemed to seep into the marrow of our bones. Even Happy was subdued with his head on his pillow as he listened and watched for lurking bears. If we ever forgot our worries, the fresh hole in the window screen surrounded by powder marks served as a good reminder. Finally, Len spoke. "I've been thinking that you best keep your rifle in your cabin today. I'll be wearing the pistol."

I nodded, but did not answer. I knew what he meant. Len did not trust me to do the right thing when the time came. My cereal felt like a cold lump in my throat when I swallowed.

"All right," said Len as he pushed himself away from the table. "We best be going." I got up and put my dishes in the sink. Then I followed Len outside. We walked in silence to the mill. Happy tagged along close behind us. As we approached the mill, Happy stopped and began to furiously sniff the air. Suddenly, he started barking at something in the woods. Len and I froze and searched the forest for danger. Happy continued to bark and lunge into the trees, and then dart back to the road. After looking for a few minutes and seeing nothing, we continued to the mill. Happy maintained his antics unabated.

"I guess he's got the spooks," commented Len.

"I don't know, Len," I said as we approached the woodpile. "Something seems to have gotten Hap's attention." I watched Happy dart back and forth and bark loudly at the same location. My intuition formed from a lifelong association with dogs told me Happy had found something worth investigating. I turned to Len and said, "Len, I'm going to find out what is troubling him." Without waiting for a reply, I jogged back to Happy.

Happy quieted as I ran up to him and sat facing the woods. I knelt beside him and put my arm around his massive back and scratched his barrel chest. Then I put my head next to his so I could see exactly where he was looking. Only a week ago, Happy would have taken my head off if I had dared to embrace him. Now, after the events of the past day, Happy deemed my attention acceptable. I whispered to him, "What do you see, boy?" Happy responded with a deep rumbling growl that emanated from his chest as he stared transfixed at some unseen object. My eyes strained to see through the dimly lit forest and find the subject of Happy's discord. A few shafts of light filtered through the thick forest canopy and illuminated a stump about a hundred feet away. As I focused on the stump, I suddenly realized that it was actually a big head with an ear sticking up. Happy had found the bear!

I hollered to Len, "Len! Come quick. You got the bear! It's right here!"

Len gave me a quick look of disbelief before running to us. He squatted down and peered into the forest. "Okay. What do ya got?" he asked.

I pointed at the head and said, "Right there, Len. See? It's the head of the bear lying on its side about a hundred feet in."

Len said nothing for a few minutes as he stared and stroked his chin. Finally he said, "I want you to run back to your cabin and grab your rifle. Then we'll go after it."

I spun on my feet and sprinted across the camp to my cabin. In one fluid motion, I jumped onto the porch and swung open the door. I snatched the rifle from the wall and raced back to Len. Len had his pistol drawn and the hammer cocked when I arrived. He nodded to the rifle and said, "Check that the safety is off and the chamber is loaded." I did as I was told and found the rifle loaded, cocked, and ready to fire. "Okay," continued Len, "this is what we are going to do. I want you to walk up to the right side of the bear. I'll be on the left. If that beast even twitches once, I want you to shoot as fast as you can and don't stop until I tell you. Got it?"

I nodded. The adrenaline concentration in my bloodstream was off the scale. An emotional cocktail of fear, excitement, and a sense of duty overwhelmed my brain. I was bound and determined not to be a coward. I knew if Len had another option he would have taken it, but I was his only backup and he was going to use me.

With the decision made, Len said, "Let's go."

We approached the bear with slow steady steps. Our weapons were drawn. Len was holding his pistol outstretched with both hands. I had the rifle butt planted into my right shoulder and the bear's head framed in my rifle sights. Happy walked between and several steps behind us with a tense and careful stalk. Time seemed to hang in suspension as we approached the bear. As we got closer, the bear appeared to be lying on its side sleeping peacefully. "Stop!" barked Len. He took two more careful steps until he stood directly behind the bear. Then he kicked it hard in the rump. The body scarcely moved from the impact.

Len lowered his pistol with a look of relief on his face. "It's dead," he said. Happy began circling the bear and growling ferociously at it. I lowered my rifle, slipped the safety on, and felt my adrenaline rush fade. My body was exhausted from the previous night of stress and misgivings. Now that the danger was over, I could finally relax.

We knelt down and examined the body closer. Flies and mosquitoes coated the bear's unseeing eyes and nostrils. Len's bullet had entered next to an eye and exited through the back of the head, shattering the skull. I was amazed that the bear had run over three hundred yards with such a mortal wound.

Len appraised the situation and said, "We need to back the tractor in here as close as we can. Then we'll drag it out and bury it away from camp. We don't want the carcass to attract other predators."

We got up and walked back to the road where we met Pat walking slowly toward us. She had seen me grab my rifle and run back and she knew that meant trouble. Pat had thrown on a hooded sweatshirt and cautiously followed me. Her face was racked with fear and concern and she hugged herself for support. Len's face softened when he saw her. He holstered his pistol and put his arms around her and said, "It's dead. Happy and Mike found it. If Mike had not investigated what Happy was barking at, we probably would have worked looking over our shoulders the whole day."

Pat smiled as she looked at me while I slipped the rifle sling over my shoulder and said, "That was a brave thing to do."

Her words slew me. My eyes misted up as I choked out a reply, "Hap found it. I just listened to him, that's all."

Len smiled, slapped me on the back, and said, "Come on. Let's get that bear out of there and buried. Get some rope from the shop and I will back the cat to it. We'll drag it away from here." I nodded and went to get the rope. After some tight maneuvering, Len was able to drive the tractor within 20 feet of the bear. I tied the rope around the bear's leg and the other end around the tractor hitch. Then I helped slide the carcass around trees and stumps and finally on to the road. Happy marched triumphantly behind with his head and tail lifted high as if he had single-handedly killed the beast.

Len stopped the C60 and jumped down. He bent over the bear, grabbed one of its front paws, and spread its toes. "Look at the size of these! A couple of swipes and you're done." The paw was the size of a dinner plate with curved sharp claws. Len looked at me and said, "Do you want a souvenir?"

"I guess," I replied not knowing what Len meant.

"Okay," continued Len, "go get an axe and I'll remove a couple of claws. Maybe you can make a necklace out of them." Len's proposal intrigued and repulsed me. The thought of having an authentic bear claw necklace was highly appealing, but the notion of chopping them off this dead bear was revolting. Not wanting to be labeled a lightweight, I quickly retrieved a double-bladed axe. Then Len removed the claws with a couple of well-placed strokes. "Here you go," said Len as he handed me two claws with bloody remnants hanging from the knuckles. "Clean these up and make them into a necklace or a neck tie. You'll be the envy of your friends."

Len had that right. I eventually made them into a necklace that I would cherish for the rest of my life.

Chapter 7

The Responsible Man

I have always been a morning person. I like the freshness of the early day—full of promise with quiet moods, singing birds, and no one around. Thus as I stepped out of my cabin at 6 a.m. with a small backpack and my rifle slung over my shoulder, I felt excitement and wonder at the gorgeous day.

Early-morning hunting was the start of my daily routine. Happy met me outside and together we walked down to the runway and up the Kokrines Trail. So far we had not stumbled across any caribou, but that did not disappoint me. I was in awe of the land. It looked so wild and inviting that it captured my imagination and I would lapse into a dreamlike state of adventure. I did not worry about dropping my guard because Happy always growled at the slightest hint of danger.

As we rose in elevation, the blueberry bushes became thick. The berries were finally ripe and plump. Pat had given me a Tupperware bowl with a sealable lid to hold blueberries. After a final look around for game, I would pull out the bowl and begin filling it with handfuls of sweet juicy blueberries. Every sweep of my hand through the bushes produced a healthy helping of fruit. I took a break every few minutes and munched mouthfuls of berries. I could not get enough of the sweet berry taste.

In a short time, I filled the quart bowl, sealed the lid, and placed the heavy container in my pack. Then Happy and I wandered down the mountain and back to camp. By the time we got to the cabins, Pat was cooking breakfast. I would hand her the bowl and she would incorporate the fresh berries into her meal preparations. The berries would enhance the pancakes, hot cereal, or coffee cake that she made.

This morning, Pat was stirring up her sourdough pancake batter when I walked through the door. "Just in time, Mike," she said with a sunny smile.

Len was sitting comfortably in his chair sipping his coffee. He smiled as he watched me give her the berries and asked, "Got skunked again?"

I shrugged and answered, "Yep. I liked the walk though. Happy and I went up the trail again. We didn't even find tracks this time."

Len nodded and said, "Caribou are nomadic creatures. They might not look like it, but they are constantly on the move. We'll get a few bands moving through here yet."

We sat down to a sensational breakfast of pancakes and bacon. My early-morning jaunts ramped up my appetite even higher than its usual ravenous state. If Len or Pat objected to the volume of food going down my gullet, they never showed it. I think they became accustomed to my eating habits and thankfully accommodated it.

As we were cleaning up, Len announced it was time to move the cooking and eating utensils and furniture into the lodge. Pat smiled and replied, "It's about time. The new kitchen has a lot more room to work and will make my life easier."

The inside of the lodge was mostly done. There were still an endless number of finishing touches such as molding, caulking, and staining to complete, but the lodge was totally functional. Hot water flowed through the pipes and toilet. When plugged into the generator, electricity energized the sockets and some lighting. The fireplace was the only glaring unfinished feature. Len and Doug had completed its massive foundation of creek rocks and mortar that rose from the ground and penetrated the floor. The fireplace insert sat on the foundation with a stove pipe extending through the ceiling. Len said that he planned for us to build the rest of the fireplace and chimney later this summer. I shuddered at the thought of hauling the gargantuan amount of rock from Hot Springs Creek by wheelbarrow to complete it.

We spent the morning hauling cans of food and furniture to the lodge and stocking shelves and arranging the table and chairs. Len and I swept the floor in the main room and picked up bits of wood, wiring, and scraps of plumbing. By the time we were done, the lodge took on a domestic atmosphere that felt like a home.

Pat celebrated by officially cooking the first meal in her new kitchen. She fired up her new woodstove and made a big pot of moose-meat soup. We ate it on the dining table in the main room with Pilot Bread biscuits. Afterwards, Len and I battled on the cribbage board, where I almost won and clearly rattled Len's confidence.

In addition to Len and Pat still sleeping in the old cabin, we also listened to the Pipeline of the North and Trapline Chatter there because the radio was hooked to a large antenna to improve reception. The front room seemed cavernous with the removal of the kitchen table and chairs. As we waited for the shows to begin, I stood looking out the north window at the mountain across the creek. It rose about 2,000 feet and peaked with a prominent finger of rock that jutted about 100 feet above the summit. Although I had stared at it several times in the past, this time it seemed to beckon me to climb it. I turned to Len, who was nested in his favorite chair reading a Zane Grey pocketbook and asked, "Len, has anyone climbed that rock?"

Len put down his book and craned his neck to look up the mountain. "I don't know. I've been to the base of it, but I couldn't find a way up. I don't know if Doug has climbed it either. Maybe no one has."

An unscaled peak! *I've got to do it*! "Ah, Len," I said studying the route up, "is it okay if I climbed it tomorrow? You know, being Sunday and all."

"It's all right by me," answered Len. "Just be careful so I don't have to haul you off the mountain. I'm getting too old for stuff like that. I recommend you cross the creek at the ford that I showed you when we fished with the shrew flies. You can carry your hiking boots with you and stash your hip boots on the other side. Also, I suggest you travel light. It's a long, steep climb."

Late Sunday morning, after finishing my chores, I assembled my gear for the assault on the unnamed peak. I stuffed a stocking cap, gloves, a camera, my knife, one sandwich, and a quart of water into my small backpack. I tied my hiking boot shoe laces together and slung them around my neck and then put on my hip boots. A quick check and I was ready to go. Then I walked into the old cabin to tell Len and Pat that I was hiking up the mountain.

"Good luck, Mike," said Len. He held up his pair of binoculars and proclaimed, "We'll be watching for you. Don't forget to wave."

I laughed and replied, "I won't. I hope you can see me."

Len looked seriously at me for a second and then remarked, "I notice you are not taking a gun."

"I thought it was kind of heavy to lug up a mountain, Len. I'll be careful."

Len nodded in agreement and said, "Can't blame you. I used to walk all over this country without one, but it does come in handy in a pinch. You should be all right, though. Just pay attention."

I smiled and said, "I will, Len. See you guys in a few hours." I bounced out the doors to begin a new adventure. Happy met me and followed me to the ford. He sat on the streambank and watched me gingerly cross the creek until I got to the other side. Then he spun around and headed back to camp.

The climb was steep and slow. Partway up the mountain I intercepted a game trail that seemed to head to my destination. The trail helped me skirt the dense alder thickets, but my visibility was limited.

As I turned a corner, I noticed a fresh moose track with water seeping into it. This indicated the track was only thirty seconds old and thus, the moose was very close. I glanced furtively around but could not see it. I felt my anxiety rise as I pressed upward.

As I rose in elevation, the vegetation changed. The alder gave way to tall spruce and eventually poplar trees. As the trees thinned, my visibility improved and my uneasiness lowered. The sparser vegetation allowed a light cool breeze to circulate. It felt like heaven against my skin. I had already stuffed my jacket and shirt into my backpack, but sweat drenched my undershirt. The mountainside pitched steeper until I could touch the slope in front of me. My breath was ragged in my throat as I gulped air to fuel my climb. After climbing for an hour without a break, I felt my legs aching for a rest. I stopped by a wind-blown log and sat down.

As I took out my water bottle, I surveyed my surroundings. I still could not see very far uphill. However, I had a jaw-dropping view of the valley below. The trees prevented me from spotting the camp, but judging from the elevation of the mountains across from me, I could tell I was more than halfway to the rock peak. The view was breathtaking. I could just imagine what the view was like on top of the peak.

After a few minutes, I struck out again. By using the mountains around me for reference points, I navigated toward the peak. I hiked nonstop for another thirty minutes when I suddenly broke out of the tree line. Dead ahead was the peak. As I approached it, I noticed it resembled a rock pillar rising straight up to a point. It looked daunting to climb.

A half an hour later, I finally reached the column base. I stopped for a moment to assess the structure. The rock was weathered and contained many cracks—some extending almost to the top. I searched the east side for a route and found a series of rock ledges that I could negotiate. I took a deep breath and jumped up to the first ledge. I caught the edge and hauled myself up. I repeated this maneuver until I came within 20 feet of the top. A smooth rock wall halted my progress. *I'm too close to turn back*, I thought as I searched for handholds. I located a few notches in the wall and tried to scale the last remaining feet. I could make only another 10 feet until I ran out of options and nerve. The top was tantalizingly close, but I did not want to get stuck on the rock face with no escape route. I reluctantly pushed away from the wall and fell back to the ledge.

"There has got to be a way," I said out loud. I decided to look for another route. I slid off the ledges and walked to the west side of the column. I discovered a steep rock slide that rose through a rock cleft. I scrambled up the ramp and found some easy handholds that brought me directly to the summit. I stepped onto the three-foot-wide peak and yelled to the world, "I did it!" The vastness swallowed up my triumphant shouts. Then I looked out at the spectacular panorama and felt its enormous splendor engulf me. My perch rendered a 270-degree view that left me speechless and with the feeling that I was on top of the world.

I sat down on the ledge and let my legs dangle over the edge. As I unscrewed the top of my water bottle, I marveled how calm I felt. An extreme fear of heights from man-made structures had plagued me for my entire life. On family vacations, my brothers would swing freely from rails of bridges or the balconies of state capitol buildings and mock me for my reluctance to come near the abyss. For some unexplained reason, I sat comfortably on top of an unstable rock ledge one hundred feet above the terrain without the least bit of trepidation.

I peacefully ate my sandwich while I gazed at the wild country before me. I looked up the valley and saw Hot Springs Creek wind and taper into a blue thread over the horizon. Wolf Mountain rose in the background like a stark pyramid. Len had told me that his son Dan had climbed that mountain. He had completed the round trip from camp in two very long days. The distance and height of the journey gave me a healthy dose of respect for the feat.

After a half hour of gawking at the vista, I decided it was time to go back, but before I said goodbye to this special place, I had to memorialize it. I took out my Kodak Instamatic camera and snapped an aerial view of camp. Years later, I would shake my head in disbelief at the height of my perch. I stood up and waved to the camp below before making my way off the rock.

The trip back went much quicker and with less strain than the trip up the mountain. In less than an hour, I made it to the mountain base and retraced my steps to my hip boots. Happy was waiting for me on the other side, wagging his tail and motioning with his head to follow him back to the cabin. We came through the arctic entry together with Happy in the lead as if he had gone to find me and successfully brought me back. Pat held up the binoculars and announced, "We saw you sitting on top! Congratulations!"

I smiled and replied, "Thank you! It was a great adventure. The trip up took some work, though."

Len nodded in agreement and said, "I bet it did. We were surprised how fast you made it to the top. I was also wondering why you failed to plant a flag."

"Uh?" I asked bewildered, "Why did you say that?"

"Because you could have named it. You know, like Travis Peak or something like that. A flag would prove you climbed it."

I felt my chest deflate as the triumph left my body. Crestfallen, I wailed, "Oh, no! I didn't think of planting a flag. You mean I've got to climb it again?"

Len shrugged, "It's up to you. A flag kind of cinches your claim."

I slumped down in my chair and contemplated Len's words. *Travis Peak. It had a ring to it*, I thought. I took a deep sigh and realized I had to climb it again. After all, how many times could a guy get a peak named after himself?

Pat was applying the finishing touches to dinner when we heard Norman's airplane buzz the camp. Len looked at Pat and asked, "Do we have enough to invite Norm to dinner?"

"Yep," she replied. "We've got plenty."

"All right, then," said Len as he rose from his chair and reached for his cap, "Mike and I will walk down and invite him up." I got up with Happy and followed Len out the door. By the time we got to the airstrip, Norman had his airplane parked and was swatting mosquitoes while he waited for us. Len raised his hand above his head and waved to Norman as we approached. "Howdy, Norm! How about joining us for dinner? Pat has got it ready."

Norman smiled and replied, "Thank you! That sounds great. Before we go, I got some important-looking mail for you." He reached behind his seat and pulled out a thick pile of envelopes held together with a rubber band. He handed the mail to Len.

Len took the bundle and waved it in the direction of camp. "Come on. Dinner is waiting." As we started walking back to camp, I saw Norman give me a quick glance like he was surprised I was still here. Len continued the conversation. "We had a little bear trouble last week. Had to kill a grizzly that tried to crawl through the window. I shot it, but it ran off. Mike and Happy found it the next day."

Norman raised an eyebrow and shot me another glance. "Really?" he said. "That sounds like a close call."

Len smiled back and replied, "Yep, but no closer than the last time. At least I didn't shoot this one in the arctic entry." I remained silent as Len and Norman exchanged small talk while we walked back to the lodge.

After dinner, Norm looked appreciatively around the inside of the lodge as he sat at the dining table drinking coffee. "First time I've been in here. You guys have done some good work."

Len looked up distracted from sorting the mail. "Ah, thanks, Norm. It took some elbow grease for sure." He flicked an envelope to me and said, "Here you go, Mike. Here's a letter from home."

I caught the letter and recognized the handwriting on the front. It was my mother's. I felt a sudden flood of excitement and homesickness gush through my heart. I immediately ripped it open and read:

Okay, Michael.

Let's try this again. I want to know the following:

1. How do we get ahold of you during an emergency?

2. How was your trip?

3. Where do you sleep?

4. What kind of work do you do?

5. Are the Veerhusens trustworthy?

6. Do you have any idea when you will come home?

Doug came over with your first paycheck yesterday. He seems like a man of his word. Mickey misses you as she keeps staring down at the basement at night hoping you will come back so she can sleep with you again.

Your brother Steve got a job at Fairbanks' first McDonald's. He's cooking hamburgers. He wasn't supposed to work there because he's not 15 yet, but the owner thought he was big enough to hold his own, so he bent the rules. The place is busy! They got people lined up out the door every night. I guess no one here has seen a McDonald's before. Poor King Leo's Hamburger Drive-In next door is dying. No one goes there anymore.

Greg spends his time riding the motorcycle at a makeshift track next to the Goldstream Theater. Jeff has been helping out around the house. He is kind of bored because he has not met many kids his age.

We love you! Be careful!

Love and prayers,

Mom

I looked up from my letter teary-eyed and realized for the first time I was missing an integral part of my family's activities. I suddenly felt isolated. I brushed away my tears and said to everyone, "I'll be right back. I've got to write back to my family."

"Okay," answered Len as he scarcely lifted his head from intensely reading an official-looking letter. His face formed a scowl as his eyes flicked across the pages.

I ran back to my cabin and retrieved my writing pad. Then I sat down and addressed each of my mother's points. I ripped out a four-page letter, signed it, and stuffed it in a pre-stamped envelope. Knowing that Norman would not wait for me, I ran back to the lodge to hand him the letter. I heard Len's angry voice before I opened the door.

"Who in the hell do those BLM guys think they are?" Len was shaking the document in the air as Norman leaned back in his chair and nodded in agreement.

Norman took another sip of coffee and said, "It's just another form of taxation. The government is always trying to take something from the common guy."

"Now, honey," soothed Pat, "I think you should go talk to them. Maybe someone made a mistake about the new lease rate."

Len's face turned bright red. He threw the paper on the table and bellowed, "They can't justify increasing the rate like that. I swear to God! I'll burn this place down before I let those thieves get their hands on this property!" Len's proclamation silenced us as we considered his words. Finally, Len harnessed his temper, turned to Norman and said, "Pat's right. I should go back with you and pay BLM a visit in Fairbanks."

"Sounds good to me," answered Norman as he set his cup down and pushed away from the table. "I'll get the plane ready while you pack." He stood up, thanked Pat for dinner, and strode out the door.

"You're leaving?" I asked Len, astonished.

"Yep," answered Len standing up and facing me. "I gotta get this sorted out. You think that you can handle things around here while I'm gone?"

"Sure, Len," I replied in a nervous voice. "What do you need done?"

Len smiled and answered, "Help out Pat and keep an eye on the place. We still got some logs that need peeling and that sawdust pile ain't getting any smaller. I should be back in three or four days."

I nodded as I handed him my letter and said, "Okay, Len. I can do that. Could you please mail this when you get the chance?"

"Sure," replied Len as he took the envelope from me. "I best be packing." He put his arm around Pat and walked her to the old cabin. A few minutes later, they came out of the cabin with Len toting a small suitcase. Happy and I met them outside and we walked down to the airstrip. Norman had the airplane untied and preflighted.

"Ready to go?" asked Norman.

"About as ready as I'm going to be," answered Len as he handed Norman his suitcase.

Norman secured the bag in the rear seat, turned to Len, and said, "I've got about thirty gallons of gas that I can sell you. Are you interested?"

Len scratched his chin and replied, "It wouldn't hurt. I've got an empty drum stashed in the alders next to the runway."

"I'll get it, Len," I said. "I found it during one of my walks." Before Len could reply, I jogged down the strip and located the empty drum. Then I balanced it on my shoulder and walked swiftly back.

In the meantime, Norman had retrieved his hand pump and inserted it into the wing tank. Len took the bung off the drum and slipped the pump hose inside. Norman cranked the pump nonstop for several minutes before jumping down and checking his fuel gauges. "That should be it," announced Norman. "Time to go."

Len screwed the bung into the drum and we both rolled it to the side of the runway. Len stood up and said, "Well that does it. Sorry. I should have anticipated getting gas from Norm. I would have had you bring the trailer down and helped you load it. Think you can handle it by yourself?"

I stuck my hand out and said, "No problem, Len. I'll figure out something." Len smiled and easily shook my hand. Then he kissed Pat goodbye and climbed into the passenger side of the plane. Pat, Happy, and I stood off to the side and watched Norman fire up the airplane and taxi to the end of the field. Then he aligned the airplane with the runway and fire-walled the engine. The roaring airplane picked up its tail and came bouncing down the rugged strip. The plane rose above the ground and soared past us as we waved. We stood watching the airplane until it disappeared down the valley with its engine noise echoing off the hills.

Suddenly, a feeling of loneliness descended upon our tight little group. We were minus our leader and it felt like a giant void. We stood quietly—uncertain of our next move. Pat broke the silence by asking me, "What should we do about the gas?"

"I'll run up to the shop and get the cat and trailer," I replied. "Then we'll load it and bring it back."

"Okay," said Pat, "Happy and I will wait here for you."

I jogged down the runway and up the hill to the shop. The C60 was parked with the trailer hooked to the hitch. Before I started the tractor, I had the presence of mind to load two timbers onto the trailer. Then I fired up the cat and drove it back to Pat. I stopped next to the drum and jumped down. I pulled out the timbers and made a makeshift ramp. Then the two of us tipped the drum onto the timbers and rolled it onto the trailer.

"Good thinking, Mike," exclaimed Pat. "I would have thrown my back out for sure if I had to lift it."

I smiled and said, "Thanks, Pat. Unloading it should be easier. I can handle that myself. I'll meet you back at camp." I drove back to camp and off-loaded the drum. Then I spent a few minutes ensuring the shop doors were shut, all equipment was secure, and things were put away before I retired for the evening. I entered the lodge and found Pat putting the dishes away.

"Everything okay?" asked Pat as she closed the cupboard door.

"Yeah, I walked around and made sure everything was set for the night," I answered. I sat down at the dining table and looked longingly at the cribbage board. There would be no battles with Len tonight.

Pat seemed to read my mind. She retrieved her knitting and joined me at the table. "So, tell me, Mike," she asked as she put her knitting needles to work, "what are you going to do when you turn eighteen? Are you going to run to Canada or are you going to Vietnam?"

Her question blindsided me. *Where did that one come from?* I asked myself. "You mean if I am drafted?"

"Yep," she replied, barely looking up. "Don't tell me you support the war."

I had never discussed my political views with anyone in my life. Until this moment, I never thought I had a political opinion, but the thought of being a draft dodger was repulsive to me. So, I answered, "I'd go. Only cowards dodge the draft." I had said stupid things in the past to my mother and watched the fuse of anger burn until she exploded in rage. I now saw the same sparks fly behind Pat's eyes. I noticed her knitting became more exaggerated and pronounced.

Pat waited an uncomfortable minute before replying. When she did, her voice contained steel. "They are brave conscientious objectors. If they chose to rebel, it's their right."

At this moment, I could have chosen to be silent and nodded with feigned agreement, but I lacked diplomatic skills. So, I plunged forward with a righteous feeling burning in my chest. "With that attitude, no one would have fought in any of our previous wars. If people chose to live in America, then they have a duty to answer the call of our president." I was about to learn an important life lesson—nobody wins a political argument.

Pat slammed her knitting down on the table, looked me straight in the eye, and said, "If my son, Michael, decided to bolt to Canada, he'd go with my blessing. I can't believe you honor such a despicable man as Richard Nixon!" Then she leaned forward, pointed her finger at me, and hissed, "Mark my words. That man is guilty as hell over Watergate! He will leave office in disgrace and bring shame upon this country!"

I sat speechless after Pat's declaration. Pat took my silence as surrender, picked up her knitting, and strode for the door. With a voice that contained ice, Pat said over her shoulder, "Good night, Mike."

That's just great! I thought to myself as I watched the door swing shut. Part of me felt stupid for angering my closest ally, but another part of me felt she was way off base. With my mind swirling with conflicting thoughts, I got up and went to bed.

—◆◆◆—

As I entered the lodge in the early morning, Pat was busy making breakfast. She smiled at me as I came to the kitchen and asked, "Did you sleep well?"

I sighed internally with relief. Her voice held no animosity over last night's discussion. I shrugged and answered, "Okay. I slept a little longer than usual, though. I didn't pick any blueberries for breakfast."

"That's all right," replied Pat. " I'm getting kind of sick of blueberries. A day or two without them would do me good. How does cornbread muffins and cereal sound to you this morning?"

"Sounds fine." I helped set the table and Pat laid the food out. I inhaled the cornbread and washed it down with canned milk.

After breakfast as we were putting away the dishes, I asked Pat, "What do you have planned today?"

Pat thought for a moment before replying. "I'm going to set up the back bedroom in the lodge in case we get visitors. Then I need to wash clothes. So, I will need you to start up the generator and pull the washer machine out."

I nodded and answered, "Okay. I'll be shoveling sawdust by the mill. Please come and get me when you are ready." Then I gathered up my gear and headed out for the day.

As I walked around the lodge to the mill, Happy joined me. High grey clouds covered the sky and a cool breeze blew out of the north. This meant fewer bugs and less sweat while I shoveled sawdust into the trailer. Around ten o'clock, my back began to ache. As I paused to catch my breath, I saw Pat walking from the lodge to me. "Hey, Mike," she called, "wanna take a break and help me set up the washer machine?"

"Sure," I said as I sank my shovel into the sawdust and left it. Pat could not have come at a better time. I was beat. I followed Pat to the old cabin and wiggled the tub washer machine out of its crevice. Then

I strung the extension cords between the generator and the washer. After I plugged everything together, I told her I would start the generator and she would be all set.

A thought struck me as I entered the shop. *Why not charge up the sawmill battery while Pat was washing clothes?* So I continued down to the mill with the wheelbarrow and retrieved the battery. Within a few minutes I connected the battery to the alligator clips that led to the generator. I gave the generator a last-minute check before firing it up. The oil level was acceptable, but the fuel was low. Knowing Pat was waiting, I quickly grabbed the gasoline can and poured the fuel into the tank without a funnel. I sloshed a little fuel around the intake and it dribbled down to the support timbers below. The spilt gas did not worry me. *It's not much*, I thought as I put the can away and secured the fuel cap.

I grabbed the starter cord, wrapped it around the crank, and set the choke. As I readied myself to yank the cord, I noticed one of the alligator clips had slipped. I set the cord down and wiggled the clip back on the battery post. A spark snapped from the post and ignited the gasoline fumes emanating from the timbers. Flames exploded around the generator and licked the shop ceiling.

I threw myself backwards away from the fire and looked up in horror at what I had done. My mind shouted, *You have to do something before the shop burns to the ground!* I fought panic as I frantically searched the shop for something to douse the flames. My eye caught the edge of a canvas tarp bunched in a corner. I jumped for it and wrenched it out. As I threw it over the generator, I saw the fire was starting to spread across the timbers and the ceiling was seconds from igniting. The tarp muffled the flames over the generator, but did not cover the timbers. I quickly threw dirt on to the wood and snuffed out the fire. Then I used the tarp to tamp out small persistent flames around the fuel line and the wiring. Within a minute, the fire was out as fast as it had started. Just to make sure, I grabbed a water jug, ran down to the creek, and filled it. Then I sprinted back and poured the water over the smoldering timbers.

When I was done, I fell to my knees and started to shake. Because of my haste, I had come perilously close to burning down a critical component of my employers' camp. The loss of the shop with all the equipment would have cost the Veerhusens thousands of dollars to replace. I was certain that my irresponsibility was grounds for dismissal. Suddenly, I heard Norman Yaeger's voice echo tauntingly through my mind, "*He hasn't burned the place down, yet, has he?*" I put my face in my hands and wailed, "Len is going to fire me!"

I stayed in the kneeling position for a few minutes longer as I struggled to contain my tears and thanked God for preventing an all-out disaster. Then I knew I had to tell Pat what happened. She was probably wondering what was taking me so long. Like a convicted man shuffling down the final corridor to the executioner, I got up and walked back to the old cabin.

Pat was standing outside waiting for me to signal that the generator was running. She did not look impatient as I anticipated. She looked scared. Pat solemnly watched me approach and stop in front of her. I tried to put on a calm face, but Pat saw through my facade and asked nervously, "What happened?" Then she looked closely at me and alarm spread across her face. "You're burned! Your eyebrows are singed!"

I struggled to keep my voice from quavering, but my emotions leaked out. "Pat, I am so sorry. I made a bad mistake." She kept silent as she braced herself for what I was about to tell her. "I should've been more careful, but I caught the generator on fire. I was able to put it out and the damage is minimal. I think you should come and see."

Pat put her hand to her mouth as she heard the news. After an uncomfortable moment, she nodded and followed me back to the shop. I showed her the charred timbers and the blackened ceiling. She stood quietly as she assessed the scene. Then she asked, "Does the generator work?"

"I think so, Pat," I replied. "I need to put electrical tape around the wires that lost some insulation, but it should be ready to go."

Pat nodded and said, "Okay. Let's see." I taped the exposed wires and made sure everything else was in working order before pulling the

starter cord. The generator started on the second pull. It idled smoothly like nothing had happened.

Pat sighed, smiled as she looked at me, and said, "Looks like we
skated by disaster again. You did fine, Mike. If that had happened to
me, I think I would have stood there and watched it burn. Come on.
I'll put some ointment on your face and get you some lunch. Then
we'll try the washer machine again."

I was relieved. I thought for sure she was going to yell and tell me to
pack my bags. I killed the generator and followed Pat back to the cabin.

———————

The evening dinner was a solemn affair. I still felt terrible about
what I had done. Pat elegantly avoided the topic. After dinner, we retired to the old cabin to await the nightly broadcasts of Pipeline of the
North and Trapline Chatter.

We listened to Country KIAK while we waited. Pat had her knitting
and I half-heartedly skimmed a dog-eared Louie L'amour pocketbook.
It was a good story, but my mind kept wandering back to the nearly
incinerated shop. Pat sensed my uneasiness and quietly began to tell
me a story while she worked on her sweater.

"You know, Mike, we have had our share of near misses and failed
adventures. It's just something you live with and keep going. You look
back at it and try to learn something. Then live on. Did Len or I ever
tell you the time we tried to snowmachine from Fairbanks to here?"

Intrigued, I put my book down. "No," I replied, "I don't think I
heard that one. It must have been a hard trip. How long did it take
you guys?"

Pat smiled as she continued knitting and answered, "We didn't make
it. The trip ended up being one of our biggest failures. We had some
heavy freight that Len needed for construction during the spring. So,
we hatched the bright idea of hauling it ourselves from Fairbanks."

Pat guffawed and shook her head as if she could not believe how
naive they had been to attempt such a feat. She continued her story

without missing a loop in her knitting. "So, Len, Happy, and I flew to Fairbanks to organize the trip. Len built two wooden sleds to carry the freight—a large one for equipment and a smaller one for supplies. We purchased a big Alpine Ski-doo to pull the heavy freight sled and a smaller Olympic Ski-doo for me to drive and pull a smaller sled with a cage for Happy."

"Our plan was to drive right out of Fairbanks on the Chena River, down the Tanana River, down the Yukon, up the Kokrines Trail, and arrive home four hundred miles later. Easy, right?"

Pat guffawed again before resuming her story. "So, we got things all set to leave as soon as the sun rose from Pike's Landing, which in early February was around 10 a.m. A friend of ours tipped off a local reporter about our trip and he met us on the Chena River. The reporter interviewed us and took our picture. Well, that delayed us and we got cold standing around. It was at least ten below zero.

"Finally, we shoved off and headed down the river. At first, things went smoothly except we traveled slowly because Happy refused to sit quietly in his cage. So, we let him out and he ran behind the machines. After a couple of hours, Happy began to drag. We stuffed him back inside the cage where he sat nice for only a few miles before he began to cry and get agitated again. Happy started rocking the cage back and forth, which caused me to veer off the trail and get stuck. Each time that happened, Len had to unhook the sleds and pull my machine out. It took forever! I thought Len was going to shoot Happy and throw his carcass to the wolves.

"We struggled on for three days and made about 150 miles until disaster struck. Len broke a brace on his ski and could not control his Ski-doo. So, there we were. Stuck out in the middle of nowhere on the Tanana River. It's starting to get dark and it's cold, too."

I was mesmerized. *Do these people ever stop having incredible stories?* I swallowed hard and asked, "What did you guys do?"

Pat inspected a couple of loops on her knitting needle before answering. "Using my snowmachine, we dragged the sleds and the crippled snowmachine to the riverbank and made camp. Then the next day, we stashed the Alpine, the larger sled, and all the supplies in a brush pile so it would be hidden from view and headed upriver to Nenana. I held Happy tight between us so he couldn't wiggle out. We made Nenana in a couple of hours and called our friend to help us retrieve the Alpine and the freight. We ended up flying the freight to here after all. It was an expensive lesson."

I shook my head in amazement. "That's a great story, Pat."

Pat put her knitting down and said, "I think I got a copy of the newspaper article that the reporter wrote. It was published after we returned." She rustled through some folders on her desk until she produced a neatly folded newspaper. "Here it is," she said and handed it to me.

I carefully opened the paper. A picture of Len and Pat petting Happy, who looked unsure of himself perched on an Alpine Ski-doo seat was prominently displayed on the front page of the *Fairbanks Daily News Miner*. The date was February 16, 1972. The subtitle under the picture read, "BUSH BOUND - Pat and Leonard Veerhusen prepare to leave on a 400-mile trip from Fairbanks west to their lodge at Melozi Hot Springs on the Yukon River. She is 52 and he is 59."

Until now, I had only estimated Len and Pat's ages. Now I had confirmation that I was in the ballpark. The article stated they were grandparents "eight times over." It briefly described Pat's rescue when she became paralyzed and Len's rescues when he broke his leg and when he fell off a rafter while building the new cabin and broke his back. Then the article described their life at Melozi. Amusingly, the article ended with this paragraph: "Len handmade a pair of wooden sleds, which they tow loaded with supplies and materials, as well as a large wire cage for their dog, Happy, who is also making the journey. He prefers normally to run with the sleds, but when he gets tired, Happy can ride in comfort behind Mrs. Veerhusen. Traveling at an average of 20 miles per hour, they expect the trip to take about five to seven days depending on weather, and going via Nenana, Manley Hot Springs, and Tanana."

Pat saw me smile after reading the last paragraph and said, "We took off with some bad assumptions. Twenty miles per hour! We were lucky to make five!"

The KIAK deejay interrupted us by announcing the start of Pipeline of the North. We sat quietly as we listened to the messages and were rewarded with the following broadcast: "And to Pat at Melozi Hot Springs. From Len in Fairbanks. All done. I'll be coming home tomorrow. Love, Len."

Pat turned to me and smiled. I could tell she missed him deeply. "Good!" exclaimed Pat. "It'll be good to have him back so soon. I thought he would stay longer."

I just nodded and thought, *I bet he'd stay longer if I wasn't here.*

As if she could read my mind, Pat reached out and touched my hand as she said, "Don't worry. Len will understand, but you are going to have to do the responsible thing and tell him yourself. Okay?" I nodded again in agreement and kept silent as my stomach twisted with anxiety.

<hr />

Norman returned with Len the next afternoon. Anticipating that Len would maximize the trip by bringing supplies, I brought the dozer and trailer down to the airstrip while Pat and Happy bounded ahead. When I rounded the bend and came onto the strip, I saw I had guessed right. Norman and Len were stacking boxes next to the airplane.

As I approached the airplane, I waved to Len, swung wide to miss the wing, and pulled alongside the airplane. "Hi, Len," I said as I jumped down. "Good to see you again." Then I gave Norman a curt nod and addressed him, "Norm." Norman gave me a nod and resumed unloading the plane.

Len smiled broadly, stuck his hand out to me, and said, "Hi ya, Mike! How did everything go?" He looked genuinely pleased to see me.

I felt a wave of guilt wash over me as I gripped his hand, shook it, and lied, "Just fine, Len. I'll load the boxes in the trailer." The three of us made short work of loading the supplies. Norman was in a hurry and bid us goodbye. Within minutes, he was roaring down the valley and we were making our way back to camp.

I stopped the tractor at the lodge and carried some boxes of canned goods inside. Pat was handing Len a cup of coffee and laughing at something he said. She looked at me as I came inside and motioned for me to sit down and join them. I carried the boxes to the kitchen and then came back to the table. After some small talk, Len summarized his trip. "I got BLM squared away, but I think they want their greedy hands on this place. So help me God, I will burn it down before they get it. I swear I will."

His declaration again silenced us. Then he continued, "I had a chance to see Doug. He has decided to sell his share of the lodge. He can't keep up his side of the bargain and help build the place, so he's trying to find someone interested in going into the lodge business. He said he had a lead on a guy in Fairbanks looking to live in the Alaska wilderness. I don't know. We'll see."

Len looked over to me and said, "Doug asked how you were working out. I told him you were a good hand." Unbeknownst to Len, he could not have picked a worse compliment. My eyes misted up and I turned my face away.

Pat understood my angst and said gently to Len, "Len, Mike has something he's got to tell you. Go ahead, Mike. Tell him."

The room went silent as I looked back to Len. His face showed a trace of concern and a little fear. I swallowed and said as evenly as I could, "Len, when I started the generator yesterday, I spilt some gas and it ignited." Len's eyes flew wide open and he sat up straight in his chair. I had definitely gotten his attention. "I smothered it out with a canvas tarp. Some wiring got scorched, but everything else appears okay. I wrapped the wiring up with tape and was able to start it. I'm sorry Len. I should have been more careful."

The cat was out of the bag and I felt strangely better for it. I sat calmly and waited for Len's verdict. To help the outcome, Pat put her hand on Len's arm and said soothingly, "I told Mike that I would have just stood there and watched it burn."

Len licked his lips and looked hard at my face for a second before replying, "I thought your eyebrows looked a little singed." Then he broke out laughing and I felt relief wash over me. Len stood up and said, "okay. Let's go down to the shop and take a look. Then we'll finish unloading the trailer."

I stood up to follow Len outside. As I was leaving, I turned to Pat and mouthed, "Thank you." She gave me a smile that said, *See? I told you.* I felt like part of the family again.

Sunday fell on July 29 and Len announced it was high time to visit the fishing hole upstream of camp. We packed our day packs with clothing and picnic food. Len strapped on his pistol and I slung my rifle over my shoulder. With fly poles in hand, we struck out on the game trail. Len led the way with Pat in the middle and I brought up the rear. Happy raced up and down the trail sniffing at spoor and scat and chasing squirrels across the tundra. The blueberries were still thick on the bushes and delicious wild raspberries were sporadically available. Each of us often leaned out, scooped up a handful of blueberries, and munched them as we walked.

The day was cool with high overcast clouds and it felt refreshing. We arrived at the pool with the roaring water boiling into the bluff and made our way through the boulder patch. Pat found a comfortable rock to sit on while Len and I assembled our rods. Happy played watchdog as he sat high above the bank where he was lord over all he saw.

I watched Len whip his rod into motion with strong full strokes. He gently laid his black gnat fly 50 feet upstream and against the bluff. The current sucked the fly down to the depths of the pool. Instantly, his line snapped taut and his rod bowed. Len let out a laughing shout and played the fish to the bank. It was a whopper! Len kept it in the water and gently removed the hook. The grayling finned in the tranquil backwater between the rocks while it rested. I could see the long iridescent dorsal fin with a red edge swirl along its back before it darted back to the safety of the pool. "We'll only keep the ones that are hooked too bad to release," said Len as he prepared to fish again.

Len and I attacked the pool and caught so many fish within the next twenty minutes that it felt like a frenzied battle. Then the fish stopped biting as quickly as they started. During the lull, Len saw we had kept four fish—all more than 12 inches long. "That should be enough," announced Len. "Let's get a fire going and eat."

Len started the fire while I cleaned the fish. Pat shook each fish in a bag of seasoning she had brought and wrapped them in foil with butter. When the fire had burned down to cooking coals, she laid the fish on them. Then she used a stick to turn them every few minutes. I could barely contain myself when she announced they were done. With Happy looking over our shoulders, we carefully opened the foil to reveal a steaming delicacy. I inhaled it. When I was done, Pat motioned for me to take the fourth fish, which I did and made short work of it.

After lunch, Len said, "Let's try some exotic flies. I'm curious what these grayling will hit." I selected a Royal Coachman dry fly and Len grabbed a purple rooster-tail-looking streamer. Although not as productive as the black gnat, each of our selections produced an abundant number of strikes. Finally, the fish wised up and stopped biting. "Well that about does it," said Len as he reeled in his line for the last time and broke his rod down. He looked over to Pat, "Are you ready to go, honey?"

"Yep," replied Pat, "just as soon as we put out the fire, we can leave." Using our water bottles, we carried enough water from the creek to adequately smother and cool the coals. Then we marched back to camp completely contented from our fun and relaxing outing.

◆→※←◆

After another rousing game of cribbage where Len brilliantly pegged out at the last second, we settled back for some quiet time before the radio broadcasts. I was too spun up after Len snatched certain victory from my hands to read. So, I asked Len a question that had plagued me since the first time I heard the name. "Len, who is Hobo Benson?"

Len looked amused as he put down his paperback book. Pat laughed and shook her head as she continued with her knitting. Her work was beginning to look like a sweater. Len took his time answering by retrieving a can of tobacco and rolling two cigarettes. He lit them with a wooden match and handed one to Pat. Then he sat back in his chair with his left arm draped over the back and his right arm propped on the arm rest lazily holding his cigarette. He was now ready to fully answer the question.

"Hobo's real name is Frank. He grew up in a little Michigan town named Hubbell. How he got his nickname is anybody's guess. He actually flew P-40s in France during the war. You would never know it by looking at him."

"His brother Leonard coaxed him to join him in Alaska in 1949. After tending bar for three years in Anchorage, Hobo opened a plumbing and heating business. In 1955, he diversified into selling bar equipment. He came to Galena to work a two-week plumbing job at the air force base in 1959 and ended up staying. That's when he met Norman 'Buckets' Burgett.

"Buckets is the most enterprising man that I know. If there is a way to make a buck in Galena, Buckets is all over it. He and Hobo became fast friends and started a bar together called the Yukon Inn. How they got a liquor license is beyond me, but they started the only bar on the Yukon to the Bering Sea. People flocked to it from hundreds of miles to tie one on. Fights broke out every night, but everyone seemed to have a grand time.

"Sometime in 1961, Hobo bought Buckets out and people started calling the place Hobo's Bar. The name stuck and became famous throughout Alaska." Len took a long satisfying drag on his cigarette and blew the smoke to the ceiling before continuing.

"Hobo had to go back to Anchorage in 1962 to close down his plumbing business and buy supplies for the bar. During that trip, he met a woman named Yvonne Worthington in a restaurant. Yvonne told Hobo that she was a commercial artist from Seattle up for a visit. Hobo took a shine to her and convinced her to accompany him to Galena.

"Hobo started the town's tongues a wagging when he arrived in Galena with Yvonne on his arm. She looked like a whorehouse madam with her makeup and jewelry, not like an artist. Hobo loved every bit of the town's attention and rumors. Yvonne walked into the bar and was immediately appalled at the bare plywood walls. She acquired some colored chalk and asked Hobo what he wanted illustrated on the walls. Hobo told her that he was a big fan of Robert Service and wanted the 'Shooting of Dan McGrew' surrounding the bar. Yvonne promised to draw the entire ballad.

"To give her credit, Yvonne was true to her word. She worked hard for three years carefully shaping the scenes on the wall. However, she turned out to be a woman of many talents. When she wasn't drawing, Yvonne helped out as a cook and bartender. She was also an expert poker player and pool shark. She would win at the card table while she smiled sweetly at the men. After picking their pockets clean, she'd get up and hustle the men standing around the pool table. After faking a few losses, she laid down a wad of money on the table and snookered her victims in matching the bet. Then she cleared the table and walked away with their money. This happened night after night. You would think the men would wise up, but pride kept them for admitting defeat. So, they tried again and she'd clobber 'em again. The men nicknamed her 'Side Pockets Sadie' for her skill and wily ways."

A broad smile crept across my face as I listened to Len tell this incredible story. Pat was chuckling and shaking her head in amusement as she continued knitting her sweater. She occasionally stopped her work to take a drag on her cigarette she left smoldering in an old butter can.

Len continued his story. "Yvonne turned out to be an incredible artist. The characters she drew came from the unusual patrons who frequented the bar. Customers would come in and spot themselves or someone they knew in the murals. Under each scene, Yvonne wrote a verse from the poem. When she was done, the story of the Shooting of Dan McGrew wrapped around the entire bar. You could spend hours looking at it. Yvonne left Galena shortly after finishing the project."

"What happened to her?" I asked.

Len shook his head as he answered, "Yvonne traveled around Alaska a bit. She got herself into a little trouble in Nenana, where she ran a gambling operation called the Missile Club. Apparently, she was also showing adult movies in the back and got caught selling raffle tickets for a night with a prostitute. After that, she started traveling again and was killed in a bush plane accident in 1969. After her death, customers at Hobo's claimed the murals started fading and her artwork was haunted. Some even stopped visiting the bar. Funny how people blame ghosts for natural causes."

Intrigued, I asked, "What do you think caused the murals to fade?"

Len laughed as he emitted smoke from his mouth. "How about a couple of fires and two floods? Heck, when Yvonne was drawing one day, she claimed she smelled gas. So, one of the brilliant customers volunteered to investigate and eventually made his way into the trailer attached to the side of the bar. He couldn't see a lick, so he decided to light a match. Turned out a propane tank was leaking. The resulting explosion knocked him out of the trailer and blew out all the windows. More sober customers managed to put out the fire that started along the wall where Yvonne was working. That was a close call!

"Then came the floods. Every spring the Yukon River swells during breakup. Every once in a while, the river ice jams downstream of Galena and forms a dam. When that happens, the water rises quickly and high. In the midsixties, the water rose four feet high in the bar. But in 1971, the water eventually rose to the ceiling. Hobo refused to leave. He put a chair on the bar, sat down, and started drinking. People in boats outside pleaded for him to swim out to them and he would cuss at them and throw bottles at the door. Finally, after the water rose to inches from the ceiling, his trusted friend and hired hand, Ronnie Franklin, put on scuba gear and swam through the submerged arctic entry and rescued him."

Len took another drag on his cigarette as he concluded, "So, you see, fires and floods don't do chalk drawings a whole lot of good."

I shook my head and said, "That was an incredible story, Len."

Pat put down her knitting and added, "That's not the whole of it. Hobo decided to get married last year to a gal half his age. They were married in the bar and had their reception at the community hall. The hall was built on a post and pad foundation, so it sits about three feet above the ground. Well, the outside temperature fell to about sixty below zero during the celebration and the floor became ice cold. As the celebrants got drunk, they began sloshing their drinks which instantly froze on the linoleum. The whole place turned into an ice skating rink. People were slipping and falling. It's a miracle no one got hurt."

"I think they were too drunk to get hurt," Len responded. "His wife's name is Sally. She's actually a nice person, but I hear she is a tough lady and can hold her own in a fist fight. The locals call her Yukon Sally."

"Wow," I said, " do you think I could meet Hobo sometime?"

Pat replied, "Hobo usually comes out here once a summer. The poor dear needs to dry out and get away from the bar. So he comes out, soaks in the bathtub, and drinks the water from the hot springs. He claims the water has medicinal properties and cures his shakes. Then after a few days, he'll pack up and do it again. A normal person would have died by now."

We went silent for a moment—each thinking about Hobo. Len and Pat reminisced about fun times and harbored concerns about Hobo's health while I repeatedly prayed, *Please God, let me meet Hobo.*

Chapter 8

Unconventional Guests

During the last days of July, Len decided to build the swimming pool. We sat around the dining table in the lodge planning the project. "First," said Len as he drew on a pad of paper, "we've got to figure out how big to make the pool."

"So, how many sheets of fiberglass do you have and how big are they?" I asked.

Len scratched his chin and replied, "Uh, I think I have forty-two sheets that survived the trip. Each sheet is eight by four feet."

"Okay," I said as I took the pencil from Len's hand and started scribbling on the pad. "Since each sheet will give you 32 square feet, we need to multiply that number by 42 That gives us 1,344 square feet to fashion the pool." I glanced at Len and saw him nod for me to continue. "So, let's make some assumptions. If the pool was 30 feet long, 15 feet wide with a shallow end four feet deep and a deep end six feet deep, the total surface area would consist of the sum of the total sidewalls and the pool bottom." I drew a rough sketch of the pool. "See here? You would have two trapezoids and three rectangles." I drew the shapes and labeled the sides with dimensions. Then I calculated each surface area. Len watched me perform the math. Pat smiled with approval as I worked. When I finished, I looked up to Len and continued, "So, the total surface area would be 1,320 square feet, which is about as close as you would want to cut it because you have to allow for some overlap when making the fiberglass joints."

Len nodded again and said, "Fifteen by thirty sounds about right. How much water would a pool that size hold?"

I quietly thanked God for my excellent geometry teacher, Mr. DeWitt, from Lathrop High School before answering. "Well, I can estimate the volume by splitting the pool into two sections. I can construct a four-foot-deep by fifteen-foot-wide by thirty-foot-long box and a triangular box 15 foot wide, 30 foot long, and four foot high." I carefully drew the sections of the pool and labeled the dimensions. Then I multiplied the sides and totaled the volumes. "See? The total volume would be 3,150 cubic feet. Since each cubic foot holds 7.48 gallons of water, the pool would hold 23,562 gallons."

Len shook his head and asked, "How much does that weigh?"

"Well," I answered as I continued to doodle on the pad, "if each gallon weights 8.35 pounds, then the total weight will be about 196,743 pounds or, in other words, 98 tons."

Len whistled at the number. "That's heavy! It'll take some timbers to make a crib to hold that. Come on. Let's go outside and measure off the pool and dressing rooms." We got up and walked west behind the lodge, crossed over the road between the mill and shop, and stopped where Len had stacked the sheets of fiberglass.

I pulled the tarp covering back and tried to lift a sheet. I could barely budge it. "Man, these weigh a lot!" I groaned. "It must have taken you forever to move these sheets here."

Len smiled and said, "I got some unexpected help. Pat's son Michael is married to Susan. Susan's parents, Mark and Luverne Swan, own a lumber company out of Port Orchard, Washington. Mark arranged for a barge to ship out of Tacoma loaded with building supplies including the fiberglass. Yutana out of Nenana met the barge in the lower Yukon and pulled it upriver to Kokrines. Then Bob Moore and I dragged the supplies over the winter trail by snowmachine. Mark pulled some strings and got me a hell of a discount. I owe him plenty. In fact, he and Luverne are driving up from Washington as we speak. They should arrive in Alaska in about ten days. They're going to fly out here and stay for a spell."

This news surprised me. "Okay," I replied, "I didn't know that."

Len waved his hands at the brush and trees around us and said, "First thing we've got to do is clear the vegetation. Then we'll stake out the building lines and start digging the foundation. Let's get the C60 started and go to work."

I used a small chainsaw to hack away at the woods. Cutting the small black spruce trees was easy. However, the gnarly willows were much harder to clear than the spruce. Their wood was denser and their roots spread out and held fast to the earth.

"You might want to be on the lookout for a good straight piece for a cane," yelled Len as he wrapped a cable around a bunch of willow and prepared the tractor to yank it out.

His comment surprised me. "Uh?" I answered as I turned off the screaming chainsaw, "What do you mean?"

Len pointed to the willow and said, "These trees are known as diamond willow. If you treat it right, you can peel off the bark and sand the knotholes. The wood is white and the knotholes turn red. Put some varnish on it and you got yourself a good-looking walking stick." Len grabbed a three-foot-long branch that was a couple of inches in diameter and said, "Here. Watch this." He opened his pocketknife and shaved the bark off one side. The wood underneath glistened white. Then he cut into a knothole and revealed a bright red wood. "See? I've seen some beautiful lamps and chairs made out of this stuff."

I was amazed. "Wow, Len, I think I will start working on one tonight." We labored through the rest of the day. By the time we broke for dinner, we had the area cleared and the position of the swimming pool and two dressing rooms marked with stakes and twine. We were tired and dirty, but satisfied at what we accomplished.

After dinner, Len dragged out the cribbage board. Without talking, he began to shuffle the cards and I placed the pegs. We played a couple of hands when Len turned a jack over on the cut. He played his first card and I pounced on his unclaimed points. "Muggins!" I yelled as I moved my peg forward two holes.

Len looked at the card in disbelief for a full second before yelling out to Pat in the kitchen, "Pat! Mike just claimed my uncounted points!" This was a first—like an eaglet flying for the first time.

Pat came out of the kitchen smiling as she dried her hands on a towel. "Well, you taught him, Len. What did you expect?"

Len looked back at me with deviltry in his eyes and declared, "Okay, son. From now on, the gloves are off!" We battled on as Len threw every trick he knew at me. I managed to counter his attack with some lucky hands. Then I pegged out and claimed my first win. Len pretended to be stunned and hurt as he said to Pat who witnessed the accomplishment, "Mike just beat me! How in the hell did that happen?" I knew he was acting, but it made me feel good.

"Well, Len," replied Pat, "I think he's wise to your shenanigans. You should concentrate on playing a good honest game and not be so sneaky."

Len pushed back from the table with faked innocence. "Why, I don't know what you mean, Pat."

"Ah, right, Len," replied Pat shaking her head. She reached out and touched my hand and said, "You did good, Mike. Congratulations for beating this bully."

I grinned and said, "Thanks Pat. It was a long time coming."

———◆◆◆◆◆———

The three of us relaxed after the card game around the dining table. Len and I read pocketbooks and Pat concentrated on her knitting. I noticed she had changed her weave to decorate the sweater. She did it so skillfully that the sweater looked factory made. "That's a great-looking sweater, Pat," I said as I put down my book.

Pat smiled without looking up and replied, "Thank you. These triple stitches are a pain, but it gives the sweater a nice touch. I should have it done by the time Sharon arrives."

"Has it been a long time since you've seen her?" I asked.

I saw a flash of melancholy cross her face before she answered, "I haven't seen all three of my kids in a while. Being out here, it's kind of tough to connect. My youngest daughter, Trish, lives in California." Pat smiled as she thought of her before continuing. "My other two, Michael and Sharon, are busy with their lives, too. That's why it's so special that Sharon and Hal are coming to visit. I want to have this sweater ready for her. I don't get a chance to sew for her often."

"When are Sharon and Hal coming?" I asked.

"The third week in August," answered Pat. "Len and Hal are going to float the Melozitna River to Ruby. That should be a good adventure."

Feeling that the time was right, I asked a long overdue question. "Pat, what brought you to Alaska?" I saw Len put down his book to listen.

Pat nodded like she was lost in thought for a moment or she was searching for the right words. When she finally spoke, she sounded like she was talking from a faraway place. "Let's just say I got divorced and wanted a new start. In 1964, Elmendorf Air Force Base in Anchorage was booming and needed clerk typists. So I applied and they hired me. I arrived with my son, Michael, and a few dollars in my pocket and went to work. We had just moved into an apartment when the Good Friday earthquake struck. I thought the whole world had come to an end!"

"I read about it," I said. "I understand it was a big one!"

"The whole earth shook for two minutes. I thought it would never stop. We were lucky in that our building was still standing when it was done. Many were left homeless."

Len joined the conversation with a laugh. "Coincidentally, I was in Anchorage, too, when it hit. I was in the Carrs grocery store off Gambell when the tremor started. The cans started shaking on the shelves. A woman who was visiting from Arizona was standing next to me and she started to scream. A stock boy came running by and said, 'Don't worry, lady. It's just a small shake.' Then all hell broke loose and the aisles started swaying. We both fell down and the cans poured over the top of us. After a few minutes, it quit. The woman sat up and said as cans slid off her head, 'If that's a small shake, I'd hate to see a full earthquake!'" We all laughed hard at Len's story.

Pat wiped the tears from her eyes and continued, "Things were hopping all over this state after the earthquake. Emergency contracts were let to start rebuilding. The Air Force had me working ten to twelve hours a day, seven days a week, typing contracts and orders. It took months to catch up. Finally, I had enough and wanted a break. The Air Force had an opening in Galena. The position paid more and required fewer hours. So I took it."

"One of the contracts I typed up when I was in Galena was for an uncouth rascal named Leonard Veerhusen. It seemed this unsavory character was fleecing the government for removing snow from the runway. I took it upon myself to expose his unscrupulous business practices. When the Air Force management failed to curtail his activities, I executed the only reasonable course of action. I married him."

I did not see that one coming. I shot Len a glance. He shrugged and said, "And see where that got you?"

Pat smirked, looked up from her knitting for the first time, and asked sweetly, "Could I bother you for a cigarette?"

Len made a comical showing of throwing his book down and scrambling to make a cigarette. I was not in the mood for smelling smoke, so I thanked Pat for her story and excused myself to go hunting for the perfect piece of diamond willow for my new cane.

Happy and I walked to the woods behind the swimming pool construction site where I saw a tangle of diamond willow. Armed with a bow saw, we entered the thicket and I carefully scanned the slim branches. Some were long enough, but had few diamonds. Others were too crooked to make a staff. After searching for half an hour and Happy vigilantly standing guard, I finally found a candidate. I carefully sawed it off from its base and dragged it back to the clearing. The branch had at least six good knotholes and it bent slightly at the end to form a handhold. The bark was fresh and would easily peel away from the wood.

I carried the branch back to my cabin with Happy following close behind and we sat down on the steps. I pulled out my pocket knife and began to shave off the bark in long strips to expose the bright white wood underneath. I labored for nearly an hour removing the bark and gently shaving the knotholes smooth. The whittling was strangely relaxing and soon my eyes grew weary.

I got up, petted Happy, and then stashed my cane in the shop before saying good night to Len and Pat. As I walked back to my cabin, I gazed at the mountains surrounding me. They radiated magnificently in the waning evening light that took my breath away. I continued up the steps with the soothing sounds of Hot Springs Creek babbling in the background and fell gently asleep.

———◆◆◆◆◆———

The next two days consisted of digging the foundation for the swimming pool. Len drove the C60 and I had to remove the boulders that the blade unearthed. This meant I had to drop down into the excavation each time Len backed up and lift the stones out. Then I scampered up the crumbling walls as Len drove forward and pushed the blade down. By lunch, I was covered in dirt and could barely lift my arms.

During the early afternoon of the second day, we finished the excavation to the depth and size needed to set the pool. Len shut down the cat and we began to discuss the next phase of construction when we heard an airplane flying up the valley. We both looked to the west and soon spotted Norm's red 185 approaching the camp. He buzzed the lodge before doubling back and setting up his approach to the airstrip.

Pat came out of the lodge and said, "Why don't you guys meet Norm and invite him up for coffee?"

Len looked like he needed a break so he heartily agreed. "That's a great idea, honey. Come on, Mike. Let's see what's up."

We and Happy walked down to the strip and saw Norman and two men unloading the plane. As we drew closer, we could see Norman looking at his passengers with disdain, which only piqued our curiosity. Then we saw the men clearly for the first time. My first thought was that they resembled the rock band *The Grassroots* that I had seen perform on the Ed Sullivan Show. They were both tall—about an inch or two taller than I. They had long brown hair that tumbled down to their shoulders under wide-rimmed felt hats. Their hair complemented their full beards. They were both dressed in flannel shirts and Levis. Happy gave them a deep growl.

I saw Norman mouth the word *hippies* behind their backs and shook his head. Len was strangely silent as he strode up to meet them. One of the men set down the box he was carrying and addressed Len. "You must be Len Veerhusen. My name is Bob Ford. I'm interested in taking over Doug's share of the lodge." Bob stuck his hand out and Len took it.

Len spoke in a businesslike tone, "Glad to meet you, Bob. And who's your partner?"

The other man stepped forward and replied, "My name is Skip Kittredge. I am just along for the ride." I immediately liked Skip. He had an easy smile and a nonthreatening demeanor. I think Len sensed it, too, but Happy did not. He gave Bob and Skip a threatening glare and circled the plane.

Len shook Skip's hand and said, "Glad to meet you, Skip. This is Mike. Doug hired him to help us out this summer. Come on. We'll give you guys a hand with your stuff." Bob and Skip slipped their backpacks on and we each grabbed a box. Len wagged his head toward the lodge and said to Norman, "Norm, we got some fresh coffee for ya at the lodge. Do you have time to come up?"

"Nope," Norman answered bluntly, "I gotta get going. I'll be back in three days to pick these . . . these . . . these *guys* up." After uttering that proclamation, he turned his back to us and prepared to leave.

"Suit yourself, Norm," replied Len. "We'll see ya when you come back." The four of us struck out for the lodge carrying our loads.

I looked over the box I was carrying and asked Bob, "What's in here? It's heavy."

Bob smiled and answered, "Oh, I thought I should bring some stuff that you guys probably don't see very often. Perishables like fruit, milk, eggs, cheese, and fresh meat."

Len replied, "Thank you, Bob. That was considerate of you, but we don't have refrigeration out here. We are probably going to have to gorge ourselves for the next couple of days or else it'll spoil."

Skip was carrying a cooler and judging by the strain on his face, it must have been heavy. "Do you need a hand with that cooler, Skip?" I asked.

Skip smiled and replied through clenched teeth, "No problem. I've got it." We marched the rest of the way to the lodge in silence with Happy walking carefully behind us. Pat saw us coming and walked outside to meet us. I saw no trace of concern on her face when Bob and Skip approached her.

Len made the introductions. "Pat, this is Bob Ford and Skip Kittredge. Bob has been talking to Doug about buying his share of the lodge. They decided to fly in and see the place for themselves."

Pat gave them her warmest smile and greeted them. "Pleased to meet you. Please come in. We have some coffee and a table to talk around." Then she asked Len, "Where's Norm? I thought he would come up for a visit."

Len shook his head and simply replied, "He had to go." Pat gave him a puzzled look before waving her hand at us to come inside the lodge. We walked inside and carried the boxes into the kitchen.

"What's this?" asked Pat.

"Groceries," I answered.

"Okay," replied Pat, "we'll tend to it after socializing for a few minutes. Please show our guests to the chairs." I motioned for Bob and Skip to sit down in the dining chairs. Then I cleared the cribbage board and cards off the table. Pat brought mugs of hot coffee for them. I mixed up my usual glass of Tang and sat on a stool in the corner.

The conversation started with small talk and soon maneuvered to business. Bob asked, "What do you guys foresee as the future of Melozi Hot Springs?"

Len responded, "We eventually want to offer a full-service wilderness resort. I don't want this place to become a hunting lodge. If people are going to pay good money to come out here, they are going to want to see wildlife and a hunting lodge is not compatible with that. We will eventually have five or six summer cabins to house people plus a few rooms in this lodge. We've got a good start on building a swimming pool that will be heated by the hot springs."

"How would you advertise?" asked Bob.

"Pat's been talking to a couple of travel agents in Fairbanks. Also, Norman Yaeger and Harold Esmailka, who own flying services will help spread the word. If the Alaska Department of Highways ever gets off their butts and builds the Nome Highway, it will pass within a couple miles of this place. That will really help lower our operating costs and getting customers here."

Len's vision impressed us. I could tell Bob was becoming excited. "Len," asked Bob, "when do you think you will be ready to operate at full throttle?"

Len answered with confidence, "Within three years." Bob sat silent as he stroked his beard and contemplated Len's words. Len took Bob's silence to mean he was done talking. Len stood up and finished his coffee in one large gulp before saying, "Let's go for a walk and I will show you around." The men stood up and left with Len.

I stayed behind to help Pat with the food. Pat rummaged through the boxes and whistled. "This is such delicious-looking stuff. We haven't seen fresh apples, oranges, and bananas in a while. We need to make sure we eat all of it before it spoils. So, Mike, what are we going to do about the milk, cheese, and eggs?"

An idea flashed in my head. "Pat, I'll take two of those one-gallon milk jugs that you got stored and fill them up with ice-cold creek water. Then we will put the food in a cooler with the jugs. I'll refill the jugs every day with fresh water. That should keep it cool for a while."

Pat smiled and said, "Good idea. I'll get the jugs." Within a few minutes, we had the food properly stored. I grabbed a banana and went out the door to find the guys. Happy met me outside and led me down to the lumber mill, where Len was explaining the operation. I felt strangely intruded upon. I had essentially worked out here with only Len and Pat for more than a month and I had grown accustomed to their solitary attention. Now I had to share that attention. I shook it off and joined the group.

Len had just finished describing the milling process. "Okay," said Len as he turned to walk to the excavation, "Now I'll show you where I plan on building the pool." We walked to the clearing. Len spread his arms and said, "This here will be the swimming pool and changing rooms. We'll heat it with the hot springs. The pool should be a big hit for visitors." Bob and Skip tugged at their beards and nodded. Len continued, "Let's take a walk over to the shop."

I followed as Len gave them a tour of the place. We concluded outside the lodge. Len turned to me and said, "Mike, show these guys to your cabin. I'll get a cot so all three of you will sleep there."

That cinches it! I thought. I almost blanched at the idea of sharing my cabin with these two guys. It was all I could do to nod and wave my arm for Skip and Bob to follow me. They retrieved their packs and carried them into the cabin. The three of us plus gear filled the front room. Len arrived shortly with a folded cot. We set it up along the bare south wall. Bob rolled out his sleeping bag on it.

The rest of the day was shot, so I helped Pat prepare dinner and then retreated to my cabin steps with my diamond willow cane. I finished whittling the bark and smoothed the diamonds with my knife. Then I retrieved a pad of medium sandpaper and started the laborious process of sanding the entire staff smooth. By the time I tired from sanding, Skip and Bob were calling it a day and were coming to the cabin for the night. I awkwardly got ready for bed while Bob tried out the bathtub. The cabin seemed unusually warm, so I opened the windows and tried to settle into my normal peaceful sleep. As ludicrous as it seemed, I felt like I was falling asleep in a crowded dormitory.

———— ◆━▶◀━◆ ————

Pat cooked a huge breakfast using as much of the fresh produce as possible. She made a towering stack of sourdough pancakes, at least a dozen fried eggs, and a gigantic bowl of cut-up mixed fruit. I washed it down with a quart of fresh milk—the first I had had for more than a month. Following some after-meal discussions, Len suggested Bob and Skip try their hand at working on a construction project. They kept silent but nodded. Len decided to use the extra manpower to build the swimming pool cribbing.

The four of us dragged two-sided logs to the excavation and then lowered the logs to the bottom. As Len directed the construction, Skip and I took turns hauling washed gravel from the creek in a wheelbarrow to provide bedding for the timbers. The cribbing slowly took shape as we worked nonstop until Pat signaled lunch was ready. We were tired and sweat streaked dirt down our faces.

We washed up and sat down to a hearty lunch of moose meat stew. Instead of Pilot Bread crackers, Pat opened a fresh loaf of sliced bread, which we devoured with butter. As we gobbled down our food in silence, I saw Pat gazing out the window. Without looking back, she asked, "Mike, where's the dog?"

I swallowed and answered, "He's sitting next to me."

"That's good," replied Pat, "because we've got a bear in the yard." Everyone bolted to their feet and ran to the west window. We saw a big shadow move through the woods toward the airstrip.

"Let's take a look," said Len as he started to walk out the door. Skip, Bob, and I followed closely behind. As they started to walk past the shop, I diverted to my cabin, grabbed my rifle, and checked the magazine. It was loaded and ready to go. I walked briskly outside and saw the men and Happy disappearing around the corner of the trail to the runway. I slung the rifle over my shoulder and trotted after them.

Suddenly, I saw the men bunch up. Happy came screaming by them with that same gut-wrenching, eye-popping look of being chased. Skip, Bob, and Len spun on their toes and came racing back. Each had their mouths open with a frozen scream stuck in their throats. Then I saw an enormous dark colored grizzly come loping after them. Time slowed as adrenalin surged through my veins. I came down on one knee, unslung my rifle, and flicked off the safety as Happy soared past me. I brought the rifle up and leveled the sights on the bear's chest, but held my shot because the men were in the way. Skip and Bob blew by me with Len coming up close behind. Len knocked the barrel up and yelled, "No! Run!"

I wasn't one to argue. I spun around and ran after him. Skip and Bob rocketed to the top of the shop roof with Len and me scampering up behind them. With all four of us standing along the front of the building, the bear stopped, rose up on his hind legs, and shook his head back and forth in rage. We were speechless as we watched the spectacle. With his point made, the bear dropped down and slowly sauntered back toward the creek. We watched it go in silence until I teased Skip, "You and Bob made it up here in record time!"

"Oh, yeah," answered Skip with glee in his eyes, "We had no problem!" We all broke out laughing.

Len caught his breath and said, "We better make sure he's wandering off for good. Let's be careful, though. I don't want him to come charging again." We jumped off the shop and slowly walked down the trail to the runway. Happy did not join us this time. We spotted the bear making his way down Hot Springs Creek and left him alone.

When we got back to the lodge, Pat was waiting for us in the kitchen. I marched up to the table and gulped down my Tang. Then I put down my glass, wiped my mouth off with the back of my sleeve, and said to Pat, "You know, Pat, this job sure beats being a box boy." Without waiting for a response, I walked back outside to put my rifle away. Days later, Pat surprised me by showing me my words that she had written down. Len and Pat thought my quote was hilarious.

◆➤✕◀◆

Norman arrived as promised the next afternoon. After we shook

Bob and Skip's hands goodbye and they loaded into the plane, Norman addressed Len. "Len, two air force servicemen would like to come out here for three or four days. Is that okay with you?"

Len scratched his chin and answered, "Sure. That'll work. We could use some extra cash."

Norman smiled and said, "Okay. I kind of thought you might. I'll bring them out in two days. If something changes, I'll tell you on Trapline Chatter."

"Thanks, Norm," said Len and shook his hand. Norman climbed into the pilot's seat and fired up the plane. Within minutes, he was whisking our young visitors away.

As Len and I walked back to the lodge, I took advantage of our time alone to ask Len some questions that were rattling around in my mind. "So, what did you think about Bob, Len? Do you think he'll buy out Doug?"

Len pursed his lips as he thought about my question for a moment. Then he replied, "Well, I think Bob is a romantic. You know, the guy who thinks he can carve a life out of the Alaska wilderness with an axe. Then he gets a jolt of reality when he finds out just how tough it is to make something happen in the bush. I also doubt that he has the resources to help make this operation work. I've got a feeling we'll never hear from him again."

Then I asked Len what was really on my mind. "Len, why did you tell me not to shoot?"

Len smiled with a look that he knew I would eventually ask him about it. "Because the bear was chasing us half-heartedly. If Happy had not riled him up, I doubt the bear would have done anything. In a situation like that, it's better to get away from it than to try to put it down. A bear of that size is tough to stop with one shot. Only shoot a charging bear when you have no choice." As usual, Len gave me sound advice that I carefully filed away for future use.

When we got back to the lodge, Pat had a chair sitting in the middle of the front room with newspapers spread underneath it. We both stared at it not knowing what she had in mind. She answered our questions by showing us scissors, a comb, and a pair of hair shears. "Time for haircuts, gentlemen," Pat announced. "Who wants to go first?"

Len looked amused. "So, what caused this?"

Pat answered, "I decided that I don't want you two to look like Skip or Bob. You both have hair longer than my taste. Take off your shirts and sit down." I looked at Len. His hair was scruffy, but it still did not touch his ears. My hair was only an inch over the tops my ears. I hardly thought we were hippies.

Len shrugged and said to me, "Better do as she says or there will be hell to pay." He took off his wool shirt and undershirt and dutifully sat down in the chair. Pat carefully approached him with the scissors and comb as she analyzed the best method of cutting.

After a couple of failed starts, Pat turned to me and said, "Here, Mike. Why don't you do it? You are much more mathematical than me."

"Me?" I replied with disbelief. "I've never cut hair in my life!"

Pat replied, "Well, there is no better time than the present." She handed me the scissors and comb and stepped back. I walked uncertainly up to Len.

Len grinned and said, "You do realize I get to cut your hair next? So, you better do a good job. Paybacks are hell." I gulped and nodded before proceeding. The next fifteen minutes were the longest in my life, but when I stepped back and appraised my work, I was pleasantly relieved. Len's hair was balanced and cut evenly short.

Pat smiled and said, "Good job, Mike. That's way better than I could do it. I'll trim his neck." Pat put shaving cream on the back of Len's neck and carefully shaved it to produce a neat finish.

Len grabbed the hand mirror and scrutinized his haircut. "Nice job, Mike. Okay. Your turn. Take a seat." I gulped again, took my shirts off, and sat down. Len immediately attacked my hair with absolutely no trepidation and little forethought. I watched in horror as my hair fell to the newspaper like snow. Within a couple of minutes, Len declared himself done and handed me the mirror. I blanched at the unbalanced image staring back at me. The sides of my head were sheared to my scalp and I had a flop of hair hanging over my forehead. I sorely wished I had gone first because I would have creatively cut Len's hair in retaliation.

"I'll shave your neck, too," announced Pat. She put shaving cream on my neck and expertly shaved it smooth. When she was done, Pat stepped back and said unexpectedly, "You know, Mike, when you grow up, you are going to be a big man." I blushed under the comment. Pat smiled and said, "No, really. You've got a long lean torso. When you fill out, you are going to have a powerful build."

I muttered, "Thank you." And hastily put on my shirts. All my life I had been considered skinny, and until now no one had ever mentioned that I would grow out of it. Pat quickly rolled up the newspapers and swept the stray hairs off the floor. She seemed to sense that I was a little sore about my butchered hair. So she announced that she was going to start dinner and that Len and I should fight each other on the cribbage board while we waited.

"That's a good idea," I said with relish as I grabbed the board and slammed it down on the table. Len got the cards, but rolled a cigarette first before he shuffled the deck. The wait was agonizing. I cut the deck and the fight was on. I lost the first game by a point, but won the next two. For some odd reason, it made me feel better.

During dinner, Len asked me, "How's the cane coming?"

"Pretty good," I answered. "I'm almost done with the sanding."

"So, what are you going to do to make it unique?" asked Len.

"Huh, what do you mean?" His question intrigued me.

"Well," explained Len as he helped himself to more gravy and potatoes, "you see diamond willow canes all the time, but sometimes you see an artist carve or add something unusual to make it special. I was just wondering if you had given it some thought."

My fork stopped in my mouth as I contemplated his words. "I hadn't," I finally said, "but I will now." Pat smiled as she watched me frozen in thought with a lump of hair swinging over my forehead. Suddenly, an idea flashed in my mind. I quickly finished my dinner and excused myself.

I hurried to the shop with Happy in close tow and retrieved a hatchet. Then we marched into the dense black spruce forest that followed the small stream that bordered the camp. I walked slowly as I scrutinized each slim trunk until I found the object of my search—a knotted burl. For various reasons, black spruce will sometimes develop rock-hard globules of wood along their trunks. Properly treated, the burls will display their unique swirls of wood and become attractive art pieces. I was determined to find a small one to crown my cane.

Several trees ahead of me had burls of various sizes growing out of their trunks. I examined each one until I found the perfect candidate— a small symmetrical growth about four-inches in diameter. With my prize found, the real work of chopping it off the tree began. Not only did I have to hack through the iron-like wood, I had to remove the burl without nicking the surface. As I focused on my task, Happy stood guard. After nearly an hour of chipping, I finally removed the burl and headed back to my cabin.

On my cabin steps, I carefully whittled the bark away and cleaned out the grooves. By the time I was ready for bed, the burl was ready for the final shaping and sanding. I would do that tomorrow.

———————◆◆◆◆◆———————

The next morning, Len and I began setting the foundation for the changing rooms next to the pool. We built a string grid to mark the position of each support post. As Len set the angles, he asked, "How do you know that your corner is square?" I picked up a carpenter's square and showed it to him. Len shook his head and said, "No. That tool is too small to extend along a floor. You could be off by a half an inch and you would never know it. Now, think back to your geometry class and remember what a right angle looks like. What would you measure?"

I stopped and thought about it for a moment before realizing what Len was telling me. I grabbed a measuring tape and demonstrated how to set a right angle. "A right angle, Len, has the dimensions of three to four to five. So, I would measure three feet along this wall, four feet along the outer wall, and the hypotenuse connecting the two points should be five feet. If it's not, then I would need to realign a wall until it does."

Len nodded and replied, "Not bad, except in real life, measuring three and four feet is not long enough to get a truly square wall. Think of the lengths as a ratio. So six to eight to ten or, better yet, 12 to 16 to 20 works much better."

I smiled and thought to myself, *That's good advice*. We measured each angle and adjusted it accordingly until the grid was square. Then we began the laborious task of digging each posthole four feet into the rocky ground. This effort took most of the day. Placing the posts into position took only an hour.

Len wiped his forehead with his dirty sleeve and said, "That should do it for the day. Tomorrow, we will connect the posts with stringers and set the beams for the buildings." I wearily stepped back and appraised our work. It looked disappointingly sparse for our back-breaking work, but the posts looked plumb and square with the world. I was looking forward to the construction ahead.

Norm sent us a message on Trapline Chatter. Weather was deteriorating in Galena and was forecasted to be down for a couple of days. He would bring out our Air Force guests when it lifted. I looked out the window and saw heavy, dark clouds moving up the valley. This usually meant heavy rain was a certainty in the near future.

I excused myself and walked down to the shop. There I retrieved my burl and secured it within the bench vise. Then I used a rasp to grind the bottom flat. Afterwards, I drilled a two-inch-diameter hole two inches into the bottom with a hand brace. I removed the burl from the vise and then pressed it onto my cane. It fit perfectly and transformed my cane into a grand scepter.

"Now, this is what I call a cane!" I exclaimed as I proudly lifted it above my head. I could hardly wait to show it to my family when I returned. That thought caused me to stop and think for a moment. I would probably be going home within the next two to three weeks. Not that far away. The trials and tribulations of my arrival seemed ages ago—a mere fleeting moment. I was suddenly overcome with conflicting emotions. I ached to see my family again, but I had grown to love this place and the Veerhusens. I was going to miss them.

I looked down to Happy who was busy sniffing my cane. I rubbed his head and said, "Yeah, I'm even going to miss you, boy." He responded by licking my hand and giving me a short wag of his thick curled tail. "Time to go to bed, Hap." I put my cane away and closed the shop door for the night.

I awoke in the morning to the sound of rain pelting the window. The trees were swaying and the sky looked angry. I got up and dressed in warm clothes to brave the elements and met Len and Pat in the lodge for breakfast. Len was drinking his coffee and staring out the windows at the storm. "Well, it's here," he said as he surveyed the scene. "The rain finally caught us."

"Yeah," I said as I mixed a glass of Tang, "it will make working outside hard."

"I agree," said Len as he walked to the unfinished fireplace. "So, I was thinking we should start working on this beast." Len wagged his mug over the rock base. "Doug and I built the base before completing the floor and erecting the walls. We had to so we would have room to work. See? We cut the plywood to match the protruding rock face."

I came over and closely looked at the structure. It looked solid with rounded river rocks firmly encased in mortar. The base was about 10 feet long and five feet wide. It rose about four feet above the ground and stood about six inches above the floor. The foundation contained a gargantuan amount of rock. "It must have taken you guys a long time to build this," I thought out loud.

"About a month," replied Len. "One hard, long month."

I looked up to the ceiling and spotted the metal roof insert for the chimney. I estimated 12 feet between the base and ceiling. "A lot more rock is still needed to complete it. That is going to take some time."

Len nodded and said, "It will at that. I thought we would start chipping away at it. A little bit at a time will add up."

After breakfast, we put on raincoats and hip boots and went to the shop and brought both wheelbarrows to the lodge. Len walked one up the ramp and into the lodge. "We'll mix the mortar in this one," Len said. "Now, let's take the other one down to the creek." We went downhill between the two cabins to Hot Springs Creek. Len brought two aviation gasoline cans with the tops cut off. I looked at them questioningly. Len explained, "We'll fill the cans with sand for the mortar."

I left the wheelbarrow on the steep bank. We first scooped sand from the banks and filled the cans. Then we fished rocks from the creek and loaded them into the wheelbarrow. When it was half full, Len motioned to stop. "Better to quit now, otherwise you will never push it to the top." Len was right. It took all my strength to wheel the load up the embankment and into the lodge. Len carried the cans.

"Okay," said Len as he took off his coat and hung it on a peg on the wall. "Now it's time to mix the mortar. I need you to get two 5-gallon jugs of water. I'll get the screen ready." A few minutes later, I came back dragging the two jugs of water. Len smiled as I came in the door and said, "Why don't you take your coat off and stay awhile?" He had placed a window screen over the wheelbarrow. As I took off my coat, Len began to shake the wet sand over the screen. It clumped and stuck to the screen. "We might have to dry the sand before screening," said Len as he sat the can down. "That will really slow us down."

We began to rub the sand across the screen. Slowly, the fine particles fell into the wheelbarrow. We periodically halted to scrape the oversized rocks and vegetable matter off the screen and into a waste can. After an hour of carefully screening, we had enough sand to mix with the powdered mortar and water. Len and I took turns stirring the mixture with a trowel. After fifteen minutes of mixing, the mortar finally attained Len's desired consistency.

Len centered the fireplace insert on the base, grabbed a rock, and scooped up a trowelful of mortar. "This is all very unscientific," Len said as he slapped some mortar on the base and laid the rock on top. "It's like a gigantic jigsaw puzzle. You just do the best you can." He grabbed another rock, put some more mortar down, and set the rock next to the first one.

Len continued the process until he had used most of the rocks in the wheelbarrow. I unloaded the rest and went back to the creek for more. I soon worked out a system supplying Len with rocks, sand, and water. I spent half my time outside in the drenching rain and the other half drying off in the lodge. After a hard day of gathering rocks, sand, and water, we had increased the height of the fireplace by a foot. As Len appraised our day's labor, he said, "It'll go faster once we clear the firebox. Then it will neck down to the chimney." His words were not encouraging.

We went back at it again the next day. My arms felt like they had been stretched another two feet longer from the heavy wheelbarrow and the water jugs. The day dragged on with agonizingly slow progress. Then, in the early afternoon, we mercifully heard an airplane buzz the camp. "Must be our visitors," exclaimed Len. "Let's get this stuff cleaned up and go down to the strip and meet them." I dumped the leftover rocks outside and Len scraped the last of the mortar from the wheelbarrow to place a final rock before declaring himself done. Pat quickly swept up our mess and set things right inside the lodge.

Len, Pat, Happy, and I walked down to the plane to welcome our guests. The rain had quit and the clouds had lifted some. Water had pooled in the low spots on the runway. Tire tracks indicated where Norm had touched down and thrown mud across the airstrip. Norm had parked his 185 at the far end of the strip where it was drier and was offloading his passengers and their luggage.

"Hi ya, Norm!" greeted Len as we approached. We saw two men standing next to Norm as he handed them their bags. One was taller and older than the other. They sported military haircuts and clean-shaven faces. The younger one looked scarcely older than I. Pat and I greeted them as Norman gently grabbed Len's arm and pulled him to the side for a private discussion.

"Welcome to Melozi Hot Springs," said Pat as she smiled warmly to them. "I'm Pat and this is Mike." The two men smiled back and shook our hands.

The older man spoke first, "I'm Tom and this is John. We're stationed in Galena and wanted to experience Alaska while we were here. Mr. Yaeger said he would pick us up in four days, weather permitting."

Pat replied, "That sounds fine with us. We'll help you carry your—" Len's wail cut Pat off in midsentence.

"No! It can't be! Not Barney!" Len's voice dripped with disbelief. Pat instinctively came to her husband's side. Len was clearly agitated. He turned to Pat and said, "Norm says they found Barney Nollner dead in the Yukon River. He was in his pickup!"

"Oh, my goodness!" replied Pat as she put her hand to her mouth. She turned to Norman and asked, "What happened?"

Norman looked uncomfortable delivering the morbid news. He shuffled his feet as he shook his head and answered, "I don't know. Barney went missing a few days ago. People started searching for him and someone noticed a tailgate sticking out of the water. So they dragged the truck out and found Barney in the cab. He had been there for a while. No one knows if he fell asleep or was drunk and drove off the road and plunged into the river. The troopers flew his body to Fairbanks for an autopsy. Maybe we will know something in a few days."

Norman's announcement threw a pall over the arrival of our guests. Tom and John awkwardly looked at each other as they shouldered their backpacks. Pat, sensing their discomfort, put on a weak smile and directed them to follow her to the lodge. I stayed behind with Len. I am glad I did because I then witnessed a rare display of sympathy from Norman.

Norman reached out to Len, held his shoulder, and said, "I'm sorry, Len. I know he worked for you at the air force base."

Len lowered his head and nodded. "Yeah, he was a good guy. A hard worker. Damn! He couldn't have been more than forty-five."

"Forty-six," corrected Norm. "Yep. Much too young to die." We stood around kicking the dirt in silence for a minute until Norman sighed, reached into his airplane, and brought out a handful of letters. He handed them to Len and said, "Here you go, Len. I'm sorry for the bad news."

Len recovered from the shock and nodded as he said, "That's okay. I appreciate you telling me. Barney was Rosie's uncle wasn't he?"

Norman nodded and said, "Yeah. Rose is busted up about it. He was her mother's brother. She's helping her mom with the arrangements."

We stood silent for a few more minutes as Len and Norm contemplated the gravity of the situation. Len finally spoke. "Well, you best be going. Fly safe and we'll see you in a few days." Norman and Len shook hands and, to my surprise, Norm shook mine, too. We watched Norm climb into his plane and fire it up. He taxied to the end of the runway dodging mud puddles all the way. Then he spun the airplane around and fire-walled the engine. It roared like a lion as the plane charged down the bumpy strip and vaulted into the sky. We waved as he soared past us.

As we watched the plane go, Len slapped me on the back and turned to walk back to camp. I walked alongside him in silence. I did not know what to say and thought it best to keep my mouth shut. Len appeared to be in deep thought. As we began to walk up the hill, Len finally spoke without looking at me, "I want you to entertain our guests while they're here. You know, take them hiking or fishing up at the fishing hole. That will free me up to continue building the dressing rooms. Is that okay with you?"

No. That's not okay with me. I thought. I wanted to help build the swimming pool. I loved carpentry work. And I was not a happy camper about taking these strangers to my special fishing hole. No way! I set my jaw firmly tight and stared straight ahead as I struggled with my selfish emotions. Then I thought, *Don't argue. Len just lost a friend. After all, Len's the boss.* I took a deep breath and finally replied, "All right, Len. If that's what you want me to do. I'll do it." Len shot me a sideways glance at my reply, but kept silent.

As we approached the lodge, Len thumbed through the mail and handed me a letter from my family. "Here you go," he said. "A letter from home." I examined the elegant handwriting on the envelope and knew it was from my father.

"I'm going to my cabin to read it," I told Len. "I'll be over shortly." I

185

ran to my cabin, sat down on my bed, and carefully opened the letter with my pocketknife. I unfolded the crisp tablet stationery and revealed my dad's perfect cursive handwriting. He had formed each letter with exquisite care and spaced each word perfectly. I loved my father's handwriting and wished that I had inherited his style. My penmanship looked barbaric next to his. I hunkered down and read every word.

Dear Michael -

We enjoyed your letter. I am so thankful that everything is working out. I knew that I took a chance by approving your travel to people we never met. It's a huge relief to know that the Veerhusens are good people and that you are enjoying your adventure. It's important that a young man develops confidence to strike out on his own. I am proud of you.

We just finished with Golden Days which celebrated the 71st anniversary of Felix Pedro's discovery of gold just north of here. One of the guys at work thought it would be funny to lock us up in the traveling jail. People showed up outside the Flight Station dressed as cowboys and saloon girls threatening to arrest us. I pointed out that our arrests would cause a safety hazard to pilots. So, they let us off, but I still had to pay five dollars because I did not have a Golden Days button.

Since McDonald's just opened their first restaurant in Fairbanks, they flew their Ronald McDonald clown up to participate in the festivities. He was the grand marshal for the parade. Steven had to endure three days of his shenanigans at work. Steve said once Ronald was asking him questions about life in Fairbanks when a telephone started ringing. Ronald answered a phone in his shoe and then ran off squirting people with his fake flower. The whole crew was glad to see him go.

The newspapers are saying that Lathrop High School is going to have their very first football team this year.

Practice starts in a week. If you want to play, you must come home soon.

I think your dog misses you. She stands at the top of the stairs every night hoping you will come home and tuck her into bed.

Love, Dad.

With tears streaming down my face, I reread Dad's letter three times before refolding it and putting it away. My father was right. It was time to start thinking about going home. I would need to sit down with Len and Pat soon and discuss it with them. I wiped my tears away with the back of my sleeve and got up to meet our guests in the lodge.

As I entered the lodge, I saw Tom standing in the dining room holding a mug of hot coffee. John was sitting down rubbing his hands together and already looking bored. Len saw me come inside and wagged his head toward John like he wanted me to do something with him. I sighed and asked, "Len, should I put these guys up in my cabin?"

Len replied, "That's a good idea. Why don't you show these two to their quarters?" I waved to Tom and John to follow me. They picked up their packs and we walked out the door. They set up in the same beds Bob and Skip had used. The whole process ate up only ten minutes and then they both looked at me expectantly as if I was a tour guide.

This is going to get old quick, I thought. I scratched my head for minute like I was deep in thought before saying, "Well we got about two hours until dinner. How would you guys like to try your luck at fly-fishing?"

John energetically shouted, "Yeah! I'd like to give that a whirl! How about you, Tom?"

Tom was more reserved than John. He stood with his hands in his back pockets and said, "That sounds good to me. What kind of fish are we going for? Trout?"

"Nope. Arctic grayling," I answered as I walked out the door. I glanced over my shoulder and saw them looking at each other with puzzled expressions. They obviously had never heard of grayling. I set up the two fly rods and grabbed a few of Len's flies. Then we walked to the hot springs. They gazed into the springs with amazement for a few minutes before I directed their attention to the creek below the bluff. Shielding my eyes with my hands to minimize the glare reflecting from the water, I searched the depths for fish. Soon I spotted a few swimming close to a short backwater channel. "There," I said as I pointed to the channel. "If you guys cast just upstream of that backwater, you'll nail 'em. Ready?"

Tom and John squinted into the water and failed to see anything notable. I handed each a rod and a black gnat fly. "You guys know how to fly-fish, right?" They both looked at me and shook their heads. I realized that I had my work cut out for me. "Okay," I continued, "Let's start with tying a fly to your leader. Here, I'll show you." I showed them how to tie a bleeding clinch knot to attach the fly. Tom struggled and I eventually tied his knot for him.

With the fishing rods ready to go, I led them down to the creek and gave them a quick demonstration of fly-fishing. "I'll show you a simple technique. First I'm going to pull some line out of the reel like this." I spooled about 10 feet of line and let it float in front of me. "Then flick your rod straight out so your line and fly kick out into the water." Using a slow stroke, I flipped my line out and my fly landed in the water. I let it float down to the side channel and over the fish that I saw finning. A grayling immediately slammed it. Tom and John stood wide-eyed as I gently pulled it to shore. Keeping the body in the water, I unhooked it and showed them the long blue dorsal fin. I could tell by the expressions on their faces that this was the first time they had seen a grayling. I released it and said, "Okay, guys. Your turn."

They eagerly took their poles to the creek and began to flail the water. I stood far back to prevent being hooked and let them go at it. They eventually got their flies to float past the side channel. John got the first strike, but he jerked his rod back too quickly and lost it. Tom finally set a hook into another and reeled it to shore. I tried to help them release the fish properly, but after an hour, we kept two fish that were too hurt to survive. I cleaned these and brought them up to the lodge.

Pat was just setting the table when we arrived. She eyed the fish and said, "Put those in the sink and I will fry them up for our guests." Tom and John were pleased at her willingness to cook them.

During the course of dinner, we learned that Tom was a sergeant and John had just completed basic training. This was the first time they had been to Alaska. Len and Pat smiled when Tom said Galena was the strangest place he had ever been stationed. We also watched in amusement as Tom and John devoured their grayling with relish.

I helped Pat clean up after dinner as our guests found some interesting pocketbooks and relaxed for the evening. After a few quiet hours, Tom and John decided to retire for the evening. Tom wanted to try out the pink bathtub and soak in the hot mineral water. I stayed behind to talk with the Veerhusens.

When the time seemed right, I addressed them carefully. "Len and Pat, my dad wrote in his letter that Lathrop High School is going to have a football team this year and I would like to try out for it." They looked sad at the news, but at the same time seemed to anticipate it.

Len replied, "Yeah. We knew school would be starting up soon. When should you be home?"

"I was thinking the middle of the month would be fine. Is that all right with you?"

Len answered, "That will be fine. In fact, you could leave on the flight that brings Hal and Sharon. Okay?"

I nodded, relieved that we amicably discussed my departure plans. I stood up to go to bed, but halted to say something else that was heavy on my mind. "Len and Pat," I said with thick emotion, "thank you for putting up with me for these two months. I know I wasn't what you wanted when I stepped off the plane. I appreciated your patience. I also enjoyed getting to know you and learning about Alaska." The lodge went silent. Len looked at me with his mouth slightly open like he was searching for a reply. Pat's eyes brimmed with tears as she put her knitting away.

"Michael," replied Pat, "we have enjoyed having you. You have made us feel like a family." Len kept silent and nodded. "In fact," continued Pat, "I'm going to write you a letter of recommendation that you can use for future work. You did the work of a man."

I was stunned. I never thought my work even approached that of a man. I managed to emit a fumbled thank you before excusing myself for bed. Even the crowded cabin I shared that night with our guests could not dampen my feelings of joy.

◆ ✦ ✕ ✦ ◆

By midmorning, Tom, John, and I were striking out for the fishing hole. Tom and John were ecstatic, but I was a ball of mixed emotions. As we hiked out of camp, I saw Len walking toward the swimming pool to start construction. I sorely wanted to help him instead of guiding two strangers to my special fishing hole. I did not want to play nursemaid for the day. Even Happy refused to go. Tom and John carried the fishing poles. I wore a backpack filled with extra clothes, fishing gear, some food, and Pat's folded tinfoil with butter and seasonings. I also strapped Len's pistol to my waist, which seemed to add to Tom and John's adventure.

We arrived at the fishing hole in less than an hour. Tom and John stood in the boulder patch with eyes filled with awe as they took in the incredible scenery and their ears filled with the roaring water crashing into the bluff. I let them survey their surroundings for a few minutes before removing my backpack and getting down to business. "You guys ready to assemble your poles?" I asked as I walked between them.

They put their fly poles together, threaded the line through the eyelets, and surprised me by correctly tying their flies to the leaders. I pointed to the pool. They responded by marching up to the creek and started horsing their line into the water. After several failed attempts, they managed to land their flies upstream and let them float into the pool. Both got instant hits. John let out a whoop and Tom gritted his teeth as his pole bent double.

I spent the next hour unhooking fish, changing out flies, and butchering grayling that were hooked too bad to release. After cleaning the sixth fish, I called a halt to fishing. "We got enough for a meal," I said. "Let's build a fire and cook these up for lunch." Tom and John gathered some firewood and I built a fire within the boulders. As the wood burned into coals, I smeared the fish with butter and sprinkled them with seasonings before wrapping each one in tinfoil. The guys watched me with deep fascination. When the wood finally yielded cooking coals, I placed the fish on them and frequently turned the fish with sticks.

I served lunch with Pilot Biscuit crackers and water. Tom and John ate like ravenous wolves and smacked their lips when they were finished. Lunch was a big hit. I let the fire burn out as they practiced their fly-fishing techniques throughout the afternoon. We closed up camp, broke down the fishing poles in the late afternoon, and walked back to the lodge.

Len and Pat smiled at us as we entered the lodge. They were pleased that Tom and John had satisfied looks on their faces. "You guys had fun?" asked Pat.

"Yes. We sure did," answered Tom. "That was the best fishing I ever had in my life!"

"It sure was!" exclaimed John. "And that fire-cooked fish was great, too. I had a good time."

Len shot me a "good job" look before asking, "No bears, huh?" The guys solemnly shook their heads and watched me unbuckle the holster and hand the pistol to Len. Len made a show of pulling the pistol out of the holster and checking the chambers. His actions capped their wild adventure.

After dinner, John stood looking out the window at the rock peak across the creek. Without taking his eyes of the rock, he asked, "Has anyone ever climbed that column?"

I joined his stare and said, "Yep. I did it last month. Great view."

Still staring at it, he asked, "You want to do it again?"

"Yes," I replied. "Yes, I do. I want to plant a flag on it and name it Travis Peak."

John looked over to me excitedly and said, "Then, let's do it tomorrow. What do ya say?"

"Okay," I replied, "we'll climb it tomorrow. It's steep, but I'm sure you'll outclimb me since you just came out of basic training."

"Huh, right," replied John with doubt in his voice as he looked back to the rock. "It should be fun."

———◆◆◆◆———

John and I started our climb in midmorning. Each of us carried a day pack that held a water bottle, sandwich, a hat, and gloves. At John's insistence, I strapped the heavy pistol to my waist and I was not happy about lugging the extra weight. I also carried a five-foot pole I had made from a dead black spruce tree. I had ripped one of Len's old tee shirts in half and tied it to the top of the pole with the words *Travis Peak* scrawled in permanent black marker across the ragged cloth. My pack also contained a pint jar with a screw-on lid. The jar held a note that read, "Mike Travis climbed this peak on August 5, 1973. I named it Travis Peak."

We waded across the creek in hipboots and stashed them on the other side. Then I led John across the foot of the slope until I found the game trail that would lead us up the mountain. John stayed close behind—his eyes darted at the fugitive shadows around him. "Here we go," I announced as I put my head down and started trudging upward.

We hiked in silence for fifteen minutes before John rasped, "I gotta take a breather."

"Okay," I said as I turned around to study him. "We got all day. Take your time." John was bent over with his hands on his knees drawing ragged breaths. I pulled out my bottle from my pack and took a swallow. "You tell me when you want to go and stop. It doesn't matter to me." John nodded without saying a word. I gazed at the overcast sky. The air was cooler than normal and I could smell rain coming.

John pointed up the trail and said, "Let's go." I led us at a slower pace, but still John called a halt every few minutes to rest. We slowly made our way out of the thick forest and into the alpine vegetation. After a long hour and a half, we made it to the base of the rock pillar. John leaned against it as he caught his breath. "How do we climb it?" he asked.

I pointed to the west side and answered, "We've got to make our way around the left side to a rock slide. Then we will climb up the ramp to the top. Are you okay?"

John nodded and said, "Yeah. I'm fine. Lead on."

We walked around the base of the rock until we found the ramp and then we scampered up to the top. I stepped back and let John stand on the peak. All exhaustion fell from his body as he took in the panorama before him. He stood silent with a light breeze blowing through his short hair as he gazed at the vast valley floor and the mountains beyond. After several minutes, I heard John whisper, "This is incredible!"

"That it is," I answered. "Go ahead and sit down. We can have lunch and rest a spell." John sat with his legs dangling over the edge while I sat against some rocks slightly below him. Then we pulled the sandwiches Pat had made from our packs and began to eat. With a mouthful I asked John, "So, where are you from?"

John answered as he stared out into the vastness, "Kansas."

I asked in a deadpan voice, "Does Kansas look like this?"

John slowly shook his head. "No. No, it doesn't. I've never seen anything close to this place."

"Ain't that the truth?" I replied.

We sat quietly for another half an hour until I deemed it time for my makeshift ceremony. I stood and grabbed my flagpole. John turned around to watch. Trying to imitate a painting I had seen of an explorer planting a flag on a remote shore, I stood tall with my chest forward. I lifted the spruce pole above my head with the tee shirt waving in the breeze and proclaimed, "I name this rock Travis Peak!" Then I rammed the pole into a rock cleft. John and I jammed rocks around the base to secure it. Then I wedged the jar into a small crevice by the pole. Stepping back, I appraised our work. The flag fluttered fully in the wind. To me, the flag looked as official as a government sponsored expedition—not a rough spruce pole with a tee shirt tied to it.

The ceremony concluded our visit. We packed up our belongings, took a final look around, and started heading down the mountain. During our descent, John required two stops to rest his aching legs. We hit the bottom of the mountain and found our way to our stashed boots. As we waded across the creek, I noticed Len, Pat, and Tom standing outside the old cabin waving. Len had his binoculars and was pointing up the mountain. Puzzled, we climbed up the bank eager to determine the reason for their excitement.

Len yelled, "You did it! Take a look."

I looked up the mountain to where Len was pointing. There, flapping high above us, was my flag. The white cloth shone brightly against the sky. The sight gave me a rush of satisfaction, but I also felt some sadness creep into my heart. I had accomplished a goal that I had wanted to complete before I left. Now I knew my time here was drawing to a close.

Chapter 9

The Swans

Len, Pat, and Tom walked in front of John and me as we strolled down to the airstrip to meet Norman. Norm had sent a message through last night's Trapline Chatter that he would be by at 2 p.m. to pick up Tom and John. Despite myself, I had come to enjoy John's company the past few days. Although he was two years older than I and came from a completely different background, we had become friends because we shared a love for adventure. I was sorry to see him go.

"So, what's waiting for you in Galena?" I asked.

John rolled his eyes and said, "Oh, the usual dork jobs that the sergeants can't get anyone else to do. Sweep the barracks, pick up trash, and wash trucks. You know, all the exciting stuff."

I shook my head and asked, "That sounds like a bummer. What do you do for fun?"

John shrugged and answered, "Not much so far. This trip was about it. Maybe I can rent a riverboat with a couple of guys and explore the Yukon." We talked for a few minutes longer until we joined the rest by the airstrip. Norman arrived a half an hour late, which was punctual on bush time.

Norm rolled to a stop and taxied back to us. After he shut down the engine, I helped him load the baggage. Afterwards, Norm took off his cap and wiped his forehead before speaking to Len and Pat. "Mark Swan called me this morning. They made it to Alaska yesterday and are planning to be in Fairbanks on the seventh or eighth. They would like to be brought out here on the ninth. I thought you might want to know their status."

Len nodded and replied, "Thank you, Norm. We were kind of wondering when they might show up. We'll be ready for them."

"Okay," said Norm as he put his cap back on, "I'll see ya in a few days." We shook Tom and John's hands goodbye and watched them load into the plane and strap themselves into their seats. We waved to them as they flew off, and turned to walk back to the lodge.

As we were walking back to camp, Len told me what to expect in the next few days. "Mike, Pat and I were discussing the sleeping arrangements when the Swans arrive. We were thinking it would be best that we put them up in your cabin and move you to the old cabin. We will take the bedroom in the lodge. How does that sound to you?"

I shrugged and answered, "Sounds okay to me. When do you want to make the switch?"

Pat chimed in, "We were thinking we should make the moves tomorrow morning. That will give me time to clean and make things nice." I nodded but kept silent. To me, the whole camp seemed to be in flux. I decided to go with the flow.

❦

The following day, I gave my safe, snug cabin a goodbye sigh and carried my luggage to the old cabin. Pat made up a bed in the front room and I unloaded my gear around it. "There now," Pat said as she patted the bedspread and smoothed it out, "this won't be so bad, will it?"

"I guess not," I answered. My sleeping arrangements were not a as private as the small cabin, but it would work out. Then I helped Pat and Len carry their belongings to the lodge. Pat set the bed up and Len completed the shelving for their clothing. Their occupancy gave the lodge a more complete look.

Len had a sudden thought that proved to be fortuitous. "I was just thinking," he said as he took his cap off and rubbed his head, "we should set up a couple of wall tents in case we get some unannounced guest. You never know around here."

"Okay, Len," I said. "Where were you thinking of putting them up?"

Len pointed toward the shop and replied, "I built two wood platforms with frames to hold the tents across from the shop. We'll set the tents up there." We walked down to the shop and retrieved the canvas tents. Each tent was almost too much for us to carry. We lugged each one to the platforms and set them up. When secured, the wall tents created a dry and snug shelter.

Len stepped back appraising our work and said, "That will do it. We'll set up some cots, then we'll have extra beds in a snap."

When Len and I went back to work on the swimming pool dressing rooms, Pat cleaned out the new cabin and made the beds with fresh sheets. Then she adorned the windows with bright-colored curtains. By the end of day, the Veerhusens were ready for their special guests.

The next day was August ninth and Pat whittled away the hours by fussing over small details in preparation for the Swans. When Norman failed to arrive by the late afternoon, Pat contacted Rose Yaeger by the sideband radio and asked for an update. I could hear Rosie's voice crackling from the speaker as she told us that the wind had been gusting hard all day making flying difficult. To complicate matters, the Wien F27 the Swans were taking out of Fairbanks was delayed until seven thirty. She would meet the Swans at their plane when it arrived. Either they would try to get them out to Melozi then or put them up for the night and try again the next day. Pat looked crestfallen as she thanked Rose and signed off.

"Darn!" exclaimed Pat as she hung up the microphone. "Flying in the bush is such an iffy thing. You got to wait for weather. Then the airplane breaks down. Then the pilot has got other pressing business and you get bumped to the bottom of the pile. You can't ever set your watch to a schedule."

We had dinner and afterwards Len and I played cribbage to pass the time. Pat tried to knit, but could not sit still. Finally, as we were preparing to listen to Pipeline of the North, we heard an airplane coming our way. Len and Pat jumped up smiling and made their way to the door. Len stopped and said to me, "Why don't you fire up the tractor and bring it down with the wagon? I got a feeling they may have lots of bags."

"Okay," I replied as I jumped off the ramp and jogged down to the lumber mill where we parked the rig. By the time I drove down to the runway, Len and Pat had finished their greetings and hugs with the Swans. I also noticed a different pilot had flown them. He was tall with a full beard—almost the exact opposite of Norman.

I pulled up beside the plane, shut the engine down, and jumped off the tractor. The pilot smiled at me, stuck out his hand, and said, "Hi. My name is Lou Mass."

"Hi," I replied as I grabbed his hand and shook it. "My name is Mike. Good to meet you. I'll help you load the bags into the trailer."

Our greeting seemed to remind Pat that I had not been introduced. She put her hands on the Swans and directed them toward me. Pat said, "Mike, let me introduce you to the Swans. Mark and Luverne, this is Mike Travis. Mike has been helping us this summer. Mike, their daughter, Susan, is married to my son, Michael."

I stuck my hand out and Mr. Swan enthusiastically shook it. "Pleased to make your acquaintance, Mike," he said.

I smiled at his energetic greeting and replied, "Good to meet you, too, Mr. Swan." I liked Mr. Swan. He appeared to be in his early 70s, but he had a spunk that radiated from his body. Mrs. Swan stood next to him with a regal stature. I judged her age to be close to Pat's. She looked kind and practical with the influence of culture. I turned to Mrs. Swan and carefully extended my hand. She gently received it as she gave me a gracious smile.

"Hello," she said.

Without thinking, I bowed slightly and replied, "Welcome, Mrs. Swan." My greeting appeared to be appropriate, but for some reason it embarrassed me. I muttered something to cover up my discomfort and started loading their luggage onto the trailer. I noticed one box had "PERISHABLE" and "EGGS" written several times in bold black letters. I nestled this box between two bags to protect it.

The Veerhusens and Swans laughed and talked their way back to the lodge while I rambled behind on the tractor. I stopped at the used-to-be-my cabin and carried their bags inside. Then I lugged the box of perishables into the lodge. Pat was already busy cooking them a late supper. I showed Pat the box and she pointed to a safe place on the floor. I gently set the box down and then found a corner to sit and quietly observe our company.

The Swans were polite and amicable. We all laughed as Mr. Swan retold their trek to Alaska and their delayed flight to Galena. Mrs. Swan gently corrected her husband when she thought he was exaggerating or embellishing the truth. Her moderation only added to the colorfulness of the discussion. Deep down, I could sense that Len and Pat missed the interaction with people from their generation. They seemed to connect with them more than I had ever seen them with past visitors. This awareness made me feel happy for them and, at the same time, a little left out. There was a gulf of years between us that could not be bridged with laughter. I sadly accepted this fact and excused myself for the night.

I met Happy outside the lodge. He looked upset and ignored, so I sat down on the ramp and petted him. The interaction made us both feel better. When weariness overtook me, I gave Happy a final pat and went to bed.

———————

I awoke the next morning to rain and fog. I got dressed and stepped outside. The cold air slapped me across the face. This was the coldest day so far since I had arrived in Melozi. The weather felt like November in Montana instead of the second week in August. I ran to the lodge and jumped inside. Len was sitting at the table with a mug of steaming coffee in his hand. For the first time in my life, I sincerely wished that I liked coffee. I could picture the hot liquid warming my body.

"Sleep well?" Len asked.

"Yes. Like a log," I answered as I sat down at the table. "Len, it's cold outside. It feels like winter is coming!"

"Yep," replied Len, "we've got a cold front moving through. That is probably what caused the wind yesterday. It will hang around for two or three days before it breaks. I wouldn't be surprised if the mountains get a dusting of snow. It'll melt off, though."

Wow, I thought, *snow in August. Short summer.*

"Good morning, Mike," Pat said from the kitchen. "I've got a surprise for you, courtesy of the Swans." I walked into the kitchen and noticed Pat had opened the perishable box. Inside she had found a can of Hershey's hot chocolate mix. "Want some?" she asked. "I can put a little milk in it, too."

I answered with deep appreciation, "Oh, thank you, Pat! Hot chocolate will hit the spot this morning." Within a few minutes, I was sipping from a steaming mug at the table with Len. The day did not seem so bad. In addition, Pat filled the entire lodge with scrumptious smells of bacon, eggs, and her world-famous sourdough pancakes.

The Swans entered the lodge a few minutes later. They looked rested and freshly scrubbed. Mr. Swan was crisply shaved, causing Len and me to subconsciously run our hands across our faces. Len had course stubble and I had a few long wisps. We felt shabby. Then we smelled Mr. Swan's aftershave as he walked by us, which accented our filth.

"Good morning," bubbled Pat. "How did you guys sleep? Did the creek keep you awake?"

Mrs. Swan smiled and replied, "We slept sound and cozy. The creek lulled us to sleep with its quiet babble. Very restful."

"Great!," said Pat as she waved them to a table. "Take a seat. You guys like coffee or tea in the morning?"

Instead of sitting, Mrs. Swan came over to Pat and said, "Mark likes coffee and I would like some tea. Pat, your breakfast smells marvelous. What are you making?" Within a heartbeat, Pat and Mrs. Swan launched into an intimate conversation that excluded men.

Mr. Swan gave us a mischievous grin and said, "Looks like I got to get my own coffee."

Len shook his head and replied, "A man has got to fend for himself out here."

Mr. Swan grabbed a mug and poured himself a cup of coffee from the stove and brought the pot to Len for a refill. The women scarcely noticed him. He motioned to me, but I shook my head no. When Mr. Swan had settled at the table, he asked Len, "What do you have planned today?"

Len motioned with his steaming cup to the unfinished fireplace and said, "On a day like today, I thought we would continue building this monster."

Mr. Swan looked intrigued. He carried his mug to the fireplace and studied it for a moment while sipping his coffee. Finally, he asked, "What's involved in building this monument to mankind? Looks like you got a lot of rock and mortar into it."

Len and I joined him. "We do at that," answered Len, "and we got a lot more to put in before its finished. I was thinking the three of us could ramp up our production a little by taking the tractor and trailer down to the strip and loading flat rocks from the creek. We could also load up cans of sand, too. Then drive the whole works back up to the lodge. That way we could mix the mortar and build quicker."

Anything is better than hauling rock in a wheelbarrow, I thought.

After wolfing down a great breakfast, Mr. Swan, Len, and I put on rain gear and went outside to gather rock and sand. I serviced the tractor and started it. The C60 was reluctant to start in the cold and chugged to life after lots of coaxing. After it idled for fifteen minutes, I motioned to Len that I was ready to go. He swung his arm forward and I followed him to the airstrip.

We spent two hours loading the flattest rocks we could find into the trailer. When we were done, the tires bulged and springs compressed under the weight. Then Len brought out the old Av-gas cans and we filled them with sand. Each can weighed at least 30 pounds when full. With ten cans balanced on top of the rock pile, the trailer was loaded to its breaking point. To emphasize the point, Len told me to take my time driving it back. "Only use low gear," he said, "especially when driving across the streams."

I started the tractor, put it into first gear, and slowly let out the clutch. The tractor tires churned into the wet sand and dirt until they found purchase and wrenched the trailer forward. Len and Mr. Swan walked alongside to ensure nothing spilled out and to assist the trailer out of ruts. The trip back to the lodge seemed to take forever and I thought for sure the trailer would bust in half over the rough stream crossings, but we returned with only a broken side plank from the shifting load.

We then shuttled the rocks and sand into the lodge with wheelbarrows. Len and I did most of the loading. Mr. Swan was exhausted from our outing and sat at the kitchen table with a cup of coffee. We joined him after we carried enough building materials inside.

Len took off his sopping wet cap and placed it on his lap. Pat brought him a mug of coffee. He gave her a smile of thanks and said, "Well, that went pretty good. We'll start screening sand in a few minutes. Then we'll mix the mortar and start building." Len's proclamation proved tough to fulfill. The wet sand plastered the screen and plugged it. We tried coaxing the sand through the screen with an old hair brush with limited results. After two hard hours of screening, we finally got a wheelbarrowful to mix the mortar.

Len sat back on his knees and wiped his brow with the back of his dirty hand. "I am afraid that we are going to have to dry the sand to speed this up. I've got some small sheets of metal in the shop that we can spread the sand on."

"Why don't you guys do that after lunch?" interjected Pat. "In fact, I have got a task for you and Mike to do that will help with the meal."

Len got up from where he was kneeling and asked, "Okay. What do you have in mind?"

Pat smiled at her husband and said, "I saw some mushrooms down by the creek that looked ready to pick. Why don't you show Mike how to identify them and pick us a bunch? I'll make soup out of them for lunch."

The thought of mushroom picking concerned me. Boy Scouts had taught me to stay far away from mushrooms because many poisonous species looked similar to edible ones. I had some trepidation about so nonchalantly grabbing mushrooms outside for lunch.

Len, on the other hand, had no reservations. He readily agreed and Pat gave him a large Tupperware bowl. Len looked at me and said, "Let's put on our gear again and go." We walked into the thick black spruce that lined the small creek that flowed across the path to the airstrip. We did not go far until Len pointed out our prize. "There's one," he said as he dropped to his knees into the wet spongy ground. He reached down and carefully pulled up a big light brown mushroom. The top was about six inches in diameter and lightly colored with greenish blue bands. "This is a nice one," Len said as he dropped it into the bowl I was carrying. "There should be a few more around here."

"Wow," I said as I studied the mushroom, "that's a big one. What is it called?"

Len shrugged and replied, "I don't know. We had a plant guy stay with us once and he pointed them out. We've been eating them ever since. We sometimes get short of breath and have hallucinations, but other than that, we've had no problems." I shot Len a look of, *are you serious?* Len smiled and winked to show he was joking and struck out to search for more. We quickly stumbled upon many more nestled within the spruce and filled the bowl. "That should be enough for the five of us. Let's get them back to Pat so she can work her magic."

Our pile of mushrooms greatly impressed Pat and Mrs. Swan. Pat quickly cleaned them and made a mouth-watering soup out of them. My reservations evaporated after the first spoonful and I decided if the mushrooms were poisonous, I had four adults to share my agony.

After lunch, Len, Mr. Swan, and I mixed the mortar and continued building the fireplace. We soon ran out of mortar, which forced us to sift more sand. Len finally threw up his hands, marched down to the shop, and brought back several metal sheets. We spread the sand about two inches thick across each sheet and left it to dry in the lodge. "I don't know what else to do," exclaimed Len. "Let's clean up the place and start again tomorrow."

I filled the rest of the day with small chores while the Swans picked a quart of late blueberries. Pat cooked up a great dinner of moose meat stroganoff. Afterward, the Swans introduced the Veerhusens to a card game called canasta—a four-person adult game that excluded sixteen-year-olds. They played all evening long and were still hard at it when I went to bed. This time Happy followed me into the cabin and sank down on his old pillow to sleep.

———— ✦◆✕◆✦ ————

The clouds lifted the next morning with patches of blue sky. As I walked out of the old cabin and surveyed my surroundings, I was surprised to see snow on the top 500 feet of the southern mountains. I shook my head in wonder about getting snow on August eleven and continued to the lodge. Len was drinking his usual cup of coffee and Pat was busy in the kitchen. "You were right, Len," I said as I sat down. "It snowed yesterday in the mountains."

Len nodded as he took another sip and replied, "Yeah, it happens from time to time. It seems a little early though. Today should be a little warmer. Looks like the rain stopped."

Pat brought me a steaming mug of hot chocolate. "Thank you, Pat. This hits the spot!" I took a few sips of the delicious cocoa before asking Len, "What do you think we should do today?"

Len answered, "I was thinking that we should mix up some mortar with the batch of dried sand and put a layer of rocks on the fireplace. Then, spread some more sand for drying and go outside and work on the swimming pool."

The Swans entered the lodge again freshly scrubbed. Mr. Swan had shaved again and Len and I simultaneously touched our rough faces.

Mrs. Swan raved about taking a bath in the sunken tub. "It was luxurious, just luxurious!"

Mr. Swan rubbed his smooth jaw and said, "I decided not to wear aftershave this time. I think it attracts bugs, so I'm going without, but I always get a cold sore when I don't use it. I'll see what happens."

Breakfast was a huge affair with Pat trying to use as many perishable foods as possible before they spoiled. I gobbled down the fruit and her homemade cinnamon rolls. I noticed that no one commented on my gargantuan intake of food when perishables needed to be eaten. It was like I was doing them a favor.

After breakfast, we laid another layer of rocks on the fireplace before the mortar ran out. Then we spread more sand for drying and went outside to the swimming pool. With the help of the C60, we started digging the leach field that would drain the pool. Like the pool excavation, the digging was slow and onerous. Mr. Swan helped as he could, but he could not climb around the pit and remove boulders when Len uncovered them.

Late in the morning, we were getting ready to break for lunch when I heard a whopping sound above the roar of the tractor. I looked up to the sky and saw a red and white Bell Jet Ranger helicopter fly around us. I pointed to it and Len and Mr. Swan looked up. Len shut down the tractor, jumped off, and waved his arms for the pilot to land. The pilot set the helicopter down on the trail between the shop and the pool.

We waited for the pilot to shut down the aircraft before approaching them. Len walked up to it as the pilot opened the door and said, "Welcome to Melozi Hot Springs! What brings you guys out this way?"

The pilot smiled and replied, "We're out prospecting for oil. Seen any?"

"I've seen only hot water bubbling out of the ground," replied Len. "Why don't you guys come up to the lodge for lunch?"

One of the men who exited the back of the helicopter showed Len a paper bag and said, "We've brought our lunch, but we could use a cup of coffee if you have it."

"We've got some," offered Len. "Come on." Four men including the pilot followed us up to the lodge. Pat and Mrs. Swan smiled graciously at them as we entered the dining room. Two of the men paused at the fireplace and admired our work before sitting down at the table.

While they ate their lunch and shared ours, we learned that the three men with the pilot were geologists. One man worked for Gulf Oil and the other two were employed by Union Oil. They were based in Galena and were looking for oil reserves within the Melozitna River drainage. Len immediately inquired if they needed logistic support. The pilot and geologists discussed their needs in-depth and determined if Len could store a drum of Jet A fuel for emergency use, they would greatly appreciate it.

I could see Len's crafty eyes scheming for a second before he began to lay out a proposal. "I would be happy to do that. I'll roll the drum inside my shop to keep the elements off it. Now, I was wondering if you guys could do me a favor. I'm sure you saw the excavations and construction next to your chopper?" The men nodded. "Well, that's going to be a swimming pool. So, the next time you come out here, you can go for a swim. How does that sound?" Again the men nodded, but smiled this time. Len looked at them before continuing, "Well, we're building the leach field now and I need the sewer pipe to finish it. Otherwise, it won't be until late next year that you can swim."

The pilot saw where this conversation was going. He asked, "Where do you have the pipe stored? It's just PVC pipe, right?"

Len nodded enthusiastically and replied, "Yep. It's light weight PVC pipe. Some of the lengths have holes in them to pass water. I've got them stacked by Norman Yaeger's office. Do you know where that is?"

The pilot smiled and answered, "Oh, yeah. We know Norm." The geologists chuckled at the comment. Then the pilot asked, "Do you think the pipe would fit between the landing struts?"

Len answered, "I think it will. I don't have a lot of it."

The pilot went silent for a moment as he thought about the problem. "You know, I could lash the pipe to the bottom of the helicopter on Sunday evening. We are supposed to be in Fairbanks Monday morning. We could leave Galena at 6 a.m. and be here by seven. It shouldn't take too long to unload."

Len threw his hands in the air and presented an offer to seal the deal, "I'll tell you what. We'll throw in breakfast. Land here around seven, Mike and I will unload the pipe and you guys can have breakfast here in the lodge before continuing to Fairbanks. What do ya say?"

The men looked at each other before readily agreeing to Len's offer. "Okay," said the pilot as he stood and drained his coffee cup, "we'll be here before seven on Monday." The geologists got up and followed their pilot to their aircraft. We said our goodbyes and watched them fly away.

Len turned to Mr. Swan and me and said, "Well, we better get the leach field ready for the pipe before they come back."

Mr. Swan nodded and said, "Okay. What needs to be done?"

Len pointed to the excavation and said, "We need to finish the pit. It's almost deep enough. Then we have to fill the first couple of feet with boulders. Then place a layer of sand on top of the rock to bed the pipe. Let's finish the pit and then hunt for boulders to line the bottom." Completing the pit took another four hours and Mr. Swan and I were spent. Pat and Mrs. Swan came down to inspect our work and call us to dinner. The expressions of their faces told me that we were expected to clean up before coming to the dinner table.

Dinner was fantastic. Pat had cooked the lamb steaks that the Swans had brought. After eating moose meat for two months, it was a welcome change. Then Pat presented a mouth-watering butterscotch pie for dessert. The meal greatly improved my mood.

As the dinner conversation diminished, I could tell the adults were about to launch into a raging game of canasta. So, I told everyone to hold off for a moment because I had something to show them. I ran down to the shop and recovered my stashed diamond willow cane. I marched into the lodge and proudly showed them my handmade art piece. Their eyes told me that they were truly impressed.

"Now, that's what I've been talking about!" exclaimed Len. "You've got yourself a unique staff. One of a kind!"

Mrs. Swan studied the cane with intense interest. Finally she asked, "What else could you make from that wood?"

Len replied, "Lamps, stools—heck, I even saw a diamond willow bed once. Why do you ask?"

She looked at Len and said, "I would like to make a lamp. Where could I get a piece big enough to do that?"

Len pointed to the creek and said, "There is a whole grove of willow out there. We'll find the perfect piece for you."

Mrs. Swan thanked Len and shivered. "My it's cold in here! I need to wear thicker clothes."

Pat got up, walked to her new bedroom, and said over her shoulder as she left, "Luverne, I've got a nice sweater for you to wear. I knitted it last year. It should fit you."

As Pat looked for the sweater, Len said to Mr. Swan, "Mark, let's slide this table over to the kitchen next to the stove. It will be warmer to play cards." I could tell that everyone was preparing for a long card night. So, I excused myself and walked back to the old reindeer cabin for the night.

———◆◆◆◆———

I awoke to the sound of rain blowing against the windows. It caused me to smile in my warm bed because the inclement weather meant no leach field work. Since it was also Sunday, Len probably would take it easy today. I slept a little longer than normal before getting dressed. I fired up the Coleman stove, heated some water, and used it to shave my carefully nursed chin hairs. I had to admit that an occasional shave did improve my appearance. As I walked out of the arctic entry, I was surprised to see my breath hang in the cold wet air. I looked south and saw the snow line had lowered several hundred feet during the night. Winter seemed to be right around the corner.

As I walked into the lodge, I saw Len drinking coffee and staring out the window. "Good morning, Len," I said. "Another cold and wet one today."

Len turned to me, smiled, and replied, "Yep. Probably just as well since it's Sunday and all."

Just what I wanted to hear, I thought. Then I noticed Len had shaved, too. He looked ten years younger. Len continued, "I was thinking we should focus on drying sand today. This wet stuff just slows down the whole process. A day's worth of drying should give us enough for a day or two of building."

The Swans arrived a few minutes later again looking fresh and clean except I noticed Mr. Swan had a rugged face. After closer inspection, I also saw that he had a cold sore at the corner of his mouth. Mr. Swan saw me looking at it and gently put his finger on the sore. He shrugged and said to me, "Happens every time I don't use aftershave. Now I have to let my beard grow for a couple of days before I can shave again."

I smiled at him and replied, "Then you will fit right in with us." Pat fed us a hardy breakfast of blueberry sourdough pancakes and bacon. Then all of us participated in drying sand. We laid metal sheets with thin layer of sand on the lodge floor and in my cabin. Then we fired up the woodstoves and let them roar. The lodge and the cabin soon became unbearably hot, which Mrs. Swan seemed to relish. Len, Mr. Swan, and I took turns all day swinging the splitting maul to chop firewood for the ravenous stoves. By late afternoon, we managed to dry a wheelbarrow-full of sand. This would be enough for a full day of building.

Pat walked up to Len with her hands on her hips and announced, "I've been so busy, I forgot to get some meat ready for supper. Do you think you guys could catch us some fish?"

"Oh, I think we can arrange that," replied Len with a grin. He looked over to us and asked, "So, you guys think we can bring home some meat for the women?"

Mr. Swan laughed and answered, "I'm willing to give it a try, but we may starve if you have to rely on my fishing skills."

I looked outside at the cold rain and light wind. *This is not ideal fishing weather*, I thought, *and we might be hard pressed to coax a strike.* I turned to Len and said, "We better dress warm. We will probably be hard at it for a while." Len nodded and retrieved several raincoats for everyone. We put them on over our coats and long-sleeved shirts and buttoned up. I gathered up the fly poles.

Mr. Swan, Len, and I walked a short distance upstream of the camp in the freezing drizzle to a series of small side channels. Our breath steamed off our faces when we stopped. I helped Mr. Swan assemble his rod and tied a fly on his line. "Here you go," I said.

Mr. Swan looked uncertainly at his gear and asked, "So, how do you do this?"

"Just flip your line out and let your fly drift down the creek," I answered as I pointed toward the water. "It will take a few tries to get the hang of it." I watched Mr. Swan experiment with ways to cast his line. He seemed to intensely attack the problem with the goal of softly landing his fly in the water. Then I assembled my gear and chose a black gnat wet fly.

I walked to the mouth of a side channel and laid my fly upstream of it. The fly sank and tumbled along the bottom toward the channel. A grayling darted from the undercut bank and grabbed the fly. I set the hook and the battle commenced. Mr. Swan and Len watched me play the fish and finally bring it alongside. I picked it up and announced, "One."

"Very good," said Len. "At least we didn't get skunked. Now let's see if we can wrangle up a couple more." Len and Mr. Swan labored on, casting and retrieving their flies for half an hour until Len finally hooked a grayling. "Got one!" he said as he lifted a 12-inch fish in the air. "Mike, have you had any more luck?"

"Some," I replied. "I've caught four more."

"What?" cried Len. "You've been holding out on us!"

Mr. Swan smiled and said, "That sounds good to me. I'm getting cold and we've got enough for supper. I say we cut our losses and get back to the lodge."

"Okay," replied Len, "but first Mike and I need to clean the fish before bringing them back." Len and I took fifteen minutes to scale, gut, and behead our catch. Then we carried the fish back to the lodge. Pat thanked us as she received the fish. Mrs. Swan looked impressed and told her husband so.

Mr. Swan pointed to me and said, "Don't thank me. Mike caught all but one of them. I just flailed the water!"

After Pat's incredible dinner, the adults assembled the chairs and table for another rousing game of canasta. I was hoping to sneak in a game of cribbage with Len, but I could tell that wasn't going to happen. I noticed for the first time since arriving in Melozi I was battling boredom. Since I had no one to talk to or play card games with in the evening, I was on my own to fill my time. In addition, I knew football practice in Fairbanks had started and chances of making the team were diminishing with each day I spent in Melozi. My situation gave me a restless feeling.

The rain had stopped, so I grabbed my rifle and called Happy. He looked dejected, too. Together we hiked our four-mile loop looking for game. We returned empty-handed but feeling better, and retired for the night. I had to get up early the next day to meet the helicopter.

I awoke to bright sunshine as my alarm clock rang. I reached over, turned the alarm off, and checked the time—6 a.m. "Okay," I said as I rose, "got to get up." I threw on my clothes, stepped out the arctic entry, and felt the frozen air rush into my lungs. "Wow!" I exclaimed as I looked around me. The ground was covered with a killing frost. Even the water in the wheelbarrow was frozen solid. *Hard to believe it's only August thirteenth*, I thought as I walked to the lodge. The surrounding mountains radiated white against the brilliantly blue sky.

Pat and Mrs. Swan were already busy making breakfast for the helicopter crew that was due within a few minutes. Len was drinking coffee. "Good morning," he said. "Are you ready to unload some pipe?"

"Yep," I answered as I walked to the kitchen. "Especially if I can get a cup of hot chocolate before they come." Pat was way ahead of me and was preparing one as I spoke. "Thank you, Pat!" I said with sincere gratitude. "It's just what I need for a cold morning like this."

Pat answered, "You're welcome. I almost cried when I saw the frost this morning. I'm sure that I lost some vegetables and flowers last night. I would have brought some inside if I had known we were going to get a hard frost."

"Len," I asked as I walked back to the table, "is this an unusually early frost?"

Len stretched his limbs as he responded, "Not too terribly early. We get nipped from time to time. It'll warm up though and we'll have some more summer days yet."

Half an hour later, we heard the helicopter approaching the camp. "Right on time," smiled Len as he drained his cup. "We should go down and make sure they land close to the swimming pool." We rose and got to the landing zone just as the helicopter circled overhead. Len waved them to the spot where he wanted to unload the pipe. As the helicopter landed, I saw the bulky load of pipe sandwiched between the landing struts.

Len greeted them, "Welcome to Melozi." I was surprised to see that only one of the geologists was with the pilot this time. He also had two new guys—a helicopter mechanic and an air force man grabbing a free ride to town. Len introduced himself to them and said, "Breakfast is ready, gentlemen. Just walk up to the lodge. We'll unload the pipe while you eat."

"Okay," responded the pilot, but he first opened a luggage compartment on the side of the fuselage and retrieved a cardboard box. He presented it to Len and said, "Here's some fittings, solvent, and glue. Norman reluctantly gave it to me when I told him I was taking the pipe."

"Thanks," replied Len. "I wouldn't have gotten too far without it."

I got down on my knees and peered under the helicopter. The pilot had ingeniously used bungee cords to strap the eight-foot lengths of pipe to the underbelly of the craft. Len and I unhooked the cords and the piping fell to the ground. Then we carried the light weight pipe to the side of the leach field excavation. We were done within ten minutes.

When we got back to the lodge, the men were wolfing down their breakfast like they had not eaten in three days. My stomach growled as I watched them shovel down pancakes and bacon. Len addressed the pilot. "Thank you. You managed to get all the pipe I had stacked at Norm's. You saved me a bunch of money and time to get that stuff out here."

The pilot smiled and replied with a mouthful of pancakes, "Not a problem. Happy to do it." Within twenty minutes, the men were done eating and were thanking Pat and Mrs. Swan for the great breakfast. Then they hastily returned to their helicopter and took off to Fairbanks.

After their departure, the five of us sat down and had a leisurely breakfast. Len was in a festive mood. "Man, I am happy to finally get that pipe out here. Now I can finish the leach field and concentrate on other things before the snow flies. So I was thinking that we should get that pit done today and install the piping."

I drank my Tang and thought, *This is going to be a long day*. It was.

We struck out right after breakfast. I hitched the trailer to the tractor and drove it down to the airstrip. There we searched for two-foot-diameter boulders in the creek and loaded them onto the trailer. When the trailer could hold no more, I carefully pulled the load to the leach field where we threw the rocks into the pit and repeated the process. We worked until late that afternoon when Len thought we had filled the pit with enough rock to start laying the sand and pipe. Using rakes and shovels, we pulled sand and gravel from the stockpile and spread it over the boulders. Len used the tractor blade to help spread it. Finally, we were ready to set the pipe.

Mr. Swan looked beat, but never complained. It was now early evening, but Len showed no sign of quitting. He was a man on a mission. I helped him assemble the pipe into a large trident. Each prong consisted of a perforated pipe. Then we connected the rest of the pipe and laid it in a trench that connected the leach field with the swimming pool excavation. We placed sand under the pipe to slope it toward the field. When everything was assembled, we carefully buried the piping with the overburden. We finished the project around 9 p.m.

I was bushed and Mr. Swan stumbled as we dragged ourselves back to the lodge. Mrs. Swan and Pat gave us pitying looks as we arrived and never once remarked about our filthy clothes. Pat had cooked a huge pot of dumpling stew made from her frost-killed vegetables. To cheer us up, she had also made us a pineapple upside-down cake.

After satiating my appetite, I suddenly felt sleepy. Len and Mr. Swan looked tired, too. I excused myself for the night and staggered to bed. I whispered a prayer as my head hit my pillow, "Thank you, God, for taking away my boredom. Please do it again tomorrow." I would learn that God sometimes answers prayers quickly.

Chapter 10

Hobo

Len predicted the weather right. Tuesday, August 14, was a beautiful and warm summer day. As I stood outside and absorbed the sun rays, I found it hard to believe that it froze yesterday. However, all I needed to do was look around and see the snow-covered mountains to remind me. I walked into the lodge and found it quiet. Len and Pat were not up yet. I thought this was unusual, but I figured everyone was slow from the past long, arduous day. I fired up the Coleman stove and fixed me a cup of hot chocolate. Then I sat down at the table and waited.

About half an hour later, Len stumbled into the kitchen. He looked rough with his hair matted and his face grizzled. He nodded a greeting, splashed some water on tired eyes, and took a sip before talking. "I'm feeling yesterday like a bad night in Mexico. How are you faring?"

I shrugged and answered, "Not bad. No soreness or anything."

"Hum," grumped Len as he shuffled to the table. "To be young again."

Pat came in shortly after Len. She looked fresh and ready to face the day. "Good morning, Mike," she said in a cheery voice. "You look a far sight better than Len this morning."

I wanted to say, *That's not saying much*, but I decided to keep my mouth shut and just smile. Then I looked around and said, "I think the Swans are moving slow, too."

Len replied, "I can't blame them. Mark was a trooper yesterday. Never slacked off or complained. I hope I can hold my own when I'm in my seventies."

Pat brewed the coffee and I savored our quiet conversation. It had been a while since it was just the three of us. Pat slowly made breakfast. We ate, laughed, and enjoyed our small world. The Swans arrived about an hour later. Mrs. Swan looked her typically clean and fresh self, but Mr. Swan looked like he had tumbled out of a foxhole. His posture was slumped and he moved stiffly. Len gave him a sorrowful look—like he caused his misery.

However, Mr. Swan's eyes danced with humor. Conscious of his crippled look, he announced, "War casualty entering!" We all laughed and a large smile broke across Mr. Swan's face. Pat served them breakfast and coffee. We talked for another hour before Len thought we should do something useful.

Len looked at Mr. Swan and said, "I was thinking we should take it a little easier today."

"Okay," answered Mr. Swan, "what do you have in mind?"

Len casually waved over to the swimming pool and said, "I thought Mike and I would work on the dressing rooms. There's a few more logs that need peeling if you don't mind."

"I don't mind at all," Mr. Swan responded.

Mrs. Swan raised her hand and said, "I've got a request! I'd like to get a piece of diamond willow to make a lamp. Can someone help me find the right piece?"

Pat lowered her coffee cup and said, "I'll help you. We'll go into the grove next to the creek where Mike found his." Then she turned to Mr. Swan and asked, "Mark, maybe you could chop the tree down for us?"

Mr. Swan smiled and gave Pat a mock bow as he said, "At your service, my lady."

The day warmed into the seventies and the sun felt good on my back as Len and I finished the floors on the dressing rooms. Mr. Swan peeled logs close by us and I noticed Len checking on him every now and then. I loved building and especially with Len tutoring me. He showed me how to frame the walls and make sure they were plumb and square. Raising the walls gave me deep satisfaction.

Mr. Swan took a break and helped Pat and Mrs. Swan chop down a diamond willow they had flagged. Then he cut the six-inch-diameter trunk into a three-foot length. The resulting log sported several twists and many deep rich diamonds. Mrs. Swan look pleased with her trophy.

We quit early and had a relaxing dinner of leftover stew and mouthwatering blueberry pie from berries picked by Pat and Mrs. Swan. We engaged in light banter after the meal and then the subject of canasta bubbled to the surface. I saw the looks of competition flare in the grownups' eyes and knew it was time to leave.

Since the evening was still warm and bright, I thought it perfect to go hunting along my four-mile circuit. I grabbed my rifle and called Happy. He seemed pleased to go for a walk. We strode down to the airstrip and began looking for tracks along its length. Happy put his nose on the ground and zigzagged in front of me searching for recent activity. I found some caribou tracks, but they were a few days old. Happy paid no attention to them.

We eventually made our way to the end of the runway when I heard an airplane coming. I looked down the valley and spotted Norm's 185 flying toward us. *Norman is paying us a surprise visit*, I thought as I called Happy to the edge of the runway. I sat down on a log and petted Happy while Norm lined up his plane to the strip and landed. Norman stopped the plane in front of us. I waved to Norm and I saw him nod through the windshield. As he turned the plane around, I noticed it was filled with passengers. I followed him back to the runway threshold where he shut the plane down.

As I approached the plane, I watched it bounce sideways and up and down from commotion boiling inside the aircraft. Then I heard kids screeching and Norman shouting at them to calm down. The passenger door swung open and a cardboard box tumbled out and crashed to the ground. I heard glass breaking and saw fluid gush from the side. Then a man's voice cried out, "Oh, God no! Not my precious champagne!" This outburst was immediately followed by a small wiry man falling out of the plane in a heap in front of me.

I looked toward the back passenger seat and saw Rose wave to me with her children strapped to each side of her. The kids were squirming to get out. Norman had his hands full trying to control them and could not help his fallen passenger. I threw my sling over my head so the rifle rode diagonally across my back and knelt down next to the man.

He was cradling the box and rocking it back and forth like an infant as he blubbered, "No, No. What an unfitting death!" I thought he was at least 60 years old with light brown unruly hair and week-old stubble growing from his gaunt face. When he sensed my presence, his demeanor instantly changed. He looked up at me with bloodshot, mischievous eyes, grinned, and asked, "And who are you, my strapping young lad?"

The smell of stale alcohol wafted across my face and almost made me vomit. I answered, "My name is Mike Travis and I work for the Veerhusens. Who are you?"

The man gave me a toothy smile and proclaimed, "I am Frank Benson. Others know me by the affectionate name of Hobo. You may call me by either."

"Hobo?" I repeated in a reverent voice. *This is Hobo?* I thought. Just then, Norm's kids, Vicky and JJ, came screaming by me, laughing and screeching excitedly as they chased Happy. Happy wanted nothing to do with the little demons and high-tailed it for the hills. Norman and Rose walked next to me and looked down as I again asked, "Hobo?" Norm remained silent and nodded.

Hobo smirked and said to me, "Instead of repeating my name, Michael my boy, how about being a jewel and helping me up? Careful with the box though. I think a bottle or two survived." I put my arm around Hobo and felt his fragile ribs poke through his pale skin. Then I carefully lifted him to his feet while I balanced his precious champagne box with my other arm. Hobo held tightly to me like he was afraid of falling.

We looked toward the trail and saw Pat with the Swans walking to meet us. "Take me to her," whispered Hobo. So, I shuffled down the runway dragging Hobo as I went. Pat did not seem to comprehend what was happening until I drew nearer. Then Hobo shouted, "Patricia, my dear, you look ravishing as ever!"

Pat put her hand to her mouth and cried, "Oh dear God, it's Hobo! Frank, what have you done to yourself?" She ran to him and hugged him fiercely. Hobo seemed to like the embrace and found the strength to stand by himself. He kept smiling as Pat grabbed his shoulders and said to his face, "And you're skin and bone. I bet you haven't eaten a decent meal in weeks."

Hobo swayed as he grinned and said, "It's good to see you, too, Patricia. And who is this lovely creature next to you?" Mrs. Swan instinctively stepped behind her husband in response. Mr. Swan seemed to think the whole situation was hilarious.

Pat kept a hand on his shoulder as she introduced him to the Swans. They cautiously shook his hand. Then Pat turned her attention to the Yaegers. "Rosie, it's so good to see you!" They embraced and then Pat appraised the kids. "Rosie, they're sprouting like weeds! Look how JJ can run now!"

Rose gave Pat an easy laugh and said, "Yes, it's tough to keep clothes on them and they're a handful, too. Norm thought that since he was flying Hobo out, we could tag along and stay for the night. Is that all right with you?"

Pat put her arm around Rose and hugged her again. "Yes. You are always welcome, Rosie." The sound of the chugging tractor caused everyone to look toward the trail. Thinking that Norman was delivering gasoline, Len had fired up the C60 and pulled the trailer with a drum down to meet the plane.

Hobo grinned and proclaimed, "Ah, my chariot arrives!" Seeing the commotion around the plane, Len looked puzzled as he pulled up and shut down the tractor. Then Hobo bellowed, "Leonard, my stalwart fellow, I have come to dwell in your humble domicile and heal my afflictions."

Len took a step back when he recognized Hobo. Then I saw sincere concern etched across his face before he grasped Hobo's shoulders and squeezed them. "Frank," he whispered so only Hobo could hear, "you really did it this time, didn't you?"

Hobo maintained his brazen grin as he replied, "Couldn't help myself, old friend. I thought a few days with you and Pat would rejuvenate my soul."

Len shook his head as he smiled and said, "You are always welcome here, Frank. You might as well load yourself onto the trailer. I'll haul you and the kids up to camp."

"Ah," laughed Hobo as he spilled onto the trailer, "a hay ride! Just like the old days in Michigan." Len and I loaded Vicky, JJ, and Hobo's limited luggage on the trailer and Len slowly pulled it back to the lodge. The kids squealed with delight as the rest of the grownups minus Hobo walked alongside.

I helped Hobo walk inside the lodge and sat him down at the dining table. Pat had a pot of coffee on the woodstove, so I poured a cup for Hobo and offered some to Norman and Rose. Norman accepted the offer and Rose declined. Len, Mr. Swan, and I entertained our guests while Pat and Mrs. Swan got the bedding ready in the old cabin for the Yaegers. Len had a surprise for me about my sleeping accommodation and waited until the Yaegers retired for the evening to tell me.

Len pulled me aside so Hobo could not hear us and quietly asked me, "Mike, do you know what the term *DTs* means?"

"No," I answered. I could tell by Len's eyes that this was a serious matter.

Len continued, "It means *delirium tremens*. It's a condition some people get when they suddenly stop drinking. Hobo has been on the heavy sauce for months, so he's probably going to have some hallucinations or nightmares as he dries out. I need you to watch over him tonight."

I recoiled in horror and asked, "Me? Why me? I wouldn't know what to do if there was a problem."

Len shook his head reassuringly and said, "You'll be fine. Just make sure he doesn't wander off in the night and every once in a while check to see if he's breathing. Okay?"

That sounds like a pretty tall order to me, I thought. I took a deep breath and nodded. "Okay," I sighed, "I'll do it."

Len smiled and said, "Good! We'll set you guys up in one of the wall tents."

I glanced at Hobo still drinking coffee seemingly oblivious to our conversation and thought, *This is going to be a long night.*

Len escorted us to the wall tent and carried Hobo's bag. Pat and Mrs. Swan had already laid out our sleeping bags, pillows, and extra blankets. "All the comforts of home," exclaimed Hobo, "Thank you, Len."

"You are welcome, Frank", replied Len. "Mike is going to sleep with you tonight because the Yaegers got his bed, but before I go I need to remove a few things."

Hobo frowned like he knew what was coming. "Oh, like what things, Leonard?" asked Hobo with feigned innocence.

"Like this," answered Len as he unzipped Hobo's bag and pulled out two pint bottles of whiskey cleverly wrapped in socks so they would not clink. "And this," continued Len as he reached inside Hobo's coat and retrieved another pint. "I think that should do it. You can keep the champagne, but you can't drink it for a couple of days."

I thought Hobo was going to howl in protest, but instead he smiled, shook his finger at Len, and said, "Busted! I should have known that you would have seen through my little ruse. I should have given it to Mike to hide. You would have done that for me, my boy, wouldn't you?"

I shook my head and replied, "Probably not, Hobo."

Hobo threw his hands up and lamented, "I'm surrounded by priests!"

Hobo's outburst caused Len to laugh. "Good night, you guys," said Len as he left. "Don't kill each other."

The night was a long one. Initially, Hobo fell suddenly asleep like he had been shot. A few minutes later, the snoring started. He sounded like he was ripping his cot in two. Then came lively conversations between snorts. "For crying out loud, Buckets! What will people think if we do that! We're going to jail for sure!" Quiet followed. "Leave him be, Ronnie, he's too drunk to know better. Just throw him outside." A few snorts punctuated more silence. "Sally, honey, I know I told you I would do that for you. I just forgot. I'm sorry. Oh, don't do that! Damn!"

I wrapped my pillow around my head to muffle the snoring and orations bellowing next to me. The night passed agonizingly slow. Hobo finally dropped into a comatose state by the early morning, which allowed me to eke out a few hours of uninterrupted sleep.

I staggered into the lodge at eight o'clock with heavy eyes and cobwebs in my brain. The Swans and the Veerhusens were already up. Their conversation stopped as I walked into the room and plopped down in a chair. Len noticed rings under my eyes and did not inquire about my night. Instead he asked, "Is he stable?"

I swallowed and replied, "Yeah. Finally. He's out cold. I doubt he'll even stir for several hours. I can't see how an elderly man can drink like that."

"Elderly man?" snorted Len. "Frank is only forty-nine."

My jaw dropped open. "You've got to be kidding!" I gasped with astonishment.

"Nope," continued Len, "booze will do that to you. He'll look a lot better when he dries out."

"I hope that's soon," I responded, "I can't take too many more nights like what I just went through."

Pat gave me the sympathy that I was seeking and served me a hot sweet roll with scrambled eggs. As I finished, Len issued our work instructions. "We really need to get this fireplace finished," Len said and he looked over the half-completed project. "I know it's nice outside, but I want you guys to stay here and work on it. You should be able to dry the sand at a steady pace outside and keep laying rock." Then Len slid the knife between my ribs by saying, "I'll continue building the dressing rooms."

My lack of sleep prevented me from masking my feelings. My displeasure must have been written all over my face because Mr. Swan smiled at me and said, "Well, it's me and you against the world. Do you think we'll make a good team?"

I could tell he was trying to make light of the situation. I thought, *I don't care if we make a good team. I want to work outside with Len and pound nails.* I took a deep tired breath and replied, "Yeah. I'm sure we will. I'll get the mortar."

Using the dried sand from past days and the stockpiled rock outside, we steadily laid and secured another layer on the fireplace. Mr. Swan and I worked out a division of labor. I supplied the rock, water, sand, and mortar. Mr. Swan mixed the mortar to the required consistency and then painstakingly chose the perfect rock for each niche. I found his last task extremely irritating. Mr. Swan would study the pile of rocks by the fireplace for a solid minute before either choosing a rock or declaring none of them were suitable and requesting that I provide more choices. This process repeated itself countless times hour after hour. I thought I was going to scream, *Just pick a rock!*

The Yaeger family came bounding inside the lodge just at the time I was about to lose my sanity. The kids swarmed over the fireplace and managed to kick over a bucket of sand and plunge a fist into the mortar. Pat and Rose got them cleaned up and sat them at the table. Then Pat and Mrs. Swan served the Yaegers a late breakfast. Unbelievably, Hobo staggered through the door. He looked like death warmed over. He shuffled to the table and fell into a chair.

Pat cooed softly to him, "How about some coffee, Frank?" Hobo nodded. Pat slid a cup of coffee in front of him and stood next to him to see if he needed help drinking. Hobo picked the cup up, saluted Pat, and sipped it, still never uttering a word. Pat left him alone and continued serving the Yaegers.

When Norman judged it time to go home, he looked to me and said, "I've got some coiled tubing in the plane for Len and I can offload some gas for you."

"Okay," I said. Relieved to take a break from masonry work. "I will take the tractor down and take the load from you."

"I think I will help you," declared Mr. Swan. He wanted to get out and enjoy the sunshine, too. While the Yaegers gathered their belongings, Mr. Swan and I took the C60 down to the plane and parked the trailer under a wing. Len took a break from his carpentry and followed us. I helped Norman pull the awkward black coiled pipe from the cargo compartment. The hardest part was squeezing it through the door. We threw it on the trailer and then Len and Norm siphoned gas from the wing into the drum. Norman had forgotten his hand-cranked pump, but once he established the siphon, it quickly removed 30 gallons of fuel.

We said our goodbyes and moved out of the way for Norman to start his plane and takeoff. Mr. Swan rode on the trailer and steadied the gas drum as we drove back to the lodge. We offloaded our cargo at the shop and parked the rig.

For the rest of the day, Mr. Swan and I labored on the fireplace. I tried to keep busy, but Mr. Swan's deliberations for each and every rock was exasperating. When Len and I worked together, we would make snap decisions, for better or worse, and lay the rocks in place. Mr. Swan considered the possibilities for several rocks before he finally chose one. This led to "Eureka" moments when he declared, "I know just the rock for that place!" In retrospect, I had to admit Mr. Swan was building a more professional-looking fireplace than Len or I. The sides were even, the corners were square, and each layer was level. It was just so agonizing to watch him build it.

By the time we quit for the day, the fireplace had risen two more feet. We were nearing the top of the firebox. Mr. Swan and I swept the floor and cleaned up our mess.

"You guys are doing a fine job!"

I looked up from sweeping and saw Hobo standing with his hands in his pockets appraising our work. He looked and smelled better. He had an unopened carton of Marlboro cigarettes tucked under his arm.

"Thanks, Hobo," I replied, "but Mr. Swan is the master mason. I just supply him the materials. He works his magic."

Hobo saw me looking at the cigarettes. He held them up and said, "Peace offering. So Len and Pat don't throw me out."

I shook my head as I thought, *They're probably better than the hand-rolled ones.*

Pat and Mrs. Swan cooked a fabulous dinner with the mouth-watering salmon steaks that the Swans had brought. Hobo ate small portions of everything as Pat watched him with concern. "What's the matter, Patricia?" asked Hobo with a grin. "Am I not eating enough? Give my portion to Michael. I've never seen anyone mow through food like this youngster can."

Pat shook her head and said, "You need to eat, Frank. You are skin and bone."

Hobo responded curtly, "Sally likes me that way." Pat dropped the subject.

After dinner, the Swans and Veerhusens prepared to play canasta while Hobo and I excused ourselves. We walked down to the airstrip with Happy and enjoyed the warm evening. The more time I spent with Hobo, the more I liked him. Under that rough exterior was a thoughtful, intelligent, and humorous scoundrel. His eyes danced with mischief when I asked him about his life.

We took turns trying to skip a rock across the creek. "Hobo," I asked as I almost got one across, "did you really only come to Galena on a two-week job and stayed?"

"Ha!" exclaimed Hobo as he snapped his wrist to match my throw. "Someone has been talking about me. I bet it was Leonard, wasn't it? Well, yeah. I had a simple plumbing job and a contract to deliver plumbing supplies to the base in 1959. Then I met Buckets Burgett and things kind of went downhill from there. Damn, that seems so long ago."

"Buckets had this idea to start a bar. I mean there was not one around for miles if you discount that flea-bitten shack in Ruby, but we had to get a state liquor license to operate it and that's hard to do. Then Buckets tells me he has this connection in Governor Egan's office who might hand-carry our application through the mill. So, we filled out the paperwork and submitted it. I couldn't believe it when we got it. So we built the Yukon Inn and the rest, as they say, is history."

I had the feeling Hobo was greatly simplifying the events, but I let it go. We talked about life in Galena as we walked back to our tent and got ready for bed. As I sat on my cot, I asked Hobo one last question. "Hobo, did you cause that water heater to explode under Len's lodge?"

Hobo threw his hands in the air and bellowed, "No! Will that simple explosion haunt me for the rest of my life?" Then he looked at me with a smirking grin and said, "I'll tell you, I hooked it up right. You want to know what I think? I think some silt seeped in from that makeshift well Leonard installed. It plugged the pressure-relief valve and caused the whole thing to take off through the floor like a Saturn rocket! Some self-appointed vigilante blamed me and beat the hell out of me in the alley. I've been branded ever since."

I could not help but laugh. "That's a great story, Hobo. Don't worry. I believe you. Good night."

"I'm glad someone does," replied Hobo as he collapsed on his cot.

<hr>

Except for a few brief senseless narratives, Hobo slept soundly through the night, which meant I got a decent night's sleep, too. I rose fully rested, dressed quietly, and left our wall tent while Hobo continued to sleep. I was met with a warm drizzle and the distinctive smell of fall. I could not believe my eyes when I saw the leaves had turned a dull yellow. I thought, *How can this be? It's only the sixteenth of August!* I hiked up to the lodge to start my day.

Len was standing with a coffee cup looking out the window as I came inside. "Little early for fall," I said as I sat down.

Len turned to me and said, "Yep. That frost a couple of days ago nipped the trees. They are going to lose their leaves early this year." Then changing the subject, Len asked, "How did Hobo do last night?"

"Much better," I answered. "He slept thorough most of the night. He was sleeping easy when I left him."

"Good," replied Len. "Maybe the worst is over. He'll probably start soaking in the tub today. Meanwhile, we need to push to finish this fireplace while you are still here. I can guarantee that as soon as you leave the production rate will drop considerably."

I shook my head in wonder as I thought, *How quickly two months go by*. I asked, "When do you expect Sharon and Hal?"

"Norman said they had scheduled a charter for Sunday. You and Hobo will go back on that plane."

"Wow!" I exclaimed, "That's only three days from now."

Len nodded and replied, "That's what I'm saying. We don't have much time before I lose you. So I was thinking about ramping up the sand drying today. We'll stoke up the woodstove in the old cabin and dry sand there and in the lodge."

After breakfast, we immediately implemented Len's plan. I started splitting wood for both stoves and got them fired up. Mr. Swan and Len spread sand on the metal sheets and set them on the floors of the lodge and cabin. Then we mixed the mortar with the last of the sifted sand and started building. Within an hour, Len experienced my frustration of waiting for Mr. Swan to select the right rock and left us to supposedly finish some pressing chores. I kept busy drying and sifting sand, stoking fireplaces, and hauling water and mortar to the fireplace.

Hours peeled away when Pat interrupted me with a request. "Mike, please go into the Swans' cabin and check on Hobo. He said he was going to soak in the tub a couple of hours ago and I haven't seen him since. I'm worried about him."

I sank my axe into the splitting stump and replied, "You bet! I'll be right back." I took off my work gloves and hard hat and left them by the woodpile before walking to the cabin. I went inside without knocking and walked into the backroom. I found Hobo immersed in the steaming sunken tub with his head back resting on the floor, his mouth open and eyes shut. He remained motionless and I could not detect any signs of breathing. Fear shot through me as I thought, *My God! He's dead!* I fell to my knees and whispered, "Hobo? Are you all right?"

Suddenly, Hobo took a deep breath, broke out laughing, and said, "Thought I was a goner, didn't you, son?"

I almost hit him. "Yeah, I sure did, Hobo," I answered with anger in my voice.

Hobo reveled in his successful joke for a few moments. Then he grabbed a glass next to the tub and said, "Watch this." He pulled the cork from the black hose and filled the glass with steaming hot springs water. He held the glass up, saluted, and unbelievably started drinking it. I screwed my face in disgust as he proceeded to drink the hot liquid down. "Ah! Just what the doctor ordered."

I shook my head and asked, "How can you stand to drink that stuff?"

"Rids my body of poisons," replied Hobo with a grin.

"You can have it," I said as I got up and left him. I didn't want to egg him on any further. Pat was waiting for me outside. I shook my head as I passed her and said, "Believe me, Pat. He's better than fine. Don't waste a second worrying about him." Then I returned to my tasks.

Late in the afternoon, I was standing beside Mr. Swan ready to strangle him. He had spent the last half hour contemplating what rock to insert into an awkward niche and now proclaimed that none of the rocks would work. I wanted to stuff him in the cavity and encase him in mortar. Just before I was going to perform a violent act, I heard a man say, "Let's go down to the river and get some more!" I turned around and came face to face with a transformed Frank Benson. He was shaved, clean, manicured, and wore brown coveralls. He looked years younger and healthier. Hobo grinned and asked, "What ya looking at?"

"Uhm, sorry, Hobo," I stammered, "It's just that you look one hundred percent better. That's all."

"Well thank you, my boy," answered Hobo. "So what do you say we go down and see if we can find some suitable rocks for Mr. Swan?"

Mr. Swan nodded and added as he pointed to the vacant cavity, "That's a great idea. Try to find something that will fit in there."

"Okay," I said getting up and cleaning off my pants, "I'll drive the tractor down and we'll fill the trailer with rocks." Hobo found Len and the three of us met at the airstrip.

After we lifted a load of rocks out of the creek, Len asked Hobo, "Why, Frank, did you feel compelled to do a little work today?"

"Oh, I don't know, Leonard," replied Hobo with a laugh. "I guess I was trying to prevent a murder." He gave me a quick wink and a wry smile.

Len caught the meaning and asked me, "Does Mark frustrate you?"

I lifted the last rock on to the trailer and answered, "He got the better of you, didn't he, Len? He does excellent work, but the progress is annoyingly slow. I try to keep busy doing other things. It's tough, though."

Len nodded and replied, "Yeah, but you guys have the firebox almost totally encased now. A few more layers and we can start on the chimney. It will go a lot faster then." Then as I was climbing on to the tractor Len offered me an olive branch. "I'll tell you what. Frank and I will relieve you and Mark for the rest of the day. Why don't you knock off an hour early?"

I smiled and said, "Thank you, Len. I might just do a little hunting this evening." Len walked up to the lodge and told Mr. Swan to stand down for the evening. Much to his credit, Mr. Swan did not argue and gracefully handed over his trowel. As Len and Hobo put another layer of rock on the fireplace, Pat and Mrs. Swan cooked an early dinner.

The meal was fun with Hobo actively engaged in the conversation. The laughter was good for my soul. Afterwards, I prepared to excuse myself when Mr. Swan surprised me and asked if he could come with me. "I need a hike being cooped up inside all day. Do you mind if I tag along?"

"Not at all," I replied. "If you get tired, we'll turn around."

"Capital idea!" exclaimed Mr. Swan as he got up from the table. "I will be back in a moment. I got to get my boots." Mrs. Swan shot him a look of concern, but kept silent.

As I waited, Len took the opportunity to tell me to take it easy. I assured him that I would. I left camp with my rifle, Happy, and Mr. Swan in tow to walk my hunting circuit. I had a feeling that Mr. Swan wanted to make amends for the trying day. He engaged me in light conversation and I found myself enjoying his company.

"So, what are you looking for?" asked Mr. Swan as we walked along the runway.

"Fresh caribou tracks," I answered. "I look along the soft areas for tracks. Happy sniffs ahead, too. Between the two of us, we look for fresh sign and then follow them." Suddenly, Happy began furiously sniffing the ground. I jogged to him and saw four sets of tracks emerge from the creek and head across the runway toward the hills to the south. "Here, Mr. Swan. Take a look. Four caribou crossed here probably early this morning."

Mr. Swan hurried over and studied the tracks. "How do you know they are caribou and not moose?"

I knelt down and moved my finger along the toe of the hoofprint and said, "Do you see how circular these tracks are? The caribou hoof splits the oval print perfectly down the middle. The hoof spreads to help them walk on tundra. Moose have pointed hoofs. These are definitely caribou."

"Okay," replied Mr. Swan as he looked to the south, "what do we do now?"

I pointed up the mountain and said, "The tracks appear to head straight up that hill. Let's go back to the winter trail and walk it up the mountain. We should cross the caribou tracks up there and figure where they're headed."

"Lead on," urged Mr. Swan. We walked to the winter trail and started climbing. Although the trail had been cleared of brush, it was still lined with tussocks. Over the summer, I had developed a gliding walk that allowed me to slide along the tussock heads. My gait was not perfect and I frequently slipped, but I could make steady progress across the shifting and uneven ground. Unfortunately, Mr. Swan did not have this skill. He floundered and fell in the cold mud between the tufts of vegetation. He was painful to watch and I felt sorry for him as he struggled to keep up.

After he fell again, I walked back to him and helped him to his feet. "Mr. Swan, let's bag it for the day. We can try again tomorrow."

"No!" shouted Mr. Swan breathlessly. "I'm fine. Lead on." I looked hard at him. He had sweat dripping off his forehead and cheeks. His breath came in ragged gulps, but he had a fierce determination in his eyes and, most importantly, pride. I respected that trait.

Against my better judgement, I reluctantly agreed. "Okay, Mr. Swan. We'll take it easy as we climb. We'll probably cross the tracks a little farther up. Then we'll decide what to do." Mr. Swan could only nod and shuffle forward. We slowly hiked the steep, muddy trail in silence. My eyes darted between Mr. Swan and the surrounding landscape. As we climbed, the importance of finding the caribou waned.

Finally, after half an hour of trudging and falling, we intercepted the caribou tracks. The second I saw them I realized something had changed. The tracks were crisper and Happy became intensely interested in them. *These tracks can't be more than an hour old*, I thought. *They must be just over the summit!* I spun around to tell Mr. Swan that I was going to run to the top, but one look at his face froze me. He was exhausted, wet, and cold. His chest heaved as he breathed through his mouth and he was shaking. Guilt ripped my excitement away as I realized we had to return immediately before Mr. Swan lost consciousness. My selfishness to bag a caribou had put us in a hard spot.

I knelt down to the tracks and showed them to Mr. Swan. "I goofed up, Mr. Swan. These tracks are much older than I thought. The caribou are probably long gone. Let's go back and call it a day." He kept silent but nodded. I could see relief in his eyes.

Happy seemed confused. He kept running in the direction of the caribou and coming back, begging me to follow. I shook my head and wagged it in the direction of the runway. Happy looked disappointed, but reversed his course and started down the trail.

I tried to stay close to Mr. Swan as we descended in case he stumbled. I managed to catch him a few times, but he still frequently hit the ground. Finally, he stayed down. "I need to take a breather," he rasped.

He's hypothermic, I thought with dread. "Okay, Mr. Swan," I said with a little levity in my voice, "but only for a few minutes. I'll never get you up if you stay longer. Then Happy will have to drag you out." Mr. Swan chuckled at the comment. *I got to keep him talking.* "Mr. Swan, I think you told me you retired. Did you sell your lumber business?"

"No," answered Mr. Swan. "I turned it over to my son. Worked out a deal with him. He's running the flagship now."

"That must give you some satisfaction."

"It does and he'll do a good job, too."

I got to get him moving again. I bent down and grabbed his fore-arms. "Okay, Mr. Swan. Up we go. We got to get down from here. Another half a mile and we'll be on easy street." I leaned back and slowly lifted him up. The effort strained both of us and reminded me that I was not strong enough to carry him. Without my urging, he put his hand on my shoulder to steady himself and we continued our journey down the trail—one step at a time. We hiked without stops until we finally emerged at the runway.

I stepped ahead of Mr. Swan as I walked onto the airstrip. Then I heard the stumbling of feet behind me. I whirled around to see Mr. Swan windmilling his arms and plunging forward. I lunged to catch him as he miraculously got his feet under him. We smacked our chests together and I held him upright. I looked at him and asked, "Are you all right?"

To my relief, he smiled and answered, "Not bad for a seventy-two-year-old man, huh?"

"Not bad for anyone," I replied. "Come on. Let's go home."

When we got back to the lodge, everyone stared at Mr. Swan as he swayed and smiled at them. Mrs. Swan rebuked him. "For heaven's sake, Mark! Can't you act your age? Come on. I'm going to get you in the tub and then to bed. You think you're twenty again."

After they left, Len looked at me and said, "I told you to be careful. What happened?"

I felt embarrassed and I had a hard time meeting his eyes. "We got caught up in chasing some fresh caribou tracks. I should have paid more attention to his health. When exhaustion hit him, he was done."

Len seemed to understand like he had stood in my shoes in times past. He nodded and said, "Well, you got him back and now he's got an Alaska adventure under his belt. I hope you learned that when you have an older man with you, you've got to be careful. Life can go to hell in a snap." I nodded. "Okay," continued Len, "let's call it a day. Maybe you and I can track another band before you leave. All right?"

"Sounds good, Len," I replied with relief that he understood. "Thank you." I excused myself and retired to my wall tent. As I lay on my cot that evening, I reflected about another lesson learned at Melozi Hot Springs.

Friday started as a hot August day. The heat inside the tent woke Hobo and me and we scrambled outside to breathe fresh air. Hobo stretched and proclaimed, "This is going to be a glorious day! Let's waltz up to the lodge and demand Pat get out of bed and fix us breakfast. What do ya say, Michael my boy?"

I laughed and answered, "Yeah! That will go over good. Len and Pat are probably up, though." We got dressed and walked to the lodge. The sky was brilliantly blue and the mountains radiated the golden hues of fall colors. It was one of those mornings that you were glad to be alive. As predicted, Len was drinking coffee as we entered the lodge and Pat was busy in the kitchen.

Hobo bellowed, "Good morning, my fine friends! And how are we this fine morning?"

Len and Pat laughed at Hobo's greeting. Pat said, "You are looking chipper this morning, Frank. Sleep well?"

"Yes," replied Frank, "until I almost roasted in the tent. We were lucky to crawl out alive."

Pat slipped a cup of steaming coffee into Hobo's hands and said, "Well, thank goodness you guys survived." I mixed myself a glass of Tang and sat down at the table.

Hobo savored the coffee for a few minutes before asking Len, "Well, Leonard, what do you have planned for this beautiful day? Digging a ditch? Breaking rocks? Flogging yourself? You know, all the fun stuff."

Len shook his head and grinned at Hobo's comments. "Depends if Mark survived Mike's abuse last night. If he did, then I thought we should work a short day on the fireplace and goof off in the afternoon. How does that sound?"

Hobo laughed, pointed his finger at me, and said, "See what you have done? The world hangs in a balance because of you." I shrugged and kept silent. Failing to get a rise out of me, Hobo turned to Len and said, "See? Michael doesn't know what to make of me."

Len laughed, "That's a good thing because Pat and I don't either!"

The Swans entered the lodge about an hour later than normal. Hobo and I were screening sand as they arrived. Mrs. Swan looked great, but Mr. Swan was dragging. He had circles under his eyes. "Sorry folks," Mr. Swan said as they sat down, "but I had a hard time rising this morning."

"That's all right," replied Pat as she came to the table, "Are you feeling okay? Would you like some coffee and breakfast?" Mr. Swan nodded.

Mrs. Swan shook her head in dismay and said, "I keep telling him to take it easy. He sees young men like Mike having fun and wants to join right in. Now he's paying for it."

Mr. Swan raised his hand and said, "Guilty." Everyone in the room gave him a knowing laugh. Hobo, Mr. Swan, and I continued to sift sand and build the fireplace until the early afternoon. Pat and Mrs. Swan helped by heating sand to dry and hauling water for the mortar while Len worked on the swimming pool. Finally, Len arrived and called a halt to our labors.

Mr. Swan looked beat and sat on his haunches as he surveyed our progress. "Looks like we can start on the chimney tomorrow."

Len agreed and replied, "Yep. We need to install the stovepipe from the firebox to the ceiling first to guide you."

Pat and Mrs. Swan cooked us an early dinner. Hobo could not help himself and begged Len to retrieve his precious champagne bottles. Only two had survived his grand entrance four days before. When Len presented the bottles, Hobo looked at them in dismay and asked, "Only two bottles made it? What a shame! I ordered them special from France. Well as they say in the bush, 'What the hell!'

234

How about being a sport, Len, and bring me a corkscrew so we can partake in this precious fluid during dinner?"

Len scratched his stubble as he contemplated Hobo's request and said, "I'm sorry, Frank. That's one thing we don't have."

Hobo took a step back and said, "No corkscrew? Well, we will just have to improvise, won't we? Any ideas?"

Len went silent for a moment as he thought about the problem. I took this pause as an opening and blurted, "I've got an idea!" Everyone gave me an expectant look that embarrassed me. "Well," I continued uncertainly, "I could get a pair of channel locks and a wood drill bit from the shop. Then all you have to do is turn the bit into the cork until it holds and then pull the cork out with the channel locks."

Everyone stared at me for an uncomfortable second before Hobo yelled out, "Eureka! Problem solved. Mike go get the instruments and I shall employ them." I got up and left before Len could shred my idea with common sense. I ran back with the drill bit and channel locks and gave them to Hobo. He started to screw the bit into the cork when Pat stopped him.

"Uh, Frank," she said with authority, "I don't want you spraying that stuff all over the dining room. How about taking it outside until you have it under control?"

Hobo gave her a bow and replied with a smirk, "Your wish is my command. Come on, Michael. Let's see how this works." We went outside and, sensing that this was a Kodak moment, I quickly retrieved my camera. Hobo posed against the sweeping vista of Hot Springs Creek and the valley with his precious champagne in his left hand and the channel locks in his right. Then I took a memorable picture of a healthy and happy Frank "Hobo" Benson.

———◆●▸◀●◆———

Saturday was cloudy and warm. Hobo slept soundly through the night and that meant I did, too. After an enjoyable breakfast, Len told us, "You two need to have your bags packed in case Sharon and Hal arrive. They are due in anytime now and I am sure Norm ain't gonna wait for you to get your stuff together."

Hobo saluted and shouted, "Immediately, Commandant! And then we'll come back and fiddle with the fireplace." Hobo only had a small bag, so he took this time to smoke while I scurried between the old cabin, the shop, and the wall tent to assemble my gear. I gently packed my bear claws, retrieved my diamond willow cane, and filled my backpack and duffel bag with the remnants of my clothing. After two months in the field, some shirts and underwear had rotted off me.

After packing, we started walking back to the lodge when Len stopped us and said, "We might as well go down to the airstrip and get some more rocks and sand. Mike, you drive the tractor down and Hobo and I will meet you there." I assembled the trailer and loaded it with the empty Av-gas cans for the sand. I threw a couple of shovels on it and then drove down to the creek. As I approached Len and Hobo, I saw them laughing and Hobo slap Len's back.

"What's so funny?" I asked as I shut down the C60 and jumped off.

Len shook his head, but Hobo answered as he wiped the tears from his eyes, "Oh, it's nothing. We were just reminiscing about times past." I had a feeling it was some shady hilarious secret that they would take to their graves. Their past seemed to bind them tight and emphasized the depth of their friendship.

We labored for two hours selecting rocks, loading them, and shoveling sand. Hobo took frequent breaks and entertained us with humorous stories. When the trailer was loaded to its breaking point, I chugged the teetering load back to the lodge. Mr. Swan was waiting when I arrived and immediately selected some choice rocks for the next layer.

Len got a ladder and we installed the stovepipe from the firebox to the chimney insert located in the ceiling. I connected the pipe to the metal insert while Len steadied the ladder. He seemed relieved that I had volunteered to work on the higher sections. Afterwards, Len directed Mr. Swan and me on how to build the base for the chimney. With our instructions made absolutely clear, Len left us alone to build it. Hobo supervised us from the background.

I soon discovered that Mr. Swan's past deliberations were lightning fast in comparison to his decisions to build the chimney. He agonized over each and every rock placement. The frustration in the air was so thick you could cut it. Finally, Hobo could not take it any longer and declared, "Well, I'm going fishing! Michael, my boy, could you please set me up with a pole and point me in the direction of the fish?"

"Sure," I answered with relief and thankfulness for the diversion. I went outside into the sweet and relaxing air and assembled a fly pole for Hobo. I tied a mosquito to his line and handed it to him. "Hobo, I'll walk you to your fishing spot. By the time I get back, maybe Mr. Swan will have laid a rock in place."

Hobo smiled and said, "Lead on, my boy." I led Hobo upstream of the hot springs to the sloughs.

"Here you go, Hobo. Cast your fly above these channels and let it drift down. You'll get a few." Hobo nodded and flicked his line out. I was surprised at his casting skills. He knew what he was doing. I watched for a few minutes before going back to the torment of the fireplace. As I approached the lodge, I met Pat and Mrs. Swan leaving the building and carrying cans.

Pat saw my questioning eyes and said, "Mark wants smaller rocks than what you guys brought up this morning. So, we are going to the small creek to fetch some."

Figures, I thought as I walked up the ramp and entered the lodge.

During my absence, Mr. Swan had managed to lay only one rock in place. I felt my anger rise. He pointed to the fireplace and said, "I need some smaller rocks to make the base."

That's what mortar is for, I thought as I walked to the kitchen and mixed some Tang to cool off. Then I sifted more sand as Mr. Swan waited for the women to return.

Soon, Pat and Mrs. Swan entered the lodge each carrying an Av-gas can full of creek rocks. Mr. Swan eagerly received these materials and rubbed his hands together in delight. "Just what I needed," he said and he selected a choice rock. His progress increased a little and we managed to add another foot on the fireplace before Hobo stumbled inside with a stringer of uncleaned fish hanging from a willow branch.

He proudly showed off his catch and said, "I slew them!"

Pat pointed to me and commanded, "Mike, handle that!"

I laughed, took Hobo's fish, and said, "Come on, Hobo. Let's get these cleaned up and then bring them back to Pat." Hobo looked crestfallen but followed me to the base of the hot springs where we properly gutted and scaled the fish.

We had moose-meat spaghetti and Pat's world-famous fried grayling for dinner. After the meal, Len and Hobo traded stories about their life in the military and their adventures throughout Alaska. Both were excellent storytellers and they drew my imagination into their past world. By the end of the night, I felt compelled to explore Alaska. I had to see this marvelous land and fascinating people for myself. Little did I know that this evening would become a defining moment in my life.

As Hobo and I got ready to walk down to our wall tent, I noticed Pat looking wistfully out the window at the evening sky. Len also saw her and asked, "What's the matter, honey? How come you look so disappointed?"

Pat shook her head like she was trying to rid herself of misgivings and replied, "I was hoping Sharon and Hal would have arrived today. I can't wait to see them."

Len slid his arm around her and said, "Don't worry. They'll get here when they get here. There is nothing we can do about it." Pat nodded and moved away from the window.

———◆◆◆◆◆———

As we flipped the tent flap open, the morning greeted Hobo and me with rain and low-lying clouds. The air was warm and humid and filled with the smells of autumn. The clouds formed halos over the golden leaves and gave the valley a mystical ambience. Hobo smiled and said sarcastically, "Looks like a fine day for flying! Let's go up to the lodge and find some sustenance. What do ya say, Michael my boy?"

"Okay, Hobo," I replied stepping out of the tent, "but be warned, Pat may be sleeping in today because it's Sunday." Hobo waved us onward. When we entered the lodge, I was surprised to see Pat busy cleaning and baking so early in the morning. "Good morning, Pat," I said. "You are getting a jump on the day."

Pat smiled and said with enthusiasm, "Sharon is coming today. I just know it. So, I want to get everything prepared for her."

Hobo nodded as he poured himself a cup of coffee and said, "Do you think they will make it in today? Not exactly flying weather out there."

Pat's demeanor was unfazed. "Yep. Things change, Hobo. You and Mike should be packed and ready to go."

I sat down, drank my glass of Tang, and thought about Pat's words. Today was just shy of two months since I had arrived. I found it hard to believe time had flown by so quickly. I was anxious to see my family again and try to salvage the football season, but I also felt sad to leave. I had a gnawing feeling that I was going to miss out on exciting adventures and significant accomplishments if I left. As I took another sip, I realized that I felt some pride in what we had built this summer. I also marveled at the lessons Len and Pat had taught me from their school of hard knocks. This summer had changed me.

Len shuffled out of the bedroom rubbing his unruly grey hair. "Good morning, gents. Why are you guys up and at 'em this morning? Today is an easy day. I bet you won't see the Swans until much later."

Hobo poked me in the ribs and replied, "Because there is only so much I can take of Michael. You know how he is."

Len snorted as he poured himself a cup of coffee and said, "Yeah. Right. You guys make quite a pair." We enjoyed a leisurely breakfast and conversation until the late morning when the Swans entered the lodge. Mr. Swan looked fully rested and rejuvenated.

Our conversation extended until noon when Mr. Swan asked me, "Mike, I was hoping you would take me fishing today and spend some time showing me how to cast a fly rod. I'm just not picking it up."

I smiled and answered, "Sure! I'm ready when you are."

Mrs. Swan raised her hand and said, "I have a request. Len, could you help me clean and shape the burl for my lamp? If you could get me going, I will have a project to do."

Len put down his cup and said, "You bet. It appears we have our day planned. So, let's get to it."

I led Mr. Swan to the sloughs above the hot springs. This time I brought a handful of black gnat flies and showed him how to tie one to the line. Then I demonstrated the basics of fly-fishing. "Your goal is to roll the line over the water so your fly softly lands on the surface. To do this, you need to practice moving your pole with long full strokes like this." I pulled out some line and used two overhead strokes to smoothly cast the line upstream. "Here, you try."

Mr. Swan muttered, "Looks easier than it is." He whipped the line too hard and smacked it into the water. After an hour of steady practice, he consistently placed his fly about 30 feet upstream with some accuracy. Then unexpectedly, Mr. Swan hooked his first fish. His face exploded with excitement as he battled the grayling to the shore. I knelt next to the bank and scooped it up.

"Not bad, Mr. Swan! Congratulations!" I said as I handed it to him. Mr. Swan wanted to run back to the lodge and show everyone—especially his wife. "Why not catch more and then go back?" I asked.

"Good idea," answered Mr. Swan as he immediately returned to the creek. For the next hour, I watched him and offered advice. He managed to catch two more during my instruction. We cleaned them and Mr. Swan proudly carried his bounty back to the lodge to show it off.

As we approached the lodge, I saw Pat walk out of the old cabin wiping tears from her eyes. A stab of concern penetrated my heart as I ran up to her and asked, "What's wrong, Pat? What happened?"

"Oh," said Pat as she gave me a forced smile and wiped more tears from her face, "I just radioed Rosie and she told me Sharon and Hal called her and said they're still in Anchorage. They will arrive in Galena tomorrow and Norm will fly them out as soon as he can. I don't know why I'm crying. I guess I was so looking forward to seeing them today." Pat saw the concern in my eyes and squeezed my arm. "I'm okay," she said as she continued to walk toward the lodge. "Thank you for asking."

Pat left me with a jumble of emotions. I wanted Sharon and Hal to get here as soon as possible to alleviate Pat's longing to embrace her daughter. At the same time, I did not want to leave Melozi. I was going to miss the Veerhusens. I shook my head clear and followed Pat into the lodge.

Inside, we found Mr. Swan triumphantly showing off his catch. He saw Pat and declared, "Pat, looks like we're having fish tonight!"

Pat graciously took the fish and replied, "Very good, Mark, but we are going to need more than three fish."

Hobo leaped to his feet and offered his assistance. "Hey, Mark. How about you and me going back down there and rustle up a few more, eh?"

Mr. Swan nodded enthusiastically and said, "Okay! Let's go!" Like two little boys running to the backyard fish pond, they bolted out the door and were gone. We watched the door swing shut and heard their feet stampede down the ramp.

Mrs. Swan shook her head and said with dismay, "Mark Swan, when are you ever going to grow up?"

Len turned to me and said, "Uh, Mike. You better follow those two and make sure they stay out of trouble."

I nodded and replied, "I was thinking the same thing, Len. I'll see you guys in a bit." I walked to the hot springs and sat down in the grass by the bluff. From my vantage point, I could see Mr. Swan and Hobo prepare for battle about a hundred yards upstream. Within minutes, they were casting their lines upstream and drifting their flies down. I watched them fish with the sweeping mountains and jaw-dropping beauty of the valley behind them. I never tired of gazing at the awesome vista. The tranquility of the scene was broken only by an occasional scream of "I've got one" from the boys below me. Their yells spooked a cow moose to bolt into the creek just upstream of their location. Hobo and Mr. Swan stared at it for a moment before continuing to fish unabated.

With the additional fish they caught, we had enough for dinner. Pat had an idea to minimize the mess in the kitchen. "How about making a fire outside and cooking the fish in foil?" she asked Len.

"That's a great idea, honey" responded Len. He turned to Mr. Swan, Hobo, and me and asked, "You guys want to build a fire so we have some cooking coals?" Everyone agreed and we built a fire toward the hot springs within a ring of rocks. When the fire burned down to coals, Mrs. Swan brought us the fish individually wrapped in foil with butter and seasonings inside. Hobo and Mr. Swan looked intrigued with the cooking method. I buried the fish in the coals and nursed them with a green willow stick. Twenty minutes later, we were smacking our lips at the steaming delicious fish as we devoured them at the dining table.

After dinner, Len asked me, "Mike, tonight will probably be your last night at Melozi Hot Springs. Is there anything you want to do?"

I immediately answered, "Yes. I want to go hunting one last time. Who knows? I might stumble across a caribou this time."

"Okay," responded Len as he stood and drained his coffee cup, "let's go and walk your circuit."

Wow, I thought as I sprang to my feet, *Len wants to go with me!* I rushed to the old cabin and grabbed my rifle. As I came back outside, Hobo and Mr. Swan were standing next to Len prepared to come along.

Hobo read my mind and said, "Don't worry. We're only going as far as the runway. You and Len can have the rest." Happy joined our pack as we walked down to the airstrip. The evening was warm and sunny. As we entered the runway, Happy bolted forward and started sniffing the ground in zigzag fashion. We watched him as we talked softly among ourselves. Nothing seemed to catch Happy's attention as we strolled down the strip. The tracks we found were days old. At the end of the runway, Happy's curly tail suddenly went straight up.

"What ya see, boy?" asked Len as we jogged to Happy. Happy stepped aside and revealed fresh massive bear tracks. Judging by the crispness of the instep, they were made within the hour.

Hobo whistled and exclaimed, "Wow wee! Look at the size of those dinner plates! That is one big boy!"

I bent down and spread my hand inside the forepaw print. My fingers did not touch the sides. Len shook his head and said, "For an interior grizzly, that is one big bear. He's probably close by."

I stood up and asked Len, "Do you think he's the same one that chased us up on the shop?" Hobo and Mr. Swan stepped back in fear.

Len smiled and said, "Could be. That bear was big enough to leave a print like this. Let's keep our eyes peeled and we might spot him while we walk the circuit." This insight diminished any desire Hobo and Mr. Swan had to follow us. They bid us farewell and headed back to the lodge.

Len, Happy, and I started climbing the winter trail. We moved silently for half an hour until we crested the hill. Then we stopped at the tree line and surveyed our surroundings. As Len's eyes scanned the slopes for game, I noticed that he was barely breathing harder than normal. Years of working in the bush had hardened him. "Nope," declared Len as he turned toward me, "I don't see a thing."

"Me neither," I said. "Nice evening though."

Len smiled and said, "Yeah. It feels good to get out." Then he looked at me and asked, "You gonna miss this place?"

I nodded and replied, "Yeah. I'm going to miss everything about Melozi. You and Pat sure treated me well. Thank you."

Len laughed and put his arm around my shoulder as we continued walking the trail. "I'm glad things worked out, Mike. We're gonna miss you, too." My evening just could not have been better.

Chapter 11

Another Lifestyle

Hobo and I awoke to a deluge. The wind howled and tore at the tent walls while the heavens opened up and dumped a torrent of rain. We bundled up and dashed through the elements to the lodge. We were soaked by the time we raced through the door. Hobo bent over, grabbed his knees, and drew in ragged breaths. "I'm done," he rasped.

"It's a barnburner of a storm," remarked Len comfortably staring outside with his coffee cup in hand. "Kind of amazing how it can go from a beautiful evening to a howling storm in the morning."

I took off my coat, hung it on a peg in the wall, and said, "Well, if things don't improve, Hal and Sharon are not making it in today."

A curt reply came from the kitchen, "They'll make it." I looked up and saw Pat busy cleaning. She looked like she was on a mission. She had clothes piled for washing, fresh folded-bedding stacked, and cleaning supplies ready to be used. All three of us kept our thoughts to ourselves and watched her get organized.

Len broke the uncomfortable silence. "I was thinking that on a day like this, we should putter around the lodge. Frank, you could give me a hand with installing outlets and wiring. Mike, you and Mark do what you can on the fireplace. We've got enough sand to get you through the morning. You both should be packed to leave at a minute's notice in case that plane gets in."

Hobo lifted his coffee cup to Len and said, "Will do, boss. What time is Norman due in?"

Pat yelled from the kitchen, "Rosie said this evening. I've got a lot to do before they get here. So I was hoping you guys could fend for yourselves. Fix what you want. Just don't make a mess." For a helpless second, we men stared at each other before shrugging our shoulders and getting up to find something to eat. Mrs. Swan entered the lodge and rescued us. She whipped up a coffee cake and some eggs which gave us enough strength to start work.

Mr. Swan and I continued building the fireplace. We had risen to a level where Mr. Swan needed a step stool to reach the next layer. He quickly tired from stepping up and down and resorted to directing me where to place the next rock. This proved to be extremely trying for me. As I stood with my arms outstretched, Mr. Swan ordered me to turn each rock in four different directions, flip it upside down, and finally decided on a position before locking it in place with mortar. A couple hours of this ritual gave me an overwhelming feeling of wanting to cast my body outside into the rain and scream at the top of my lungs while I wallowed in the mud.

Fortunately, Hobo's banter carried over to our workplace causing us to laugh. He constantly teased Len and told amusing stories while he pulled electrical wire through the conduits they installed along the floor. "The one that really took the cake was when the Red Cross wanted to give me an award for raising money for the 1969 flood victims," Hobo said as he yanked on the wiring and connected it to the outlet box. "Some official-looking woman bundled up in a virtue-protecting dress that sealed her off from her neck to her ankles arrived in Galena and said she wanted to present me with a trophy. She asked me what was my secret to generating so much money so quickly. I looked her in the eye and told her that I raffled off three prostitutes from Fairbanks.

Man, you should have seen her eyes fly open as she sputtered, 'Why, I don't understand!'" Hobo used a high-pitched falsetto when he imitated her response. "Then I said to her, I'll tell you what you don't understand. Galena has got several hundred servicemen stuck here with nothing to do. So I offered them a chance for some female companionship and they damn near stampeded to the bar to buy a ticket. 'Why, that's illegal,' she said. 'Illegal, hell,' I answered. 'You snatched up the money didn't you?' She turned ghastly white, kept my trophy, and ran. Never heard from her again. I didn't get my money back either. I guess I couldn't have been too illegal for her tastes."

Hobo could really get us laughing with his off-color male humor. He made the day bearable. The rain stopped in the early afternoon leaving the ground saturated. Hot Springs Creek had risen a foot since the morning. The normally tranquil creek raged within the confines of the steep banks. I thought it was probably flooding the runway.

Pat came into the lodge and Hobo suddenly went silent. He worked with angelic grace and presented an example of a stalwart craftsman. Pat seemed oblivious to our activities as she consulted her task list on the dining table. I saw her hand go up to her face as she remembered an important item. "Michael," she said to me as she dashed to her bedroom, "I've got something for you." She came back with an envelope with the words "Michael Travis, Letter of Recommendation" typed on the front and handed it to me.

I quickly cleaned off my hands on a rag, received it, and opened it up. I removed a single sheet of fine stationary and unfolded it. Pat had typed an official-looking document with the words *Melozi Hot Springs Lodge* centered on the top. The line below read, "Letter of Recommendation for Michael Travis, August 1973." The letter described my activities and stated that I performed them well with little supervision. The final line grabbed my heart. "I highly recommend Mr. Travis for any employment that he is seeking. Sincerely, Leonard and Pat Veerhusen, Owners." Pat had signed for the two of them.

I carefully refolded the letter and reached for Pat. She wrapped her arms around me as I whispered, "Thank you."

She hugged me and replied, "You are welcome, Mike. We have enjoyed you." Pat released me and brushed back a tear.

I held the letter up and called to Len across the room, "Thank you, Len."

He smiled and replied, "Glad to do it." Suddenly, an airplane roared over the top of the lodge.

"Oh, my God!" screamed Pat. "They're early!" Pandemonium broke loose. Hobo and I ran to our tent to collect our gear. Len jumped on the tractor, fired it up, and started pulling the trailer down to the airstrip. Pat and the Swans grabbed their boots and jackets and began walking. Happy started running in circles amidst the excitement.

I threw my backpack over my shoulders and grabbed my duffel bag and diamond willow cane. Hobo had a jacket and his small bag. Together, we walked briskly down the soggy trail to the runway. Hot Springs Creek looked like a frothing river and had spilled onto the runway. Norman had slid his plane between the hillside and water, but the landing had thrown mud along the fuselage and coated the underbelly.

As Hobo and I approached the plane, we saw Norman help Sharon out of the airplane. She was beautiful with her brunette hair in pigtails. She wore a burnt orange wool jacket with matching yarn ties in her hair. Sharon squealed when she saw her mother and sprinted toward her with her arms held wide, but she slipped in the mud and fell to her knees. Pat rushed to help her and they laughed and cried as they slowly stood and embraced each other.

Hal exited the plane with more restraint, but his eyes showed he was excited to be here. He was a big-chested, capable-looking man. He gave Len a solid handshake and then stood stoically beside Sharon until she finally released her mother. With tears streaming down her face, Pat hugged Hal as she whispered to him, "Thank you for bringing my daughter to me." I saw a crack in Hal's somber face as he nodded, not trusting his voice to remain strong.

Hobo and I stood to the side and watched the emotional greetings. Norman looked strangely upset. He tapped me on the shoulder and said, "Might as well load your stuff. We gotta get going." I opened the cargo door and slid my gear inside. Then I threw Hobo's bag on top of my stuff.

"Let's go," ordered Norm as he looked at me, opened the passenger door, and slid the front seat forward. "I want you in back."

"Just a minute, Norm," I said as I walked toward Len. "I got to say goodbye." Len had just released Sharon when I approached him. I stretched out my hand and said as maturely as I could, "Goodbye, Len. Thank you for everything. I will never forget my summer here."

Len knocked my hand away, threw his arms around me, and gave me a bear hug. "It was good having you, Mike. You helped me in more ways than you will ever know." I choked back my tears and nodded.

Pat grabbed me next and hugged me fiercely. "Michael," she said into my chest, "you be good. Don't hang around with bad friends and work hard at school. Then come back to us, okay?" Again, all I could do was nod.

Pat released me and confronted Hobo. She hugged him and then grabbed his shoulders and said straight to his face, "You take care of Mike, understand? And none of your shenanigans. Do you hear me?"

Hobo grinned and answered, "Why Pat, I don't know what you mean."

Pat's face became serious. "I mean it, Frank. You make sure he gets on the first airplane to Fairbanks or you will have me to answer to. Got it?"

Hobo lifted his right hand as if he was giving Pat a solemn oath and said, "Geez, Pat. I promise. Okay?" I noticed his left hand was behind his back with his fingers crossed.

I walked to the Swans. Much to my surprise, Mrs. Swan gave me a full and meaningful hug. She released me and said to me in a gracious voice, "I enjoyed getting to know you, Mike. Have a safe trip."

"Thank you," I replied. "Thank you also for the great meals. You and Pat made sure that I never went hungry. I hear that's a big task." Mrs. Swan laughed and patted my shoulder.

I extended my hand to Mr. Swan. He shook it enthusiastically and said, "I enjoyed working with you. I don't know how I'm going to finish that fireplace without you."

I laughed and replied, "Mr. Swan, I have no doubt that you will figure out a way. I enjoyed getting to know the both of you. Please drive safely when you head back to Washington."

Then I bent down and gave Happy a hug and kiss. "Well boy, I'm going to miss you. Protect the lodge." He gave me a smooch and wagged his thick curly tail. I rose, turned around, and saw Norman chomping at the bit to leave. "All right, Norm. Let's go." I grabbed the handhold on the fuselage and pulled myself into the back seat.

Norman swore under his breath, "Next time, kid, knock the mud off your shoes before climbing in." Hobo gave me a "what's up with that" look before struggling into the front right seat. Len pulled the trailer back and the adults walked to the end of the strip. Norman fired up the engine and taxied through the mud and water to the runway threshold. I watched him set the flaps at ten degrees to give the wings extra lift. Then he fire-walled the engine and we bounced down the runway. The mud slowed our acceleration. Norm leaned forward in his seat as he eyed the end of the runway rocketing toward us. He jerked the yoke back and the stall warning screamed in protest. The right wheel struck a small boulder that marked the runway boundary and tilted the airplane to the left. Norman instinctively righted the aircraft as we buzzed over the tundra. Then he nursed the plane toward the creek and followed it down the valley. Relief washed across Norman's face as our airspeed increased and the plane rose.

When I looked back, the runway and Melozi Hot Springs had disappeared around the bend. I felt a heavy loss descend upon me.

We gained altitude and entered the clouds as Hot Springs Creek met the Melozitna River. We flew in thick bellowing clouds for the rest of the trip until Norman began his descent. We broke out of the overcast about four miles northeast of Galena.

As we approached town, we flew directly over a log home that looked like it had recently exploded. Furniture, appliances, and garbage radiated from the open front door and broken picture window.

Hobo punched Norman on the shoulder and asked with a laughing voice, "What the hell happened down there?"

Norman shouted back, "Barney Nollner's potlatch. It was a humdinger!" I still didn't know what a potlatch entailed, but it looked like something to avoid.

Norm smoothly landed the plane and taxied to his office. He shut the engine down and announced he would help us out. Norm helped Hobo exit first and then slid the front seat forward and let me out. As I was stepping down Norman yelled, "Damn it, kid! I told you I didn't want any mud on the side." He pointed to a smudge that my boot left on the door entrance. The dab paled next to the amount plastered along the fuselage.

Something clicked inside of me. I set my jaw and walked to the cargo door. "I'll do that," barked Norm. I ignored him. I opened the door and pulled Hobo's and my gear out and carried it to the steps of Norman's office. I heard Norm swear again, but I did not give him the satisfaction of acknowledgment. Hobo went inside and called a friend to pick us up. When he finished, he came back out and stood next to me. After a minute he said, "Norm has got a burr under his saddle for you."

I looked toward the massive air force hangers and said, "Doesn't matter. I let his comments slide like water off a duck's back. He's really a good person. Norm helps the Veerhusens a lot." Hobo nodded and remained silent. A few minutes later, a beat-up 1966 Plymouth Rambler station wagon pulled up.

Hobo waved to the man inside and announced, "Here's our ride, Mike. You gotta throw your stuff in the back seat. The tail gate doesn't work anymore." I threw my gear onto the dirty cushions. Dust billowed up when my pack hit it. I got in and shut the creaking door. Hobo jumped into the front seat and yelled, "Tally ho!" Our chauffeur put the car in gear and sped us to town. As we drove around the base, Hobo rolled down his window, rested his arm on the frame, and enjoyed the warm sunny afternoon. Hobo's friend brought him up to speed on events that had happened since he was gone. They talked about village decisions, people traveling, and business in general.

I looked out the window and gazed at the enormous dike that separated the runway from the village. Not only did the dike protect the air force base from flooding, it was also a barrier to trespassers wanting to take a shortcut across the runway. However, I spotted a young man scampering up the side of the dike as we entered the town. He gave us a furtive look as he glanced both ways before sprinting over the top and disappearing. "He's looking for the military police," commented Hobo. "If you can make it without getting caught, it saves you two miles of walking. If they catch you, it's a bad day."

Galena was a collection of houses sandwiched between the Yukon River and the dike. As we drove down the dirt road, I saw a flimsy aluminum building with the words "National Bank of the North" written above the door. One block farther, a stout cinder-block building with a single barred window caught my attention. "What's that?" I asked.

Hobo grinned, wagged his finger at me, and replied, "That's the liquor store. I know what you are thinking. The bank should look like this, too, but no one messes with the bank. You can't even go inside the liquor store, see?" As we drove past, I saw a large man with a pistol on his hip standing in the doorway with his arms crossed over his chest. "You tell that guy your order and he brings it out to you and takes your money."

I shook my head in amusement as we continued down the street. We passed a general store and stopped in front of a weathered brown single-story building. Its main walls consisted of four-sided logs with a lumber roof. The planks were painted a dull white with the words, "Yukon Inn" scrawled above the threshold in black cursive letters. I noticed the door was wide open to take advantage of the pleasant afternoon. The Inn had several haphazard additions that sprawled along the street. "We're here!" announced Hobo. "Grab your stuff, Mike, and we'll set you up for the night."

I pulled my gear and followed Hobo into the bar. As I walked inside, my eyes struggled to adjust from the bright afternoon to the dim interior. I felt like I was entering another world. The bar was adorned with trinkets, signs, and broken artifacts. Large beautiful murals surrounded the lounge. The place was empty except for a couple of men who sat at the bar. Hobo went straight to the counter and walked behind it. He looked like he had found his perfect place in the world.

Hobo shook hands with a big man who was tending bar and said, "Ron, I want you to meet a young man who took care of me at Melozi Hot Springs. His name is Mike Travis. Mike, this is Ronnie Franklin." I shook Ronnie's solid hand. Ronnie was about six feet tall and built like a lumberjack. He looked fully capable of handling any situation that might unfold in this establishment.

Ronnie smiled and said, "Hi ya, Mike. Are you staying for a while?"

I smiled back and replied, "Just the night. I have to catch a plane back to Fairbanks tomorrow."

Hobo interjected, "Ron, why don't you set him up in a room in back? You, know, an unoccupied one."

Versus an occupied one? I thought.

Ronnie rubbed his chin and said, "Okay. We got one at the end of the hall. Follow me, Mike." I grabbed my stuff and followed Ronnie through a door behind the bar. The hallway was even darker than the bar. I noticed several rooms on each side of the hallway. The doors were shut except one. In that room, a woman sat on a bed and looked at us expectantly. Ronnie shook his head as we passed her and led me to the last room at the end of the hallway. "Here you go," he said as he opened the door. "You can stash your stuff in here for the night. Keep the door closed while you're here, okay?" I nodded and threw my gear on the bare mattress, closed the door, and followed Ronnie back to the bar.

My eyes had fully adjusted to the interior lighting when I returned and I began to explore the lounge. I walked to the far wall behind the pool table and stared at the first mural. It was the first scene of Robert Service's ballad of "The Shooting of Dan McGrew." With dark and pronounced colors, the chalk rendition of a bawdy Klondike bar seemed to come alive like I was staring through a time portal. Can-can girls were dancing while patrons drank or conversed with the barmaids. I marveled at the detail Yvonne Worthington had put into her sketches. There were scenes within scenes—each with a story to tell.

Under each mural was a verse from the ballad. I was entranced by the size of the figures. They ranged from a few feet high to almost life-sized. Their expressions seemed to leap out of the wall and come alive. I could almost hear the gunshots ring out when Dangerous Dan McGrew and the love-crazed stranger shot each other over a dance hall girl known as Lou. I slowly made my way around the lounge and finished at the bar.

The bar still had only two patrons sitting on stools and two men sitting at a nearby table. I sat down on a stool and prepared to strike up a conversation with Hobo. Hobo pulled a cigarette from his mouth and let out a long satisfying stream of smoke before smiling and asking me, "Well, Mike. Do you want a beer?"

My mind screamed, *I'm going to be served in a bar!* I quickly calmed myself and answered in the most mature voice that I could muster, "Ah, sure. I could use one. Thank you." *I think I answered like this was old hat*, I thought to myself. Hobo smiled, reached under the bar, and retrieved a can of Olympia beer. He pulled the flip-top tab and slid it across the bar to me. I caught it like I had done it a million times before and nonchalantly lifted the can to my lips. The warm liquid tasted foul in my mouth. I struggled hard not to gag as I noticed Hobo staring at me. I lifted the can again, saluted, took another revolting taste, and smiled back at him. I do not know if I fooled Hobo, but he shook his head and continued to serve his customers.

As I sat at the bar and nursed my drink, I noticed the mural on the wall above the displayed liquor bottles. Yvonne had sketched a chalk rendition of a bar that was similar to her other murals. Feathery girls were dancing with patrons while a fistfight broke out on the floor. Again, there were scenes within scenes. I chuckled when I noticed a barmaid grabbing a man by his hair and prepared to whack him over the head with a whiskey bottle.

Hobo had placed signs around the mural. They read, "Welcome to Peyton Place of Galena, Alaska"; "This place is recommended by Drunken Heinz!"; "No Minors Served" (*Can't mean me*, I thought); and "When the White Men discovered this Country, the Indians were running it. There were no Taxes, no Debts, Women did all the work, and the White Man thought he could IMPROVE on a system like that!"

I then looked at the wall next to the door to the back rooms. I noticed a sign that said, "Yukon Inn . . . Ye Public Telephone" with arrows pointing to an area next to the door. Where the telephone should have been was a sign that read, "Out of Order." Pieces of a telephone hung on the wall with a shotgun blast pattern around it. "Hobo," I asked pointing to the debris, "what happened there?"

Hobo looked to where I was pointing and said, "Oh, that? Earlier this year, some guy lost his dime in the pay phone and took offense. He came back with a 12-gauge shotgun and blew it up. I never bothered to fix it." He shrugged like he was talking about repairing a wall panel and went back to work. I nodded in reply because the explanation fit everything else that I had heard and seen about the Yukon Inn and went back to fiddling with my horrible-tasting beer.

Within the next hour, the bar filled to capacity. All stools and tables were taken and the noise level rose to the point you had to shout to the guy next to you. Some off-duty servicemen started playing pool. Several men holding drinks stood behind me. I was still clinging to my inaugural beer can. My beer was now flat, but I could not tell the difference. Hobo seemed to come alive as the crowd got rowdier. While he laughed and joked with his customers, I noticed Ronnie keeping a careful eye on the activities around him. He seemed tense, like he knew something was about to break.

The man sitting next to me looked like he'd had six beers too many. He sat with his head hung and stared at his empty crushed can of Olympia beer. When he stood up to fish another dollar out of his pocket, his stool fell over. He either was oblivious to the fallen stool or he could not hear the crash over the cacophony around him, but he laid his dollar on the bar and proceeded to sit back down. I threw my hand out to catch him and missed. He fell backwards with a look of utter surprise, and hit the floor hard. The men behind him scarcely gave him a second look. "Hey, are you all right?" I yelled.

The man crawled back to the bar and gave me an angry drunken stare. "What do you mean by that? You kicked my chair out from under me!"

I shook my head and said, "No. You got it all wrong. You . . ." I never got another word out. The man balled up his hand into a fist and took a wide looping swing at me. I easily ducked under it. His fist went sailing above my head and smacked the man standing behind me.

At first, the man looked dazed. Then his expression changed to rage as he looked at my inebriated companion and yelled, "Cousin, why did you hit me?" He launched a lightning-fast jab to his relative's chin that sent him flying on top of the bar.

My high school science teacher once told me that a single neutron hurled at a radioactive core could ignite a chain reaction. I witnessed this exact process. The tension that Ronnie had sensed exploded into a melee. Men who just minutes ago were drinking and talking with each other were now trading blows. I rolled off my stool just as a chair smashed across the bar where I was sitting. Men had each other by the throats and were beating each other's faces. Someone threw another man across a table and broke it in half. I made it to a wall to cover my back when a cue ball thrown from the pool table crashed next to me. I glanced up to see Hobo laughing and banging his hand on the bar. Another cue ball hit the bottles behind him and exploded. Hobo ducked as liquor gushed over him. Then I saw Ronnie grab a billy club and start hammering his way toward the pool table where two men, standing on top of it, were throwing balls.

"I got to get out of here!" I screamed to myself. I tried to make it to the door, but two men locked in battle rolled in front of me blocking my escape route. Suddenly, I saw a person on a motorcycle pull up to the front of the building and park next to the door. I could not see who it was in the late afternoon glare, but the person walked inside with a confident and strong stride. As the figure emerged from the sunlight, my jaw dropped open at the vision. There in the doorway stood the strongest, meanest looking woman that I had ever seen. She wore cowboy boots with black jeans and a black blouse. I saw a pistol holstered on her right hip. She had a black cowboy hat that accented her blonde, curly hair that spilled over her shoulders. She wore a yellow scarf around her tough neck to give her outfit a hint of femininity. She wiggled her black-gloved fingers as she assessed the situation. Then she bolted into action.

Taking the first two men by the hair, she pulled them apart and said, "I thought I told you guys never to come back here." She clunked their heads together and threw them out the door like bags of garbage. Then she proceeded to clear the bar. With some of the bigger men she had to punch their lights out before grabbing them by their shirt collars and the seat of their pants and throwing them out the door.

As she cleared the bar, she came up to me and looked me up and down. *Oh, God!* I thought. *She's going to throw me out next!* Instead, she walked past me, reached over the bar, grabbed Hobo, pulled him to her, and gave him a huge kiss. Still holding him up by the shirt collar, she asked, "Frank, why didn't you tell me you were back in town?"

Hobo ignored her question, smiled at me, and said, "Mike. I want you to meet my wife, Sally. Sally, Mike here watched over me when I was at Melozi."

Sally gave me a beautiful smile that transformed her from a fighting amazon to a loving wife. She abruptly released Hobo, causing him to collapse in a heap on the bar. Then Sally extended her gloved hand to me. Still reeling from the fight, I gingerly took it. She crushed my hand in response.

"Hey, Sally," Hobo said in a laughing voice, "Why don't you take Mike to the trailer and fix him some dinner. He's probably starving by now."

Sally looked around her and saw Ronnie already sweeping up the mess and righting the unbroken chairs and tables. "Okay," she said as she started for the door. "Come on, Mike. I'll carry you down." I staggered after her and saw her mount her Yamaha 250 Enduro. She quickly kick-started it and wagged her head for me to jump aboard. I grabbed her waist as Sally popped the cycle into gear and we sped down the street. She stopped after a few blocks at a modern-looking mobile home. "Here we are," Sally said as I hopped off and she killed the engine and set the kickstand.

Sally led me into the arctic entry where she took off her boots, hat, and pistol and hung them on pegs in the entry. I slipped off my boots and came inside the home. The living quarters were spotless. The living room and kitchen were neatly arranged with nice furniture and appliances. Something delicious was cooking in the oven. Sally motioned me to the living room and said, "Make yourself comfortable, Mike. The base TV station may be working again. They get their programing by tape reels flown in from the States. So, everything is two to three days old, but it's better than nothing."

"Thank you, Sally," I said as I sat on the couch, "but I think I'll just sit here for a while." Truth be known, I did not want to touch anything that might invoke her wrath. I watched her set the table as she hummed a tune from the rock group Bread. I was having a tough time rationalizing the two opposing sides of this woman. Never in my life had I seen anyone fight as ruthlessly and efficiently as Sally. Minutes later, Sally became a loving and caring woman seemingly incapable of violence. If I had never witnessed her fight, I would have had a hard time believing her wild side.

Sally looked up at me with a smile and said, "Dinner is ready, Mike. You can wash up in the bathroom down the hall." I found the bathroom and washed my face and hands. The bathroom was also neat as a pin. In the kitchen, Sally had placed a casserole on the table. It smelled fabulous. "I hope you like tuna casserole," said Sally.

"You bet I do," I exclaimed. "It smells delicious. Thank you." I spooned up a generous helping and devoured it. My appetite seemed to amuse Sally. We engaged in small talk about the town. The bar fight was never mentioned. As the meal ended, I finally asked a question burning in my mind, "Sally, how did you and Hobo meet?"

Sally looked wistfully out the window for a second before answering. "Oh, I don't know. Mutual friends I guess. One thing led to another and we decided we would make a good match. I help him and Ronnie run the bar and straighten things out. I just wish he wouldn't drink so much. He was in bad shape when Norm flew him out to Melozi."

I nodded and suddenly felt bad for Sally. She seemed lonely, like she was the only mature adult in the whole town. Pat was right. Sally appeared to be in her late twenties—half Hobo's age. Yet being married to Hobo was probably like being married to a teenager. She was constantly trying to keep him from self-destructing. The conversation died and we sat in silent contemplation for a minute. Finally, I said, "Thank you so much for the great dinner, Sally, and I enjoyed meeting you. I should be going now."

Sally looked up with a sad smile and said, "You are welcome. It was great to talk with someone different for a change. I can drive you back."

"That's okay," I said. "I want to walk around town and see it before calling it a day. I'll make my way back to the bar."

Sally's eyes narrowed as she asked, "Did Hobo put you up in one of the back rooms?"

"Yeah, the last one. Why?"

Sally gave me a stern look and replied, "Nothing. Just keep your eyes forward when walking to your room and keep the door closed. Okay?"

"Okay," I answered with a puzzled look. "Ronnie told me the same thing." I shook her hand and walked out into the evening sunshine.

I walked down to the Yukon River and stood at the bank watching the boats glide along the surface. The river looked a mile wide with brown, turbid water moving steadily to the west. The town and river were alive with people enjoying the weather and the outdoors. Kids chased each other down the dirt streets. Adults drove three-wheeled all-terrain vehicles with small trailers filled with gear or more kids. Dogs barked and chased after the children. I glanced at my watch and it read nine o'clock. The town appeared to be getting ready for a night of fun.

I wandered through a few side streets and eventually found my way back to the Yukon Inn. The place was strangely quiet when I entered. Only two hard-core drinkers remained and they kept to themselves. Hobo sat on a stool with his legs crossed smoking a cigarette. He greeted me with, "Hi ya, Mike. Did Sally get you all squared away?"

I sat down next to Hobo and answered, "Yes. Sally was very nice and a great cook. I enjoyed meeting her."

Hobo took another puff and replied, "She's a good gal. I don't know what she sees in me." I heard a grunt of agreement come from Ronnie as he cleaned a few glasses from behind the bar. Hobo flashed him a quick grin.

My eyes felt heavy with sleep. I'd had an eventful day and my body was starting to shut down. "Hobo," I said as I started to yawn, "I've got to call it a night. I think I'll turn in."

Hobo nodded and said, "It's been a good day." He pointed toward the entrance and continued, "Ronnie will lock up tonight and bolt that door shut. Don't open it until someone comes in the morning. Understand? And don't open it for anyone no matter what they say. Got it? People are always trying to bust their way in here and steal some booze. I should be back here by ten in the morning."

I nodded and thought, *This should be an interesting night.*

Ronnie added, "I'm going to spend the night here. If something should happen, I'll take care of it."

"Thanks, Ronnie," I said as I got up to go to my room. "Good night, guys."

Ronnie put his hand on my shoulder as I walked by and said softly, "If you crawl into bed and there's a woman next to you, you've got the wrong room." I took a step back in surprise at his revelation. Then I saw the twinkle in his eyes and realized he was pulling my leg. I nodded and hurried straight down the hallway to the last room at the end.

I fell asleep hard in my sleeping bag—oblivious to the sunlight streaming though the curtainless window. I vaguely remembered hearing whispers and doors opening and closing. The tapping on the window finally broke through to my subconscious and woke me. As I opened my unfocused eyes, the tapping changed to aggressive banging.

I rolled over and saw a face pressed to the window trying to look inside my room. I remained motionless while the young man searched for someone.

He had a partner standing beside him who looked agitated. Suddenly, the man at the window yelled, "Hey! Wake up! We want to buy some beer!" I froze trying to look like I was part of the mattress. The man beat on the window again and screamed, "Hey! Wake up! We've got money!" I knew he could not see me, but I was afraid the window might break from his thrashing.

Then Ronnie's voice bellowed through the wall, "Get the hell outta here!" The man at the window jumped in response. "You heard me! Scram!"

The men seemed confused and held a brief conference. Apparently, they were desperate because the second man yelled back, "Ron, we got money. We only want a case or two. We'll meet you at the front door." Then they vanished.

I heard Ronnie swear and kick open his door. For the life of me, I do not know what I was thinking, but I threw on my pants and followed him. Ronnie stood at the doorway bare-chested behind the bar facing the building entrance and holding a small caliber pistol. I stood behind him and watched the door. Moments later, I saw an eye look through the hole that normally accommodated the door knob. Ronnie held his pistol up and waved it menacingly at him. "Get outta here! I'm not fool'in!"

Unbelievably, the man behind the door yelled back, "No! We're coming in!" And started ramming the door with his shoulder. Then I heard him take turns with his partner kicking it. Ronnie calmly lifted his pistol and fired twice into the door. The sound inside the bar was ear-splitting, but the men miraculously vanished.

Ronnie waited to hear if they came back, but after a quiet minute, he shrugged and said, "Well, they had enough for tonight. I bet their feet still haven't touched the ground. Goodnight, Mike."

"Ronnie," I gasped, "Weren't you afraid of hitting them?"

"Naw," responded Ronnie as we headed down the hall, "that's a solid oak door. This little popgun ain't gonna make it through. I do it all the time. Only thing that gets their attention. See ya in the morning." He disappeared into one of the rooms.

I was too spun up to sleep as I slipped back into my sleeping bag. I lay on the mattress with my hands behind my head and contemplated how people can embrace and let go of danger at the drop of a hat. Just this evening, I had seen Hobo, Sally, and Ronnie confront violence, overcome it, and then immediately brush it aside. None of them appeared to fret or lose a minute of sleep over it. I then realized that these people were living another lifestyle, one that I could barely fathom. Like the Veerhusens, they had the confidence to meet each day and face what life threw at them. I felt the adrenaline ebb from my blood as sleep slowly overcame me.

I was sitting at the bar when Hobo unlocked the front door. "Good morning, Mike," said Hobo with his ever-present smile. "How did ya sleep?"

"Like a baby," I responded.

"That's great," replied Hobo as he walked behind the bar. "I've got some instant oatmeal. Want some?"

"That would be fine, Hobo. Thank you. By the way, what time does Tanana Air Taxi fly back to Fairbanks?"

Hobo opened two oatmeal packets, poured them into a mug, and answered, "Two o'clock. We've got a few hours before you need to get to the airport." He flipped on an electric plate and put a kettle of water on it to boil. "Before we do that though, there is something I want to discuss with you. But that can wait till after breakfast."

His statement piqued my interest. My imagination flew over the various unusual topics Hobo would want to discuss. I ate my oatmeal as Hobo took inventory of his stock and wrote down some notes. When I was done, Hobo and I went for a walk. We strolled in back of the Yukon Inn and he showed me a junk pile. "Mike," he said with his hands in his pockets, "I need someone to go through this stuff and determine what is salvageable and what is junk. Then haul the crap to the dump." We stared at the mountain of accumulated stuff for a moment before moving on.

We walked down the street to the Yukon River where he showed me his riverboat. It was an aluminum, V-hulled, green river craft with a plywood pilothouse and shelter. An 80-horsepower Johnson outboard engine hung on the stern. On the bank were coils of copper wire strewn across the sand. Hobo turned to me and said, "Okay, Mike. Here's the deal. I am willing to pay you top dollar if you stay here in Galena for a while and clean up my mess. You would sort through that junk pile at the bar, haul off the waste, and coil up this wire and bring it back to the Inn. On your off hours, you can take my boat out and explore the river. What do you say, Mike?" Hobo stuck out his hand to cement the deal.

Never before had I stood at a life crossroads where I could clearly see two forks. One path led home to family, friends, and football. The other disappeared into an alluring world of adventure. I hesitated even though I knew I should choose the right path and go home instead of selecting the potentially wild path of being Hobo Benson's employee. I had to admit, the pull of driving Hobo's riverboat was strong. I could just see myself behind the controls. Then the seeds of reality sprouted. A vision flashed before my eyes of my dad hunting me down and kicking my tail—not to mention Pat getting her hands on Hobo's neck. I avoided Hobo's outstretched hand as I grabbed his shoulder and said, "I'm sorry, Hobo. I really appreciate the offer, but I have to go home. My family is waiting for me and school is starting soon. If things were different, I'd stay."

A wave of disappointment washed over Hobo's face. He looked down and nodded. We stood there for an uncomfortable moment before he resumed his undaunted smile. "Well, it was worth a try. Let's go back and get your stuff together and I'll arrange for a ride to take you to the airport."

I kept my hand on his shoulder as we turned to leave and said, "Thank you, Hobo, and thank you for everything. I've enjoyed getting to know you."

Hobo grinned at me and said, "My pleasure, my boy. Now, let's get you back home."

--------◆◆◆◆◆--------

The drive to the passenger shelter was uneventful. The day was shaping up to be another hot one. I shook hands with Hobo's friend and watched him drive away in the old Rambler.

A lady took the crumpled ticket that Doug had given me two months ago, weighed my bags, and recorded my weight, too. The plane arrived by two thirty, which was punctual according to bush time. I climbed aboard and looked out the window with the sad knowledge that my summer adventure was coming to an end.

As the Navajo rapidly climbed above the Yukon and headed toward Fairbanks, I realized that I had changed. The vastness below me now looked inviting and familiar like I was a part of it. Melozi had injected Alaska into my veins and I was forever hooked. At 16 years old, I knew that I could not live anywhere else in the world. My spirit would never be whole apart from this land.

Epilogue

On a November day in 1973, Len and Pat surprised my family with a visit to our Fairbanks home. They sat in our living room with my entire family plus dog sitting around our couch. They smiled at my parents in sympathy for raising four boys. Then Pat paid me the greatest compliment by telling my Dad that I had held a man's job and did it well.

The inevitable happened in May 1974. My parents moved us to Colorado. My family and I corresponded with the Veerhusens throughout the next year. I graduated from high school in May 1975 and immediately helped my parents move again—this time to Idaho. During the last week of May, I loaded two suitcases into my 1967 Ford Mustang, kissed my mother goodbye, and headed north. Because I was still seventeen, my father had given me a notarized letter granting his permission for me to return to Alaska. The Canadian guards read it and then waved me across the border. On June 1, I drove into Fairbanks, ready to start my life.

Fairbanks had changed since I was gone. It was now a pipeline boom town bulging at the seams with people and crawling with temptations and opportunity. My goal was to save enough money to help pay for my first year of college. Fairbanks merchants were screaming for help because many of their employees had abandoned their positions for incredibly high-paying pipeline jobs. I quickly landed a good job as a warehouseman with J C Penney that paid well with as much overtime as I could handle.

I wrote a letter to Pat and Len telling them that I had come back to Alaska. During the month of July, Len paid me a surprise visit at work. I was on my knees fixing a leaky hydraulic hose on a forklift when Len walked into the warehouse. He seemed pleased that I was still getting my hands dirty while working hard.

"Len, I am so happy to see you again!" I said as I wiped my hands on a rag and shook his hand.

"How is it going?" Len replied with a grin. "Are they treating you okay here?"

"Not as good as you and Pat treated me. Thank you for looking me up." We exchanged small talk.

Len brought me up to speed on the current status of the lodge. "Why, we even got the swimming pool built and flowing. It works great. You ought to think about coming back to try it out."

I shook my head in wonder and replied, "I knew you would get it going and I suppose the fireplace is finished, too."

Len laughed and answered, "Yep! It came out nice, too. Heats the whole lodge when it's cold."

I smiled as I thought about the hard, messy work of hauling rocks and water and screening sand. "So, what brings you to Fairbanks, Len? Are you rounding up some supplies?"

Len's face became serious as he touched his lower back and replied, "I've got a nagging backache and I came in to have a doctor check it out."

"What do you think it is, Len?" I asked with concern. "Could it be something related to your fall off the roof several years ago?"

Len shook his head and answered gravely, "I don't know. It might be. I should know something in two weeks." We talked a little longer until my foreman gave me the evil eye. We shook hands goodbye and that was the last time I saw Len Veerhusen.

Len died of prostrate cancer on January 1, 1976 in the Veteran's Administration hospital in Seattle, Washington. He was 62. Pat plunged into despair. Her grief was so thick that she could barely walk. Eventually, she found her way back to Melozi, where she was comforted by Tom Dome and his girlfriend Roslyn Whaley. Tom had assumed Doug DeFelice's partnership and tried to fulfill Len's dream of making Melozi Hot Springs a wilderness resort. Roslyn said she and Pat spent hours each day around the dining table drinking coffee and talking. Pat would reminisce about her life with Len. She was filled with pain.

In an attempt to stave off loneliness, Pat married Orin Johnston during the spring of 1977. Orin was Len's cousin and Pat had stayed with Orin when Len was in the hospital. In August 1977, Pat was diagnosed with lung cancer. On December 3, 1977, she died in Seattle. She was only 57.

Being young and selfish, I never wrote the Veerhusens when I attended college in Fairbanks. I learned of their passing in the early 1980s when I noticed a man exiting a truck with the words "Melozi Hot Springs Lodge" written along the side. I introduced myself to him and inquired about Len and Pat. The man told me of their deaths. The news stunned me and filled me with regret.

I never returned to Melozi Hot Springs. This book was my attempt to right my wrong and forever memorialize their lives.

Tom Dome also felt compelled to commemorate their lives. He submitted a petition to the U.S. Geophysical Survey to name the small mountain creek that paralleled the camp Veerhusen Creek. The USGS granted Tom's request. Now when visitors cross over the small stream as they walk up from the airstrip, they pay tribute to the couple who dreamed big and carved a lodge out of the Alaska wilderness.

———◆◆×◆◆———

On Wednesday, April 27, 1988, Norman Yaeger and his chief pilot, Harold "Hal" Graham, took off from Galena in a twin-engine, Beechcraft Baron en route to Anchorage. The Baron required some mechanical and electrical work. Thus, Hal requested and received a ferry permit from the Federal Aviation Administration to fly the plane to town for repairs. Under the ferry permit, Hal was granted permission to fly only in daylight and under visual flight rules.

Before they left, Norman noticed the Loran navigational equipment in the Baron was malfunctioning. Even though Hal was to fly under visual flight rules, Norm wanted the assistance of the Loran to navigate. So, he pulled the Loran from another aircraft and installed it in the Baron. They departed Galena shortly before noon with Hal flying and Norm sitting in the right seat. They flew directly toward Rainy Pass in the Alaska Range.

As Norman and Hal approached the pass, the weather deteriorated. The wind started to gust, the cloud ceiling dropped, and it began to snow. Other pilots reported heavy icing at the time. Hal concentrated on flying while Norman tried to assist him by adjusting the Loran, but a previous pilot had programmed the way points on the device and Norm was not familiar with the identifiers. Thus, they were unsure of their course as Hal flew into instrument meteorological conditions. They drifted 30 miles south of their intended route. Anchorage Center tried repeatedly to warn the pilots that they were flying into danger, but failed to contact them. At 1:18 p.m., Harold Graham slammed into a mountain two miles north of Mount Spur. According to the FAA accident report, if Hal had flown 850 feet higher, they would have made it.

Blowing snow limited visibility and prevented the military rescue crew from finding the crash site. Late Thursday night, the wind calmed allowing the rescue party to finally reach the mangled plane. They extracted the men from the wreckage and discovered Norman was dead. Rumors circulated that the rescuers had found Norm with his head and hands tucked into his jacket to stay warm after the crash. Norman W. Yaeger was forty-nine-years-old.

Hal was barely alive—suffering from internal injuries and severe exposure. The military helicoptered him to Providence Hospital in Anchorage where he died early Friday morning. Years afterward, bar patrons across Alaska nursed their drinks and wondered if the rescuers had found them on the first day, would they have lived?

———————◆▸◈◂◆———————

Mark and Luverne Swan each lived to the ripe age of ninety. Mark passed away in 1990 and Luverne in 2007. According to their daughter, Susan Schultz, "They would not have traded their Melozi experience for any amount of money in the world!" The rock fireplace inside the lodge still stands today as a testimony to their tireless and careful work.

———————◆▸◈◂◆———————

Despite continually abusing alcohol, chain-smoking, surviving a serious gunshot to the face, and another beating, Frank "Hobo" Benson finally succumbed to Lou Gehrig's disease instead of cancer or a liver ailment as everyone expected. He died at 6:45 p.m. on September 20, 1990 in Galena. He was 66.

Hobo worked in his bar every day until his final year. Complications from his disease and arthritis eventually crippled him. His hands hurt so bad that he could not strike a match to light his cigarette. So he would sit on a stool next to the bar, shove a cigarette into his mouth, and wait until someone took pity on him and lit it. He thought his plight was hilarious that he would die of an athlete's disease, and frequently told people that he had beaten the odds.

Hobo's funeral was at the town hall where he and Sally had held their wedding reception eighteen years earlier. The town buried him in the Old Louden Cemetery where the Native elders were laid to rest.

———————◆▸◈◂◆———————

During the course of interviewing and gathering information for this story, I met many wonderful and interesting people. One conversation in particular that captured my attention occurred in March 2009.

I met Rudy Scott and had lunch with him in Anchorage. Rudy, his wife Colleen, and Tom Dome had formed a corporation and taken over the Melozi Hot Springs Lodge. They ran it for eight years before personal and financial reasons forced them to abandon their venture. Rudy talked fondly of his time at Melozi and we readily swapped stories. Rudy mentioned that several times he felt Pat's and Len's spirits in the lodge supervising his activities. He especially felt their presence when he was alone on quiet winter nights.

Finally, I asked him why he left. He said that the BLM had raised the yearly lease fee until he could no longer afford to operate the business. After they abandoned the lodge, the camp fell into disrepair and was now rotting into the ground. We each ate in silence and brooded on the tragedy of Veerhusens' unfulfilled dreams. I interrupted our contemplation by asking Rudy, "Did you know what Len requested if the BLM ever got their hands on the place?"

Rudy nodded and replied, "Yeah, it was made known to me, but I couldn't do it. I just couldn't burn the place down."

Acknowledgments

I fully confess that a sixteen-year-old boy's memory and perceptions may be inaccurate and skewed. Coupled with the fact that this adventure occurred in 1973, my adult memory may be taxed, too. However, with the help of many people, old letters, a journal, and magazine and newspaper articles, I believe I correctly reconstructed the events that occurred that summer.

The following people provided crucial details that I could not have resurrected or found on my own. I am grateful for their interest and contribution to this story. I listed them in alphabetical order along with a short note on their participation.

Daniel Calkins

Daniel provided detailed editing. I am very grateful for his efforts.

Bob Cline

Bob told me many stories of life in Galena during the 1970s. He also gave me leads on where to find specific people with knowledge about Melozi Hot Springs.

Kathi Dome

She shared her experiences at Melozi Hot Springs during the late 1970s.

Tom Dome

Tom was a lodge partner with the Veerhusens and others. He gave me key information that improved the accuracy of this story. Tom also reconfirmed other facts that I originally thought too fantastic to be true.

Harold and Florence Esmailka

The Esmailkas were close friends of the Veerhusens. They gave me details of the Veerhusens' last years and some history about developing Melozi Hot Springs.

Andy and Rose Greenblatt

Rose convinced her husband Andy to deviate from his guiding and outfitting duties and fly over Melozi Hot Springs. In September of 2009, Andy hung out of a Super Cub and took many incredible and heart-wrenching pictures of the deteriorating lodge and camp. I included some of these pictures in this story.

Wolf Hebel

Wolf was a friend of the Veerhusens. He once hiked from Kokrines to Melozi Hot Springs. He gave me details of the trip.

David Heimke

Dave grew up in Hubbell, Michigan, and knew the Benson family. He gave me details and reconfirmed my recollections about Frank "Hobo" Benson's life.

Max Huhndorf

Max was a longtime resident of Galena. He told me about businesses that existed in Galena in the 1960s and 70s.

Marthy Johnson

Marthy skillfully edited my story. Without her expertise, my prose would have looked barbaric.

Skip Kittredge

Skip provided details of his visit to Melozi Hot Springs when I was there.

Charlie Parr

Charlie accessed the U.S. Bureau of Land Management Alaska Case Retrieval Enterprise System and retrieved historical information on the development and ownership of Melozi Hot Springs.

Jerry Pitka

Jerry was born and raised in Galena. He confirmed details and provided information about people I met.

Ned Rozell

During July 2009, Ned and a group of adventurous friends hiked from the Yukon River to Melozi Hot Springs and then floated the Melozitna River to Ruby. Ned graciously allowed me to incorporate some of his pictures in this book. He posted the pictures and synopsis of his adventure on his blog, *Alaska Tracks 2010*.

Rudy Scott

Rudy and his wife, Colleen, formed a corporation with Tom Dome in the 1980s to operate the Melozi Hot Springs Lodge. Rudy refreshed my memory on many details about the lodge and provided information about people of the area.

Susan Shultz

Susan was married to Patricia Veerhusen's son. She provided detailed recollections of the Veerhusens' adventures. Her father and mother, Mark and Luverne Swan, visited Melozi while I was there. Susan sent me her mother's journal that provided vivid details of my last two weeks at Melozi Hot Springs.

Dan Veerhusen

Dan is Leonard Veerhusen's son. Dan provided detailed memories of building the Galena Yukon Lodge and how his father struggled to develop Melozi Hot Springs.

Adele Virgin

Adele was a reference librarian at the Noel Wien Library in Fairbanks. She looked up obituaries in the *Fairbanks Daily News Miner* and gave me information on Yvonne Worthington.

Roslyn Whaley

Roslyn recalled her tearful days with Pat Veerhusen sitting around the lodge kitchen table and listening to her reminisce about her life with Len.

I especially want to thank my beautiful wife, Barby, and my daughter Natalie for tolerating my impromptu readings. They patiently smiled and dropped what they were doing when I came running, waving a piece of manuscript, and yelling, "Listen to this and tell me what you think!"

Finally, I want to thank my mother for reading and reliving this story. I know she blames herself for letting me go, but, Mom, I am so glad you did.

Michael D. Travis

Bibliography

BOOKS

De Laguna, Frederica. 2000. *Travels Among the Dena*. University of Washington Press. Seattle, WA. 113p.

Lund, Robert. 1955. *The Alaskan*. Bantam Books. New York. 366pp.

Rotham, Stewart N. 1975. *The Untold Story of Hobo and Dangerous Dan McGrew*. Produced by The Lens Unlimited for Ken Lavigne. Fairbanks, Alaska. 28pp.

ARTICLES

March 15, 1968. *Bawdy House Charge Dropped*. Fairbanks Daily News Miner. Fairbanks, AK. 7p.

December, 1969. *Christmas Party at Hobo's*. Stories from Alaska. www.pajbcooper.com/stories_from_alaska.htm#christmaspartyathobos

February 16, 1972. *Couple shows Alaskan spirit*. Fairbanks Daily News Miner. Front page.

June 27, 1972. *Galena - How to Win A Flood?* Alicia Patterson Foundation Newsletters of Lael Morgan. Http://www.aliciapatterson.org/APF001972/Morgan/Morgan06/Morgan06.html

July 11, 1973. *Body of Nollner found in Yukon.* Fairbanks Daily News Miner. Fairbanks, AK.

Veerhusen, Patricia. July, 1974. *We, The Intruders.* Alaska Magazine. Anchorage, AK. 47-48p.

April 29, 1988. *Crash kills 1, Injures another.* Anchorage Daily News. p B2. Anchorage, AK.

April 30, 1988. *Crash claims a second victim.* Anchorage Daily News. Section B. Anchorage, AK.

May 1, 1988. Obituaries. Anchorage Daily News. Section B. Anchorage, AK.

September 22, 1990. *Frank Benson, owner of Hobo's Yukon Inn, dies in Galena.* The Anchorage Times. page B2. Anchorage, AK.

September-October, 2002. *Harold Esmailka: A Credit.* The Alaskan Shepherd. Vol. 40. No. 5. Fairbanks, AK.

SOURCES

Bureau of Land Management Alaska Case Retrieval Enterprise System. Case Abstract AKAA 064725 Melozi Hot Springs.

National Transportation Safety Board Accident Database. Case no. ANC88FA051. Factual Report of Galena Air Service Accident. 04/27/1988.

Photos
Reflections of Melozi

Melozi Hot Springs Falls.
Photo by Ned Rozell. July, 2009

Bleached Melozi Hot Springs Well. This was
the tank Len and I constructed on my first
day in camp.
Photo by Ned Rozell. July, 2009

Inside the Lodge. Note the massive fireplace.
Photo by Ned Rozell. July, 2009

Aerial View of Lodge and Old Cabin.
Photo by Andy Greenblatt. September, 2009.

Aerial View of Camp.
Photo by Andy Greenblatt. September, 2009.

Old Reindeer Cabin.
Photo by Ned Rozell. July, 2009

Aerial of Melozi Hot Springs.
Photo by Andy Greenblatt. September, 2009.

Melozi Airstrip.
Photo provided by Skip Kittredge. Mid 1970s.

Aerial View of Airstrip and the Kokrines Winter Trail.
Photo by Andy Greenblatt. September, 2009.

Sixteen-year-old Michael Travis holding a stringer of arctic grayling.

Displaying my trophy arctic grayling next to my 8-inch pocket knife.

Frank (Hobo) Benson compensating
for the lack of a corkscrew.

Luverne Swan and Len and Pat
Veerhusen at the airstrip

The massive fireplace that caused me so much sweat and agony.
Photo by Amy Marsh. July, 2010.

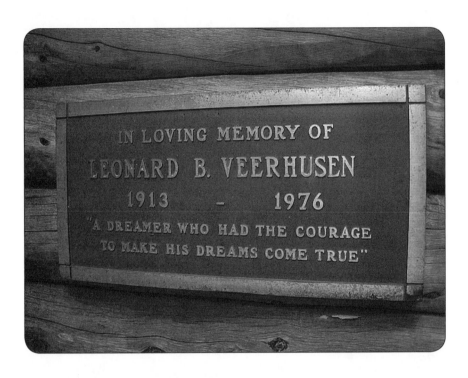

Photo by Tom Dome. September, 2009.